Discover the passion and joy of Christmas past, present, and future in this heartwarming time-travel romance by Flora Speer, bestselling author of *A Love Beyond Time*.

CHRISTMAS CAROL

Bah! Humbug! That's what Carol Simmons says to Christmas, charity, and the phantom in her room. But the specter of Lady Augusta Marlowe has only one chance to save herself from eternal damnation. Using all her ghostly powers, she takes Carol through time to three different London yuletides to transform her from a Scrooge to a Santa.

"Christmas Past"

Amid the glitter and splendor of Regency England, Carol finds herself in the body of an impoverished noblewoman—and in the arms of a dashing peer.

"Christmas Present"

Back in her own era, Carol learns that the goodness of a heart cannot be measured by the length of a family title or the size of the family jewels.

"Christmas Future"

In a bleak and distant age, Carol discovers that to receive the greatest gift of all she must first sacrifice her most treasured possession.

SPIRIT OF LOVE

"I thought I knew you well, Caroline, and knew what to expect of you. I never guessed that beneath your proper demeanor you possessed so lively a spirit." His mouth was now disturbingly close to hers. Carol knew a moment of panic.

"I have recently learned more than I care to know about lively spirits," she declared.

"Have you? This change in you grows more interesting by the moment. Perhaps you will allow me to test your newfound spirit."

"I don't think it would be wise." The cautionary words came out as more of a gasp than a firm statement.

"Why not, when I am your promised husband?" His free arm slid around her waist, drawing her closer still. "Who would dare to criticize me for sampling that which will soon be entirely mine?"

Christmas Carol

FLORA SPEER

LOVE SPELL **NEW YORK CITY**

LOVE SPELL®

November 1994

Published by

Dorchester Publishing Co., Inc.
276 Fifth Avenue
New York, NY 10001

Printed in the United States of America.

This book is dedicated to my readers, and most especially to those who enjoy time-travel or futuristic romances. We who read or write in these subgenres of romance believe that true love is not confined by the limits of ordinary time or space. Thus, I give you Carol's story, with the wish that every one of your holidays will be merry and bright and that love, which is the true spirit of any holiday, will remain in your hearts throughout all the years to come.

Part I.
Humbug.

London, 1993.

Chapter One

Considering her dislike of any occasion that required the distribution of gifts or money, it was regarded by all who knew her to be perfectly in character for Lady Augusta Marlowe to take her leave of this world on the 18th day of December. By doing so she neatly avoided having to hand out Christmas presents to her servants or to the few tradespeople who were still willing to deliver groceries, or wine or spirits, or the occasional garment, to her door. That is to say, to the door assigned for servants and tradesmen. The front door—original to the house and carved of solid oak—was seldom used anymore. Even Carol Noelle Simmons, who was Lady Augusta's paid companion, and thus might have passed with impunity through the mansion's chief portal had she chosen to do so, almost always used the servants' entrance instead. However, on Tuesday, the 21st day of December, Crampton the butler was kept busy opening and closing the heavy front door, for this was the day of Lady Augusta's funeral.

Carol was forced to admire the old girl's spunk. Early in the autumn Lady Augusta had declared with all the shrill force of which she was capable that she *would not* be taken to a nursing home or to a hospital. She absolutely defied her despairing physician on that point. Nor, as it turned out, had she intended to pay for professional nursing care at home. Thus, it had fallen to Carol and the few remaining servants to bathe and feed her, and to turn her when she became incapable of moving on her own.

Lady Augusta's fury at her ever-increasing helplessness had fallen upon all of her staff, but most especially on Carol. Cantankerous to the end, during the last few months of her life Lady Augusta had even denied Carol the free day each week that she was supposed to have.

While not daring to disobey her employer, Carol had resented the deprivation. She had precious little money to spend—Lady Augusta considered room and board to be a large part of her servants' wages and Carol was, in Lady Augusta's opinion, no more than an overpaid servant—but London offered pleasures that cost nothing at all. The only requirements were a comfortable pair of walking shoes, an umbrella, and a weatherproof outer garment. But since Lady Augusta had become permanently bedridden at the end of September, Carol's solitary walks had been denied to her. Those treasured hours could soon begin again, for Carol stood now, in late afternoon of the day of Lady Augusta's funeral, in the chilly, pale yellow drawing room of Marlowe House, bidding farewell to the mourners.

There were few of them and they departed ill-fed. When she knew her end was fast approaching, Lady Augusta had stipulated that only tea and biscuits should be served at the funeral "feast." Even in death her commandments were not to be disobeyed. Carol wondered if the servants feared Lady Augusta would return to haunt them if they opened a bottle of sherry for the guests as she herself had suggested the day before.

"Certainly not, Miss Simmons," Crampton had responded to Carol's remark with barely concealed horror. "There will be no wine served. Lady Augusta personally ordered the menu for this occasion and we will, as always, follow her directions to the letter."

And so they had. A small coal fire burned in the grate, a plate of biscuits and a pot of tea sat upon a tray on one of the delicate Regency-style tables, and Carol felt certain the drawing room was every bit as cold and cheerless as it must have been in the early eighteen hundreds when Marlowe House was first built.

Now the Reverend Mr. Lucius Kincaid, who was the rector of nearby St. Fiacre's Church and who had performed the funeral service, approached Carol. Assuming that he was about to take his leave, Carol put out her hand to shake his. But the clergyman apparently had no intention of departing from Marlowe House until he had extracted some information from Carol.

Flora Speer

"I do hope," he said, "that Lady Augusta remembered St. Fiacre's Bountiful Board in her will." He was a tall, thin man with dark hair going gray and clothes that did not fit him very well. Carol regarded him with distaste for, like her late employer, she was not interested in religion. In fact, Carol could not remember Lady Augusta ever entering a church. It was Crampton who had suggested that the Reverend Mr. Kincaid be asked to conduct the funeral service.

"We have not yet heard anything about Lady Augusta's charitable bequests," said the rector's wife, who joined them. In contrast to her nondescript husband, the blond, blue-eyed Mrs. Kincaid wore a fashionable outfit with a remarkably short skirt and a hat that might have come right out of the American West. "I must confess that we at St. Fiacre's are feeling a bit desperate right now. There always seems to be such need at Christmastime, so much that ought to be done to help the poor. We stand ready to provide what is required, if only we have the funds. Or at least a pledge."

"I am not authorized to make donations in Lady Augusta's name," Carol said coldly. "If you want money, speak to her solicitor."

"Then perhaps you yourself would care to contribute to our holiday efforts," urged the rector, giving Carol a smile she chose not to return.

"I do not," Carol snapped.

"Surely," Lucius Kincaid persisted, "having received from Lady Augusta generous recompense for your devoted care of her over these last five years and more, you will be disposed

16

at this holy season to give liberally to help the less fortunate."

Biting her tongue to keep herself from retorting that there was no one less fortunate than herself, Carol glared at the Reverend Mr. Kincaid. Until meeting him on the day of Lady Augusta's death she had not known that people still talked the way he did. With his cultivated accent the man sounded as if he belonged in the Victorian Age. How dare he hit her up for money at a funeral?

"St. Fiacre's Church," Carol murmured, taking a nasty pleasure in what she was about to say. "I know who St. Fiacre was."

"In this nation of gardeners, most people do," the rector responded, "since he is the patron saint of gardeners."

"That's not all," said Carol. "St. Fiacre was a typical woman-hating, sixth-century Irish hermit-monk. As I recall, he made a rule forbidding all females from entering his precious enclosure." She was not sure why she was deliberately being so unpleasant. She usually had better manners than she was displaying on this occasion, but something about the Kincaids grated on her. For a reason she could not understand, they were making her feel guilty. She did not like the feeling.

"Saints are notoriously difficult people, whose very saintliness makes everyone around them uncomfortable," Mrs. Kincaid said, laughing as if to show she was not offended by Carol's rudeness. "There is even a legend about a noblewoman who once broke St. Fiacre's rule. She actually dared to walk into the enclosure surrounding his hut and

17

attempted to speak with him. Of course, she immediately suffered a dreadful death. But that happened, if it happened at all, more than fourteen hundred years ago. It would take a foolish woman indeed to still be angry over attitudes that existed so far in the past. In these modern times, we ought instead to forgive poor old St. Fiacre his sins, if any, against the gentler sex, and perhaps occasionally invoke his horticultural spirit when we are having trouble with our gardens." She finished her speech with a smile.

"I don't garden," Carol said. "I never have." She watched with pleasure as Mrs. Kincaid's smile vanished.

"If you would like to learn," Lucius Kincaid offered in a friendly way, "we can always put volunteers to good use in the little garden in our churchyard when spring arrives."

"No, thanks. I'm a city girl." The Kincaids would probably expect her to donate plants to their wretched garden. Carol had no intention of throwing any money away on *flowers*.

"Look," Carol said, "it's none of your business, but just so you won't waste your time asking me again, Lady Augusta left me nothing."

"Nothing at all?" gasped the rector's wife.

"Nothing." Carol was still reacting with rudeness to what she perceived as prying questions. "Since you appear to be indecently interested in the will, let me tell you what the solicitor told me and the *other* servants this morning. Lady Augusta did leave small amounts to Crampton and to Mrs. Marks, the cook. Nell the chambermaid, Hettie the scullery maid, and myself receive nothing but room and board for one month after Lady Augusta's death, during which time we are to search for new employment."

"Dear me." The rector appeared to be in shock. "Not a generous arrangement, I must say."

"You're damned right about that. I hope you weren't expecting Lady Augusta to be generous." Carol included both the rector and his wife in her mirthless grin. "She was the stingiest, coldest woman I have ever known."

"Now, now, Miss Simmons," Lucius Kincaid ed. "Whatever your personal disappointment in this matter, one must always speak well of the dead."

"That's what I was doing. I admired Lady Augusta's stinginess, and the way she never took any nonsense from anyone. She lived and died the way she wanted and I say, good for her."

"She lived for the most part alone, and died alone, too, save for her employees," the rector noted, adding in one of his old-fashioned phrases, "One would hope to have at one's side at the end of life a close relative, or at least a dear friend."

"Instead she had me, and she didn't think I was worth much. She proved that by her non-bequest." Carol did not add what she was thinking, that everyone else she had ever known had also assumed that Carol Noelle Simmons wasn't worth much. Not unless she had plenty of money to boost her charms into something interesting. She made herself stop thinking about her own past. She had promised herself long ago to put out of her mind the uncaring man who—

Flora Speer

"Speaking of close relatives," said the rector's wife, intruding into Carol's unpleasant ruminations, "why isn't Nicholas Montfort here? I believe he is Lady Augusta's only living relative?"

"Yes," her husband put in. "Mr. Montfort is Lady Augusta's nephew, her only sister's child."

With an effort, Carol refrained from asking if her two inquisitors had been researching the Marlowe-Montfort genealogy. Instead, she offered a reasonably polite explanation for the absence of Nicholas Montfort.

"Mr. Montfort was unable to leave Hong Kong immediately. Business interests keep him there. He sent a telegram urging us to go on with the funeral in his absence. He expects to arrive in London sometime next week to meet with the solicitor about the estate."

"One would think," said the rector's wife, "that he would have wanted the funeral delayed until he could be present."

"No doubt Mr. Montfort was as fond of his late aunt as were most people." Carol's eyes narrowed as she addressed the rector. "Come to think of it, I never noticed *you* visiting Lady Augusta while she was alive. Would you have asked *her* for a donation?"

"I did, during a pastoral visit several years ago. She refused to give any money to St. Fiacre's and said she never wanted to see me in her house again. Still, in Christian charity, one would have thought—in her will—and here it is Christmastime. . . ." Lucius Kincaid paused meaningfully.

"Oh, yes." Carol could not keep the sneer out

of her voice. In truth, she did not try very hard, for her exasperation with this ecclesiastical couple was increasing rapidly. "The holiday. I am afraid I would be the last person to help you in the name of the season. I don't think much of Christmas."

"Not think much of Christmas?" Mrs. Kincaid echoed.

"That's right." Carol had had enough of being questioned. Noting the glance that passed between husband and wife, she added, "The way Christmas is celebrated these days is just an excuse for rampant commercialism. There's no real spirit left in the holiday anymore."

"If you believe that, then you have been spending the holiday with the wrong people," the Reverend Mr. Kincaid informed her. "I know of places where the true spirit of Christmas dwells all year long."

"Really?" Carol gave him a scathing look. "Well, then, you just have a happy little Christmas in one of those places. But don't ask me to celebrate with you, and don't expect me to donate to your favorite charity." With that, she turned her back on the pair, not caring if her words or the action had shocked or distressed them yet again. She had her own reasons for hating the Christmas holiday, but she wasn't about to discuss them with the Reverend Mr. Kincaid and his wife.

Carol wished that people would not make assumptions about her financial state as the rector had done. People had been doing it all her life. Young men, seeing her parents' lavish lifestyle at the pinnacle of New York City's newly rich society during the nineteen-eighties, assumed she would inherit great wealth. Carol had believed it herself. But when, through the machinations of his business associates who had involved themselves in illegal stock transactions, her father had gone bankrupt, the protestations of eternal devotion had ended abruptly and those same young men—including the one special man with whom she had foolishly imagined herself in love—had lost all interest in her. Her girlfriends had also begun to shun her. And not one of those so-called friends who had assumed that her father's wealth was endless had lifted a hand to help him in his struggles to repay his partners' debts. Her mother's response to financial ruin had been divorce and remarriage to a man who was more wealthy than Henry Simmons had ever been. The former Mrs. Simmons had then departed on a long honeymoon cruise. Carol did not know her mother's present whereabouts, and after their last bitter quarrel, she really did not care.

His fortune gone, deserted by his wife, Henry Alwyn Simmons had taken an antique gun from his collection and blown out his brains. The deed had been done on Christmas Eve, which also happened to be Carol's 21st birthday.

Left alone and virtually penniless, Carol had begun searching for a job, only to discover that in the recession-bound economy of the late nineteen-eighties, her previously sheltered life had left her unsuited to do any kind of practical work. Computers were a mystery to her. She might have taught French, which she spoke well, or English literature or history, but none of the schools to which she applied displayed interest in hiring a young woman with no teaching experience.

She worked for a few months as a waitress, but hated the job except for the food she was able to hide away in her purse each day to eat later in her rented room. She quit the job when the restaurant manager made it all too clear to her what she would have to do to earn a raise in her meager paycheck. She hadn't been hungry enough to sell herself for food or for a promise of money.

Being of a thrifty disposition, she had managed to save a little cash, but she knew it would not last long. It was then, when she was wondering if she would end as her father had done, that she had seen the ad for a paid companion. The job was in London and offered room, board, and a small salary. The chance to get out of New York had been an added incentive. After a lengthy phone interview, Carol had been offered the job. She'd possessed just enough money to buy a one-way economy-class ticket from New York to London.

Fresh from an overnight flight, with her single suitcase in one hand and the address of her new employer in the other, Carol had arrived early one morning on Lady Augusta Marlowe's doorstep. At first she'd been greatly relieved to have found a position with such a prestigious British family. She'd needed only a week of employment at Marlowe House before she understood why Lady Augusta had been forced to advertise in the United States. Her stinginess and ill temper were legendary. But Lady Augusta's character had suited Carol's mood at the time, and gradually she'd adapted to the difficult old lady's eccentricities.

In fact, the two of them had been remarkably similar. Like Lady Augusta, Carol knew—she believed it in her deepest heart—that the only thing that mattered on this earth was money. She had seen in her own life what money could buy—for proof, she needed to look no further than her many suitors and her extravagant mother—and she knew from the defections of her would-be lovers from her side, and from her mother's easy desertion of her father, exactly what happened when the money disappeared.

Which was why she so respected Lady Augusta, who'd harbored no illusions about human affections. Or the value of charity. Or the need to celebrate holidays with an extravaganza of feasting and gifts and parties. Especially Christmas, which was nothing more than commercial nonsense designed to trick ordinary, hardworking fools out of their money. Carol heartily agreed with Lady Augusta on all of these points, if not on the matter of leaving bequests to one's employees.

"That was the last of them, Miss Simmons. I'll send Nell to clear the tea things away." Crampton had entered the drawing room, and suddenly Carol realized that she had been so deep in thought that, without noticing what she was doing, she must have bid farewell to the Reverend Mr. Kincaid and his wife, to the solicitor, and to the five or six other people who had attended the funeral. "Will you be taking dinner in your room again tonight?"

"No, I'm going out on the town." Her tone was so sarcastic that Crampton's eyebrows flew upward at the sound.

"I beg your pardon, Miss Simmons?" Disapproval was implicit in the butler's voice.

"Of course I'll eat in my room. Don't I always?" When she first arrived at Marlowe House, Carol had been expected to dine each evening in the formal dining room with her employer, but after Lady Augusta had taken to her bed during her final illness, Carol had asked for a tray to be brought to her own room so she could eat there. It was the easiest way she could think of to give herself an hour or so of privacy at the end of her busy and frequently upsetting days with her irascible patient.

Leaving the drawing room, Carol started up the wide, curving staircase. As her hand skimmed along the banister, it seemed to her that the polished wood vibrated beneath her fingertips. Of course, it was just foolish imagining on her part. She was overtired and suffering from the inevitable letdown that came after a funeral. Not to mention the letdown of knowing that Lady Augusta had not chosen to remember her companion's five and a half years of honest service with a bequest.

"It didn't have to be a lot of money," Carol muttered, reaching the top of the main stairs and walking along the hall toward the smaller flight of steps that led to the uppermost levels of Marlowe House. "A hundred pounds, two hundred at the most. Ye gods, that would only have been five hundred dollars or so, and everybody knows she was fabulously wealthy. She could have let me know that she appreciated all I did for her."

A low, cynical laugh came from the direction of Lady Augusta's suite of rooms. Carol paused for a moment or two, standing at the closed door. All was silence.

"Now I'm hearing ghosts," Carol said aloud. "There is no one in that room. I know it." Nonetheless, she opened the door. Within, the curtains were drawn, so the room was dim and shadowy. Carol fumbled for the light switch and found it, and electric bulbs glowed in the crystal chandelier that hung in the center of the ceiling. "Just as I thought. No one is here. Nor in the bathroom, either. Nor in the dressing room." Carol moved from bath to mirrored dressing room and back to the bedroom, still talking to herself.

"Lady Augusta was the kind of personality that impresses itself on everything around it and hangs on after death. That's what I'm reacting to. Tomorrow I'll tell Nell to open the windows in here and do a thorough cleaning to get rid of the last traces of the old girl, including that awful lavender perfume of hers."

Carol started for the hall, then paused. Though she knew it was impossible because she had just searched the suite, a prickling sensation between her shoulder blades warned that there was someone else in the bedroom with her. She spun around, but the room was still empty. From somewhere a cold draft blew across her ankles and she caught a whiff of lavender fragrance. Quickly she turned off the light, stepped into the hall, and shut the door firmly behind her. Then she hurried to the end of the hall, where the stairs to the upper floors were. She refused to look back as she went upward toward her own room.

It had once been a governess's room, and

thus fell into an indeterminate status between outright servants' quarters and a chamber that might have been given to an insignificant guest when Marlowe House was overcrowded. The room was at the front of the house, and a pair of windows allowed Carol a view of the square, which in summer was pleasant enough with trees, grass, and a flower garden, all confined within a wrought-iron fence. At the moment a small fir tree in the center of the square was decorated for Christmas. Its colored lights shone merrily through the early evening fog and drizzle. The weather was more like Halloween than Christmastime. It was a fine night for ghosts, if Carol had believed in them. She did not. There was little Carol did believe in anymore. She closed the curtains against the cheerful holiday display.

Nell, the chambermaid, had already been in to start a fire in the old fireplace to take the chill off the room. The flames threw dancing shadows across the ceiling and the walls. It was a simple room, with an old-fashioned four-poster bed that had once boasted frayed velvet hangings. The dust and the musty odor of the antique fabric had periodically sent her into fits of sneezing, so Carol had personally removed the hangings shortly after her arrival at Marlowe House. Besides the bed, the room also contained a chest of drawers, a desk and chair, and an upholstered wing chair next to the fireplace. A floor lamp, a footstool, and a small table, all of them set next to the wing chair, completed the furnishings. The bathroom was three doors down the hall.

Carol did not care that the room was bare

of pretty objects, that the bed looked naked without its hangings, or that the old Turkish carpet and the green bedspread were both threadbare. She could think of no good reason to spend her hard-earned money on frivolous decorations. The spartan bareness of her room suited her repressed spirit—though she would not have said she was repressed. Carol thought of herself as sensible in the face of adversity.

Having no further obligations for that evening, she changed from her plain, dark dress and low-heeled pumps into a flannel nightgown and a warm bathrobe.

"Here's your dinner, Miss Simmons." Nell appeared with a tray. "Oh, are you ready for bed so soon? I wish you would come down to eat with the rest of us. It's ever so much more pleasant in the kitchen, and warmer, too. You'll freeze way up here all alone."

"No, I won't." Carol motioned to her to put the tray on the table next to the wing chair. "That will be all, Nell."

"You oughten to be alone so much." Nell took no offense at the similarity of Carol's tone to the way in which Lady Augusta had always spoken to the chambermaid. Nell's youthful warmth could not be diminished by anyone else's coldness, and her broad, rosy face showed her concern for Carol. "Especially not tonight, you shouldn't be up here by yourself. Not after the funeral and all."

"I'm tired. I want to be left alone."

"All right, then, if you're sure. But tomorrow, you ought to come to the kitchen and join our plans. We're hopin' to make a nice little Christmas feast while we're all still together, and you're invited, of course. Well, good night, miss. Sleep tight now."

"Good night, Nell." As Lady Augusta had often remarked, Nell did not know her place in the household hierarchy. According to Lady Augusta, Nell's most improper friendliness was a sign of the degenerating times. In Lady Augusta's time, servants had known their places and stayed in them. If she could have heard Nell's invitation, Lady Augusta probably would have declared that no lady's companion should have been invited into the kitchen to share a Christmas feast concocted by servants. While not entirely agreeing with Lady Augusta's undemocratic attitudes, Carol had no interest in holiday celebrations of any kind, whether above or below stairs.

Carol sat down before the fire, put her feet upon the low stool, and took from her dinner tray a bowl of steaming soup. Mrs. Marks was an excellent cook, seeming to find challenge rather than discouragement in the tight budget which Lady Augusta allowed her. Carol spooned up rich chicken broth with thin slices of mushroom in it and wondered if the staff was eating as well as she. Lifting the domed metal cover over her dinner plate, she discovered a healthy portion of the chicken itself, with peas, diced beets, and a small pile of rice. A wedge of apple tart completed the meal, along with a large pot of tea.

"Foolish extravagance."

Had she spoken aloud? Surely not. But there was no one in the room except herself to make such a remark. Save for the crackling of the fire, all was silent. The kitchen was too far away for any noise from that area to disturb her.

Or for anyone to hear her if she called.

Telling herself that she was indeed overtired as well as overstressed, Carol disregarded the odd little shiver that ran down her spine. She re-covered the plate of chicken to keep it warm, and resumed eating her soup. She certainly had good reason to be nervous, but not about being upstairs alone in a big old house. Her future prospects were enough to scare anyone. Should she look for a new job in London, or should she spend precious money to fly back to New York and try to find employment there? As Lady Augusta's companion she had taught herself to type, and she had devised a rudimentary version of shorthand so that she could tend to her employer's scanty correspondence, but she did not think either skill would be much help to her in the world outside Marlowe House.

Why in heaven's name didn't all parents insist that their daughters learn early in life how to do some kind of useful work? Carol's mother had been too busy with social life, and her father too preoccupied with business and with earning vast sums of money, to pay much attention to their child, and so Carol had drifted through her girlhood and teen years with neither goals nor ambition. All that was required of her by her parents was that she look pretty, be polite, and not embarrass them. Being possessed of light brown hair with a natural curl to it, clear gray eyes, a nicely rounded figure, and a rather quiet personality, she had never caused them any trouble.

"And I'm paying for all of that now," she muttered, staring into the soup bowl. "Until

30

six years ago this week, my life was just one long vacation. Now look at me. Oh, how I wish I had a million dollars! No—ten million. Out of all the money Dad had made for himself and others, that wouldn't be much."

What would you do with it if you had it?

"What? Who said that?" She nearly spilled her soup when she sat up straight to look around the familiar room. Of course, there was no one to be seen. She hadn't heard the words. It was just the wind, sighing down the chimney. Carol sat back again, pulling the lapels of her bathrobe closer to her throat. She dipped her spoon into the soup bowl. If she didn't finish it soon, the soup would be cold, not to mention the chicken and vegetables still awaiting her on the tray.

The wind? Half an hour ago, the night had been still and foggy with a gently drizzling rain. On such a night, how could there be wind whistling down the chimney? Or rattling her bedchamber door as it was doing now? Carol paused, soup spoon suspended halfway between bowl and lips, wondering about the sudden meteorological change. The wind howled again, shaking the windowpanes and making the faded old curtains billow into the room.

And then Lady Augusta stood before the fireplace. At first, the figure Carol saw was semitransparent. Gradually Lady Augusta became more substantial, though Carol noted that the firelight cast no illumination upon her. Whatever this apparition might be, it was a creature of shadows, not of light. Whether it was real or whether she was only imagining

31

it, Carol could not tell. Fascinated but not yet frightened, Carol stared at the figure.

Lady Augusta looked much as Carol remembered her from their first days together five and half years previously, when her employer had been old but not yet ravaged by illness and the approach of death. Her gray hair, which was surprisingly thick for a woman of more than 70 years, was pulled into her customary knot at the back of her head. She was clothed in pale lavender chiffon robes that flowed and drifted around her as if blown by a gentle breeze.

"Good evening, Carol." Lady Augusta's voice was the same as Carol remembered, yet there was a slight difference to its timbre, a muting of its usual sharp querulousness.

"What are you doing here? You're supposed to be dead." Carol's hand shook, spilling chicken broth onto her robe. The soup was now entirely too cold to eat. Carol put the bowl on the tray, then looked back at the spot where Lady Augusta had appeared. She was still there.

"I don't believe in ghosts," Carol said, keeping her voice hard and steady. "Go away."

"If you do not believe in me, then I am not here," Lady Augusta replied with indisputable logic. "If I am not here, then I cannot go away."

"All right then, you're a figment of my imagination or a message from my subconscious mind. Tell me what I ought to know and then leave."

"That is precisely what I intend to do." To Carol's further amazement, Lady Augusta now sat down directly across the fireplace from

Carol's seat, in a spot where there was no chair. Lady Augusta simply bent her ghostly ectoplasm and sat, disposing her lavender robes about her as if she were in her own elegant drawing room taking her place upon one of the silk-upholstered sofas. When she was finished, the hem of her gown still rippled in the non-existent breeze. She leaned against the back of the sofa that was not there. To Carol, the effect was most unsettling.

"What—what do you want?" Carol did not sound as assured as she intended, because her voice cracked. She swallowed hard and tried again. "Are you really a ghost, or am I dreaming?"

"Make up your mind, Carol. Am I a figment of your imagination or a dream? Is your unconscious mind trying to tell you something? Am I a ghost? Or am I real? I cannot be all of those possibilities at once." Lady Augusta inclined her head, awaiting Carol's answer.

"You have forgotten another possibility," Carol said. "Your sudden appearance in my bedroom could be a nasty trick that's being played on me. Perhaps you are a holographic projection of some kind."

"Who would do such a thing to you?" asked Lady Augusta. "The servants? They are too unimaginative. Besides, they like you, although why they should I do not know. You are almost as unfriendly to them as I was. No, Carol, in your heart of hearts you know that I am real."

"But are you really dead?"

"Oh, yes." Lady Augusta smiled. Carol could not recall ever seeing her smile while she was alive. Before Carol could recover from this new amazement, Lady Augusta continued. "Death is a most remarkable sensation. In some respects it is quite delightful. I no longer feel physical pain and that is a great relief to me."

"I'm glad to hear it. I know your last few days were awful."

"There is something far more dreadful than physical pain," said Lady Augusta.

"I can't think what that might be," Carol remarked absently. One part of her mind was still assessing the ghostly appearance of her visitor in an attempt to discover exactly how this remarkable trick was being played on her. For the life of her, she could not think how it was done, but then Carol was not well informed on the subject of electronics technology. Nor, as Lady Augusta pointed out, did she know of anyone who might have reason to do such a thing to her.

"Pay attention, Carol." Lady Augusta had raised her voice a notch, and Carol jerked her thoughts back to what the ghost was telling her. "As I was saying, worse than any physical pain is the unbearable anguish of knowing that I never fulfilled the true purpose of my life. I let youthful disappointments harden my heart against life and love, as you also have done."

"You don't know anything about me," Carol cried, grabbing at the arms of her chair and holding on tight. "You never bothered to ask about my life before I came to work for you. You were too glad to have a companion who was willing to take the job for cheap wages to make any fuss over who I might be." Carol shut her mouth on the additional complaint

34

she wanted to make, about the way in which she had been treated in Lady Augusta's will.

"You poor, foolish girl," said Lady Augusta, shaking her head sadly. "Of course I had your past investigated. Do you think that I, mistrustful character that I was in life, would take the chance of hiring someone who might rob me or murder me in my bed? Really, Carol, you are entirely too naive and, like your father, you are much too weak-spirited to fight back when life deals you a bad blow."

"Don't you dare insult my father! He was an honest man!"

"Indeed he was, and he regrets his suicidal weakness now."

"*Now?* Have you met my father? In that— that—wherever you are?"

"Where I am," Lady Augusta responded, "all motives are understood, all excuses pardoned, though earthly mistakes must be exonerated. Yes, I have been in contact with your father, and I know everything there is to know about your youthful life. I do wish you had not allowed that selfish young man to take such terrible advantage of your affection for him. He did not value you properly, you know."

"Shut up! Just shut up!" Carol was out of her chair, standing over Lady Augusta as if to threaten her. "I won't talk about Robert."

"Of course you won't. You learned through sad experience what a mistake it was to allow him so much of your heart. Robert Drummond's affection was not for you as a person but for your father's money and power. No man has ever loved you for yourself."

"Stop this!" Carol was shaking with rage. The

mere mention of Robert Drummond's name was enough to chill her blood, as though the shadow of his old betrayal could still cast its blight over her life.

"I see that I have distressed you," said Lady Augusta. "Perhaps I was wrong to raise the subject at all. Some of my former tactlessness remains with me, I fear. I must work on improving that particular trait. Dear girl, do please sit down and stop looking as if you would like to murder me. What do you think you could possibly do to hurt me now?"

Still angry, and unappeased by what amounted to a rare apology from her late employer, Carol put out her hand to grab at Lady Augusta's arm. Her hand went right through Lady Augusta's seated figure. With a frightened gasp Carol snatched back her hand, which felt as if it had been plunged into ice water.

"You can't be real," Carol insisted.

"I am real," her ghostly visitor countered, "but real in ways that you will not be able to comprehend for many years yet. Sit down, Carol, and allow me to explain why I have been sent to you."

"Sent?" Carol sat without taking her eyes off Lady Augusta.

"As I was saying, I wasted my life on earth in miserliness, and in anger and willful misunderstandings, when I might have known love and spent my wealth in bringing happiness to others."

"Sure," Carol replied with considerable cynicism. "I know all about it. If you have money and you are willing to spend it, everybody loves you. I found that much out before I turned twenty-one. But it's not real love. People just pretend, the way Robert did, because they are hoping to get their hands on your money. I admired you, Lady Augusta, because you never let that kind of parasite take advantage of you."

"I can see you have a lot to learn." Lady Augusta regarded her sadly. "Not everyone is interested solely in money. You need to learn that the heart and the spirit are what matter, not earthly possessions. Carol, have you never wondered why you have always been so unhappy?"

"I know why," Carol told her, "and since you claim to know all about my life, I shouldn't have to explain it to you. By the way, you are partly to blame."

"Because I did not leave you any money in my will?" Again Lady Augusta smiled her ghostly smile. "Yes, in that document I was entirely too miserly toward all who were in my employ. I am paying for it now."

"Good," said Carol in a nasty tone of voice. "Serves you right. You were grossly unfair to me."

"Will you be silent and listen to me, or not?" asked Lady Augusta.

"Go ahead." Carol tried to repress the anger she could still feel simmering inside her, threatening to burst forth once more. "Say what you want to say."

"Thank you." Lady Augusta inclined her head with all the graciousness of a grand duchess. "Because of the unloving way in which I misspent my life, I am now doomed to wander the

Flora Speer

earth for all eternity, observing happiness that
I cannot share, witnessing need that I am no
longer able to alleviate."

"Alleviating the needs of others never bothered you much when you were alive," Carol
observed, "so it shouldn't upset you now."

"But it does. You see, the passage from your
dimension of life to my present state changes
one deeply."

"I should think it would," Carol said,
intrigued by this unique point of view in
spite of herself.

"The heart that once was hard and uncaring
is now transformed," Lady Augusta went on,
"so that I ache with unfulfilled love. But I have
no one upon whom to lavish it. I see poverty
and injustice that I want to lighten, but I am
no longer in your world and cannot use my
wealth for good. The opportunity has passed
me by."

"You should have left your money to charity—and to your employees," Carol said. "That
might make you feel better. But it's too late
now for you to change your will."

"Precisely." Lady Augusta nodded approv-
ingly. "I am glad you understand. It is too
late for me, but not for you. I do not want
you ever to suffer as I am suffering now.
Furthermore, you, dear Carol, are my means
to everlasting bliss."

"What are you talking about?" Carol demanded.

"I have been assigned to you," Lady Augusta
said. "If I can convince you to change your
hardhearted ways, to open yourself to love and
charity and beauty—if I can, in short, change

38

you as I was never able to change, into a kind and generous and loving person—then I will be permitted to give up this eternal wandering and take my proper place in the other life."

"Whoa," Carol said, putting up a hand to stop the eager flow of Lady Augusta's words. "I've seen this plot before in an old movie. And I read something similar once in a Christmas story. This is some kind of a put-up job, isn't it? Who planned this, anyway? That's what I can't figure out."

"From whom do you think the creators of those old movies or books received the plot lines, if not from the Greatest Planner of all?" asked Lady Augusta. "Such stories linger in the hearts of ordinary folk because those good souls recognize the eternal truth in them. This is no game, Carol, nor is it a trick. What I tell you is but a truth too simple and obvious for your closed and earthbound mind to grasp. In time, left to yourself, you will understand as I have come to understand, that love and charity and goodwill toward all whom you know are the most important qualities required of any soul. But by then it will be too late for you to alter your earthly life. In any case, you cannot stop what will happen next."

"Happen?" Carol repeated weakly. "What do you mean, happen? What are you going to do to me?"

"Now then," Lady Augusta went on as if Carol had not spoken. "I have been given this special season, from the winter solstice until Twelfth Night, in which to convert you to a better life."

"I don't like that word *convert*," Carol said.

"No matter. Another word will do as well. Say *change, alter, transform,* or *transmute* if you prefer. It is all the same to me. According to your earthly time, we have the three nights until Christmas Eve in which to begin our work. Afterward, the final changes will be up to you."

"You mean, *your* work," Carol said. "I hope you don't actually expect me to contribute anything to this project. I am not in favor of donations. And I am definitely not in the Christmas spirit."

"You will be, by the time I have finished with you." Lady Augusta's pale face took on a serious expression. "You must be, Carol, for the future of my very soul depends upon your transformation. Fight the events to come as hard as you wish. The alteration in your heart will mean more to you if it happens as the result of struggle. In my place, as in your world, what comes easily is not appreciated." Lady Augusta rose, her robes billowing about her, though Carol still could feel no wind. When Lady Augusta held out her hand, Carol shrank back into the shelter of the wing chair.

"I am not going anywhere with you," Carol declared.

"I cannot give you a choice in this, lest you reject an opportunity that will never arise again for you or for me. You *will* come with me, Carol, and you will give your all—heart, soul and mind—to what transpires. Let us begin."

Lady Augusta spread her arms wide. The folds of her flowing gown whipped toward Carol, who sat clutching at the arms of the wing chair, determined not to participate in

40

what she still perceived as a farce or a trick. The lavender folds blew and drifted ever nearer, wrapping themselves around the chair until Carol and chair were both totally encompassed in fog-like, wispy fabric.

"Don't!" Carol clawed at the sheer cloth, fighting desperately, afraid she would be smothered in what was now a pale, lavender-colored, lavender-scented mist. "Stop it! Let me go!"

"Fight all you want," Lady Augusta said, embracing her. "What will happen, will happen. But I will not desert you. I will remain at your side."

"I don't want this! Go back where you came from!" Carol shrieked, still trying to push the cloth away from her nose. She could not breathe, the lavender scent was so strong it was choking her, and Lady Augusta's cold embrace almost stopped her heart with fear. Carol had never been so cold. It was like the coldness of the grave. She screamed. . . .

Part II.
Christmas Past.

London, 1818.

Chapter Two

"Caroline, my dear, wake up. How can you be dozing on such an important night?"

"Who—what?" Carol battled the last shreds of a lavender-scented mist into the background of her mind so she could determine who was speaking to her. The voice was vaguely familiar.

"Dear sister, you have been dreaming." A youthful face surmounted by short curls of pale gold hair presented itself to Carol's confused sight.

"Dreaming?" Carol repeated. Then, remembering. "No, this is Lady Augusta's doing."

"Oh, dear." The pretty girl leaning over Carol bubbled with barely suppressed laughter. "Has Aunt Augusta brewed another of her famous herbal potions and sent you to sleep when you ought to be up and stirring in preparation for the ball?"

"Aunt?" repeated Carol. "What ball?"

"The Christmas ball, silly. Oh, do wake up, Caroline. It is time to put on your gown, and you did promise that I should be the only one to help you. Come, now, out of that chair at once."

Thus urged, Carol could only obey. She was sitting in a wing chair that, save for a change of upholstery, was the same chair in which she had been sitting while eating her lonely dinner and while talking to the ghost of Lady Augusta. However, the room in which she now found herself was most definitely not the same. This was a luxuriously furnished room, a lovely and spacious chamber with pale blue walls and ornate white molding all around the ceiling. A simpler molding outlined panels on every wall. A warming fire blazed high in the fireplace, candles burned on the wide mantel to light the room, and more candles shone upon tables and in wall sconces. And the once-frayed green fabric covering the wing chair was transformed into a fresh shade of blue brocade.

"I do believe Aunt Augusta was right after all," said the blond girl, lifting the hem of the gown that was spread across the blue coverlet of a large, canopied bed. "Peach is more properly your color than white."

This charming creature was herself gowned in white, a dress made with a high waistline, a low, rounded neck, and tiny puffed sleeves. A simple gold locket hung about her neck on a thin gold chain and her earrings were tiny pearls with pearl droplets. Her sweet face appeared to be untouched by cosmetics. Though Carol had never seen the girl before, she felt a peculiar stirring of affection toward her, as if she did know her and as if the girl were important.

"Off with your wrapper," said the girl, tugging upon the sash at Carol's waist. Looking down, Carol saw that she was no longer wearing her old bathrobe and flannel nightgown, but a pale yellow silk robe with ruffled edges. When she let the girl remove it, Carol gaped at unfamiliar underwear. An embroidered linen chemise covered a light corset that felt as if it had thin stays in it. Sheer peach-colored stockings were gartered at her knees. She was wearing flat satin slippers dyed a delicate shade of peach.

"Here you are." The girl steered Carol toward the bed. "Put up your arms. Do be careful, now. It is delicate and we don't want to tear it."

Carol followed the young woman's instructions without protest, standing still while a cloud of sheer, pale peach fabric was lifted over her head and adjusted around her body. With remarkable speed Carol's companion fastened a row of tiny buttons up the back of the dress. A gentle tug pulled everything into place.

"There. Don't I make a wonderful lady's maid? My dearest, you have never looked lovelier. Montfort will be ravished by the very sight of you. Just see for yourself."

"Montfort?" Yielding to the pressure of her companion's hands upon her shoulders, Carol turned to look into the cheval glass that stood in one corner of the room. The reflection that greeted her there was a real shock.

It was her own face that Carol saw, but her shoulder-length, light brown hair was cropped into a tumble of short curls, a coiffure almost identical to the one the young woman with her was wearing. Carol's peach-colored dress was also similar in style to the white one, and a matching pair of pearl earrings dangled from her own lobes.

What was most amazing to Carol was the difference she perceived in her face, for despite the astonishing similarity of feature, the face in the mirror was not exactly hers. Except for brief periods after her infrequent walks about London, when she had some color in her face and looked alive again, Carol was used to seeing her reflection pale and wan and somewhat listless. Even without makeup, the cheeks of the woman in the mirror glowed with good health and her eyes sparkled with excitement. Or—upon a closer, more thorough inspection—was that glow a feverish flush? Were those eyes perhaps too bright? And was it a shadow of fear Carol saw in the gray depths that were so similar to her own eyes? She did not have long to ponder the puzzling reflection.

"Shall I fasten this for you?" The girl in white held up for Carol's inspection a necklace of magnificent pearls with a clasp carved from a large sapphire.

"I can't wear that," Carol gasped. "It must be worth a fortune."

"My dear, Montfort told you himself that this necklace is part of his family's jewels. You must wear it. You cannot insult your fiance on this night of all nights by spurning his betrothal gift. Besides, you have already told him how much you like it."

"I do like it. That's just the trouble." But Carol

obediently bowed her head while the necklace was fastened about her neck. She lifted her head and, gazing into the cheval glass again, adjusted the heavy clasp so it lay just at the hollow of her throat. Three strands of large, perfect pearls glowed against her skin.

"Oh, how I envy you, Caroline," said her companion with unaffected sweetness. "I sometimes wonder if Lord Simmons will ever come up to scratch. But he is the only man I will consider marrying. I don't care who else asks me."

"Lord Simmons?"

"Good heavens, Caroline, can you do nothing but repeat everything I say?" The girl laughed at Carol with open affection in her manner. "However, I am sure that on the night of my own betrothal party, I will be as slack-witted as you appear to be, so I ought not to criticize my own dear sister."

Thus chastised, Carol refrained from repeating *sister*. She was by now in a state of absolute confusion. She did not have a sister, had never had a sister, and did not want one.

"I thought you said this was the Christmas ball." It was the only thing Carol could think of to say that would not sound like the raving of a lunatic. "Now you're telling me it's for my engagement?"

"You know perfectly well it is both." The girl in white laughed again. "The three of us and Montfort together agreed on the purpose of the ball, and I must say Aunt Augusta has done well by you. So many flowers and the best musicians! But then, she likes Montfort.

49

I swear, she would marry him herself if she were young enough."

"Montfort." Carol bit her lip. This pretty girl was right; she did seem to be making a habit of repeating whatever was said to her. Only one name gave her hope that she could make some sense out of her bewilderment.

"Aunt Augusta," Carol said.

"Yes. She wants to inspect you as soon as you are dressed. Here." The girl took a pair of long white gloves off the bed and handed them to Carol. When they were on, they reached above Carol's elbows. Her companion helped Carol to fasten the buttons. "Now your fan." This was a confection of peach silk on ivory sticks, the silk painted with delicate flowers and leaves.

"Are you coming with me?" Carol did not know whether to hope the girl would accompany her, or hope she would stay behind. If "Aunt Augusta" proved to be the Lady Augusta whom Carol knew and who was the cause of Carol's present confusion, then she wanted to confront the woman without having to be careful of her words in front of someone else. On the other hand, if it was not Lady Augusta, then Carol might need some support from this girl who seemed to hold her in great affection.

To Carol, there was something tantalizingly familiar about this young person, as if she were someone she had seen and heard in a dream or, perhaps, met briefly long ago. Carol looked more closely at her, wishing she dared to ask the girl what her name was, but it did not seem appropriate to inquire as to the identity of one's own sister. Except that Carol knew perfectly well the girl was not her sister. She experienced an odd tug of regret at the thought. A sister like this one might not be so bad.

"I have already passed inspection," the girl said in answer to Carol's question about Lady Augusta. "You go along. I will join you in a few moments. I want to brush my hair one last time, so I will look my very best."

"Just in case Lord Simmons appears at the ball?" The gently teasing tone of her own voice startled Carol. She actually sounded as if she were fond of the girl.

"Oh, I do hope he will come." Soft blue eyes shone at the thought; the sweet young mouth curved into a tremulous smile. "If he does, he might ask me to dance the waltz with him."

"Now, that would be cause for excitement." Realizing she could not remain in that chamber thinking up excuses to delay going to see "Aunt Augusta," Carol stepped through the door and into a long hall lit by a series of wall sconces in which candles burned.

The hall was not familiar to her, but she went toward an area that appeared to be more brightly lit than the area just outside the bedroom she had left. And then, suddenly, she did recognize the hall. It was because of the staircase. That lovely, curving sweep of step and banister was unmistakable to one who had been up and down it several times every day for five and a half years. And there, just a few steps away, was the door leading to Lady Augusta's suite of rooms. Taking a deep breath and hoping she was not mistaken, Carol went to the door and knocked upon it. The door was opened at once by a middle-aged woman in a black dress and white apron.

"Who is it?" said a well-known voice from within.

"It's me," said Carol, brushing past the servant to enter the room.

The decor was different. The paneled walls of the room were cream and white, with pale green taffeta curtains at the tall windows and matching hangings on the bed, but it was definitely the room Carol remembered from her time as Lady Augusta's companion. The woman sitting at the dressing table with a jewel box before her certainly looked like the Lady Augusta whom Carol knew.

"Come in and let me look at you," commanded Lady Augusta. "Marie, you may leave us. I will call when I want you again."

"*Oui*, madame." With a curtsy, the servant disappeared out the door, leaving Carol alone with a woman whom she believed to be a ghost. Or perhaps, despite appearances, this was not the ghost she had seen earlier that night. Carol decided to be cautious.

"Good evening, Lady Augusta." This salutation elicited raised eyebrows from the woman at the dressing table.

"In this house, during this time," said Lady Augusta, "you would be better advised to call me Aunt Augusta. Everyone you know will begin to wonder if you do not."

"Are you who I think you are?" Carol demanded. "Because if you are, I have to tell you that I am beginning to lose patience with this game you are playing."

"What seems to be the problem, Carol?"

At the use of her real name, Carol let out a

breath of relief. Then she got angry.

"How dare you set me down all alone, without any preparation, with a girl who thinks I am her sister? If I didn't have sense enough to keep quiet and listen instead of telling everything I know, that poor girl would be scared out of her wits about now. How do you think she would react if I claimed to be the victim of a sadistic trick played by a ghost?"

"But you did not frighten her by telling the truth, did you? I wonder why. Could it be that you felt a faint glimmer of sisterly tenderness toward her?"

"Don't get your hopes up," Carol responded. "She's nothing to me. By the way, what is her name? And why did she keep calling me Caroline?"

"If she means nothing to you," said Lady Augusta, "then why do you care what her name is?"

"You brought me here against my will," Carol said, "and apparently you have given me a new identity. I am wearing clothes that look like something a character in a Jane Austen novel would wear, and a girl who claims to be my sister tells me that tonight is my big engagement party. I don't even know who my fiance is supposed to be! If you don't want me to make some dreadful mistake in public that will embarrass you and that poor girl down the hall, then you had better provide a bit more information."

"Shall I wear the rubies or the sapphires tonight?" asked Lady Augusta. "I originally thought the sapphires with this deep blue dress, but I have no wish to outshine you on your special night. Your necklace is quite remark-able, isn't it? I remember when Montfort's late mother used to wear it. Did you know that she was one of my best friends?"

"No." Carol gritted her teeth in exasperation. "I did not know. How could I?"

"Well?" Lady Augusta held up two necklaces, one glittering with rubies and diamonds, the other a heavy gold chain boasting three large sapphires set in gold with diamonds around each stone. "Which do you think?"

"Wear the damned sapphires. Just tell me what I need to know to avoid making a fool of myself at this ball I am expected to attend. Or better yet, send me back where I am supposed to be."

"You are entirely too impatient," said Lady Augusta. She held first one, then the other necklace up to her throat, testing the effect of each in her dressing table mirror. "I do believe you are right. Very well, it shall be the sapphires." She fastened the necklace, then rose and approached Carol.

"At the moment, you *are* exactly where you are supposed to be," said Lady Augusta. "The year is 1818. You are living in Marlowe House as it was at that time."

"Who am I?" snapped Carol.

"You are Lady Caroline Hyde. Your younger sister is Lady Penelope. You two have always been remarkably close, and have grown closer still since the death of your parents in a carriage accident four years ago. As your aunt, I have seen to your education since that time, and have sponsored you in society. Though at four and twenty years of age you are considered a little old for such good fortune, you have succeeded in making one of the great matches of the year. You are to wed Nicholas Marlowe, the Earl of Montfort, who, incidentally, is a distant cousin of my late husband."

"Is he any relation to the Nicholas Montfort who is your nephew?" Carol asked, her full attention caught by the repetition of the same name.

"Who *will be* my nephew in the next century," Lady Augusta corrected. "My future nephew is a direct descendant of Lord Montfort."

"Then these people you have been telling me about are all real." Carol paused to think for a moment before continuing. "Does this mean that you and I are inhabiting the bodies of other people? If we are, then where are the personalities of those people now? Have you hurt this Lady Caroline in any way? Or her Aunt Augusta?"

"While we are in this time, you and Lady Caroline, and I and the earlier Lady Augusta, are one and the same. You need have no fear for their safety. The One who sent me on this mission will allow no harm to come to either woman through us. However, the emotions you experience will be entirely your own. That is, after all, the purpose of this visit to the past—to stir up emotions long dead in you, to raise feelings you never knew you possessed."

"This whole arrangement strikes me as highly immoral," Carol insisted, unappeased by an explanation that made little sense to her practical mind. "Couldn't I ruin Lady Caroline's life by doing something stupid that would make her fiancé decide he doesn't want to marry her after all?"

"Have no fear on that score. Montfort will not break off the engagement," said Lady Augusta. "Nor, while you are here, will you be able to alter the overall course of history in any way unless you reveal that you are from the future."

"Are you sure about that?" Carol demanded, recalling a science-fiction novel she had once read that involved creating major changes in the future by making the most minute changes in the past.

"Absolutely," said Lady Augusta. "Though I am pleased to hear you voicing concern about the lives of people you do not yet know, I assure you that all you have to do is say nothing about your true origin, keep your eyes and ears and, most important of all, your heart open, and go with the flow."

"Go with—?" Carol broke off with a surprised laugh. "Now, there's a phrase I never dreamed I'd hear from you."

"Yes, it is, isn't it?" Lady Augusta looked pleased with herself for a moment, before she turned businesslike once more. "Listen carefully, Carol, for there is a great deal you need to know before the ball begins, and Penelope may join us at any moment. You will find the house somewhat different. The original Marlowe House is twice as large as the one you know. It was remodeled after the Second World War and turned into two houses so one of them could be rented." There followed a barrage of information on the Marlowe and Montfort families as they were in the early nineteenth century, along with a list of the rigid rules of etiquette at that time.

"You can't possibly expect me to remember all of this," Carol cried after ten minutes or so.

"If you become confused, I suggest that you take a deep breath, relax, and let Lady Caroline's instincts guide you," Lady Augusta advised.

"This is crazy," Carol protested. "You know that, don't you?"

"It all seems perfectly simple to me." This was said with airy complacency as Lady Augusta turned back to her mirror to don sapphire earrings that matched her necklace. A gold and sapphire bracelet followed, worn over her long white gloves. Holding out her arms, she spun around to face Carol again. "How do I look? I do so love the clothing designs of this period. A high Empire waistline can disguise those unpleasant problems of expansion about the midriff that all middle-aged women inevitably develop."

"You sure don't act like someone who is desperately trying to save her soul. I think you are actually enjoying this!" Carol surveyed the tall, slender figure garbed in deep blue. The twinkle in Lady Augusta's eyes effectively softened the harsh words that Carol might have spoken—indeed felt she had a right to speak, considering what was being done to her against her will. "You look very nice. Your hair is a different color now. It's not so gray. It's more salt and pepper. Lady Augusta—I mean, Aunt Augusta—are you sure I won't make some idiotic mistake tonight?"

"I have every confidence in you, my dear." At the sound of a light tap on the bedroom door, Lady Augusta looked over Carol's shoulder. "Ah, here is Penelope now. You are late, miss. Shall we go down? Our guests will soon begin arriving."

As they trooped down the stairs, Carol could see what Lady Augusta had meant when she said Marlowe House was different. The entrance hall, with its black and white marble checkerboard floor, was twice as large as Carol remembered. Off to one side of the hall was a reception room, which was entered through a wide, arched doorway that did not exist during Carol's twentieth-century years in the house. Beyond this reception room lay the ballroom, a glittering splendor of cream walls, gold-leaf trim, mirrors, and chandeliers decorated with holiday greenery and blazing with hundreds of fine wax candles. Gilt chairs lined the walls to provide seating for the chaperones and for those not dancing. The parquet wood floor was waxed and polished to a brilliant shine.

Double doors at the back of the ballroom opened into a grand dining room, where a late supper would be served. Another room was set up with small tables for card games. Next to the dining room, in the section of the house that Carol knew well, the library offered a quiet retreat for anyone weary of the crowd. A large walled garden lay behind the house.

Gazing around this earlier version of the mansion, Carol understood why the upstairs hall was unfamiliar to her. Lady Caroline's bedroom belonged to this other half of the building, and in Carol's own time it was no longer a part of Marlowe House.

"What a pity it had to be changed," she said softly.

"Taxes." Lady Augusta's equally low response was crisp. "Death duties when my grandfather died. The intrusion of the modern world on ancient privilege. As you say, a pity, and the more so since my father later made a huge fortune that would have allowed him to keep the house as it was. Still, at the end of the twentieth century no one holds great balls anymore." Raising her voice, Lady Augusta added, "Caroline, I do believe your fiance is arriving."

"I can't—I'm not ready—"

"Ready or not," said Lady Augusta, "here he is. Good evening, Nicholas."

"My lady." Nicholas Marlowe, Earl of Montfort, bent over his hostess's hand, then kissed her cheek.

"You ought to be doing that to Caroline instead of to an old lady like me," Lady Augusta told him, rapping his arm with her closed fan.

"It will be a pleasure, ma'am." Montfort turned from Lady Augusta to Carol and fixed his sparkling green eyes on her.

Carol nearly fainted from the impact. He was tall, a broad-shouldered, slim-waisted man. His black evening clothes were perfectly tailored in the severe style made popular by Beau Brummell. His black, curly hair was cut short, his nose was long and aristocratic, and his mouth looked made for laughing. Or for kissing.

He took Carol's gloved hand in his and bent forward to kiss her cheek as Lady Augusta had commanded. Carol caught a whiff of lime cologne.

"Will you please try to smile? I am not a monster, you know," he whispered into her ear. Through the spotless white kid of his glove she felt the strength and the heat of his fingers around hers. When he straightened, Carol stared back at him, unable to speak.

"How romantic," cried Penelope, her hands clasped at her bosom. "My sensible older sister is struck dumb at the sight of her true love."

"Hello, Penny Sweet." Montfort grinned at her. "I need not ask how my little sister-to-be is this evening. Looking as you do, you will surely send all the young men into veritable paroxysms of romantic passion."

"Montfort," snapped Lady Augusta as he chucked the giggling Penelope under her chin, "I will thank you to confine your attentions to my elder niece. Unless, of course, you intend to set up a harem."

"Oh, Aunt Augusta, what a shocking idea," cried Penelope, still laughing. "I am certain that Nicholas has eyes only for Caroline."

"For no one else, I promise you." Nicholas was drawing Carol's hand through his elbow as he spoke. "I do believe if I had proposed to you, Penny, instead of to your sister, you would have broken my heart by refusing me. If I am not mistaken, your affections are engaged by young Simmons, who, as I understand it, plans to attend tonight with the express intention of dancing the waltz with you."

At this Penelope began to blush furiously, but

Montfort did not see it. His own attention was on Carol, and she had the feeling that it was not because he was smitten with her charms. There was something calculating in the way he regarded her.

"Caroline, you seem somewhat distracted. Is anything wrong?"

"I am just a little giddy with excitement." In fact, Carol was wondering exactly what this man's feelings were toward Lady Caroline Hyde. It was plain to her that he held Lady Augusta in real affection, and his easy, teasing manner toward Penelope revealed all the fondness of a much older brother-in-law-to-be toward an innocent young girl, but Carol could not make out what the relationship was between Lord Montfort and Caroline. She wished that she had thought to ask Lady Augusta if Caroline Hyde were an heiress—or if Montfort were rich.

"I am pleased to see you are wearing the necklace I gave you." Montfort's eyes were on the pearls and the sapphire clasp. Then his gaze moved lower, toward the deep neckline of her gown, and Carol knew he was admiring the swell of her breasts. She sensed a slight tremor in the muscular arm where her fingers still rested. The involuntary motion communicated itself to her and ran through her body so that she began to tremble.

Ye gods, Carol thought, *what has Lady Augusta gotten me into? How can I possibly resist this man if he has decided that he wants to make love to his fiancee before the wedding? Or are Montfort and Lady Caroline lovers already? Why do I care? These people are nothing to me.*

She did not have long to worry over the problem for their guests were beginning to arrive. Lady Augusta shepherded her nieces into the reception room, where they formed a line to greet those who were invited to congratulate the newly betrothed couple. Montfort stood between Lady Augusta and Carol, with Penelope on Carol's other side. Carol was not pleased by this arrangment, since it provided no opportunity for Lady Augusta to whisper information to her about the various people she was meeting, most of whom she was apparently supposed to know by sight. Carol took refuge in polite chitchat, which seemed to her to be remarkably similar to the conversations held at the large cocktail parties her parents had once given.

Growing more aware with every passing moment of Montfort's masculine presence at her side, Carol listened with a polite smile and a definite lack of serious attention while an elderly gentleman, whom Montfort addressed as Lord Falloner, informed her that the weather was unusually cold for so early in the season. He could tell from the aching of his gouty big toe, said Lord Falloner, that a heavy snow would fall before Christmas Day dawned.

"Dear me," Carol said to the aged lord, "I have been so busy lately that I have quite forgotten the date. How long is it until Christmas?"

"Just three more days," came the response. "I'll wager Montfort, here, has some special gift planned for you. Hah! Hah! I know what I would give you if you were *my* wife-to-be."

Carol did her best not to blush at this, and she carefully did not look at Montfort to see his reaction. Instead, she gave her hand to the next person coming along the line. There were so many guests that she thought she would faint from sheer exhaustion before they all passed through the receiving line and into the ballroom. She began to wonder if her face would crack from the effort to keep smiling. At least she could do little to embarrass herself or anyone else while she stood in line. Her first real difficulty arose when it was time for her to open the dancing with her fiance. Taking her hand without a word, Montfort led her to the center of the polished ballroom floor.

"I hope this is a waltz," Carol said to him, annoyed by his continuing silence and worried about what would happen in the next few minutes.

"You know perfectly well that the first dance at any ball is always a minuet." Montfort's voice was frosty. "I believe the exact music for the opening dance was decided upon some days ago."

"If it was, no one told me about it." Carol stopped right where she was, with all the guests staring at them. She did not know how to dance a minuet. Nor did she know what other kinds of dances were popular at this time in history. She imagined complicated steps involving groups of people, and she was certain if she were to attempt such a dance, she would make a complete fool of herself. She would probably also annoy her fiance. However, she did know how to waltz.

"Caroline." Montfort's eyes were dark with anger, and now Carol was sure that he did not care about Caroline Hyde. He was marrying her for some other reason than love. Carol did not have to look far into her own past to decide what that reason must be. She drew herself up, lifted her chin, and looked Montfort square in the eye.

"I will dance a waltz, or I will not dance at all," she said. "This is *my* betrothal party. I will begin it as I wish."

She could see he was furious. She could see something else, too. There was a faint spark of humor deep in his eyes, and perhaps a gleam of dawning respect.

"Madam, will you also try to change the vows we take when we stand at the altar?" he demanded.

"We shall see about that," she said. "And about what happens afterward, too."

"Indeed?" After studying her face for a few moments, Montfort turned on his heel and strode away from her. Not knowing what to do, fearing that he meant to leave her there alone in the middle of the dance floor, Carol remained where she was standing while Montfort spoke to a servant, who hurried away toward the musicians' gallery. Then, to Carol's great relief, Montfort returned to her.

"If you will but grant the musicians a moment to make the substitution," he said, "they will play a waltz."

"Thank you, my lord." Carol tried to keep her voice level and unwavering. Then the music began and she was swept into Montfort's strong arms. Now she was forced to follow his lead, but she did so gladly, for he was an expert dancer.

"You amaze me," Montfort said as they

whirled across the ballroom floor.

"Why is that, my lord?" Carol decided the safest course for her to follow with this man was to maintain a cool, detached attitude toward him. She had known since the first moment of meeting him that Nicholas Marlowe was a danger to her. If she was not careful he could shatter the emotional stability she had achieved with such difficulty after being badly hurt by a man she loved. She had vowed long ago never to allow that to happen again. Even if she were to relent and allow herself to feel something for another man, it would be the height of lunacy to let her emotions run wild in her present situation.

"I believed I knew you well," Montfort said in answer to her question. "Now I find you behaving like someone else."

"How so, my lord?"

"You have never made any demands of me until this past hour."

"Perhaps I should have done so long ago. A demand made upon you every now and then might be good for your soul." Carol watched the corners of his mouth twitch in the beginning of a smile. The humor was quickly suppressed and he spoke with great severity.

"It was my understanding that I would find in you the biddable wife I want, who would give me the heir I need, and who would not interfere in my life."

You miserable male chauvinist pig. She almost said it aloud, but stopped herself just in time. Of course he was a male chauvinist pig; all men were in the early nineteenth century, and especially aristocratic Englishmen, who believed the world belonged to them. He probably had a couple of mistresses set up in nice little flats right there in London, and he would think nothing of leaving his wife's bed to visit them. Carol decided to strike a blow for Lady Caroline.

"Good heavens, sir," she said in a mocking voice, fluttering her eyelashes at him as she spoke. "What is a wife for, if not to interfere with a man's pleasures?"

"I expect you to keep to the terms of our agreement," he responded.

"And if I do not?" Carol stopped dancing, leaving Montfort poised on one foot in the middle of a step. For a split second his face was like a thundercloud and she almost expected him to hurl a destructive bolt of lightning at her. Then, inexplicably, he smiled at her. Catching both of her hands in his, he raised her fingers to his lips. The onlookers must have thought he was greatly amused by something she had just said and was saluting her wit. But when he spoke it was through clenched teeth and in a voice so low that Carol could just barely hear his words.

"I do not know what game you think you are playing, Caroline, but I will not allow you to create a spectacle to feed the gossips."

"If you don't like the way I am behaving, then cancel the engagement," Carol retorted.

"I will not cry off," he said, still smiling that beautiful, blazing, false smile and speaking in a way that would suggest to those watching them that he was now whispering words of tender love. "Nor will I allow *you* to cry off. We made a bargain, Caroline, and you will keep it. All of it."

Of course she could not break off someone else's engagement. What she was doing could put Lady Caroline into an unhappy situation after Carol departed to her own time and after Lady Caroline was married to this man. Carol did not know much about the marriage laws of that period of history, but she suspected that a husband would have control of his wife's person and her fortune—and he could probably control every minute of her daily activities, too. For Lady Caroline's sake, Carol would have to be more careful. But she wasn't going to knuckle under completely.

"I find I am a bit faint from all the excitement," Carol said. "If I could just have a few minutes alone to collect my thoughts, I am sure I will feel much more like myself. I think I will go to the library."

"Make your curtsy, madam, and I will take you there." Montfort bowed gracefully and Carol, in response to his action, made a dancing-school curtsy.

As he led her off the ballroom floor the musicians struck up a new tune. There were other men who crowded around Carol to beg for dances with her, but Montfort made her excuses before Carol could say anything for herself. Their progress out of the ballroom was followed by the knowing looks of the guests. A few elderly ladies whispered behind their fans.

"Is it quite proper for you to close the door?" Carol asked when she and Montfort were alone in the library. "Shouldn't I have a chaperone?

Aunt Augusta, perhaps?" she added hopefully.

"I shall claim the right of a betrothed husband and say I want to have you to myself for a short time," Montfort responded. With the door closed, he approached her with the tread of a man determined to dominate their meeting. "Now, Caroline, I want you to understand that I will not allow you to go back on your word to me."

"I have never in my life gone back on my word, any more than my father ever did," Carol told him. "I am insulted that you might think I would."

"I am glad to hear you say so," Montfort told her. "There are some men who believe a woman has no sense of honor. I am not among them, and I will expect honorable behavior from my wife."

"Montfort, are you marrying Lady Caro—I mean, are you marrying me for my money?"

"Hardly, since my fortune is so much greater than yours." He looked at her as if he were trying to decipher all her secrets. "You have known about my fortune for most of your life. Why do you ask about it now? Caroline, you are not at all like yourself tonight."

"That is certainly true," Carol said. Relieved by his claim to wealth, she continued in a more agreeable way. "I am sorry. I spoke without thinking."

"Tell me what is wrong and I will try to help."

"If I did, you really would think I'm mad." Responding to the slight softening she detected in his probing gaze, Carol seriously considered revealing her true situation. She quickly decided against the idea. She did not think Montfort would believe her outlandish story. Furthermore, if Carol were to be returned to the twentieth century in the next few hours, poor Lady Caroline would be left to make explanations for incredible events that she could not possibly comprehend. People might think Lady Caroline was the mad one.

This business of thinking for two people at once—and of voluntarily and without expectation of any payment considering another person's welfare before her own—was a completely new experience for Carol. It was also tiring. She raised one hand to rub her forehead. Montfort responded to the weary gesture by moving closer to her, as if he wanted to protect her in some way.

"Surely you know by now that you can trust me?" he urged.

"Can I? How I wish I could be sure of that."

"Why this sudden uncertainty now, when you expressed no qualms at all on the day when you agreed to our bargain?"

"Refresh my memory, Montfort. Explain to me exactly what this bargain is, and why I consented to it."

"You cannot have forgotten details so important to your future," he objected. "Or to your sister's future."

"Perhaps I want to hear you tell me in order to be certain that *you* have not forgotten." Carol waited, hoping he would reveal at least a few facts that would help to keep her from making any mistakes for which the real Lady Caroline would later have to pay. She looked deep into his eyes and smiled. "Indulge my foolishness, Montfort. Please."

"Are you flirting with me? This is most unlike you, Caroline." He looked puzzled. Then: "Very well, if you are determined to hear the facts once again, here they are. Your father and mine were lifelong friends. After your parents' death my father did his best to see that you and Penelope were well settled in life. It was my father who suggested to Lady Augusta that she allow you and your sister to live with her and that she should sponsor you in society. She was unwilling at first, believing such an arrangement would cause her too much trouble and would also be expensive. I do not need to tell you that Lady Augusta can be foolishly miserly at times. However, I do not think she has ever regretted taking you in, and she has done her best to launch you into the world in proper style and to find husbands for both you and Penelope.

"When my father died and I became Earl of Montfort in his place, his obligations fell upon me." Montfort paused.

"Are you saying that you are marrying me out of pity?" There was a challenge in Carol's voice that made him look at her sharply.

"Not at all," he said. "Save for the lack of a large fortune, you are an eminently suitable choice as a wife, and one my own father would have approved. You and I have always been on cordial terms. Since I am now in need of an heir to my title, our marriage seemed the sensible solution to several problems."

"I am to provide an heir," she prodded when he fell silent.

"And one or two other children," he added, "since babies do not always outlive their first few years. It is best to be certain there will be at least one adult heir to survive me. In return I have arranged a handsome settlement for you, so that even if I should die at a young age, you will never want for any material thing. While we both live I have agreed to keep you in a style befitting the Countess of Montfort."

"I see," Carol murmured. "Financial security for me in exchange for the use of my body to create your heirs. It does make practical sense, but it is an awfully cold-blooded way to arrange a marriage."

"You agreed to it as cold-bloodedly as I proposed it," he said. "In fact, you left me with the impression that you were, in your own dispassionate way, pleased by my proposal. And then, there is the matter of your sister."

"What about Penelope?" She sounded defensive, but she didn't care. That sweet girl deserved a big sister who would defend her if need be. Carol did not pause to question why she felt that way; she simply accepted the unfamiliar emotion while she listened carefully to what Montfort was saying.

"On the day we are married," he told her, "I will settle a substantial dowry on Penelope, so she can make a good match. I would not be at all surprised if Lord Simmons makes an offer for her."

"So I am marrying you for my sister's sake?"

"I did hold out some faint hope that the arrangment might please you for your own

71

sake." He now looked more puzzled than ever. "With only a small dowry, you were unable to find a husband, and since you are several years past the preferred age for marriage and have no other likely suitors dangling after you—" He left the sentence unfinished, but Carol could imagine what he might have said. This was a time and place in which the only suitable career for a noblewoman was marriage and motherhood. Lady Caroline Hyde did not have many choices. Lord Montfort was handsome, well bred, and rich. It was a perfect match— except that love did not enter into the equation between these two people. Carol felt a twinge of pity for Lady Caroline.

"What a neat little business arrangement," she mused.

"So I thought, too," he replied, placing one finger beneath her chin and turning her face toward his. "Until this evening, when you were changed into someone I scarcely recognize."

"Does the change make you angry?" she whispered, left nearly breathless by his nearness.

"It intrigues me. I know you love your sister enough to do almost anything for her sake, even marrying a man you consider to be something of a rake. I thought I knew you well, Caroline, and knew what to expect of you. I never guessed that beneath your proper demeanor you possessed so lively a spirit." His mouth was now disturbingly close to hers. Carol knew a moment of panic.

"I have recently learned more than I care to know about lively spirits," she declared.

"Have you? This change in you grows more interesting by the moment. Perhaps you will allow me to test your newfound spirit."

"I don't think it would be wise." The cautionary words came out as more of a gasp than a firm statement.

"Why not, when I am your promised husband?" His free arm slid around her waist, drawing her closer still. "Who would dare to criticize me for sampling that which will soon be entirely mine?"

Carol was all too aware of his masculine warmth, and of the muscular hardness of his body. This had to stop at once. She was appalled to discover that she was not as immune to the charms of handsome men as she had imagined. And this particular man belonged to another woman. She prepared to voice a vigorous protest.

"My lord, I do not—" It was too late. His mouth touched hers. The fingers that had been holding her chin now wove their way through her short curls to steady her head so she could not pull away. The arm around her waist tightened.

It was more than six years since a man had kissed her, and never had she been kissed with such expert skill. There was no use in fighting him. He was far too strong. The awful thing was that she quickly found she did not want to fight him. With a moan, Carol opened her lips to his thrusting tongue. With a feeling of helpless despair she put her arms around him. And then she let her emotions take control of her actions.

Montfort's mouth was fierce and hot on hers, and Carol responded to his demands with growing urgency. She was drowning in his desire. They stood pressed together, with Carol drawn up on tiptoe to reach his mouth. His hand slid downward to push her hips against his hardness. Carol did not protest. The kiss went on and on until she lost track of time and knew only the bliss of his embrace. When he finally broke off and lifted his head, his face was taut with desire and his green eyes spoke of needs too primitive for civilized existence.

"My God, Caroline," he rasped. "How could I have been so mistaken about you? I never guessed that you would be so responsive. Oh, how I want you."

He buried his face in her bosom, his hands now at the sides of her breasts. Carol's arms were still around him. She held his head where it was, accepting—no, demanding— the kisses he was placing along the curve of peach fabric where her gown barely covered her breasts. Her own murmured words sounded like an echo of his surprised exclamation.

"I had no idea—I didn't know—oh, Montfort!"

"Nicholas," he groaned. "My name is Nicholas. I wish you would use it."

"Nicholas," she repeated, her eyes closed to better savor what was happening between them. She felt his hand inside her gown, slipping beneath the chemise, lifting her left breast. And then his mouth was on her nipple, sucking.

"Ah!" Carol could not control herself. Her body jerked in response to his tugging, and her hands were tight in his hair, holding his face against her breast. "*Nicholas!*"

"Nicholas indeed," said Lady Augusta's disapproving voice. "Montfort, what are you doing to my niece?"

Nicholas lifted his head from Carol's breast, and for an instant she saw the primitive emotion in his eyes again, this time expressed as blazing fury. She knew just how he felt. She, too, was angry at the interruption. She wanted to scream at Lady Augusta to go away and leave them alone.

"Well, Montfort?" Lady Augusta's voice was sharper than before and from the sound of rustling silk across the room, Carol suspected that she was coming closer to them.

Nicholas straightened slowly, keeping his broad shoulders between Carol and Lady Augusta, thus blocking Lady Augusta's view. His eyes rested on Carol's bosom, where one hard little nipple peeked above the neckline of her gown. Nicholas cocked an eyebrow, smiling, while Carol hastily stuffed herself back into the dress. When she was finished, Nicholas turned slowly, still shielding Carol with his body, giving her time to recover her wits sufficiently to enable to her to think and act like a rational person once more.

"Montfort, I spoke to you!"

"I beg your pardon, Lady Augusta. I did not hear you at first because I was kissing my intended wife."

"I see." Lady Augusta shot a questioning glance in Carol's direction. Thanks to Nicholas's delaying tactics, Carol was able to look back at her with some degree of calmness. "I trust you enjoyed it," Lady Augusta said to Nicholas. Her sharp eyes were still on Carol.

"I found it a most enlightening experience," Nicholas replied. "One which I plan to repeat as often as possible."

"Caroline, I wish to speak with you." Lady Augusta had not taken her accusing gaze from Carol's face.

"You must excuse us, ma'am," said Nicholas. "Caroline has promised another dance to me and I refuse to be disappointed." Turning to Carol, he held out his hand.

"My dear lady," he said, his eyes speaking of a conspiracy of desire between them, "I believe the next dance is mine."

"Yes, my lord." Carol placed her fingers upon his wrist, allowing him to lead her past an openmouthed, speechless Lady Augusta and thence out of the library.

Chapter Three

During the rest of the evening Nicholas danced
three more times with Carol. Since they were
affianced, this caused only mild comment from
the chaperones, but all the while she was in
Nicholas's arms for a waltz, or was handed
from person to person during a more intricate
dance, Carol could feel Lady Augusta's eyes on
her. She knew she would have some explaining
to do for that kiss in the library, but she discovered that she did not much care if Lady Augusta
did scold her. The kiss that never should have
taken place had released in her a spurt of rare
joy that lingered for hours afterward, so she
was able to smile and laugh and talk as if she
belonged in the ballroom of Marlowe House—
as if she were born to dance there.

She quickly discovered that the dances were
not as complicated as she had feared. Once,

when she was in her mid-teens, the parents of one of her girlfriends had given their daughter a square-dance birthday party, complete with instructors to teach the steps to the young guests. Now Carol found most of the dances being performed in Lady Augusta's ballroom were similar to those square dances, and the steps she did not know she quickly learned.

"You look so happy tonight," Penelope remarked during a brief interval between dances. "Caroline, I do not think I have ever seen you so lively." Those soft blue eyes were a bit too penetrating for Carol's comfort. She tried to deflect Penelope's interest.

"Nicholas said much the same thing," Carol responded, linking her arm through Penelope's. "I told him it was the excitement of the evening. I hope you are also enjoying yourself. Has Lord Simmons arrived yet?"

"Oh, yes, and Nicholas was right. Lord Simmons told me he came here tonight especially to dance the waltz with me. He even asked Aunt Augusta if he might take me in to supper." Penelope's cheeks were bright pink as she glanced over Carol's shoulder.

Curious, Carol turned to find Nicholas approaching with a man perhaps a year or two older than Penelope. Once again she was expected to know who an unfamilar person was, but from Penelope's reaction to him it was easy to deduce that this must be Lord Simmons. Carol studied the young man's features intently. Despite the fact that he bore her family name, she could detect in him no resemblance to any relatives she could remember. Lord Simmons was tall, fair-haired, and good-looking. Since the two men were obviously on excellent terms, Carol could not help wondering if Montfort had made Lord Simmons aware of the dowry he was planning to bestow on Penelope and if it was that knowledge that made Lord Simmons so attentive to the girl.

When the next waltz began and she was in Montfort's arms once more, Carol asked him about it. To his credit he did not laugh the question away, nor did he become angry when she insisted on an answer.

"I am sure Simmons does care for Penelope," Montfort said. "However, I know him well enough to believe he would never displease his overbearing father by offering for a girl who would bring to her marriage only a small dowry. The settlement I will provide for Penelope will simply allow Simmons to follow his heart. It will also give Penelope what she most desires. You cannot disapprove of this arrangement, since you and I privately agreed to it weeks ago."

"I just want her to be happy," Carol said, "and not only for a few months or for a year or two, but for the rest of her life. She is such a lovely, sweet girl. I don't think she has ever had an unkind thought about anyone."

"I agree." Montfort gave her a deliciously teasing smile. "However, I regret that I cannot say the same about you, my dear. I do believe you have, on several occasions, harbored unkind thoughts about me."

"I cannot deny it, my lord." This response was greeted by a deep, appreciative chuckle.

"Caroline, if you continue as you have been

doing this evening, I will endeavor never again to give you cause to think unkindly of me."

"Is that a promise, my lord?" She meant it as a joke, but the words came out more sharply than she intended.

"A most solemn promise," he responded at once. "I find this new quality in your character to be most remarkably fascinating." His eyes were a smoky green as they gazed into hers, and Carol could sense the leashed passion in him. She could tell that he wanted to kiss her again. And afterward he would put his mouth on her breast. . . . She shuddered in memory, and saw understanding in his face.

"As you are tonight," he said, "you could easily fascinate me for all eternity and to the exclusion of all others."

"Eternity is a long time," she murmured.

"Nevertheless . . ."

The dance ended just then, and Penelope and Lord Simmons were left standing right next to them, so Carol and Montfort were forced to break off their too-intimate conversation, but Carol had the impression that Montfort would pick it up again as soon as he could. The way he looked at her, and stayed right beside her when the four of them went in to dinner together, the manner in which he neatly cut off the attentions other men would have paid to her, all convinced Carol that the fascination he claimed to feel for her was no empty compliment. With a bravado completely out of character for Carol Simmons, and from what she had learned of the lady, a bravado that would have been beyond the comprehension of Lady Caroline Hyde, Carol decided that while she was in nineteenth-century London, she might as well enjoy the masculine attention.

The dining room was a large space that could have been coldly formal, but that was on this night made intimate with decorations of candles and greenery, and with white and red flowers in honor of the season. Instead of one long table, small tables for four or six people were set up around the room.

Carol, Montfort, Penelope, and Lord Simmons occupied one of these tables by themselves. The gentlemen brought plates of ham and roast beef and salad for the ladies, and then sat drinking wine while the women ate. Throughout the light, casual conversation, Carol was conscious of Montfort's continuing attention. She was also aware of Lady Augusta's piercing gaze, and knew that at some point in the near future she was going to have to account for her behavior in the library.

In spite of these concerns, Carol was having a wonderful time. Lord Simmons was witty and gallant, and within a few minutes of sitting down at the table with him Carol was firmly convinced that he was in love with her sister. She caught herself in that thought. Sweet though Penelope was, the girl was not *her* sister, so why should she feel this tenderness and this need to protect her? It was an emotion that Carol could not put aside, though she tried her best to do so.

And then there was Nicholas. His attentions were flattering, and Carol could not deny her response to him. She sat through the supper hour in a state of heightened awareness of everything that was happening around her, wishing she could sink into Nicholas's arms and experience the pleasure of his lips on hers once more. From the looks he cast her way she thought he wanted the same thing.

It was an impossible situation. Carol gathered that the real Lady Caroline had always held her fiance at arm's length. Would he be hurt if Carol returned to her own time and Lady Caroline once more took over the body that belonged to her, and then proceeded to reject Nicholas when he tried to make love to her? The thought of hurting him sent a stab of pain into Carol's bleak heart.

With the pain came anger at Lady Augusta. As a ghost who clamed to know everything important about her, Lady Augusta must have been aware of how much of Carol's emotional energy over the last six years had been devoted to avoiding any feeling that might cause the least bit of distress. How, then, could Lady Augusta now subject Carol to the possibility of real anguish? It was a nasty thing to do, and terribly unfair.

And yet, despite her resentment toward Lady Augusta and her feeling of being misused, Carol had to admit to herself that there was no place else where she would want to be on that particular evening. Of all the changes worked upon her during the course of that astounding night, this was the most surprising change of all—that she was happy to be where she was.

The late supper was followed by more dancing, which did not end until the early morning hours. By the time the last of the guests were leaving, Carol was so sleepy she could hardly keep her eyes open. She gave Nicholas her hand

and let him kiss her politely on the cheek while she tried to swallow the yawn she could not prevent. Of course, he noticed.

"I will assume it is the result of the late hour and not caused by my presence," he teased, taking advantage of her distraction to place another kiss on her opposite cheek, this one a bit too close to her mouth for Carol's peace of mind. "May I call for you during the afternoon and take you for a drive?"

"Oh, do, Nicholas," said Penelope before Carol could answer for herself and before Lady Augusta could offer any objection. "I am sure Caroline would enjoy it, and we have no engagements before dinner because Aunt Augusta insisted we should be quite worn out after tonight. But I do not expect to be the least bit tired, and I don't think Caroline will be, either."

"Caroline?" Nicholas watched her with raised eyebrows.

How could anyone, even Lady Augusta, expect her to refuse his offer? Carol smiled and nodded her assent, and Nicholas took his leave.

"Caroline," said Lady Augusta in a stern voice, "we must have a little talk."

"Not now," Carol retorted, surprising even herself with her firmness. "I am much too tired to get into a heated discussion tonight. We can talk later if you want. For the moment, I am going to bed."

And if you take me back to the twentieth century before we get a chance to talk, she added silently to herself, *then whatever you are planning to say to me won't matter.*

"Very well, I will expect to see you in my boudoir shortly before noon." Lady Augusta began to climb the stairs to the upper floor. "I absolutely insist on speaking to you before you go out for your drive with Montfort. Now, it is time for both of you to be in your beds."

"Yes, Aunt Augusta." It was Penelope who answered, Carol being occupied with another large yawn. Laughing at Carol, Penelope added in a whisper, "Dear sister, I want to talk to you, too, and hear everything that Montfort said to you this evening, but I am nearly asleep where I stand. Aunt Augusta sounds remarkably irritated, so in contrast to the lecture she no doubt plans for you, I shall cheer you up with the most delightful news."

"Let me guess," Carol retorted. "Is it something to do with Lord Simmons?"

"You will have to wait until tomorrow," said Penelope. She embraced Carol warmly and then all but danced down the corridor to her own room, which Carol only now discovered was just next to the chamber occupied by Lady Caroline.

When she awakened the next morning Carol was surprised to find herself still in the lovely blue and white bedchamber, and thus still in the nineteenth century. She had fully expected to open her eyes to the dreary, bare room in which she had slept and taken most of her meals for more than five and a half years.

After the maidservant pulled the draperies back to reveal the pale sun of a late December day, Carol lay quietly, looking around the room. There was something remarkably soothing about her surroundings. The blue and white porcelain vases on the mantel were so pretty, the blue brocade chair was comfortable, the rug was designed with a pleasing pattern of roses and ribbons, and the taffeta and sheer lace curtains at the windows were fresh and crisp and let in a softened light.

"Good morning, my lady." The maid presented a small tray containing delicate pieces of china in a pink and blue pattern, including a fat little teapot. "A plain roll and tea, just as you like your morning meal." Pushing herself up to a sitting position, Carol accepted the tray, letting the maid place it across her lap.

"I never noticed what a nice room this is," Carol said. "Or how sleeping in such comfort can improve even the most irritable disposition."

"Oh, my lady, no one could ever call you irritable," the maid responded. "Quiet and mild you are, and a great favorite with all the staff, if I may say so."

"Am I?" Carol did not think the staff who maintained Marlowe House in the twentieth century would say the same about her.

"Oh, yes," said the maid, "and we're all so pleased to know you'll be marrying such a great nobleman. He's a lovely man, Lord Montfort." Her sigh made it plain that she fully appreciated Montfort's manly attributes.

When the maid was gone, Carol stayed in bed for a while, sipping her tea and thinking over the remarkable events of the previous day. Apparently there were still more to come; otherwise she would have been returned to the twentieth century.

Nicholas. The thought of him propelled Carol out of bed and across the room to the wardrobe to pull out a dress she hoped would be suitable for daytime wear. The maid had brought a pitcher of hot water as well the breakfast tray. Carol was washing her face when the chambermaid returned.

"Oh, my lady, I didn't know you were getting up so early. No, don't try to dress yourself. That's what I'm here for. Don't you remember when you first came to London and thought you ought to take care of your own clothes and brush your own hair, and how we agreed that you would let me take care of you as the maid of a great lady ought to do?"

"You do have a point. I can't seem to twist my arms around enough to button up the back of this dress. Is it the thing for morning?"

"Exactly right, my lady. Now you just stand still and let Ella take care of those buttons."

The dress was yellow and white striped muslin, scarcely warm enough to afford protection from the winter cold, but Ella did not appear to think her mistress ought to be wearing a more substantial garment. She did drape a flower-patterned yellow and green shawl around Carol's shoulders. From its warmth and softness, Carol decided the shawl must be woven of cashmere.

"Now, my lady," Ella said when Carol was clothed to her satisfaction, "I know Lady Penelope is waiting for you in her own room. I finished helping her to dress just before I came in to you."

Penelope's bedchamber was much like Carol's, except that it was decorated in pink and white. When Carol entered, Penelope was sitting at a dainty lady's desk, using a quill pen. Catching sight of Carol, she threw down the pen and rose, hurrying forward.

"Oh, Caroline, I gave my solemn word I would tell no one but you, so you must promise to keep my secret," she exclaimed.

"What secret?" But Carol thought she could guess. She was immediately proven correct.

"Alwyn—that is, Lord Simmons—has declared himself," Penelope announced. "He says he loves me."

"Has he asked you to marry him?"

"Of course not, dunce!" Penelope began to laugh. "You know he cannot in honor ask for my hand until he has his father's permission. Alwyn is always perfectly correct where his father is concerned."

"Then I am surprised hear he was incorrect enough to speak to you before discussing the matter with his father," Carol said.

"Alwyn told me that Montfort did advise him to wait, but he was afraid someone else would ask for me in the meantime, so he revealed his feelings to me while we were waltzing last night. You do recall that he came to the ball specifically to waltz with me?"

"I remember Montfort saying that Lord Simmons would be there." Carol began to wonder what part Nicholas was playing in this particular romance.

"Well," Penelope went on, "Alwyn wanted to be certain that my affections were as firmly engaged as are his."

"And you assured him they were?"

"Oh, yes." Penelope's face was aglow with

excitement. "I know we cannot make a public declaration of our betrothal until Alwyn's father has agreed, and Aunt Augusta, too, but at least we can each be certain of the other's love. Alwyn says Nicholas is strongly in favor of the match, and has promised to go with Alwyn when he speaks to his father about me. With someone like Lord Montfort supporting his cause, Alwyn has every hope his father will approve."

"It would seem as if Montfort and Lord Simmons have our lives neatly arranged between them," Carol murmured.

"Well, of course they have. Men are supposed to arrange these things. You cannot object, Caroline, since you wanted a good marriage for me, and now both of us have found wealthy and titled husbands. What noblewoman could ask for more? You are happy, aren't you?"

"Divinely happy." Penelope missed the dry tone of Carol's voice and went on cheerfully talking about her plans for a blissful future as the wife of Lord Simmons.

Carol was unwilling to spoil Penelope's happy mood by discussing what she knew about Penelope's dowry. Since she wasn't sure whether Penelope knew of this arrangement or not, a certain amount of discretion seemed to be advisable.

After her revealing talk with Nicholas on the previous night, Carol was aware that he was using her sister's dowry to exert a subtle pressure on Lady Caroline. He would not actually make that all-important settlement on Penelope until after Caroline had fulfilled her part of their bargain by marrying him—

and, Carol was sure, by allowing Nicholas to consummate their marriage so he could have at least some hope of an heir. The Earl of Montfort was far from being a mustache-twirling villain, yet he had Lady Caroline exactly where he wanted her.

"Excuse me, my lady." Lady Augusta's personal servant, Marie, stood in the doorway. "My mistress would like Lady Caroline to attend her in her chamber at once."

"Oh, dear," said Penelope in mock terror. "Caroline, shall I go with you to protect you from the dragon?"

"I think I ought to handle this one by myself." Carol gave the girl a quick hug and a kiss. "We will talk more about your plans later. If you are happy, and if you are sure of Lord Simmons's affection, then you have my blessing and I wish you all the best."

Carol was halfway down the hall to Lady Augusta's room before she realized what she had just done. She could not remember the last time she had hugged someone out of pure affection. But hugging Penelope felt good. There was an unfamilar warmth around her heart as she knocked on Lady Augusta's door. Unfortunately, it did not last long.

"I have been waiting for more than an hour to speak to you." Lady Augusta did not waste time on small talk. "Kindly explain to me just what you thought you were doing with Montfort last night."

"He wanted to kiss his fiancee. I could hardly object, could I?"

"What I saw appeared to be considerably more than a mere kiss."

It had indeed been more, and at the memory of Nicholas's demanding mouth on hers, Carol began to feel again some of the tumultuous emotions she had experienced on the previous night. There seemed to be no way for her to prevent her own reactions to him. The realization of her own susceptibility made her angry. Telling herself the anger was for Lady Caroline's sake, she attempted to explain the incident to Lady Augusta.

"Lord Montfort believes he is in complete control of his relationship with Lady Caroline," she said. "He is apparently loaded with money, so he thinks he can do whatever he likes. Did you know he is providing a dowry for Penelope? But only after Caroline marries him."

"Yes, I do know. It is not an entirely uncommon arrangement, not when a man is as rich—and as generous—as Montfort. Do you expect me to believe that what you were expressing in the library last night was gratitude for his consideration of your sister's happiness?" The hint of sardonic amusement in Lady Augusta's voice made Carol wonder just what this irritating ghost was really up to.

"I was trying to show him that Lady Caroline has some backbone," Carol retorted. "I was hoping he might treat her better."

"I am not aware that he has been treating her badly." Lady Augusta's eyes bored into Carol's. "I very much doubt that your motives were as altruistic as you pretend. Montfort is, after all, a devastatingly handsome man." She paused, still watching Carol.

"I am not interested in handsome men,"

Carol said. "I had my fill of them six years ago."

"In more ways than one," Lady Augusta agreed.

"If you intend to stand there and throw that old incident with Robert Drummond in my face again," Carol told her, "then I am going to leave."

"Carol, you *must* learn to be honest with yourself. It is the very first requirement for the success of my project. Admit to your true feelings for Montfort."

"I don't have any feelings for him," Carol declared. When Lady Augusta sadly shook her head, Carol threw up her hands. "All right. If you want me to say it, I will. He's handsome. He's sexy. He is also manipulative and demanding. Is that why Lady Caroline has been cool to him?"

"Has she been cool to him?" Lady Augusta tilted her head to one side, apparently fascinated by this disclosure.

"That's what he said."

"Why do you suppose that is, Carol?"

"How should I know? You're the one who has all the information on this situation. And you are the one who hasn't told me what I need to know about the relationship between those two. I had to talk Nicholas into revealing what little I do know about their arrangement. It's just a business deal. But you knew that, didn't you?"

"What do you intend to do about it?" asked Lady Augusta.

"Do?" Carol stared at her. "You tell me. This is your mission, not mine."

"I suppose it is too much to expect you to understand all of it at once," said Lady Augusta.

"I don't understand *anything*, because you aren't telling me what I need to know," Carol cried. "You haven't really explained what our purpose here is, you only set me down among strangers and left me to figure things out for myself. It isn't fair. Look, do me a favor. Just send me back to my own time."

"Neither of us can return until we have accomplished what we were sent here to do."

"*What* were we sent here to do?" If there were something at hand to throw, Carol would have thrown it at the older woman in outraged frustration.

"We will know it when we have done it," Lady Augusta responded with infuriating calmness. "Now, you must excuse me, Carol. There are household duties to which I must attend." She waved a hand in dismissal. Carol refused to move.

"Is this all you wanted to say to me?" Receiving no answer, Carol asked another question. "How long will we be here?" she demanded.

"As long as it takes," was the cryptic answer. Lady Augusta turned away, thus discouraging any further probing on Carol's part. As if by magic, the servant Marie appeared to hold the door open and stand waiting until Carol passed through it.

This interview left Carol, once she calmed down a bit, with the sense that in spite of the tart inquiries Lady Augusta had made, she did not really disapprove of what Carol had done in the library with Montfort. *Why* she did not disapprove, Carol could not guess, and she was pretty sure that Lady Augusta was not going to supply any more clues. What Carol needed to know about Lady Caroline, she was going to have to find out on her own. The only fact of which she could be certain was that she would remain in the nineteenth century for a while. Which meant she would see Nicholas again, when he came to take her for a drive that afternoon. The pleasant anticipation she felt at the prospect frightened her.

"I don't know what to wear," she said to herself as she made her way down the corridor toward her bedchamber. "More important, I don't know what to expect or how to behave." When she reached Penelope's door she stopped and knocked on it.

"Help me," she begged as soon as Penelope opened the door. "What shall I wear when Nicholas comes?"

"I knew you would ask," Penelope said, laughing. "You always do. And I always give you good advice, don't I?"

With Penelope's assistance, and by pretending to be a bit distracted and sleepy after the ball in her honor, Carol got through a morning and early afternoon that included calls by three young women who claimed to know the Hyde sisters well. These visitors were full of the latest gossip about betrothals, marriages, and social events amongst the aristocracy. Carol listened avidly to their conversation and tried to remember everything she heard. When her responses weren't right, Penelope was there, gently laughing, to supply sisterly aid. Carol discovered that though their visitors were a bit silly and giddy, Penelope was dependable. She was beginning to treasure Penelope.

She did not even mind Penelope's teasing over the arrival of a huge bouquet of flowers sent to Lady Caroline by Nicholas. Carol was able to respond with a pointed comment of her own when, a short time later, a slightly smaller offering was brought to the door for Penelope from Lord Simmons. It was so delightful to have a companion to whom she could talk, whom Carol knew cared about her, that for an hour or two Carol almost forgot she was not Lady Caroline Hyde.

Thanks to Penelope's suggestions, by the time Nicholas called for Carol in late afternoon she was properly dressed in a gray and blue striped gown with a long, dark blue woolen pelisse buttoned over it and a matching blue bonnet that had a large bow arranged beneath her chin.

She had not the faintest idea what kind of carriage Nicholas was driving, but the single seat to which he handed her was by Carol's standards a high and precarious perch and she held on tightly at first. He drove with such assurance and ease that after a while she began to relax, understanding that this light, sleek conveyance was the early nineteenth-century version of a young man's sports car. Before long she could even begin to enjoy the ride.

Taking her cue from Nicholas, she bowed and smiled at the people they passed. As they rode along she also watched Nicholas out of the corner of her eye, waiting to catch the right moment to raise an important issue with him. She was planning to strike another blow for Lady Caroline. In the meantime, she could admire the imposing figure he presented in his bottle-green, many-caped greatcoat and beaver hat.

Nicholas turned into the park, where he slowed the horses and moved into a line of carriages of various types, all of them carrying people who were out to see and be seen while enjoying the fine, cold day. This, Carol decided, was as good a time as any to speak her piece.

"I have a bone to pick with you, sir," she announced.

"I beg your pardon?" He sent a surprised glance her way. Carol bit her lip, wishing she had been more careful in her choice of words. Nicholas had probably never heard that particular expression before this day.

"What I mean to say," she corrected herself, "is that I believe you and Lord Simmons are manipulating Lady Caro—manipulating me and my sister in order to force me to marry you."

"Caroline, have you gone mad?" He gave her another quick look before turning his attention back to the horses. "Simmons and I are attempting to provide Penelope with the happy future she wants and deserves. You cannot object to my efforts in her behalf, because you have repeatedly endorsed them. As for you, our betrothal is publicly known. I have no need to manipulate you into anything."

"Doesn't a woman have any right to make her own decisions?" Carol cried.

"Certainly, she has," Nicholas replied. "You could have refused to marry me."

"I see." Carol spoke sharply. "Case closed, then. There is nothing more to discuss."

"On the contrary, I think there is a great deal more to say," he responded in a low, compelling voice. "We *will* marry. The kind of marriage we have is up to us. I do confess that I began by expecting the usual polite arrangement we see so often in society. After last night, however, I have begun to hope for more."

"More, my lord?"

"I have begun to dream of a marriage in which my wife expresses the warmest feelings toward me," he told her. "I know it is not fashionable for husbands and wives to care deeply for each other, but I now believe that you and I could do so, once we learn to know each other completely. Are you willing to try, Caroline? Will you trust me not to betray your heart?"

In the instant when he leaned toward her to look into her eyes, Carol saw beneath the veneer of dominant male and calculating man of the world to a reservoir of kindness and tenderness that lay hidden deep within the man. Nicholas wanted to love Lady Caroline, if only she would let him. But Carol was not Lady Caroline and could not answer for her.

"I—I don't—I'm not sure—" In vain she fumbled for the right words. She could not find them. With grief she watched him pull back and saw his eyes turn cool again.

"I am aware that the idea is new to you," he said. "Perhaps you will think on it and give me your answer at some later time."

Before Carol could make any further response, they were hailed by a voice from a carriage moving past them in the opposite direction. Nicholas pulled his horses to a halt, and the other carriage stopped, too.

"My Lady Falloner. Lord Falloner." Nicholas raised his hat. "Good day to you."

In the carriage now halted next to them Carol recognized the elderly lord with the gouty toe and his wife who had been at Lady Augusta's ball. Carol bowed to them in imitation of the nobles she had been observing during this drive.

"Well, well," cried Lord Falloner to Carol. "You are as rosy and pretty as ever, I see. Late hours never do seem to affect the young. Tell me, my dear, are you planning to attend Lady Lynnville's ball tonight?"

"Aunt Augusta, my sister, and I will all be there," Carol replied.

"I wish I could ask you to save a waltz for me," Lord Falloner said, "but my gouty toe will not allow me to dance. Would you inform your aunt that I hope to partner her at the whist table this evening?"

"Of course, my lord. I will give her the message. Do you also intend to play cards, Lady Falloner?"

"I shall be busy serving as chaperone to my niece," the lady replied.

When the other carriage moved on, Carol returned her attention to Nicholas. She was grateful for the interruption. It had given her a chance to catch her breath so she could turn the conversation to less intimate subjects than the future marital relations between Nicholas and Lady Caroline.

"Will you also be at Lady Lynnville's ball?" she asked.

"I am planning to attend." Leaning closer to

her Nicholas added, "I wish I could ask you to save every dance for me."

"If you want me to, I will." Good intentions or no, she could not help her response, not when he was looking right into her eyes. He really was remarkably handsome when he smiled in that teasing way.

"It would be most improper." Taking the reins into one hand, Nicholas used the other to cover her fingers. Through the leather of his gloves and hers she could feel his warmth. The sensation left her weak. "Lately, Caroline, you have become the most tantalizing woman. Is it your intention to create a scandal?"

"Could we?" She grinned at him. His hand tightened over hers. "I mean, can an engaged couple actually become social outcasts just for dancing together too often?"

"I begin to think that for your sake I would gladly flout all propriety," he said. When she curled her fingers around his, he added, "Have a care, Caroline, or you will drive me mad."

"I don't know how long I will be here," she murmured, thinking out loud. "This won't last forever, and when I am gone, I will never again have the chance to learn what this life is like, or what it's like to know you."

"I hardly expected philosophical speculation from you," he responded, looking surprised.

"I want to discover everything I can about you before it's too late," she said. "Nicholas, where will we live once we are married?"

"In my house, as we have already decided," he said. "At Montfort Place."

"Is it here in London?"

"Yes, Caroline, you know it is. Has this

something to do with our earlier conversation?" She could tell he was perplexed by her odd questions. She was also aware of the flare of renewed hope in his eyes. It was painful to remind herself that the hope was for Lady Caroline, but having made up her mind to learn as much as she could about him, she would not stop.

"I want to see your house." She took his hand in both of hers and held it against her bosom. "Please, Nicholas. I want to know what it looks like so I can imagine you living there when I'm not—" She caught herself and stopped speaking just in time to avoid revealing too much.

"Very well," he said. "But you must release my hand before we cause any more raised eyebrows amongst the *ton*. People are staring at us."

"Is everything we do food for scandal?" she asked.

"You know how you ought to behave in public," he replied with just a touch of severity in his voice. "While I welcome your expressions of warmth in private, I do not want us to become the subject of gossip. This caution is for the sake of your reputation, my dear."

"Of course. I should have realized." What she had seen and heard while in the drawing room of Marlowe House with Penelope and her friends earlier in the day ought to have taught her that young women were expected to be more restrained. Letting go of Nicholas's hand, Carol folded her own hands together in her lap. "I am sorry, Nicholas. I wasn't thinking. But will you show me your house?" she asked again.

"If you wish, we will drive past it," he said. "You know I cannot take you inside without a chaperone."

"I understand."

The house was in Mayfair, an ornate white wedding cake of a place. Nothing about it struck a chord in Carol's memory, though she had walked along that particular street many times during her ramblings around London.

"It's huge," she whispered.

"I feel certain you will know how to manage it," he told her. "Your mother raised you to be the competent mistress of such an establishment."

By the time Nicholas returned her to Marlowe House, Carol felt as if her brain would burst from all the information she was trying to sort out. As she watched him drive away, she was certain of only one thing. She could scarcely wait to see him again that evening at Lady Lynnville's ball.

Chapter Four

Carol, Penelope and Lady Augusta went to the theater first and then on to Lady Lynnville's ball. The ballroom was large and it was badly crowded with elegantly dressed people.

"What a crush," gasped Penelope. "Lady Lynnville must be delighted to know her affair will be considered a huge success."

"Must social success be dependent upon how uncomfortable the guests are?" Carol demanded, trying to push her way through the throng. "If that's the case, then we didn't make the grade last night, did we? There was plenty of room at Marlowe House."

"Do you mean you didn't notice?" As usual, Penelope was laughing, and her pretty blue eyes were twinkling merrily. "I vow, you had eyes only for Nicholas and saw no one else. And then, you spent so much time in the library with him."

101

"There is a charming library in this house," a voice at Carol's shoulder said, interrupting Penelope. "I will be happy to show it to you, my dear."

"Nicholas," Penelope exclaimed, "you ought not to make such suggestions." Looking at the man with him, she added with a slight blush, "Good evening, Lord Simmons."

Within a few moments Penelope and Lord Simmons were dancing and Carol was swept into Nicholas's arms. This second evening in early nineteenth-century London passed in a blur of overcrowded, overheated rooms, of constant frivolous chatter and dances claimed with her by men whom Carol did not know. Through it all Nicholas frequently returned to her side, and Carol began to regard him as the one stable element in an unfamiliar, shifting, and confusing scene. Penelope was spending most of her time with Lord Simmons, except for a few dances with other men in order to assuage the demands of propriety. Lady Augusta seemed to have disappeared, possibly into the card room with Lord Falloner. Nicholas was the only constant.

"Are you feeling unwell?" he asked sometime after midnight, when he discovered her standing on the terrace just outside an open French door.

"It's too hot in the ballroom," she answered, taking a deep breath of the bitterly cold fresh air, "and everyone is wearing so much perfume. I wanted to clear my lungs."

"You will end with lung fever," he cautioned. There followed a moment of silence until he asked, "Shall I take you home, Caroline?"

"Now?" She turned toward his tall, dark figure. He was wearing black again this evening. In the shadows where they were standing, only the pristine white of his linen and the pale shape of his face were visible. "Are you telling me we can leave this—this fearful crush, as Penelope calls it, without causing an uproar among the chaperones, or hurting our hostess's feelings?"

"It can be arranged," he said. "If an early departure is what you wish."

Something in his voice told Carol that more than transportation back to Marlowe House was included in his offer. Suddenly the prospect of several additional hours spent dancing with men whom she would have to pretend to recognize, or conversation with young ladies who were chiefly interested in snagging rich and titled husbands, was unbearable.

"I find that I am most dreadfully tired," she said in her best imitation of one of those ladies. Spreading her fan, she fluttered it gracefully. "I do believe I feel the beginnings of a headache. Not to mention a cough that may presage development of a serious inflammation of the chest."

"All excellent reasons for you to return home as soon as possible." He spoke with complete seriousness, but she could tell he was amused.

"Would you be good enough to arrange a speedy, yet quiet departure?" she asked.

"It will be my pleasure. Allow me to offer you the support of my arm."

He handled their leave-taking beautifully. He found their hostess, explained Lady Caroline's indisposition, and begged Lady Lynnville to excuse them. Meanwhile, Carol drew Penelope aside and whispered her own explanation so her sister would not worry. Lady Augusta was nowhere to be seen, but Penelope promised to transmit the message to her.

"I cannot think where she could be," Penelope said. "I looked into the card room a few minutes ago and she wasn't there. Lord Falloner is trying to find her, too."

Carol could not help wondering if Lady Augusta had herself departed the ball in order to make a brief visit *elsewhere,* there to receive further instructions on how best to torment her victim.

She did not dwell on that thought. Never had she felt less like a victim. After wrapping her in Lady Caroline's warm, fur-lined cloak, Nicholas hurried her out of Lady Lynnville's mansion and down the steps to his waiting carriage. This was not the small, open conveyance he had driven earlier in the day, but a closed coach with someone else to drive it and two footmen to help them in and out of it. Inside, the coach was luxuriously appointed with well-padded gray leather upholstery and with a fur rug to cover her knees. Nicholas tucked the rug in around her, then sat back on the seat beside her.

"This is lovely," she said. "Thank you for taking me out of there. It was all a bit too much."

"I do recall you saying once that you do not care for large gatherings," he replied.

"I never have." It was perfectly true.

"I am glad to hear that in that much at least

you have not changed, since as you know I, too, prefer a quiet life in the country over the constant round of tedious social events."

"You keep telling me how much I have changed." Carol paused, hoping he would let slip a few more facts about the real Lady Caroline. She got more than she expected. He seized her hands and held them tight, and when he spoke again it was with a barely suppressed passion.

"I do not know why you are so different now from your usual cold and unemotional self, but I beg you, Caroline, never change back to what you were before last evening. I could not bear it if you did."

"It seemed to me at first that you disapproved of my new warmth," she said, trying to chose her words carefully so as to avoid making any further mistakes that might prove detrimental to Lady Caroline.

"I was surprised by it," he said. "The change was so sudden. Caroline, we barely touched on the subject when we agreed to marry, and you evaded an answer this afternoon. Now I must speak of it again. I know my proposal pleased you for practical reasons, because you told me so. And I knew from your own lips that you liked and respected me. But I received the distinct impression that you regarded certain of your future marital duties with some trepidation—not to say distaste."

"Is that what you thought?" Carol tried to play for time until he could reveal more about the exact direction in which the relationship between the Earl of Montfort and

Lady Caroline had been going prior to her own arrival on the scene.

"Dare I hope that you have had time to warm to the prospect of—shall I say it aloud, Caroline?—of sharing a bed with me? Your recent behavior makes me hopeful that this is the case. Otherwise I would not have spoken so boldly this afternoon."

"My lord, you will make me blush," Carol murmured, still stalling in hope of learning more. What in heaven's name was wrong with Lady Caroline that she did not respond to this man? Was she frigid? What kind of upbringing did girls have in this period of history? From what she had been able to observe so far, Carol knew young women were taught to repress any youthful exuberance in public, and she had no doubt, considering the tight supervision they were under from numerous chaperones and from all the rules of propriety, that most well-bred girls were virgins when they married, but how were they instructed to behave when alone with their fiances—or their husbands? She had no idea.

"You were not blushing last night after I kissed you," Nicholas said, the sudden note of steel in his voice reminding her that, however sensitive he might appear to be in regard to his fiancee, at heart he remained a tough and rather arrogant nobleman. It was dark in the coach, but she could see by the light coming in through the windows that he was sending a meaningful sidelong glance toward her. His tone did not change when he spoke again. "Answer me honestly, Caroline."

"You are right," she said slowly. "I have

changed. Knowing our future together is settled, knowing I don't have to wonder anymore—"

"Yes," he interrupted. "You did tell me when you accepted my proposal that for some time you had been worried about your future, and about Penelope's."

"Do you actually remember every word I spoke?" she asked, prompting him to reveal that conversation.

"You said you were willing to become Lady Augusta's companion, or to endure the humiliation of taking a position as governess, if that were the only respectable path open to you, but you did not want such a life for your sister. As I recall, at the time you were planning to turn your own small dowry over to Penelope, to add to the one left to her by your parents, in order to enable your sister to make a good marriage. Fortunately, I was able to convince you that Penelope would surely refuse such a scheme as unfair to you, and so you agreed to my proposal of marriage instead. I believe my offer of a substantial dowry for Penelope was the deciding factor in your decision."

"Anyone would wish the best in life for Penelope," Carol said.

"It was your affection for your sister that first endeared you to me, Caroline. Having no brothers or sisters myself, I view the love between you and Penelope as beautiful and sacred."

"*Am* I dear to you?" she whispered.

"You are becoming more so every day."

"Oh." Carol smothered the quick little spurt of jealousy that was the result of knowing she would not be present to be the recipient of Nicholas's love. She had no right to be jealous of Lady Caroline. It was not Lady Caroline's fault that Carol Simmons was presently living in a nineteenth-century body.

In fact, Carol was beginning to like Lady Caroline Hyde. In a time of limited possibilities for females, a woman who was willing to marry in order to secure a comfortable and happy future for her beloved sister was a woman worthy of admiration. Carol just wished she knew what Lady Caroline's true feelings toward Nicholas were. From her own point of view, marrying Nicholas, going to bed with him every night, and bearing his children was definitely not a fate worse than death. Life with him might well be an interesting variation on life in heaven.

"You cannot claim to be frightened of me," Nicholas whispered, his breath warm at her ear. "Not after last night."

"I'm not afraid. Not in the way you mean. It's just that there are things you don't know about me—I mean, about the real me. I'm not what I appear to be."

"Whatever you are, I want you. I want to hold you in my arms, and I pray that when we marry, you will come to me with hope and bright anticipation. I cannot tell you how glad it would make me if you were to admit that you feel a warm affection for me. After the way you responded to me when I kissed you, I think you are not unmoved by my advances. You need not be ashamed of your reaction, my dear. I assure you, it was perfectly normal."

"You are speaking of physical love." She

could scarcely whisper the words. Her heart was beating hard—she could hear it in her ears—and she was trembling. This was more than the reaction of Carol Simmons. This had something to do with the body of Lady Caroline. Carol could not understand what was happening to her, and she could not stop shaking. "I ought to tell you—to explain—"

"Dare I hope that you might look forward to that part of our marriage, now that we are beginning to know each other better and to explore the possibilities that lie between us?"

"Well, you see—" She wanted to tell him everything, all about Lady Augusta and the way she had moved Carol through time. She wanted to confess her stupid and emotionally destructive teenage indiscretion with Robert Drummond. And when Nicholas knew the truth, she wanted him to tell her it didn't matter. She wanted him to know all of it and still make love to her because he wanted *her*, Carol Simmons.

She tried to tell him, only to discover that she could not. Lady Augusta's warning, combined with her own fear of the historical repercussions if she violated that warning, kept her from speaking the words forming in her mind and on her tongue.

"It's all so complicated," she whispered.

"Then let us discover together how best to simplify matters." Nicholas gathered her into his arms and kissed her hard.

Carol did not protest. Because it was what she wanted, too, she ignored the continued shaking of her body and the peculiar, panic-stricken little voice deep inside her mind that told her she ought to find the touch of any man repulsive. Another, stronger, voice overcame the first to insist that nothing about Nicholas could ever be repulsive. Carol welcomed his kiss, opening her mouth for him, accepting him in a surge of spiraling desire.

While they were still locked in that first, long kiss, Nicholas unfastened the clasp of her cloak. His hands slid beneath the heavy folds, pushing back the thick wool and fur so he could draw down the top of her gown. She was wearing a yellow, gauzy dress this evening, with not much of a bodice between the low neckline and the high waist, so it did not take much effort for him to get it off her breasts. The air was cold on her bare skin and his mouth was hot. And his hands—never had hands touched her so gently, or wreaked such havoc upon her senses.

Carol moaned, pressing herself upward into his hands, feeling her nipples harden against his palms. He pushed down upon the yellow gauze again. Within a moment she was fully revealed to him from waist to chin, his to touch and kiss and fondle. And adore.

"Beautiful," he murmured, though he surely could see nothing in the darkness of the carriage. Now it was his mouth caressing her breasts, first one and then the other. Carol was filled with a sweet, surging warmth. His hand moved lower, over her hip and between her thighs. "Exquisite. Caroline, Caroline—"

Carol slid down onto the gray leather seat with Nicholas on top of her. His hand stroked her inner thigh with a slow, circling motion. The thin fabric of her gown offered no barrier to erotic sensation. She shifted her legs hoping, but not daring to ask, that he would press upon and thus ease the aching fullness between her thighs, which was beginning to make her uncomfortable.

Nicholas's crisp linen shirt was scratchy against her breasts; the diamond head of the stickpin fastened in his cravat was like ice on her lips as she strained upward, searching for his mouth . . . and found it . . . and let him devour her. . . .

The carriage jolted to a stop. As if it were happening far away, Carol heard one of the footmen jump to the ground and begin walking across crunchy ice and snow toward the door to open it.

"Dear God, Caroline, what am I doing?" Hastily, Nicholas hauled her to a sitting position and pulled the bodice of her gown upward. Carol heard a ripping sound as the fabric gave way. She fumbled with her cloak, trying to cover herself before the door was opened. Her gloved hands were shaking so hard that she could not get the clasp hooked. She uttered a sob of frustration, which was not caused solely by the recalcitrant clasp.

"I have it." Pushing her fingers aside, Nicholas fastened the clasp and drew the edges of the cloak together just as the footman flung the carriage door wide and let down the step. There were torches flaming at either side of the entrance to Marlowe House. Carol saw their fiery light reflected in Nicholas's eyes. Then he was out of the carriage and turning to hand her down.

His self-control was amazing. Not by the faintest crack in his haughty expression did he reveal what he and Carol had been doing. He saw her safely inside her door with all the cool self-possession of the born aristocrat.

"I have no doubt we will meet again tomorrow evening," he said, bowing while the butler looked on in open appreciation of Nicholas's good manners. "At yet another ball. Will you save the first waltz for me? And allow me to take you in to supper?"

"Certainly, my lord." Taking her cue from him, she gave him her trembling hand to kiss. "If I have counted the days correctly, tomorrow is Christmas Eve."

"It is indeed. When we meet at the ball I shall take the opportunity to wish you an especially merry Christmas." For an instant a glowing fire in his eyes flared and sparkled for her alone, giving a private meaning to his words before he resumed his cool demeanor. "Until then, good night, my dear."

The butler closed the door after him and turned to Carol.

"Your cloak, Lady Caroline?" He stood with his hands outstretched to receive the garment.

"I think I will keep it on until I get to my room and can take it off in front of the fire," Carol told him. "I am badly chilled after the cold ride home." Actually, though it was true she was trembling, she was far from cold. She was still burning from Nicholas's kisses and his entirely too intimate caresses. Not knowing what damage he might have done to the fragile fabric of her evening gown, she was afraid to remove the cloak until she was in a more private place than the entrance hall.

She should have known that for aristocrats

there was seldom a private place. The maidservant Ella was waiting for her in Lady
Caroline's bedroom, and there was no reason not to let Ella take the cloak from her
shoulders.

"I think I stepped on my skirt when I got
out of the carriage. I may have torn the dress,"
Carol said, making up the excuse on the spur
of the moment.

"It's only a little tear." Ella did not dispute
Carol's explanation. "It can easily be fixed. Oh,
you are shivering so hard! Into bed with you,
my lady, and I'll put a warm brick at your feet
so you don't develop a chill."

Eventually, following half an hour or so
of Ella's well-meant ministrations, Carol was
granted the privacy she sought. Having tucked
her mistress between warmed sheets, and after
repeated assurances from Carol that she was
perfectly well, Ella left the room.

The hot, flannel-wrapped brick at Carol's feet
did not ease the shaking that seemed to come
from the very marrow of her bones. She sensed
that it had something to do with Nicholas's
lovemaking, because it had started when he
began to talk about sharing a bed with his
future wife.

"Lady Caroline," she whispered, having no
idea where the words were coming from save
that she felt them in her heart, "he will love you.
You don't have to be afraid anymore. Nicholas
will never hurt you. You can trust him."

Slowly, very slowly, the shaking subsided. It
was as though a terrified, caged bird had been
soothed and gentled into a weary sleep.

What happened just now? Carol kept perfectly

still, not wanting by any movement or another whispered word to reawaken the frightened creature that must be Lady Caroline's consciousness. *Lady Augusta said we would be one entity, and that I could not cause her any harm. Why, then, did she wake up in abject fear when Nicholas began to make love to me?*

Carol lay for a long time watching the firelight cast flickering shadows around Lady Caroline's beautiful room. She tried not to think about Lady Caroline, or about Lady Caroline's fiance. That last attempt was a hopeless cause, for by now Carol knew with painful certainty that she was never going to stop thinking about Nicholas. She was falling deeply in love with him—with a man who was not hers to love and never would be.

Marlowe House was in the process of transformation. While the public rooms—the reception room and ballroom and the great dining room—had been decorated for Lady Caroline's betrothal ball, those parts of the house daily used by the family were traditionally decorated on the morning of Christmas Eve Day so the decorations used would be fresh for the holiday itself.

Coming down the stairs and into the hall, Carol nearly collided with a footman whose vision was obscured by the huge vase of fir, ivy, and holly he was carrying.

"Beg pardon, my lady. I didn't see you." The footman set the vase down on the table in the center of the hall and hastened away to follow the latest instructions from Lady Augusta's butler.

The cream and white drawing room was fragrant with greenery. Knowing that Christmas trees would not become a part of holiday decorations until later in the century, Carol did not expect to see one. All the same, she was dazzled by the festive appearance of bunches of evergreens, holly, and red and white hothouse flowers, all tied with bright red ribbons.

In addition, the daily bouquets sent from Nicholas to Lady Caroline and from Lord Simmons to Penelope were also crowded into the drawing room, to add their fragrance and color to the Christmas decor.

"Nicholas." Carol picked up the card that accompanied the bouquet meant for Lady Caroline. She touched one of the deep red roses with trembling fingers. "What am I going to do about you? How can I keep on lying to you?"

"Aunt Augusta has gone out." Penelope poked her head around the drawing room doorway. "Since you were still asleep, she ordered me to supervise the decorating, but it is almost finished. Come join me in the breakfast room, where it is quieter and we can talk."

Penelope put an arm around her waist and Carol went with her, sliding her own arm around the girl. Carol had been alone, or at least left to herself, for so much of her life that until recently she'd thought it was normal. She had scarcely known how much she missed and longed for the pleasures of ordinary companionship. In Penelope she had found a true sister. Not even the knowledge that she would at some point have to return to her own time could mar Carol's enjoyment of the hours they spent together.

In the cheerful, pale yellow breakfast room frosty sunlight streamed through the windows to touch the porcelain bowl of holly sitting in the exact center of the table. The sideboard was laden with kidneys, bacon, eggs, and assorted breads. One of the servants poured coffee for Carol as soon as she sat down at the table.

"Did you talk to Aunt Augusta before she left?" Carol had not seen Lady Augusta since the previous evening and she was beginning to wonder what was going on. She was almost getting used to Lady Augusta watching her, so it seemed strange for her ghostly companion to absent herself. Carol wanted to talk to Lady Augusta about the sensation of Lady Caroline's presence that she had experienced. Perhaps Lady Augusta would have an explanation for that occurrence.

"She told the butler she had some business to transact," Penelope said, biting into an iced bun. Carol smiled at her, amused to see Penelope's small pink tongue appear to lick a particle of sugar glaze off her lower lip. Penelope possessed a ready sweet tooth. Carol had noticed that wherever Penelope was, a sweet bread or pastry, or a dish of candy, was always near at hand. Penelope swallowed her bite of currant-stuffed bun and spoke again. "Now that the decorating is nearly over, we are left to our own devices this morning."

"Morning?" Carol laughed. "It's more like early afternoon. What would you like to do, Penelope?"

"Shopping," was the immediate answer. "I do need several pairs of gloves. They dirty so quickly that I never have enough. And Mary

Anne Hampton told me last night that Madame la Salle has the most delightful new bonnet in her millinery shop window. I want to try it on. We can take Ella with us."

"Then, shopping it is," Carol agreed readily, glad for the distraction. She hoped the excursion would help to keep her thoughts off Lady Caroline for a while—and off the disturbing subject of Nicholas.

The two young women spent a pleasant hour in the shops along Bond Street. Carol enjoyed the opportunity to compare the elegant shops to the ones she knew on the same street in her own time. She bought gloves when Penelope did, and also a small vial of rose-scented perfume for herself. She was not altogether successful in her efforts to put Nicholas or Lady Caroline out of her mind, but she did try her best to pay attention to what Penelope was saying.

Penelope talked with delighted anticipation about the Christmas Eve ball to be held that night at one of the great London houses, about the plans for Lady Augusta and her two nieces to attend a church service on Christmas morning, and about the holiday meal Lady Augusta had arranged.

"I do so love Christmas dinner," Penelope went on. "Cook and her assistants are busy preparing the food. I looked in on them this morning before you were out of bed, my dear. We shall have a wonderful, plump goose to eat, and cakes with sugar icing, and the biggest Christmas pudding you ever saw! There is so much food that it's a good thing Nicholas will join us. We will need a manly appetite to help us eat it all. Aunt Augusta said she is inviting Lord and Lady Falloner, too, and their niece. I wish Alwyn's father would not insist that he remain at home for the day."

"Perhaps it's just as well," Carol said with great seriousness. When Penelope looked at her in a questioning way, she added, "If Lord Simmons ever realizes just how many sweets you consume, he will certainly break off your engagement in utter despair."

"Caroline, do not tease me!" Penelope dissolved into laughter.

On their way from shop to shop they paused now and then to greet other ladies they knew, and there were a few gentlemen strolling along Bond Street, too. Carol was not at all surprised to recognize Lord Simmons among them. Upon spying Penelope he came to her at once, and though his greeting to Carol was polite enough, it was plain to her where his real interest lay.

"May I invite both of you to join me for chocolate and a pastry?" asked Lord Simmons.

"Oh, yes," breathed Penelope, her blue eyes fixed on his face. "I should like it above anything."

When Lord Simmons looked toward Carol as if expecting her to agree to his invitation, she made a fast decision. She suspected this meeting with Lord Simmons was not entirely by chance. She also believed that Lord Simmons and Penelope were responsible young people who would not trespass beyond the boundaries of propriety. And then there was Ella, who stood behind Carol with her arms full of packages. Penelope would be perfectly safe with Lord Simmons, and with Ella present as chaperone no one could question her discretion.

"I still have several more errands to complete," Carol said to Lord Simmons. "But there is no reason why Penelope cannot go with you. I will just finish my shopping and then hire a coach to take me back to Marlowe House so Penelope can use our carriage." She could tell from the startled expressions of her two companions that it was not quite the thing for a lady to hire a carriage for herself, but Carol did not care. She was finding all the restrictions placed upon unmarried ladies increasingly tedious, and she had just decided upon a particular errand for which she did not want any company. First, she had to find out where Nicholas was.

"I might discover Lord Montfort in one of the shops," she said brightly. "He could escort me home." She kept her gaze on Lord Simmons as she spoke, and he responded at once.

"I do not think it is likely," he said. "Montfort told me last night that he has business to transact at Montfort Place today, so he will be at home until he leaves for the ball this evening. You see, Lady Caroline, in the days just before Christmas men with large properties tend to be somewhat busier than usual. Montfort will be deciding on holiday gifts for those in his employ."

Having learned what she wanted to know, Carol smiled and nodded at this patient masculine explanation of a simple business fact. She did like Lord Simmons, and from the way Penelope was looking at him, there could be no doubt that Lady Caroline's younger sister was happily in love.

"Well, then, I shall find my way back to Marlowe House on my own. You need not worry about me; I will be perfectly all right." Carol gave the two young people a radiant smile, wished them the joy of their chocolate and pastries, and took her leave of them. She did not think they were terribly sad to see her go. As soon as they were out of sight she began to look for a coach she might hire, but most of the carriages she saw were private ones, and those that were for hire apparently were not stopping for women who were alone. It was worse than trying to find an empty cab on a rainy afternoon in New York.

After a while Carol gave up and decided to walk. It was not terribly far to Nicholas's house. She knew this area of London and she had walked much farther on many a day. Unfortunately, the shoes she was presently wearing were not intended for serious walking, and soon her feet were wet and cold. She slipped a couple of times on patches of ice. Once she came near to falling in a most undignified way, until she regained her footing just in time. She was sure it was more than an hour after leaving Bond Street before she finally marched up the steps of Montfort Place and pulled at the bell.

The butler who opened the door stared at her as if he did not know what to say. Or perhaps he wanted to say that ladies, in his experience, did not appear upon a nobleman's doorstep on foot and without an escort. Carol had a pretty good idea what kind of woman he must think she was, in spite of her elegant clothes.

But Carol had learned a few things about aristocratic behavior during her two days in this earlier time. Sticking her nose into the air, she brushed right past the butler and into the entrance hall.

"I am Lady Caroline Hyde," she informed the butler. "I wish to see my fiance at once, on a matter of great importance."

"My lady." With a perfectly straight face the butler inclined his head. "I was not aware that Lord Montfort was expecting you. If you would care to wait in the reception room just over here, I will inform him that you have arrived."

The butler conducted her to a small, simply furnished reception room that opened directly off the hall. The location made Carol think the man still wasn't sure she was who she claimed to be. At least he was going to call Nicholas, and that was all that mattered to her. She was determined to see Nicholas, and what she had told the butler was no more than the truth. It *was* a matter of great importance.

Throughout the busy morning, while she was outwardly occupied with other matters, Carol had slowly been working her way toward a difficult conclusion. She had decided that she was tired of deception. She loved Nicholas, and because she loved him, she could not continue to lie to him. Despite Lady Augusta's warning, and despite her own fears over what full disclosure might do to the course of history as well as to her relationship with Nicholas, Carol was now determined to reveal the truth to him. She was going to tell Nicholas that she had come to him from the future.

Chapter Five

"It *is* you. I could not believe it when Bascome told me you were here." Nicholas did not look pleased to see her. "What can be so terribly important that you would risk your reputation by coming to my house without a chaperone?"

"Please don't be angry with me. There is something I must tell you. This is so difficult. I don't think Lady Augusta will back me up. In fact, I'm sure she won't because she doesn't want you to know. You probably won't believe me, but I have to say it anyway." Carol noticed the butler and a second man standing in the entrance hall just outside the doorway to the room where she and Nicholas were. Both men were staring at her. She fell silent.

"Caroline, you are distraught." After a quick glance toward the men in the hall, Nicholas

122

gave her his full attention. "In heaven's name, what has happened?"

"Could we go someplace more private? I don't want to say this in front of other people." Seeing him start to shake his head, seeing his lips part with what she feared would be a refusal, Carol begged, "Please, Nicholas. If I am dear to you, as you said last night, then hear me out." He gazed at her for a moment more, as if wondering what to do with her, before he nodded.

"Wait here until I have finished with my secretary," he said, and left her. Carol heard his voice in the hall when he spoke to Bascome, his butler. She heard the front door open and close and the murmur of further conversation. A few minutes later, Nicholas returned. "Come with me."

There was no one in the hall or on the great stairs when he led her up them to the next level of the house.

"Did you send your secretary away to protect my good name from scandal?" Carol asked. "And all the servants, too?"

"It seemed the sensible thing to do," Nicholas responded. He showed her across a wide landing and into what was obviously his private study. Bookshelves lined the walls, there was a desk cluttered with papers, and there were a couple of leather chairs and a table with decanters and glasses on it. A fire burned in the fireplace, warming the room.

"Please close the door." Carol tugged at the ribbon that held her bonnet. She pulled off the hat, flinging it upon one of the chairs, then ran her fingers through her short curls.

Realizing that she was still wearing her gloves, she took them off, too, and tossed them on top of the bonnet along with her reticule. She turned around to see Nicholas watching her as if she were doing a complete striptease act. She stopped with only the first few buttons of her deep blue pelisse unfastened.

"Close the door," she said again. "I don't want anyone else to hear what I have to say to you."

"It is for the sake of your reputation that I have left the door open, Caroline. However, if you wish, I will close it. Now, then"—he came toward her—"what matter is serious enough to make you willing to risk that good reputation?"

"Give me a minute to catch my breath. Now that I'm here, I'm not sure how to begin. I'm not sure that you are going to believe me, either."

"I will believe you." He was facing her, standing just a few inches away from her with his hands at his sides, poised and tightly controlled, as if he expected to hear some earth-shattering announcement.

Carol experienced a stab of fear. What she planned to say *was* going to shatter his world, and suddenly she wasn't sure she could do that to him.

"Caroline?" His green eyes searched her face. He waited.

"I have to begin my confession," she whispered, "by telling you that I love you. If you believe nothing else I say here today, believe that much."

"There was a time when I would not have believed this could happen," he said. "Though after the last few days, I was beginning to hope." She saw him relax and begin to smile at her, and she knew she would have to complete her revelations quickly, before he got the wrong idea.

"I haven't finished. There is more," she told him.

"I don't care that you came here alone." He seized her in his arms. Raw emotion roughened his deep voice. "All that matters is that you love me and you were willing to admit it to me."

"Nicholas, wait," she pleaded. "You are not going to like the rest of my confession."

"Whatever it is, it will amount to nothing in comparison to the gift you have just given me."

Carol choked back the words she needed to say. When he bent his head to kiss her she responded eagerly, wanting to revel in his affection for just a few minutes more, before she shocked him and perhaps permanently destroyed his tender feelings for her. His embrace quickly grew warmer, the passion aroused between them on the previous evening flaring anew.

"You are trembling," he murmured. "My poor darling, your hands and cheeks are like ice. Take off your coat and stand closer to the fire." His fingers worked at the buttons of her pelisse.

"You are the fire," she whispered, shrugging off the woolen outer garment. At the moment, what she had initially intended to say to him seemed unimportant. It could wait a few minutes more. "Warm me, Nicholas. Hold me close. Don't let me go."

"Never," he breathed. "Never, till life's end. Come, it's warmer here." There was a thick Oriental rug in front of the fireplace. Kneeling, Nicholas drew her down beside him. They knelt there, holding hands and gazing at each other, until Carol spoke again.

"Kiss me once more, before I tell you everything."

"Gladly. Don't look so frightened, my dear. Don't you know by now that I will never turn away from you no matter what you say? Whatever your problem is, we will solve it together."

"Not this problem." Her words were lost in his mouth.

She could not stop kissing him. Apparently he could not stop what was happening either, because within a heartbeat more they were lying together on the carpet and his hands were on her breasts and then at the buttons runing down the back of her dress. The gray and blue striped fabric was whisked away as if by magic. Her shoes and stockings were gone, along with her chemise. Nicholas was pulling off his jacket and then his shirt. He paused with his hands at the waistband of his trousers.

"Caroline?" She knew what he was asking.

"I am sure," she whispered. "Don't stop."

A minute later his warm, firm body was stretched out next to hers. Nicholas pulled her close, then paused, giving her time to adjust to the sensation of his naked flesh against hers. She trembled in brief panic at the intimate contact, before she deliberately closed off the part of her mind that was once more cringing and shaking like a terrified little animal. Carol did not know if this terror was another break-through from Lady Caroline's consciousness or if it came from her own past. Whichever it was, she would not let the fear prevent her from fully experiencing her love for Nicholas. She forced herself to relax.

Nicholas felt her hesitation. Catching her chin on one finger, he raised her face so he could look into her eyes.

"I will be gentle," he whispered, "but if you have just discovered that you do not want to do this after all, we must stop now. A few kisses more and it will be too late."

"You can't hurt me, and I wouldn't care if you did," she cried, pressing herself tightly against him in an attempt to prove how much she wanted him.

All the same, he was remarkably careful with her, as if she really were the innocent, untouched young woman he believed her to be. He awakened her body's passion with skill and with the gentleness he had promised. He took his time, at first doing no more than kissing her softly and holding her. After a while his kisses deepened and his hands began to roam over her shoulders and her arms. Where his hands went, his lips immediately followed. It was amazing how erotic the touch of his tongue in the crook of her elbow was. Even more astounding was the way heat boiled deep inside her when he drew her fingers into his mouth and sucked on them, slowly, one by one.

"I don't understand," Carol groaned. Her breasts felt tight and heavy. She thrust them at him, silently begging him to take them into his hands and caress them, into his mouth to suck on them.

"I was right," he whispered. "You are the passionate woman I dreamed you could be. Do not attempt to restrain yourself, Caroline. Set your emotions free. Give yourself to me without fear. I will keep you safe."

"This is not safety," she gasped. "Not when I feel as if I am going to explode at any moment."

"It is freedom," he told her. "Freedom to say and do whatever you want while we are together like this. From what you are doing just now, I assume that you want me to touch you . . . *here*."

She began to writhe in a state of painful delight because his hands were finally on her breasts, stroking their softness with a light, skimming motion. She soon discovered the touch she had craved only made matters worse, and she began to believe that she would completely lose her mind.

Slowly Nicholas worked his way along her body, caressing and kissing every part of her, generating more and more heat until Carol thought she and the fire in the fireplace were one and the same. Molten heat sang through every nerve and blood vessel, her bones melted in pure joy at his touch on her skin.

She was half crazed with desire by the time he knelt between her thighs and pushed hard against her aching, eager softness. She lifted herself a little to meet his thrust and her body opened to him at once, easily and naturally, as if they had been meant to come together since the beginning of time.

"Caroline?" He paused, not yet exactly where she wanted him to be, and the look on his face was one of puzzled concern along with barely contained passion.

"It's all right. You aren't hurting me," she responded, surprised at how easy his entry was. Why there was no discomfort when she was in Lady Caroline's virgin body she could not imagine, but she did not have time to wonder about that particular phenomenon. Passionate need clamored within her and she gladly gave in to its commands. "Oh, Nicholas, I love you!"

She pulled him closer still, until he was completely buried inside her and her heart was singing in anticipation of what would happen next. She was not disappointed. His restraint and his skill were working their desired effect on her. Even now his caresses and his hot, demanding kisses continued. She was shivering and quaking beneath him before he finally released all control to take her with a stormy abandon that brought her to a throbbing, shuddering release. Turning her head aside to gasp for air, Carol looked into the flames in the fireplace and felt herself and Nicholas become one with them, cracking and burning with a searing, blinding heat.

It was a long time before either of them was able to speak again. Nicholas lifted his weight off her and gathered her tenderly into his arms, holding her so her back was toward the warming fire.

"Hush, my dearest, don't cry." He wiped a tear off her cheek. "Surely you know that I love you, too, and I will not leave you or think less of you because of what we have just done."

"Do you mean that?" She wasn't certain he heard her, because he continued as if he were musing aloud to himself.

"How can this have happened to me, when I never loved before? But I do love now, and more completely than I ever dreamed was possible. Caroline, I think I would die without you."

It was then, at that exact moment, that Carol realized she could not tell him the truth after all. Sooner or later, she was going to have to go back to the twentieth century, while he would have to remain where and when he was and marry Lady Caroline. And while he might think he would die without her, Carol knew she would go mad if she left him to suffer for the rest of his life from the loss of the woman he loved. The pain he would feel at her absence she would feel too, for they were bound together beyond the limits of mere time or space. The only solution, the best thing for Nicholas, was to let him go on believing that the woman he loved was the real Lady Caroline.

"What an unexpected joy," he murmured, stretching luxuriously while keeping Carol still within the circle of his arms, "that having made up our minds to be practical and do our respective duties, we have found love."

After a long, sweet kiss, he withdrew his arm from beneath her shoulders and propped himself up on one elbow so he could look down at her. He spoke softly, gently, as if he wanted to quell any fears she might still have after the last, tender hour.

"Caroline, my dear, there is something I must

ask you. Please do not be embarrassed, and do not be afraid to tell me the truth. I believe it is what you wanted to tell me last night during our carriage ride, and what you have been trying to say since you came here today. Only something so vitally important could lead you to disregard the rules of proper conduct. You see, for all the recent changes in your actions, I do still know you fairly well." He ended with a smile.

"What do you want to know?" Carol did not think he could suspect the truth. Something else must be bothering him.

"I could scarcely believe my discovery," he said, still speaking softly, "because you have always, until the last few days, been the very model of a well-brought-up young lady."

"Have I said or done something to offend you?"

"I cannot answer that question until after I have heard your explanation. I am aware that there may be some innocent explanation, Caroline, and I am willing to listen to it without anger, and without blaming you."

"What are you talking about?" She sat up, putting a little distance between them, so she could think without the distraction of his warm skin against hers.

"My dear," he said quietly, "you were not a virgin."

"Oh, my God. You could tell? Of course you could. That's why you stopped for a second right in the middle of everything, isn't it? Oh, what you must think of me. I know how important a bride's virginity is to the men of this time. Nicholas," she gasped, "does this

131

mean you want to call off the engagement?"

"It means I want to know what happened to you. Some girls ride a lot, and that can make a difference, but you have never been particularly fond of horses. Well, Caroline?" He was sitting up, too, now, facing her directly. He did not look angry, but Carol thought he must be awfully disappointed in his fiancee.

"I don't expect you to think well of me after I've come here in defiance of all the polite rules of society. Certainly, you can't want to marry me after discovering that I am—what shall I call it, Nicholas? Used? Would that be an appropriate word?" She saw him wince at the harsh term.

"Just tell me what happened," he said. "I have a right to know, and I am willing to listen."

"I guess you are being a lot nicer to me than most men would be at a time like this. How could I have been stupid enough to ruin everything for you and for Lady—" She broke off, staring at him. His face was pale and his eyes were hard. When she moved, trying to put even more distance between them, he caught her arm to hold her where she was.

"*Answer my question, Caroline.*" So compelling was his manner that she did as he demanded. She told him the truth.

"I thought he loved me. He said he would marry me. But then my circumstances changed, so he left me."

"When?" he said. "When did it happen?"

"It was almost eight years ago."

"Eight years? You were only sixteen? You were still a schoolgirl! Caroline, where were your parents? How could they allow this to happen?" When she did not answer, he went on in a deadly cold tone of voice. "How long did this affair last?"

"It wasn't an affair," she cried. "It only happened once. It was very fast and not at all pleasant for me. In fact, it was painful. And bloody. He left me feeling dirty and emotionally numb. After that one time, I wouldn't let him get close enough to do it again. But I still thought he would marry me. I actually thought he loved me in spite of the fact that he had taken what he wanted without regard to my feelings. Some girls are incredibly foolish, aren't they?" There were tears running down her face, but she ignored them.

"Who was he?" Nicholas demanded, and she could tell he wanted to kill the man. At least that wasn't going to be a problem.

"His name was Robert Drummond," she said. "You don't know him.".

"Sir Robert Drummond?" His voice hardened. "I am aware of the man's existence, though I have refused his acquaintance in the past."

"No, it's not possible," she groaned, fearing the worst. Ever since the terrible night when Robert had so callously taken her virginity, Carol had sensed that he was not finished with her. He had disappeared from her life when her father's bankruptcy became public knowledge and she had never seen him again, yet his memory went with her wherever she was, like an evil shadow standing behind her.

"It is fortunate that he left the country last year or I would be obliged to call him out," said Nicholas.

"Left England?" she repeated, wondering how there could be two such cold, uncaring men as Robert Drummond. With all the pain of her unhappy past in her voice, she added, "I hope he went straight to Hell."

"In point of fact, he emigrated to America rather than fight a duel with an outraged father. From what I have heard, the case was similar to yours, my dear. I am sorry you were so badly used, Caroline, and so poorly protected by your family. Your parents must be held partly responsible for what happened to you, you know."

"I suppose you will want to cancel our engagement now," she whispered, gazing down at her own hands rather than at his face. "I know that noblemen feel they have the right to demand virgin brides, so they can be absolutely certain their heirs are actually their own children."

He lifted her chin so she was forced to look at him, though she was so consumed with shame at having proven to be less than he wanted her to be that she would have preferred to keep her face hidden. He was silent for a long while, looking deep into her eyes. When at last he spoke, he did not say what she expected to hear.

"How can I reject you when I have just done something similar to you?" he asked.

"Not similar at all," Carol protested. "This time, instead of hating what was happening, I cooperated. You gave me several chances to say no. If I had said no, you would have stopped. And you saw to it that I enjoyed what we did. Those are very big differences, Nicholas."

134

Christmas Carol

"Now I know why you were always so cool to me, and why you were cold toward other men, too. No wonder you reached four and twenty with nary a proposal. It was because in your heart, you wanted nothing to do with men after that tragic betrayal of your innocent trust. I consider it little short of a miracle that you were able to overcome your distaste for an act that you must, ever since that terrible day, have regarded as horribly brutal. I will never forget that I am the man you loved enough to trust me not to hurt you when I possessed you." One finger traced along her cheek to the corner of her mouth. "I understand so much more about you now. Caroline, I want to change the terms of our agreement."

"I know. You don't want to marry me." She met his eyes with a touch of defiance. "All right, Nicholas. Thank you for the kind words, but they really weren't necessary. I will agree to break the engagement without making a big public fuss, so you will be spared any scandal. I know by now how important a good reputation is to you.

"However," Carol went on, determined to salvage something out of the debacle she had created by giving way to her foolish passion for this man, "I do place one condition on my compliance with your wishes. You must promise me that you will still settle that dowry on Penelope so she can marry Lord Simmons. Penelope should not have to suffer for my youthful transgressions. And I don't want her to know the real reason for the end of our engagement either. We can tell her it was a mutual agreement."

135

"Caroline." Nicholas was grinning at her. When he continued, she could not believe what she was hearing. "I am amazed that I have only recently begun to appreciate what a wonderful person you are. I thank heaven that you were finally able to overcome the coldness that was your heart's protection against the terrible thing that was done to you.

"Penelope will have her dowry. Never fear on that score. Penelope will always be like a sister to me."

"Thank you." Carol wished he would stop smiling at her in that crazy way, when she felt like crying her eyes out. Not only had she ruined everything for herself, she had succeeded in ruining Lady Caroline's life, too, in spite of Lady Augusta's ghostly predictions that Carol would be unable to change the past. It was unforgiveable, when Lady Caroline had never done anything to hurt Carol.

"I believe, my dear," said Nicholas, still grinning, "that you have misunderstood me. I do not wish to break off our engagement, nor to change the financial settlements. I only want to renegotiate the personal terms."

"What are you saying?" Carol gasped.

"I think you know. I entered this betrothal as you did, seeking only practical gains. I wanted an heir to my title, while you sought economic security for yourself and a dowry for your sister so she could follow her heart. We both forgot the emotional aspects of marriage.

"Caroline, I will say it again. In these last three days, I have fallen deeply into love with you. Nothing I have learned this afternoon has changed my feelings."

"You love me in spite of my awful history?" she exclaimed, still disbelieving.

"I am as surprised as you are," he said ruefully. "Caroline, I tell you in all truthfulness, if someone had proposed today's events to me as a hypothetical problem, I would have said that I would reject the woman in the case. But I find I cannot reject you. Yes, I do love you, with all my heart, and all the more because you were willing to flout convention to come to me in order to confess your sad past. Have you any idea what your trust and honesty mean to me?" Kneeling before her, he took both of her hands in his.

"Lady Caroline," he said in a formal voice, "I want to make a new betrothal, here and now. I do solemnly promise that I will love you and protect and care for you for the rest of our lives. And I will be a faithful husband. I swear it on my honor."

"Nicholas, are you absolutely sure about this?" she cried, dismayed by his misreading of her intentions in coming to him and wondering what would happen when he found himself wed to the real, presumably virginal, Lady Caroline.

"I have never been so certain of anything in my entire life." Lifting her hands to his lips, he kissed them both, and then kissed her mouth to seal what he referred to as their new betrothal.

"I love you, too," Carol murmured. "I will always love you, no matter where or when I find myself."

"You will find yourself always at my side," he whispered, "because after we are wed, I will never let you be anywhere else." He drew her down to lie on the carpet again while he made love to her once more. This time he told her repeatedly what was in his heart and Carol, bound to him forever by her own love, responded with a depth of emotion that left both of them shaken yet completely satisfied.

Later, after he helped her to dress, Nicholas called for his carriage and took her back to Marlowe House.

"Do not forget the ball this evening," he reminded her as they waited for Lady Augusta's butler to open the door.

"I won't." she responded.

"Now that we are properly betrothed," he added, smiling into her eyes, "I am permitted to issue commands to you."

"Are you, indeed, my lord?" She could not help smiling back at him. "And what are your commands for tonight?"

"You are to save every waltz for me," he told her, "in memory of the waltz you demanded on the night of our betrothal ball. It was then, Caroline, when I first saw the new spirit shining in your eyes, that I fell into love with you."

"Nicholas," she promised, "I will never dance the waltz with anyone but you."

"My lady," the butler informed Carol as soon as the heavy front door closed upon Nicholas's departing figure, "Lady Augusta is in the drawing room. She gave orders that she wishes to see you the moment you return from shopping."

Gowned in high-waisted, long-sleeved dark

138

green, Lady Augusta stood still as a statue against the background of holiday decorations, watching Carol enter the drawing room.

"I need not ask what you have been doing during your absence," Lady Augusta said in the chilling tone Carol had heard too many times during her future employment as a companion in twentieth-century London. "One glance at your glowing cheeks and shining eyes and the dullest imbecile would know you have been making love with Nicholas."

"I won't deny it, no matter what punishment you are planning for me. I am not ashamed of what I did this afternoon." All the same, Carol kept some distance between herself and Lady Augusta. "The only thing worrying me about what I did is the possibility that I may have managed to change history just enough to ruin Lady Caroline's life."

"Why should that possibility disturb you?" Lady Augusta's eyes seemed to burn into Carol's very soul. Under that intensely focused gaze Carol could only respond with truth directly from her heart.

"Lady Caroline never did anything to me. After living in her body for these last few days, I have begun to like her. I respect her determination to make it possible for her sister to have a happy life. I don't want to do anything to hurt her or to leave her life in a mess as a result of my actions."

"I am pleased to learn that you are now capable of caring about another person. Your concern for Lady Caroline signifies an important development in your own character."

"Not entirely." Finding Lady Augusta's penetrating eyes no softer in spite of her approving words, Carol was still compelled to speak the truth. "I have fallen into love with Nicholas. I will always love him."

"That is a pity." Lady Augusta did not sound the least bit sorry.

"Why?" Carol demanded.

"Because it is time for us to return to the twentieth century," said Lady Augusta.

Chapter Six

"Go back now?" Carol cried. "No, please, not yet."

"You did not want to come into the past in the first place," Lady Augusta reminded her. "No sooner did you arrive than you wanted to return to your shabby little room and your emotionally arid existence."

"I know. But that was before I met Nicholas."

"Whom you claim to love," said Lady Augusta distainfully.

"I do love him. You can't change that."

"Perhaps I do not want to change it." Lady Augusta's penetrating eyes watched for Carol's slightest reaction as she asked a cool and pointed question. "Exactly how much do you love Nicholas?"

Carol wished Lady Augusta would look somewhere other than into her eyes so she would have at least a slim chance of lying about her feelings and getting away with it. She was afraid there could be some unknown danger, to her and perhaps to Nicholas, too, in Lady Augusta's knowledge of the extent and depth of her love for him. She could not lie, nor could she evade an honest answer by quoting an old verse she knew, to the effect that if she could say how much, she did not love at all. She was being forced to tell the truth.

"I love him with my heart and my soul and—yes—with my body, too," she said.

"Do you love him enough to give him up so he can have the life he was meant to have?" asked Lady Augusta.

"What do you mean by that?"

"While you were unable to change the course of history by your presence in this time, you *were* able to change the way Nicholas feels about his fiancee."

"He loves *me*," Carol said. "He fell in love because his fiancee is different now. He told me so. And that difference is *me*."

"Do not mistake your situation," Lady Augusta warned. "Nicholas is meant for Lady Caroline. He will marry her, not you. She, not you, will bear his children and live with him into old age."

"Then why did you bother asking me if I love him enough to give him up?" Carol demanded. "It is obvious that I am not going to be given a choice in the matter, so what difference can it make whether or not I am willing to let him go?"

"You have done what you were meant to do in this time."

"That's no answer. It seems to me that all I've done here is hurt some very nice people. Thanks to me, Nicholas now believes Lady Caroline gave up her virtue to another man." Recollections of the afternoon flooded over Carol—the memory of Nicholas's passionate embrace, of his startled comprehension that the body he was entering was not virgin, and then his remarkable understanding when Carol revealed her hasty, unhappy, prior experience with Robert Drummond. But in confessing the incident, Carol had been speaking of her own past, not Lady Caroline's.

"Lady Caroline did not give up her virtue," said Lady Augusta in a kinder voice. "It was taken from her by force and by falsehood, in much the same way in which you lost your virginity."

Carol gaped at her, dumbfounded by this disclosure until she realized that of course Lady Augusta would know the details of what the twentieth-century Robert Drummond had done to Carol Simmons. Lady Augusta was in a position to uncover any facts that might be useful to her.

"Lady Caroline's brief and violent acquaintance with the early nineteenth-century version of Robert Drummond," Lady Augusta went on, "left her emotions frozen, so she has been unable to express love toward any man. Today you have rectified that sad event in her life. In so doing, perhaps you have begun to heal the wound in your own life, since you, too, love Nicholas. It is only through love that such healing is possible."

"So the same thing happened to Lady

Caroline and to me, and in both our cases, it was done by a man with the same name and the same kind of character. Is that why I immediately felt so familiar with her?" Carol wondered, not doubting for a moment what Lady Augusta was telling her, though she was surprised by the odd coincidence. "That must be why I was able to sense her terror whenever Nicholas and I seemed to be getting into a passionate embrace. That poor, terrified woman! I know exactly how she felt."

"As I said, your actions today have resolved and forever banished the fears Lady Caroline had about lovemaking," Lady Augusta told her.

"Then I have helped and not hurt her? I am glad." Carol was afraid she would start crying from all the various emotions warring within her.

"The last and most important thing you can do for Lady Caroline," said Lady Augusta, "is relinquish the hold your love has on Nicholas. There is a subtle difference between you and Lady Caroline. Nicholas expresses his subconscious uneasiness with that difference by declaring repeatedly that you have changed, because he perceives the difference as a change in his fiancee. Unless you are willing to voluntarily withdraw your love from him, he will never fully accept or love his wife-to-be, because after you have gone from this time, he will be aware of a missing element in her personality. There is only one way to resolve this problem. You must set him free, Carol."

"If you are telling me to stop loving him,"

Carol said, "then I can't do it. I can't just turn off my emotions."

"I did not say 'stop loving him,'" Lady Augusta responded. "I said 'give him up.' *Willingly*. Your willingness to sacrifice your own selfish desires for the sake of another's happiness is one of the most important aspects of your experience in this time."

"I suppose you think it will make me a better person," Carol grumbled with a touch of her old sarcasm.

"I know it will. The choice is yours, Carol. You, and you alone, can free Nicholas to love the woman he will marry." Lady Augusta waited tensely, her sharp eyes still fixed upon Carol's face.

It took Carol less than a second to make her decision. The ease with which she made it surprised her, but still, the decision hurt.

"How could I do anything that would make Nicholas the least bit unhappy?" she asked. "Or cast a shadow on his future with Lady Caroline? I will give him up. I cannot do it happily, but I will do it willingly, as you require."

"Excellent." With a deep sigh, Lady Augusta relaxed. "You have learned this first lesson well. We leave immediately for the twentieth century." She lifted her arms as if to embrace Carol as she had done once before, when removing Carol to this other time.

"No, wait!" Carol made an abrupt motion to stop what Lady Augusta was going to do next.

"What, a change of heart? So quickly?" exclaimed Lady Augusta, regarding her with raised eyebrows. "For shame, Carol. I was beginning to think better of you."

"I will still go back with you," Carol said. "Just not this minute. Look, I did what I was supposed to do in this time. You said so yourself."

"Without knowing what your purpose here was," Lady Augusta reminded her. Carol chose to disregard that comment because what she was going to ask was so important to her.

"I want something in return for all I've done," Carol said.

"So, you are selfish still." Lady Augusta's pale face went cold and hard.

"It's not much to ask," Carol said. "Just a few hours more. Let *me* go to the ball tonight. Let me have a waltz with Nicholas, just to feel his arms around me one last time. After tonight, I will never see him again." Her voice broke and she stopped, unable to continue for the emotions that were threatening to choke her.

"I am not sure it would be wise." However, Lady Augusta did appear to be thinking seriously about Carol's request. "There is always the chance that you will say something you should not."

"I won't," Carol promised. "I'll be careful of every word. I want to give Penelope a last hug, too. It's strange the way I have begun to think of her as my real sister, and in so short a time.

"Please, Lady Augusta, I'm begging you. This means so much to me. Give me one dance with Nicholas, and the instant the dance is over, you and I can go. I won't make a scene. You can handle our leave-taking however you want. Just grant me this one wish, so I can say good-bye to him in my own way. He will never know, but in my heart I will be able to end it and to know my time with him is over."

"Swear to me that you will guard your every word," demanded Lady Augusta.

"I have already said I will, but yes, I swear it on my love for him."

"I am not entirely happy with this request of yours, but I can see that you do truly love Nicholas. You may not think so now, when you are in such pain at the thought of parting from him, but you are fortunate, Carol. In my many years on earth, I never loved as you do today. Perhaps if I had allowed myself to care so wholeheartedly, I would not be in my present predicament. Very well, I will grant you the hours from this moment until the first waltz of the ball is finished. However, mark me well. When the last note of music dies at the end of that waltz, we will be gone."

Hurrying toward her own room after her interview with Lady Augusta, Carol found Penelope loitering in the upper hall.

"I have been waiting for you," Penelope called out as soon as she saw Carol. "Did Aunt Augusta tell you my wonderful news?"

"No," Carol replied. "We only spoke about Nicholas. What has happened, my dear?" It seemed perfectly natural to put her arms around Lady Caroline's sister as if the girl were in truth Carol's own sibling.

"After we drank our chocolate and ate the most delicious pastries, Alwyn—that is, Lord Simmons," Penelope corrected herself with a blush. "Lord Simmons escorted me home and then he spoke to Aunt Augusta. He insisted that I be present, even though Aunt Augusta said it would not be proper. Lord Simmons told us he has obtained his father's permission to marry me, on the sole condition that Aunt Augusta must also approve the match." Penelope paused for a moment before concluding her announcement.

"Caroline, Alwyn formally asked for my hand, right there in front of me, and Aunt Augusta agreed. We are to be married in the spring, shortly after you and Nicholas are wed."

"Oh, Penelope." Carol embraced and kissed her. "Be happy all your life, my dearest sister. You are the sister of my heart."

"Caroline, are you actually weeping for my joy?" With careful tenderness Penelope brushed the tears off Carol's cheeks. She could not know that they were not only for her happy betrothal, but were also tears of parting. This was their farewell, for though Carol would be with Penelope and Lady Augusta at a dinner party that evening, after which they would all go on to the ball, the two of them would not be alone together again. While she might be ignorant of the true cause of Carol's tears, Penelope was not blind.

"Caroline, you are in some disarray," Penelope observed. "It is most unlike you to be untidy. Is something wrong? I was worried when I arrived home with Alwyn and Aunt Augusta told me you were not yet here. Where have you been?"

"I went to see Nicholas. We spent the afternoon—we spent it talking." Carol could feel herself blushing.

"You went to his house without a chaperone?

148

From the look of you, the two of you weren't just talking. Has Nicholas been taking liberties with your person?"

"I didn't mind at all," Carol said with perfect truth.

"Caroline," gasped Penelope, giggling a little, "how could you?"

"Because I love him."

"Oh, what a relief!" Penelope let out a long breath. "And here I thought you were marrying him for my sake, to get a larger dowry for me."

"You weren't supposed to know. How did you find out?" Carol asked.

"Do you think I am a complete dunce? I guessed, of course, after Aunt Augusta revealed to me weeks ago that I was to be handsomely provided for in your marriage settlement. I thought I was the only reason you agreed to marry Nicholas."

"She never told me that you knew! I have been trying so hard not to say a word that might give you the slightest hint about the arrangements being made for you. Are you telling me that we have been hiding the same secret from each other?" Carol cried.

"It seems so." Penelope gave one of her quick, little laughs. "What a fine joke! And all this time I have been wondering how to thank you for your willingness to sacrifice yourself for my sake after you have claimed for years that you never wanted to marry anyone. It is good to know that Nicholas was able to change your mind—and your heart."

"I love you, Penelope." Carol found it remarkably easy to say what she felt for this sweet girl.

149

Flora Speer

"I love you, too. You are the very best of
sisters," Penelope responded, adding with a
bright smile, "Isn't it fortunate that Alwyn
and Nicholas are such good friends? And their
country estates are near to each other, too. We
won't be separated by our marriages the way
some sisters are."

"I cannot think of anything in this world that
would keep your sister apart from you," Carol
replied, knowing with absolute certainty that
Lady Caroline would agree.

The Christmas Eve ball was held at yet
another of the great London mansions to
which Lady Caroline, her sister, and her aunt
were regularly invited. This particular mansion
was even more heavily decorated for Christmas
than was Marlowe House. Thick garlands of
evergreens were hung around the mirrored,
gilded ballroom and the smaller nearby cham-
bers. Vases of hothouse flowers added their
sweet fragrance to the sharper scent of the
abundant greenery. Hundreds of fine beeswax
candles in glittering chandeliers shone their
light upon the richly dressed crowd as the
guests wandered about exchanging holiday
greetings before the dancing began.

Carol found the seasonal cheerfulness a sad
contrast to her state of mind, though on the
surface she did not think anyone could notice
anything different about her. She was wearing
a gown in a soft shade of rose silk and with it,
the sapphire and diamond necklace Nicholas
had given to his fiancee.

On this festive evening Lady Augusta was
resplendent in lavender draperies and pearls.

150

The first sight of her as they were preparing to leave Marlowe House sent a chill to Carol's heart, reminding her of the costume Lady Augusta had worn on the night when she first appeared in Carol's bedchamber. The prospect of being wrapped into those draperies a second time was almost too much for Carol to bear, and all the more so because she knew when the moment came she would be torn from people for whom she had learned to care deeply.

The three ladies greeted their host and hostess and then moved on into the ballroom, where Lord Simmons immediately appeared to salute them with a warmth and charm that made Carol understand why Penelope was so attracted to him. He promptly filled Penelope's dance card for the three dances allowed by the rules of etiquette, and wrote his name on Carol's card, too, for two dances.

"May I stretch propriety a little and claim a fourth dance with Penelope, since she is to be my wife?" he asked Lady Augusta. "Let the gossips say what they will tonight, the news of our betrothal will soon be out and then everyone will understand."

After Lady Augusta assented, Lord Simmons led Penelope away to take their places in the first dance. With a sense of finality Carol watched them go, certain that she and the girl whom she now thought of as her sister would never speak together again.

"Tell me about them," Carol murmured. "About their future lives."

Lady Augusta did not answer at once. Like Carol, she was watching Penelope and her new fiance. After a long wait, she spoke with her gaze still on the young couple.

"They will marry, of course," Lady Augusta said, "and will produce four sons and a daughter."

"What about the name?" Carol asked. "Lord Simmons's given name, Alwyn, was my father's middle name."

"Ah, yes," said Lady Augusta, "I thought your guess at that particular truth would be accurate. Thirty years from now, the youngest son of Penelope and Lord Simmons will journey to America and settle there. Those two dancing together are your great-grandparents many generations past."

"Penelope is my ancestor?" Carol's eyes filled. She blinked hard. "Thank you for telling me. What about Nicholas and Caroline?"

"Indeed, what of Nicholas and Caroline?" said a beloved voice from just behind Carol. Nicholas continued, teasing the women, "Are you two rearranging our wedding plans? If so, I implore you to name an earlier date. I find I am becoming impatient." This last was said with a glance into Carol's eyes that almost broke her heart with its tenderness.

"Actually," said Lady Augusta. "we were speaking about Penelope and Alwyn."

"Is it Alwyn now?" Though he was speaking to Lady Augusta, Nicholas was still smiling into Carol's eyes. "Does this mean the attachment is official?"

"They received my approval late this afternoon, as you very well know, since you helped to ease the path to their hearts' desire," said Lady Augusta. Her voice suddenly taking on a sharpness that must have seemed odd to

Nicholas, she added, "I assume you have presented yourself in order to claim this next dance with your fiancee. I believe the dance cards say it will be a waltz. I shall now retire to the card room to join Lord Falloner for a game of piquet until you have finished."

Carol wanted to tell Nicholas to wait, to sit this dance out with her and not take her onto the floor until the next waltz, but with Lady Augusta looking hard at her she did not dare attempt a delay that would give her more time with him. Her heart aching with love and grief, she put her hand into his and stepped to the center of the floor. Nicholas took her into his arms and they began to dance.

Carol knew she would have only a few minutes more to touch him and to memorize his strong, handsome face. She kept her eyes fastened on him as they whirled about the floor. His steps were sure and she followed him easily, without having to think about what she was doing. They were meant to be together like this, with Carol safe in his arms and Nicholas gazing at her with an affection he did not trouble to conceal. For these last, brief moments they moved along together, twirling and gliding in their own enchanted space into which the rest of the world—and the rest of time—could not intrude.

"I love you so much," Carol whispered. "Whatever happens in the future, don't ever forget that, and never doubt that I am grateful for the way you treated me this afternoon. I do not regret what we did together and I never will."

"I am not sorry for those hours either." His

tender smile almost reduced her to tears. "I love you, Caroline." He said more, but the music was just ending and his voice began to fade in her ears.

"Nicholas?" She wasn't sure he could hear her. What Carol heard instead of Nicholas's words was Lady Augusta's voice, though Lady Augusta was still in the card room. By now it was probably the real Lady Augusta who was sitting at the piquet table with Lord Falloner, both of them completely unaware of what was happening. The Lady Augusta whom Carol knew was there in the ballroom with her, and this Lady Augusta was invisible.

"The dance I allowed you as a special favor is finished," Lady Augusta said. "Now we must leave."

For an instant or two Carol could still feel Nicholas's arms around her, before his figure started to blur. To Carol's eyes, the ballroom began to grow dark and the musicians, who were just striking up for the next dance after the waltz, seemed to her to be more and more distant and off key.

"Please, Lady Augusta, wait for just a moment," Carol begged. "Let me see him happy with her. Let me know my breaking heart isn't a waste."

"I cannot permit a further extension of your time here," Lady Augusta began, but she was interrupted. Another, deeper voice spoke with a sound that reverberated through Carol's head like thunder and yet was gentle as a sigh.

"Because you love honestly," said the voice, *"your wish is granted. Behold."*

The darkness now surrounding her parted

and Carol could see the ballroom again, bright with candles and Christmas decorations. She saw Lady Caroline standing with Nicholas's hand holding hers. As she watched, Lady Caroline swayed, putting her free hand to her forehead. Nicholas bent toward her with open concern on his handsome face. Lady Caroline said something and Nicholas smiled. Taking the hand he held, he tucked it into his elbow and led her off the dance floor, toward a row of French doors that opened to the gardens. Every line of Nicholas's body conveyed the same loving protectiveness as the expression with which he was now regarding his fiancee.

"They will be happy," said the voice in Carol's head, *"and that happiness is your doing."*

"Thank you." Carol said the words aloud, though she believed the owner of the voice would have heard them even if she had only spoken them in her mind.

"Come, Carol." That was Lady Augusta. "We have overstayed our time."

Lady Augusta's arms were around her. On this second occasion, Carol was better prepared for the chill of her companion's embrace. This time, the bitter cold could not compare to the grief of parting forever from her only love, or to the knifelike pain of the loneliness now filling her heart.

"Nicholas!" The cry tore from her lips like the wail of some lost soul consigned to the outer regions of darkest hell.

"Oh, Carol," murmured Lady Augusta, "you do not yet understand. There is more . . . so much more still to come. . . ."

Part III.
Christmas
Present.

London, 1993.

Chapter Seven

The cold draft blowing around her feet wakened
her. At first Carol sat perfectly still in the old
wing chair next to the dead embers of the previous night's fire while she tried to remember
where she was. Her body was cold and stiff, as
if she had been sleeping in the same position for
a long time without a blanket. Confusion filled
her mind, making clear thought difficult.

When she noticed a faint gray light coming
in around the edges of the windows, she got
up to push aside the curtains and look out on
the little square in front of Marlowe House.
The fog was gone, the sky was sunny, and
the brightly colored lights on the Christmas
tree in the square glittered as the branches
moved in the morning breeze. A few early risers
walked purposefully across the square. They
were wearing twentieth-century clothing.

"What has happened?" Turning from the cheerful outdoor scene, Carol surveyed her dingy, unattractive room. "What am I doing here? I should be in the blue bedroom, with Penelope just next door. This must be a servant's room, but why am I in it?"

Not until she flung open the bedroom door and stepped out into the hall did her memory begin to return. Looking down the hall she could see the wall that, since soon after the end of World War II, had divided the once-spacious Marlowe House into two smaller houses. The blue bedchamber—Lady Caroline Hyde's bedchamber—lay on the other side of that thick wall, one level down from where Carol presently stood.

"Was it all a dream? But how could it have been when it was so long and so detailed?" Deep in thought now, though still confused, Carol went back into her room and closed the door again. "It must have been a dream. Anything else is impossible. Lady Augusta's ghost? Ridiculous. I don't believe in ghosts. No sensible person does. Something I ate must have upset my stomach. Spoiled food can cause nightmares."

A half-eaten bowl of chicken soup sat on the table beside the wing chair, a thin, blackened slice of mushroom floating on top of the broth. Upon lifting the domed metal lid from over her dinner plate, Carol discovered a congealed mess of cold chicken and vegetables. The untouched wedge of apple tart did not look much more appetizing. Carol quickly replaced the dome.

"If I didn't eat any of my dinner, then it

160

can't have made me sick," she reasoned. "I don't recall ever hearing of an empty stomach causing bad dreams. More likely, it would keep me awake. So, what did happen here last night? *Was* it last night? Or have several days passed?"

She sank down into the wing chair again, thinking hard, trying to remember every detail of her sojourn in the early nineteenth century. There had to be a rational explanation for the events she was able to recall in such vivid detail. Lady Augusta's ghostly late-night appearance . . . Penelope . . . Nicholas—

Nicholas. Pain flowed over her, grief and a terrible loneliness filling her heart. In the midst of lingering confusion she was sure of only one thing. The emotion she felt for Nicholas was real.

"Nicholas," she whispered. "Oh, my love. My dear, lost love." Tears poured down her cheeks. She did not bother to wipe them away. She cowered in the wing chair, seeking comfort in its familiar shape. She did not stop crying until Nell, the chambermaid, knocked at her door and entered, bearing a tray with Carol's breakfast on it. Then Carol hastily wiped her face on the sleeve of her bathrobe and sat up a little straighter, trying to appear more composed than she actually felt.

"Are you up already?" asked Nell in surprise. After a closer look, she said, "No, you're up *still*. You haven't been to bed, have you? You've been sittin' in that old chair all night long. Oh, miss, you'll catch pneumonia or something worse if you don't keep warm."

"I am not sick. I am just a little chilled." It

161

was all Carol could do to make herself respond, but she did not want to worry the maid. Nell had done everything she could to make Carol's existence at Marlowe House a pleasant one, and Carol knew she hadn't been very nice in return. For the first time, she felt guilty about that.

"You just drink your tea now, and eat something, and you'll brighten right up," Nell advised. "A nice, hot bath will help, too," she added, pouring out a cup of tea and handing it to Carol.

As she looked at the maid through the rising wisps of steam from her tea, it seemed to Carol that Nell was remarkably like Ella, the maidservant who had been taking care of her for the last few days.

"Nell," Carol asked, "what day is today?"

"It's Wednesday," Nell responded, "the twenty-second of December. Just three more days till Christmas. I shouldn't wonder if you've forgotten what day it is, with everything you've been doing lately, seeing to Lady Augusta's care and then arranging for the funeral and all that."

"The funeral," Carol repeated. "Nell, did you or anyone else in the house see or hear anything strange last night?"

"What do you mean, strange?" asked Nell.

"Just unusual sounds, or perhaps someone who shouldn't be here," Carol said.

"Like an intruder? No, Crampton saw to all the locks as soon as the funeral guests left, and he turned on the alarm system. You know how Lady Augusta was about using that system. She thought she was going to be robbed and then murdered in her bed if it wasn't turned on every night, and Crampton isn't likely to change old habits now." Nell paused, and Carol thought she went a little pale. "Why do you ask, miss? Did you see something? My old grammie used to say that sometimes the ghosts of people recently dead come back to their houses just after their funerals. They aren't quite ready to go to heaven yet, you see, or to the other place, either. Can't blame them for that, I say. Heaven's bound to be strange for most people after livin' on earth for years, and as for the fires below—well, who would want to go there at all?"

"I'm not sure exactly what it was I thought I saw and heard," Carol said. "Perhaps it was just the wind."

"There wasn't any wind last night," said Nell, "only the clear sky and one or two stars. But after all, you can't expect to see many stars with all the city lights shinin' so bright, can you?"

"I must have been dreaming, then," Carol said, unwilling to continue the conversation. Nell claimed the previous night had been clear, but Carol distinctly recalled a thick fog. And she *had* heard the wind. "I was so tired that I fell asleep in the chair and, as you guessed, I never did get into bed."

"That uncomfortable old chair would give anyone bad dreams," Nell agreed. "You take my advice, miss, and have a nice soak in a tub of hot water."

"I'll do that," Carol promised. "I am planning to be out for most of the day, so would you tell Mrs. Marks I won't be here for lunch?"

"I'll tell her." Picking up the dinner tray, Nell

left Carol to her usual breakfast of tea and a plain roll.

After eating, and after indulging herself with a long, hot bath, she did feel better. Upon entering her bedroom from the bathroom down the hall, Carol took a good look at the place where she had been living for years. Until this morning the decor of her room had suited her mental state, but now she saw that it was filled with depressingly worn and faded furnishings.

During her brief stay in the nineteenth century she had been learning all over again to appreciate comforts she had once taken for granted. After her father's bankruptcy, and especially after his suicide, she had given up elegant furniture, good clothing in pretty colors, fresh flowers, music, the theater, and all other material pleasures as if she were a medieval monk putting on a penitential hair shirt. She had reacted to her father's misfortunes and to his death as if she were the one to blame for them.

Now, sensibilities newly awakened to the pleasures of Lady Caroline Hyde's daily existence made Carol chafe at the lack of beauty in her own life. Recalling Lady Caroline's blue and white bedchamber, her finely made gowns, her rose perfume, and most of all, the frequent sight of Nicholas's broad-shouldered form attired in perfectly tailored clothing, Carol heaved a deep sigh.

"Nicholas, your presence in that borrowed life was the greatest pleasure of all. If I had known that living without hope of ever seeing you again would hurt so much, I'm not sure I could have given you up. No, not even for your own good."

The slightly musty smell of her room, to which she was so accustomed that usually she did not even notice it, suddenly irritated her beyond enduring. Carol flung open the windows, letting in cool air and watery December sunshine.

"How could I have lived like that?" she muttered to herself. "After I started working for Lady Augusta, I wasn't completely without money. I could have bought a few pillows or a new comforter to brighten up my room, or treated myself to a restaurant dinner once in a while."

Standing by the window, she gradually became aware of the springlike warmth of the weather. The sun and the pleasant temperature drew her like a magnet. She took her unattractive but serviceable old brown coat out of the closet and, after a last glance around her room, headed for the outdoors.

On her way out of the house Carol hurried past Lady Augusta's suite on the next floor below her own room. Nell was busy cleaning and had the door and all the windows thrown wide. There was just the faintest trace of lavender perfume borne on the fresh breeze blowing through the door and into the hall.

"I'll have this suite spit-and-polish clean by the end of the day," Nell called, catching sight of Carol. "Then, when Lady Augusta's missing nephew finally gets here, he'll have a nice place to sleep. These are the best rooms in the house. Lady Augusta was stingy elsewhere, but she kept her own rooms in good shape, at least till she got so sick at the end.

"Go on now, miss," Nell urged when Carol hesitated as if she would enter the rooms. "You've been indoors too much lately, takin' care of Lady Augusta for all these weeks. Get some fresh air and sunshine and go for a nice long walk like you used to do and you'll sleep better tonight than you did last night."

"I suppose you're right."

As she started down the great staircase toward the entrance hall Carol paused, overcome by memories and seeing Marlowe House with eyes in which the past and present flowed together in a thoroughly disorienting way. The black and white checkerboard floor in the hall remained the same, but the hall itself now looked pathetically small to her. Just the day before, she and Penelope had come down these same steps together, laughing and planning a day of shopping, each of them secretly hoping to encounter a beloved man during their excursion to Bond Street.

Carol had to fight back the urge to pound against the wall that cut the hall in half. She had the oddest feeling that if she could only break down that wall, or in some way pass through it, she would find on the other side of it the people she loved and the life she had been living for the last few days.

"Not days," Carol reminded herself. "One night. That's all the *real* time it took for me to fall in love."

Even as she stood at the foot of the staircase, glaring at the wall with one fist raised as if to strike it, her common sense reasserted itself. In the other half of Marlowe House there currently lived a businessman with his wife and two small children. Nothing waited for Carol there. *Nothing.*

With Crampton not in sight, Carol opened the heavy front door herself and stepped outside. Pausing on the top step to catch her breath and steady her nerves, she recalled Nicholas bringing her home and acting so terribly proper in front of Lady Augusta's butler, though he had just been doing the most wonderful, outrageous things to her in the privacy of his carriage.

With as much strength of will as she could muster, she told herself that all of it had happened 175 years in the past. If it had happened. If what she thought she remembered was not a dream.

"No," she said aloud, her voice breaking a little. "I know it was real. I would never feel this loss and this aching sensation in my heart if it were only a dream. The emotions I experience when I have been dreaming last for a few minutes, or for an hour at most, after I wake up, and then they disappear. These memories are just growing stronger the more I think about them. It really did happen. I love Nicholas and I will never see him again. I have to accept that. I have to learn to live without him. The trouble is, I'm not sure I can."

Consumed by memories of Nicholas, Carol spent the day walking around London while she looked for sights familiar to her in that previous time. The glittering, present-day Christmas decorations she saw everywhere mocked the sorrow she felt and made her yearn for the simpler evidence of the holiday season in the lost world of Regency London to which she longed to return.

She saved the most important spot for last, walking to it from Bond Street as she had walked to it on an afternoon so far in the past, yet in her mind and memories only 24 hours earlier. Getting there was easier today. She was wearing her sensible walking shoes and there was no ice or snow to impede her. She found the right street at once, but Nicholas's house was no longer there. Pretending she was a college professor doing research on the Regency period, she stopped an elderly, well-dressed man and asked him if he knew what had happened to Montfort Place.

"I know the house you mean," the man told her. "I remember this area from my childhood. It was a very different neighborhood in those days. The original buildings on this block were bombed into rubble during World War II. You do know about the Blitz?"

"I do." The lump in her throat prevented further speech.

"You must be terribly disappointed not to find the particular historic house you wanted to see," said the old man. "But there are other interesting spots in London still surviving from the Regency period."

When Carol nodded and thanked him, he passed on down the street, leaving her to stare at the uninteresting modern building that now took the place of the lovely white house in which she and Nicholas had once made love.

"So long ago," Carol sighed, "and yet only yesterday for me. Oh, Nicholas, why can't I *feel* your presence here? Where have you gone? Into

168

the afterlife with Lady Caroline, I suppose," she said, answering her own question sadly. "You are dead now—grown old and feeble, dead and buried more than a hundred years ago." Unable to bear that thought, she hurried away to walk unseeing through the busy streets until the early December twilight brought her ramblings to an end.

Her way back to Marlowe House in late afternoon took her past a small florist's shop. Just as she reached it the shop door opened to discharge a customer. The scent of holiday greenery mingled with the fragrance of roses wafted outward to Carol's nose, stopping her when she would have hurried by. Once again, memory assailed her. The drawing room of Marlowe House had smelled like that long ago, on a day shortly before Christmas.

"Perhaps spending money on flowers isn't a waste after all," Carol said to herself. "How much I enjoyed receiving the bouquets that Nicholas sent to me."

Irresistibly drawn by the sight of numerous containers within, all filled with bright flowers, and by the sparkling white and green display of miniature Christmas trees in the window, she entered the shop. There she purchased a few red roses and some evergreens. Then, acting on an impulse, she also bought a red glass bowl of paperwhite narcissus bulbs set in white pebbles. The buds at the top of each stem looked ready to burst into bloom.

When she reached Marlowe House it was almost dinnertime. Carol did not use the front door. Instead, she pushed open the gate in the iron railing at the front of the house and went down the outside stairs into the sunken area where the servants' entrance was. Opening the old-fashioned, glass-paned door, she stepped through the tiny vestibule and thence into the kitchen. The cook looked up in surprise at her unexpected appearance.

"Good evening, Mrs. Marks," Carol said. "Would you have a small vase I could use for these flowers?" Carol looked around at what were obviously preparations for the holiday. Certain spicy aromas suggested that gingerbread was in the oven, and two fine, high loaves of white bread were cooling on a rack. A second rack held a batch of cookies onto which Mrs. Marks was just sprinkling red and green sugar. Hettie, the scullery maid, was busy chopping celery and onions.

"I suppose we could find something. Hettie, put down that knife before you cut off a finger and go see if you can locate a vase in the everyday china closet."

Mrs. Marks was, as always when dealing with Carol, polite but not particularly pleasant. Carol had long suspected the cook of disliking her. It had never bothered her before, but for some reason on this evening the cool glance Mrs. Marks gave to the flowers in her hand irritated Carol.

"Actually," Carol said, pulling back the wrapping a bit and holding out the flowers, "I bought them for the table down here. Nell told me you are planning a Christmas feast and I thought you might like a centerpiece." She had thought no such thing while purchasing the roses, intending them for her own room.

"Oh, ain't they pretty?" Hettie returned from

the china closet with a vase. "I do like red and green together. So Christmasy. Thank you, Miss Simmons. They'll look ever so nice on our holiday table, where we can all enjoy them."

"The feast we are planning," said Mrs. Marks in a repressive tone of voice, "will not take place for two days yet. These flowers will surely be dead by that time."

"If they are," Carol replied, seeing Hettie's face fall at this prediction, "then I will go out and purchase another bouquet."

"You could eat with us on Christmas Eve," Hettie suggested, oblivious to Mrs. Marks's scowl of disapproval. "I know Nell has asked you, 'cause she told me so."

"I'm sorry," Carol replied. "I won't be able to do that. I have plans for Christmas Eve, and for Christmas Day, too. Some old friends from the United States will be in London for the holiday and I am eager to see them again. Hettie, I leave the flowers with you, to arrange as you think best." Thrusting the bouquet into Hettie's hands, Carol made her escape from the kitchen.

"Humph," she heard Mrs. Marks mutter behind her departing back, "I didn't know Miss Simmons had any friends."

"Oh, what a shame. Everyone should have friends. I hope she's not lonely," Hettie responded. "Anyway, the flowers are beautiful."

By the time Carol reached her room she was furious with herself.

"Why did I make such a stupid excuse? Now I'll have to go out on the holiday even if I don't want to, or they'll know I was lying to get out of eating with them. I don't feel like pretending anymore. Most of my life has been pretending and I'm sick of it." With a rough motion Carol tore the paper off the bowl of narcissus. A stem rising from one of the bulbs lifted half-open buds into the air. Carol sniffed at them appreciatively. "At least they don't smell like lavender."

That thought stopped her with the bowl in her hands before she could put it down on the table beside the wing chair. Lady Augusta's last words to her before removing Carol from the nineteenth century had indicated that there was still more to come, which suggested the probability of another ghostly visitation. Carol did not want to see Lady Augusta again. She wanted to try to forget what had happened on the previous night. She did not think she would ever be able to forget Nicholas, but putting the unexplainable events firmly into the past and shutting the door on them seemed to her to be the only way to maintain her sanity. Still, she had to admit that the ghost of Lady Augusta held a certain fascination.

"She is more interesting dead than she ever was alive. When she was living, she was just a miserly, argumentative pain in the neck." Carol put the bowl of narcissus on the table and stood back to judge the effect. "It doesn't look right there. Perhaps on the bedside table." She picked up the red glass bowl and headed toward the bed.

"Miss Simmons?"

"Ye gods, Nell, don't creep up on me like that!" Carol exclaimed. "I nearly dropped this."

She did not mention her relief that Nell was not a ghost.

"Oh, those'll be pretty when they open." Nell regarded the narcissus with approval. "Yes, they belong there, right next to your bed, so you can see them first thing every morning. Hettie told me you gave her the roses. She says she's never had a nicer Christmas present."

"It wasn't a present, just something for all of you to enjoy."

"Don't tell Hettie that or you'll break her heart. She thinks you are wonderful." Nell set down the tray she was carrying. "Mrs. Marks said you'll be out Christmas Eve and Christmas Day, so we aren't to make meals for you then."

"That's right." Again Carol cursed herself for making an impulsive excuse that was going to be extremely inconvenient. She wasn't certain any restaurants would be open on the holiday, and even if she could find one, it would mean buying a meal that she could have gotten free at Marlowe House.

"Be sure you don't skip dinner tonight the way you did last night," Nell admonished, lifting the metal dome off the tray to reveal a plate heaped with seafood curry, rice, and peas. A small bowl of chutney sat beside the dinner plate. Dessert was a fresh pear and gingerbread.

"It smells wonderful," Carol said, "and I am hungry. I am just going to get a glass of water to put on the narcissus, and then I promise to eat every bite."

But when she returned from the bathroom all thought of food was swept from Carol's mind the instant she stepped through the bed-chamber door. She stopped short, clenching the filled water glass in both hands so she wouldn't spill it. The visitor who was bending over the bowl of flowers straightened and turned around when Carol kicked the door shut. With only the lamp beside the wing chair lit, most of the bedroom was in shadow. Even though she could not see the figure clearly, Carol knew at once who it was.

"Good evening," said Lady Augusta. "I have been waiting for you."

Chapter Eight

"What do you want with me now?" Carol demanded. "Haven't you done enough harm already?"

"It is my opinion that I have done only good to you," Lady Augusta responded, "and will do still more good on this night."

"I refuse to become involved in another time-travel excursion," Carol stated. "I haven't recovered from the last one yet."

"I do understand how difficult it is to change your heart," Lady Augusta said in a surprisingly sympathetic tone. "While I lived I was never able to do so, though I had many opportunities to alter my ways. You may take comfort in the knowledge that during your visit to the past you learned a valuable lesson or two, and you prevented much grief for those whom you loved in that time."

"A famous woman once said that no good deed will go unpunished." Carol could not keep the bitterness out of her voice. "I am paying now for my generosity to Lady Caroline."

"Yes, you were generous," said Lady Augusta. "You will receive full credit for your actions. However, I note that you have not yet given up your essential selfishness. You have much more to learn in the two nights still to come. We shall begin at once." She moved from the bedside toward the middle of the room, passing into the light of the single lamp, and now Carol could see her clearly for the first time.

"Are you headed for a costume party?" Carol asked, surveying her unwelcome guest's appearance. "Who are you supposed to be, anyway?"

"Do you like my gown? Personally, I am quite pleased with the overall effect." Lady Augusta was wearing a robe of deep red velvet. Long strands of ivy were wrapped about the robe in a spiral pattern. These garlands were caught here and there with sprigs of red-berried holly or with small bunches of green and white mistletoe. A high collar of rubies and diamonds encircled Lady Augusta's neck, and ruby and diamond earrings fell in glittering showers almost to her shoulders. She wore wide matching bracelets on each wrist. Her shining black hair, which on this occasion displayed not a single streak of white, was piled high and decorated with a diamond snowflake ornament.

"You look like one of the Christmas trees I saw in a florist's window this afternoon," Carol said.

176

"That is altogether appropriate, since on this night you will witness Christmas in the present." Lady Augusta moved toward Carol, who backed away until she was pushed up against the door. "Come now, Carol, surely you are no longer afraid of me."

"Why don't you leave me alone?" said Carol rudely.

"Dear me." Lady Augusta sounded surprised and a bit hurt. "I hoped the lessons you learned last night would stay with you longer. I regret to see how quickly you have reverted to your earlier self."

"How could you imagine that I would be glad to see you again after you took me away from the one man I have ever really loved?" Carol cried.

"I did not remove you. You left voluntarily. You still do not understand. But then, how could you? Water your flowers, my dear, and we will go." Moving aside to let Carol pass, Lady Augusta lifted the dome on the dinner tray. "I see Mrs. Marks has been stirring up that dreadful curry recipe of hers, now that she doesn't have to feed me anymore. I never could abide the stuff." Lady Augusta sniffed, turning up her nose in distaste.

"I happen to like curry," Carol retorted, pouring the contents of the water glass over the narcissus bulbs. "But I suppose I won't have an opportunity to eat it, will I? If you insist on showing up every night at dinnertime and taking me away, I will probably starve to death before you are finished with me."

"There is little chance of that." Lady Augusta

smiled at her and Carol began to tremble.

"What are you going to do this time?" Carol asked.

"Come." Lady Augusta held out her hand. When Carol did not move, the smile turned into a scowl. "Do not be childish. We have work to do and no time to waste. If you do not take my hand, Carol, I will be forced to embrace you once more."

"Oh, all right." Reluctantly, Carol reached toward the ghost and felt cold fingers clasp hers.

"That wasn't so bad, was it?" Lady Augusta was smiling again.

"Where are we going?" Carol asked.

"We have two visits to make tonight. The first is to the servants' hall."

"Why?" Carol tried to pull her hand away, but Lady Augusta held fast to her.

"You have a habit of asking the wrong questions," Lady Augusta told her. "Just come with me and I will explain as we go along."

In an instant they were standing in the warm, bright kitchen of Marlowe House.

"How did you do that?" Carol demanded. "We didn't come down the stairs. We didn't even walk out of my bedroom door."

"Delightful, isn't it? I do so enjoy the transportation part of my assignment."

Carol scarcely heard her companion. She was staring at Nell, Hettie, and Mrs. Marks, who were all bustling about the kitchen.

"Nell, what are you doing?" asked Carol, putting out a hand to catch the maid's attention. Nell walked right by her as if Carol weren't there.

"She cannot see or hear you," said Lady Augusta.

"Why not? What kind of trick is this?" Carol cried.

"You persist in thinking that I am playing mere tricks on you," responded Lady Augusta with exaggerated patience, "when in fact, what is occurring is of an importance far beyond your comprehension. No person whom we will encounter on this night will be aware of your presence. Until your heart is finally and permanently changed, you cannot be allowed to alter the present-day course of events. What you see before you is this year's Christmas Day at Marlowe House. Your duty is to observe, to think upon what you see, and to consider ways in which you might improve the lives of others."

Carol said nothing to this. She watched as the female servants prepared and set out a holiday meal under the direction of Mrs. Marks. A small roasted turkey with chestnut stuffing, a sauceboat of gravy, bowls of whipped potatoes, cranberry sauce, and several dishes of vegetables were all carried into the servants' dining room, where the table was laid with a spotless white cloth and gilt-edged plates.

"They are using my mother's best china," Lady Augusta noted. "Well, why not? No one will know unless they break a plate, and Mrs. Marks will see to it that all is replaced where it should be when they have finished."

"Where is Crampton?" Carol asked.

"In the wine cellar," came Lady Augusta's reply just as the butler appeared with two dusty bottles.

"They are stealing your wine for their dinner?" Carol exclaimed.

"By household tradition, the servants are allowed a bottle or two for their own use on Christmas," said Lady Augusta, "and I have always left it up to Crampton to choose the wine. It appears that he is still honest. While those particular bottles are adequate for this feast, he has not brought up the best my cellar has to offer. He must know the servants would not appreciate it, while my nephew will."

Carol wasn't really paying attention to what Lady Augusta was saying. She was much more interested in what the servants were doing. As the women took off their aprons, she realized that they were all three dressed in what must be their best clothes. Crampton, who was now occupied in opening one of the wine bottles, was also properly attired in jacket and necktie.

"This is the Christmas meal to which you were invited," Lady Augusta explained, "and which you refused to attend."

"I would eat it now if I could," said Carol. Her invisibility did not prevent her from smelling the delicious aromas coming from the turkey or the vegetables and the freshly baked rolls. From past experience she knew what a good cook Mrs. Marks was, and her mouth was watering. "I'm hungry. I never did eat lunch today and now, thanks to you, I have missed my second dinner in a row."

"You would be hungrier still if you waited for this meal," Lady Augusta noted, "since it will not take place until Christmas Day. The scenes you will see tonight are of the present holiday season, unmodified by any act of yours. Listen, now."

"Ain't the flowers pretty?" asked Hettie, taking her place at the festive table. "They didn't wilt after all. It were so nice of Miss Simmons to think of us."

"It was, indeed," said Crampton, speaking right over Mrs. Marks's derisive snort.

"Miss Simmons has a real kind heart," Nell remarked. She was sitting across from Hettie, with Crampton at the head of the table and Mrs. Marks at the foot.

"Miss Simmons is a snob," said Mrs. Marks.

"Oh, no, Mrs. Marks," cried Hettie, apparently greatly upset by this point of view. "She ain't no snob. She always speaks to me."

"Be quiet, Hettie," commanded Mrs. Marks. "What could an ignorant girl like you possibly know about Miss Simmons?"

"I knows that I likes her," Hettie responded.

"Let us have no dissension on this special evening," said Crampton. "Enjoy your meal, Hettie, and be grateful for it."

As soon as Crampton finished carving the turkey, the vegetables, stuffing, gravy, and rolls were passed, and everyone at the table fell silent while the dinner was eaten.

"Mrs. Marks," said Crampton after a while, leaning back in his chair and glancing around at the empty plates, "allow me to congratulate you upon a superlative meal."

"There's still dessert to come," said Mrs. Marks, rising.

"And brandy to go with it." Crampton rose, too, disappearing into the pantry, while Mrs. Marks headed for the kitchen and Hettie and

Nell began to clear the table.

"He's got my best brandy!" cried Lady Augusta as Crampton returned bearing a silver tray with a bottle and brandy glasses on it.

"What difference can that make to you when you didn't care about the wine?" asked Carol, who had been observing the meal with a watering mouth. "Can't I just have a tiny piece of turkey? I'm starving."

"You don't have time to eat," responded Lady Augusta. "You are supposed to be learning valuable lessons from what you see before you. Have you noticed Hettie?"

"What about her?" Carol tore her eyes from contemplation of the turkey carcass and the remains of the whipped potatoes to glance toward the scullery maid. "Hettie looks fine to me. She's the same as she always looks."

"Exactly," said Lady Augusta. "The same as always. Do you know why Hettie does not change?"

"I suppose you intend to tell me," said Carol, her thoughts still on food.

"Hettie will never be more than a scullery maid because she cannot read or write."

"That's nonsense. Everyone in England has to go to school."

"There will always be children who do not learn what they should," said Lady Augusta. "Hettie was not slow enough to come to the notice of the school authorities, who are always overworked and understaffed, and who do not have the time to look for problems that are not obvious. Hettie can write her name and do simple arithmetic, but she has never mastered the art of reading fluently, and certainly she could not compose a letter or fill out a complicated employment form. She got through school by pretending she can read and by memorizing a good portion of her schoolwork, but once her schooling was over, she was qualified for little but a life as a scullery maid."

"What a shame," Carol said. "Hettie is a nice girl, and I don't think she's stupid."

"Not stupid at all," agreed Lady Augusta. "Were she fully literate, Hettie might go far in life. But she will never have the chance to discover just how far unless—"

"Unless what?" Carol asked.

"Hettie needs a teacher," said Lady Augusta. "Someone she respects might set her on the right path."

"If you're thinking that I ought to teach her to read," Carol said, "forget it. I wouldn't know how to begin."

"You could begin by offering encouragement. Or by discovering where there are schools that teach adults to read. You could volunteer your services to such a school."

"Volunteer? Look, maybe you aren't aware of my financial situation. I need to find a paying job for myself, never mind Hettie."

"What kind of job do you think Hettie will be able to find?" asked Lady Augusta.

"Hettie is not my responsibility." But even as she said the words Carol experienced a pang of guilt.

"Observe," said Lady Augusta, waving a hand toward the scene in the kitchen.

Mrs. Marks had just removed a large steamed pudding from its basin and was placing it on a silver platter that could only have come from

Lady Augusta's supply of family plate. The cook stuck a sprig of holly into the top of the pudding, then doused the whole dessert with brandy and set it alight.

"I'm ready," Mrs. Marks announced.

With Mrs. Marks leading the way with the flaming pudding, Nell following with a bowl of hard sauce, and Hettie bringing up the rear carrying a plate of decorated sugar cookies, the three women made a procession into the dining room, where Crampton awaited them.

"Well," said Crampton, beaming his approval, "this might be a Christmas scene right out of a Dickens novel. Mrs. Marks, you have provided a suitable finale for our years of employment here at Marlowe House."

As if these words were a signal, Hettie burst into tears. Nell, after casting a worried glance in Mrs. Marks's direction, all but tossed the bowl of hard sauce onto the table and took the cookie plate out of Hettie's hands before she could drop the cookies onto the floor.

"Hettie," said Crampton, "you ought not to cry on such a joyous occasion."

"It ain't joyous," Hettie wailed. "It's the last holiday we'll all be together. Next year Nell and me'll be in the poorhouse."

"There is no poorhouse anymore," said Mrs. Marks in her sternest voice. "Good heavens, girl, haven't you got any sense at all?"

"I'll be out on the streets," Hettie cried. "I'll be homeless. I'll never find another job. I ain't fit for nothin' but kitchen work. You told me so yourself, Mrs. Marks, and it's true. *It's true!*"

"Hush now, Hettie." Nell put her arms around the weeping girl. "I'll take care of you. I said

184

I would. We'll find some kind of work to do. We'll start looking on Tuesday, soon as Boxing Day's over."

"Why is Hettie so upset?" Carol asked Lady Augusta.

"For the same reason you were upset yesterday," Lady Augusta responded, "and for the reasons I explained to you earlier, Carol. Hettie knows how slim her chances of finding employment are. How is a semiliterate young woman to find work in today's harsh world? Nor will she have a home after Marlowe House is closed up and sold when my estate is settled."

"There are social services available for people like her," Carol said.

"Perhaps. I am inclined to think that what Hettie needs is a caring mentor rather than an overburdened social worker."

"Nell said she would help."

"Nell's situation is not much more hopeful than Hettie's." Lady Augusta paused for a moment, gazing at the scene of the two young servants in a tear-drenched embrace while Crampton and Mrs. Marks looked on as if uncertain what they ought to do or say.

"I know Crampton and Mrs. Marks have worked for your family since the end of World War II, so they at least must be pretty well fixed," Carol said. She was trying unsuccessfully to shake a growing sensation of uneasiness and guilt generated by the scene she was witnessing. She told herself that none of the misfortune she saw before her was her fault, nor could she be expected to do anything about it.

"I regret to say that neither my father nor I ever paid our servants adequately," Lady Augusta replied to Carol's comment. "Both Crampton and Mrs. Marks remained with me out of a combination of loyalty and inertia, and perhaps also because they did not wish to be separated from each other. Now, they are left with whatever they have been able to save out of their wages and the small bequests I made to them in my will."

"But they are all four decent, hardworking people," Carol cried. "Can you foresee their futures? What will happen to them?"

"Crampton and Mrs. Marks will pool their resources and retire together," Lady Augusta replied. "Nell and Hettie will try to find work, but there are almost no more establishments like mine left these days, where a girl could begin as a scullery maid and slowly work her way up to cook or housekeeper or lady's maid. Hettie and Nell will have to move into another line of work."

"But if Hettie can't read well," Carol protested, "then she's right. She won't find a good job."

"There is always one kind of work available to a desperate young woman. An ancient profession. Neither Hettie nor Nell is homely. With some paint on their faces and some bright, tight-fitting clothes—"

"No!" Carol cried. "Don't even suggest such a thing, not with all the terrible diseases people can be infected with these days. Prostitution would be an almost certain death sentence for them. Even if they should survive, what they would have to do each day and night would still break their hearts and their spirits. They don't deserve that."

"If no one will help them, they will have little choice." Lady Augusta shrugged her velvet-clad shoulders. The movement sent a spray of pure, icy glitter dancing from her diamond earrings across the faces and the worn clothing of the four people in the servants' dining room. Only Carol saw that supernatural light or heard Lady Augusta's next, seemingly careless words. "With workers in the social system too busy to spare more than a thought for two badly educated, jobless girls, what can you expect?"

"You are trying to make me feel personally guilty about something that isn't my fault," Carol said, angrily fighting against her own emotions. Deliberately, she turned her back on the scene in the servants' dining room, as though not seeing it could block it out of her mind. "If Hettie's situation—and Nell's—is anyone's fault, then it is yours, Lady Augusta. You are the one who took advantage of them, who didn't pay them properly, or make any provision for their futures so they would have a little money to fall back on when you died."

"Very true," said Lady Augusta, her nod of agreement sending another shower of light into the room. "I will never cease to regret my miserly actions. I know now, as I did not know during life, that we are all responsible for the helpless among us. Unfortunately, I am no longer in a position to assist Hettie and Nell. You, however, might do something, if you care enough to make an effort in their behalf."

"How do you expect me to do anything for them when I'm no better off than they are?"

Carol shouted at her. "Take me out of here. I've seen enough."

"Not quite," said Lady Augusta. "There is more. Turn around, Carol. Watch and listen."

While Lady Augusta and Carol argued unseen and unheard, Nell had succeeded in calming Hettie and had coaxed her to sit down at the table again. Crampton stood in his place at the head of the table, pouring an amber liquid into four glasses from the bottle that Lady Augusta claimed held her best brandy. These glasses Crampton passed around to the women.

"I would like to offer a toast or two," Crampton said, lifting his glass. "First, to the blessed holiday."

"To the holiday," echoed Mrs. Marks, drinking with him. The two younger women sipped at the brandy as if they didn't much care for it.

"And now," said Crampton, "I ask you to drink to the memory of our late employer. To Lady Augusta."

"To Lady Augusta." Mrs. Marks swallowed another mouthful of brandy and Crampton refilled her glass and his own.

"Lady Augusta," cried Nell.

"Lady Augusta." Hettie tipped back her glass and drank.

"Nicely done," said Lady Augusta, smiling her approval of the toast.

"Mindful of the improbability that we will all be together for much longer," Crampton went on, "I would now like to offer a toast to the entire household staff. We have worked well together, I think, and I can honestly say that I will miss those of our little group who plan to move on to other positions."

"Very well put, Mr. Crampton," said Mrs. Marks. "A sentiment suitable to the holiday. A toast to the four of us." Thus bidden, they all drank.

"I want to make a toast, too." Nell was on her feet, glass in hand. "We can't forget Miss Simmons. To her health!"

"To Miss Simmons," said Hettie, bravely trying not to start crying again.

"Custom dictates that the butler should propose the toasts," Mrs. Marks declared, sending a disapproving glare toward each of the young women.

"In the name of the holiday," remarked Crampton, reaching for the brandy bottle again, "I will drink to Miss Simmons's good health. This is not a time for pettiness, Mrs. Marks. You and I both know that the grand old days of this house are long gone. Let us participate in our last Christmas here with generosity in our hearts." With that, he refilled glasses all around, and everyone drank to Carol's health.

"It is time to go," Lady Augusta said to Carol. "We have another visit to make tonight, and the hour grows late."

"What will happen to them?" Carol whispered, her eyes and her thoughts still lingering on Nell and Hettie. "What could I possibly do to help them when I need help myself?"

"Unless the shadows I foresee are modified by kind and loving hearts," Lady Augusta told her, "the future prospects for all four of my former servants are unpleasant. However, the time for action is not yet. First, there is more for us to see."

Before Carol could offer any excuse to stay where she was, the scene around her changed. With Lady Augusta by her side, she was propelled out of Marlowe House and into the streets of London by the same remarkable process that earlier had moved her in the blink of an eye from her bedroom to the kitchen. Though it had been nighttime while she was observing the servants' Christmas dinner, Carol saw that it was now bright daylight.

"It is the afternoon of this year's Christmas Eve," Lady Augusta explained, as if she could read Carol's mind. "As in the servants' quarters at Marlowe House, so here, no one we pass will be able to see or hear us. You cannot be permitted to change the present until you yourself are changed."

"What if I don't want to change?" asked Carol with grim resistance.

"That is but the last vestige of your old self speaking," said Lady Augusta. "You are too intelligent not to change once you know all you are meant to know."

"I wish you would stop talking in riddles," Carol muttered. "I already know more than I want to know, and everything I've learned has only made me more unhappy than I was before you came back from the dead."

"I have not come back," remarked her companion. "The Lady Augusta whom you once knew is dead for all eternity."

"So is Nicholas." The words slipped out before Carol could stop herself.

"Nicholas," Lady Augusta repeated, her eyebrows raised. "Carol, you disappoint me. Surely your experience with me has taught you that the spirit never dies."

"You just said yourself that you are dead. So is Nicholas dead." Carol shook her head in disgust at what appeared to her to be a senseless conversation. "Lady Augusta, you are speaking in riddles again."

"No, I am telling you a simple truth, which you are still too blind, and too impatient, to comprehend. Ah, here we are."

They had reached an old church located not far from Marlowe House.

"I know this place," Carol said. "It's Saint Fiacre's Church. The rector read your funeral service."

"The Reverend Mr. Lucius Kincaid," said Lady Augusta. "He is a fine man."

"Really? I didn't notice." Carol grimaced, remembering the rector and his fashionably dressed wife. "He accosted me at your funeral and tried to get a donation out of me."

"And of course you refused." Lady Augusta sounded amused. "So would I have refused, once upon a time. I know better now."

As she had previously observed, while she was with Lady Augusta, Carol was able to pass through walls or move along streets in the same way as her companion and with no effort on her own part. Thus they moved through Saint Fiacre's Church, which was solidly built of ancient stones, and out the back to a tiny garden dedicated to the patron saint. In one corner of the garden stood a statue of Saint Fiacre, leaning on his shovel while he contemplated the winter-bare flower beds at his feet.

"Poor old St. Fiacre." Carol paused to look

more closely at the statue. "After so many centuries, who can be sure what crisis in your life sent you off into the wilderness to live as a hermit? I have done something similar myself, so I had no right to criticize you the other day. I am sorry for what I said about you."

"I am glad to hear you speak kindly of him," said Lady Augusta. Then she added more sharply, "However, your regrets cannot help St. Fiacre now. You would be wiser to save your concern for the living."

An instant later Carol and Lady Augusta passed through the stone garden wall and into a brightly lit, though shabby and unappealing, hall. This appeared to be a building of great age, for the plaster of the high ceiling was smoke-blackened and the walls were cracked and in need of a fresh coat of paint.

A series of metal tables was set up in the middle of this hall. Paper cloths decorated with Christmas motifs covered the tables and cheap metal folding chairs were drawn up to them. A few red and green bells were hung in the doorways, the ceiling being too high for such decorations. An artificial tree stood to one side, its ornaments of macaroni sprinkled with multicolored sparkles, painted clay angels with lopsided wings, and bright chains made of construction paper loops all attesting to the loving industry of Sunday school students.

"Where are we?" Carol asked. "I smell turkey again."

"This is the enterprise for which the Reverend Mr. Kincaid solicited your donation," Lady Augusta responded. "While you refused him, others did respond. Six turkeys were given just yesterday. At the Christmas season the public responds most generously, though these good people need help all year long."

"Help for what? Is that a buffet table set up at the back of the hall? Is this a party? If so, where are the guests?"

"They will be invited to enter in a few minutes," said Lady Augusta. "Welcome to Saint Fiacre's Bountiful Board, Carol."

"It's a soup kitchen," Carol said, finally understanding. "The people who run this place are feeding the poor."

She now became aware of a great bustle of activity in a room off the back of the hall. By the smells coming from it, Carol deduced that this was the kitchen. Out of this kitchen now filed a little band of people, some of whom Carol recognized. The similarity to the servants' procession and feast at Marlowe House was unmistakable, for the same spirit of Christmas cheerfulness in the face of harsh economic reality permeated both events.

As Carol and Lady Augusta watched, the Reverend Mr. Kincaid and his wife appeared, each carrying a cheap aluminum tray heaped with slices of roast turkey. Two elderly ladies hurried into the hall with pans of stuffing. More volunteers brought in the rest of the meal. Even three small Kincaids—distinguishable by their close resemblance to their blond, blue-eyed mother—had been pressed into service, each child bringing some portion of the feast to the buffet table.

Three or four men who were present tended to the lighting of alcohol burners under the trays of food, which were intended to keep the food hot. The men then took up positions in front of the table as if they were standing guard to prevent the expected rush of hungry folk from upsetting the table and setting the hall on fire. The elderly women stationed themselves behind the platters and bowls of food, serving spoons in hand.

"Now," said the Reverend Mr. Kincaid to his helpers, "I do believe we are ready to open the doors."

"Thank heaven it is warm enough for people to wait outside without freezing," remarked Mrs. Kincaid. "There is always so much confusion until everyone has a plate."

Mrs. Kincaid was for this occasion clad in a bright red ankle-length skirt and an equally bright green turtleneck sweater. Each of the little Kincaids wore a red or a green garment, and all were freshly scrubbed and neatly brushed. The Reverend Mr. Kincaid regarded his family with justifiable pleasure.

"How grateful I am to have all of you by my side," he said to his wife, who responded by laughing and kissing his cheek. The elderly ladies who were waiting to dish up the meal smiled and nodded their approval at this sign of domestic bliss.

"Mrs. Kincaid sure doesn't worry about spending money for clothing," Carol noted to Lady Augusta in a sour tone. "I'll bet she could make a sizeable donation to this soup kitchen if she weren't so concerned about fashion."

"You know nothing at all about the Kincaids' situation, Carol." Lady Augusta sounded remarkably sad, considering the joyful atmosphere in the hall. "Clergymen do not earn large salaries, especially those who accept assignments to parishes once fashionable but now fallen upon hard times. In Lucius Kincaid's case, he turns more than a tithe back to the parish so that he can carry out his charitable work.

"Abigail Kincaid buys almost all of her clothing, and her children's clothing, from rummage sales. She cleans and patches and irons every piece of clothing herself. What she cannot buy in that way, she sews. If she and her children appear to be dressed in the latest style, perhaps it is because she has inherited her fashion sense from ancestors who were once almost as poor as she is today. It may also be that she imagines a good appearance on her part will cheer her hardworking husband and thus bolster his self-esteem and happiness. You might be interested in knowing more about Mrs. Kincaid."

"She does sound like an admirable woman," Carol admitted. "From what you have told me, it seems I judged her too hastily."

"And misjudged her husband, too." Lady Augusta broke off, watching the activity in the hall. The front doors of the building were now thrown open and a line of people surged forward toward the buffet table. Carol stared in amazement as a steady stream of men, women, and children, black, white, and East Indian, were served plates of food and shown to places at the tables in the middle of the hall. There was no pushing or shoving. Everyone was polite, but the sheer mass of hungry people did create the confusion Mrs. Kincaid had mentioned.

"I had no idea there were so many poor people in this area of London," Carol remarked. "A lot of them are old, and some are just teenagers or little children."

"The poor we have always with us," noted Lady Augusta.

"That's hardly an original thought," Carol said, adding, "Tell me more about Mrs. Kincaid. From what I've seen while we have been standing here, it looks to me as though she is the one who organizes these meals."

"You are correct," said Lady Augusta. "Her husband is the spiritual force behind their efforts to feed the poor, but it is Abigail Penelope Kincaid's practical mind that arranges and directs these affairs so well that they never degenerate into chaos."

"Penelope?" Carol stared at Mrs. Kincaid, noticing familiar features she had missed in her first scrutiny of the woman.

"I wondered how long it would take you to see the family resemblance," said Lady Augusta. "Like you, Mrs. Kincaid is a descendant of Lady Penelope Hyde, and thus is your distant cousin. Very distant, I must admit. But then, all the world is related, if you care to trace ancestors back far enough."

"I never would have guessed if you hadn't told me. I wasn't really seeing her that first time we met. I was too involved with my own feelings to pay attention to her or to hear what she was saying to me." Carol bit her lip, watching Abigail Kincaid take the plate of an old woman at the buffet table and offer the woman her arm to lean upon as, with a smile and a cheerful word, she helped the woman to find a seat at one of the dining tables.

"A generous heart would seem to be a family

trait," Lady Augusta noted.

"Not on my side of the family," Carol said. "I was deliberately rude to her, and to her husband."

"You can rectify your previous behavior," Lady Augusta said. "An apology coupled with an offer of help will surely be accepted."

"I could donate some time, at least until I find another job here in London, or decide whether I am going to return to New York or not. Why don't you make me visible right now, so I can talk to her?"

"As I have explained to you, Carol, you may not take any action that would change the present until all of your lessons are learned."

Carol did not have a chance to make any objection, for the scene around her changed again and she discovered that she and Lady Augusta were back inside Saint Fiacre's Church. Now the candles were all lit, dozens of them in old brass candlesticks that were a legacy from the days when the church could boast of wealthy patrons who could afford to make such gifts in memory of dead relatives, or to commemorate a recovery from serious illness, or in thanksgiving for the birth of a long-awaited child.

By this golden candlelight Carol could see that the church held a finely carved walnut reredos screen behind the altar, and there was a matching pulpit. Both of these furnishings gleamed from a recent polishing by the ladies of the altar guild, and the rest of the church was swept and neat. The linen on both altar and credence table was spotless and crisply ironed. But the poverty of the parish was evident in the few evergreen branches that decorated the altar in place of flowers, and in two places along the nave there were boards covering the holes where stained-glass windows once had been set. Carol could feel in the damp coldness the absence of an adequate heating system.

"This must have been a lovely little church once," she said.

"And could be again," added Lady Augusta. "All it needs is some decent restoration work."

"Restoration takes money," Carol replied. "These people don't have any to spare, and if they did have extra cash they would probably use it to feed more of the hungry."

Lady Augusta did not speak again, for the midnight service was about to begin. Mrs. Kincaid arrived with her sleepy children in tow and took her place in the second pew. The smallest of the children, who looked as if he would fall asleep as soon as he dared, curled up on the wooden seat next to his mother. She put a loving arm around his shoulders while his brother and sister found their places in the hymn book.

There were only six people in the choir, and three of them were drawn from among the poor folk who had eaten their holiday dinner in the hall a few hours earlier. Their choir robes were darned and patched here and there, but were freshly washed and ironed in honor of the occasion. After what Lady Augusta had told her about Abigail Kincaid's industriousness, Carol suspected that this was her distant cousin's doing.

All the members of St. Fiacre's little choir sang out at the top of their voices as they marched into the church behind the youthful crucifer who carried an antique and ornate brass cross, and every one of them sang on key without the help of an organ. The three dozen or so souls who made up the congregation added their own volume to the old hymns until the sweet, joyful sounds rose to the very roof.

Lucius Kincaid's sermon was brief. There was little, he told his listeners, that needed to be said beyond the beautiful prayerbook service for that most blessed of nights. He read the Gospel in a deep and resonant voice, and said the prayers, and then he sent his little congregation home with his blessing. Afterward, Carol stood shivering in the dark and empty church.

"Lady Augusta?" Her companion was gone. Carol was alone.

Chapter Nine

"Lady Augusta, where are you?" Carol cried. "This is no time to play games. You can't expect me to find my way back to Marlowe House by myself in the middle of the night." She turned around twice, searching for Lady Augusta, only to discover that she was still alone in an empty church.

Then, suddenly, without any sense of having crossed the city blocks that lay between house and church, she found herself back in her own room. The fire Nell had built up earlier in the evening had burned down into cold ashes, and Carol's waiting dinner was also cold. Shivering violently now, Carol stripped off her clothes and found her warm flannel nightgown. Pulling it on, she got into bed, but she could not stop shaking.

"It's not from fear," she said to herself,

"because I am actually beginning to get used to being transported all over creation by a ghost. No, Lady Augusta left me to freeze in that unheated old church. Does she want me to die? What good would my death do for her in her quest to earn the place she wants in the afterlife? I thought the idea was to change me, not to kill me.

"Maybe," Carol decided after a few more minutes of thought, "just possibly, Lady Augusta was called away. Perhaps she had to make a report on her progress with me. I hope the people upstairs tell her to give up her mission and leave me alone." On that fantastic thought, Carol slipped into a deep sleep from which she did not awaken until Nell arrived with her breakfast tray.

The following afternoon found Carol back at Saint Fiacre's Church. This time she came to it on her own two feet, but once there she discovered that she could not go inside. The doors were locked, perhaps as a precaution against the group of a half-dozen or so unsavory-looking men who were loitering nearby.

"They look as if they'd steal the very candlesticks off the altar," Carol said to herself. "I'd better keep moving or one of them may hit me over the head and snatch my purse."

Keeping an eye upon the men until she was out of their sight, she walked around the corner of the church to the street behind it. There she found the entrance of the hall where she and Lady Augusta had observed the Christmas Eve dinner being served. This door was open and there were signs of activity, with people carrying bags of groceries into the building. Carol thought she recognized a few of the workers from the previous night. Since a glance at the morning paper before leaving Marlowe House had assured her that this was the day before Christmas Eve Day, Carol decided the people going into the hall must be starting the early preparations for the meal.

She wanted to join them, but again something stopped her from entering the building. It was not a physical barrier this time. She simply could not bring herself to walk inside the hall and introduce herself, to apologize to the Reverend Mr. Kincaid and his wife if they were there, and then to offer her help.

"There really isn't anything I can do for them," she said. "I would only get in the way. And I would be embarrassed after I was so nasty to them the last time we talked. Besides, I'm not sure I could meet Penelope's descendant without saying something that would make her think I am stark, staring mad."

Carol knew perfectly well that these were only excuses, yet she turned away from the hall and from Saint Fiacre's Church. Once more she walked through the busy streets of London, scarcely noticing the holiday decorations or the people who hurried past her on their Christmas errands. Her thoughts were all turned inward, and they were not comfortable. To her hopeless longing for Nicholas now was added a fearful concern for the welfare of Hettie and Nell, and guilt over the way in which she had treated the Kincaids on the day of Lady Augusta's funeral.

"One reason why I'm feeling depressed," she decided as the afternoon wore on toward tea time, "is because I haven't been eating properly. I need a decent meal, but Lady Augusta has prevented me from eating my dinner for two nights now, and she will probably do the same thing tonight. Oh, Lord, I wonder what horrors she has in store for me this time?"

Compared to her other recent trials, food seemed a minor problem, and one she could easily resolve. Before returning to Marlowe House, Carol stopped in a pub to eat a large roast beef sandwich and drink a pot of strong tea. Thus fortified against Lady Augusta's unknown plans for the evening to come, she continued along the darkening streets until she reached the far side of the square where Marlowe House stood. The day had been cloudy, and now fog was drifting between the buildings and into the square. The lights of the Christmas tree in the middle of the tiny park shone with a peculiar haziness.

Usually, there were at least a few people walking in the square and several cars parked in front of the houses. On this evening Carol saw neither cars nor people, and it was remarkably quiet. The noises of city traffic beyond the square were apparently muffled by the ever-thickening fog.

As she started along the path that cut across the square, her footsteps on the gravel sounded loud in comparison to the growing silence around her. When she reached the decorated fir tree she stopped, thinking she heard someone just behind her. She spun around, but no one was there. The silence was deeper now, and somehow more menacing. Carol thought the fog was thicker, too. In fact, the fog was making it difficult for her to breathe, and she could hear the pounding of her own heart.

In the gloom she could just make out the shape of Marlowe House directly ahead of her. There were no welcoming lights in the windows or at the front door, nor even a hint of the electric bulb she knew ought to be glowing at the servants' entrance, but Carol was familiar with the way into the house.

"I will probably trip getting down those steep side steps," she muttered, moving forward again. "I'll have a few words with Crampton as soon as I get in. Just because Lady Augusta is gone, there is no excuse for him not to turn on the lights. The house looks deserted, and that's bad security.

"Oh, good heavens." She stopped on a sudden thought and stood squinting through the mist. "What if they've all gone off somewhere to a movie or shopping? Am I going to have to go into that big old place all by myself? Perhaps I ought to go through the front door. The light switch in the main hall will be easier for me to find than the one downstairs. But why did they turn off every light in the house?"

The words were barely out of her mouth when the lights on the Christmas tree behind her went out. The fog was now remarkably cold and wet. Carol could feel beads of moisture on her face.

"A fuse must have blown," she decided. "I refuse to be frightened. There is nothing unusual about a fuse failing. I'll report it to Crampton and he will know who to call about repairing it. At least the street lamps are still on, not that they're doing much good in this pea soup fog."

The street lamps went dark.

Carol caught her breath, telling herself to stay calm.

"It must be a general blackout," she said aloud. She took a cautious step in the direction of Marlowe House. "If he is at home, Crampton will light the candles right away. I'll just work my way down the steps as carefully as I can and then bang on the servants' door and someone will hear me and let me in."

The thought of Nell's pleasant face, or even Mrs. Marks's sour one, was encouraging. The night was unbelievably dark, and the fog made it easy to imagine there was someone, or something, waiting just a few steps away to clutch at unwary pedestrians. Most unnerving of all was the total absence of sound. Carol could still hear nothing except her own breathing.

"You'd think somebody would be outside walking around, trying to figure out what's wrong," she muttered. "Why isn't there a policeman? For that matter, why aren't there any burglars taking advantage of the situation? At this point, I think I might welcome a nice, friendly burglar, as long as he was carrying a flashlight."

Stepping carefully, she kept moving. She thought she was still heading toward Marlowe House, but she could not be absolutely sure. She was vaguely aware of a large, solid shape ahead of her, and this she assumed was her destination. Or perhaps it was one of the other houses.

"It doesn't matter if I find the wrong house. I know them all, and once I reach one, I should be able to get home without any trouble."

For all her attempts to stay calm, the silence and the darkness were beginning to wear away her courage. Never had Carol experienced such a terrible and frightening blackness, or so profound a silence. She did not understand what was happening. She knew there were people living in the other houses around the square, so there should have been candlelight by now, or the glow of flashlights. There ought to be voices questioning the loss of electricity. Fighting the urge to hurry, to try to flee toward a familiar place where she would be safe, she felt with one toe, searching the ground in front of her, and then with the other toe.

She was certain the temperature had dropped by at least ten degrees. Her hands were freezing and the drops of mist on her face seemed turned to ice.

"I thought I was cold last night," she said, "but it was nothing compared to this. I hope the gas is still on so I can get a pot of tea." She knew she was talking to herself out loud so she wouldn't start screaming or crying. If she admitted to herself how frightened she was, she would not be able to control her descent into complete panic.

By the feel of the ground beneath her feet she could tell when she came to the end of the gravel walk and reached the paved street. She kept moving, walking cautiously, knowing that now she did not have very far to go. The comforting bulk looming in front of her was closer, proof that soon she would be warm and safe inside Marlowe House.

Something moved. A shape detached itself from the darkness and came toward her. Carol could make out a faint difference between the shape and the black night.

"Who is it?" she called. Immediately she was ashamed of the quavering of her voice. She tried again. "Are you a policeman? Or someone who lives in one of these houses? Do you happen to have a flashlight?"

"If I were a neighbor with a flashlight, would I be walking around in the darkness?"

"Lady Augusta!" Carol nearly fainted with relief at hearing a familiar voice. Then she got angry. "What do you mean frightening me like that? Are you responsible for this blackout? If you are, turn on the lights at once. Have you thought about the harm you could cause? There will be automobile accidents, and people stuck in elevators, and others wandering around lost and possibly hurting themselves in the dark."

"This is an improvement," Lady Augusta interrupted. "Only a day or two ago, you would have been worrying about your own inconvenience. I assure you, the other citizens of London will notice nothing amiss."

"Is this darkness supposed to be for my enlightenment?" Carol demanded.

"You are growing more witty, too."

"Why have you chosen to appear outside the house, instead of in my bedroom?"

"But you do persist in asking the wrong questions."

"Perhaps that is because you are driving me crazy. At least I've had something to eat this

207

time. What's your plan for tonight?"

"I intend to show you the future," Lady Augusta said. "As it will be if you do not take steps to change it."

"What future? Next month? Next Christmas?"

"I began by showing you the past as it was one hundred and seventy-five years ago," said Lady Augusta. "On this night you will see Marlowe House as it will be one hundred and seventy-five years in the future."

"You expect me to change what will happen a hundred and seventy-five years from now? That's impossible," Carol scoffed. "I'm not important enough to make any difference at all to the future. Especially not if I decide to go back to New York to look for work."

"Your decision whether to leave London or to stay will make a difference," Lady Augusta pointed out.

"You may not feel the cold," Carol said, "but I am freezing. Could we go inside where I can get warm? I would also like to see you while we argue about this."

"You will not find it warm in Marlowe House. However, I can arrange for a bit more light."

Carol sensed a motion from the dark shape that was Lady Augusta. Around the shape a faint white glow appeared. By its light Carol could see Lady Augusta's face and hands. Both were pale as ashes. There were dark circles beneath Lady Augusta's eyes, and her face and hands were much thinner than on her previous appearances, as if the flesh were wasting away from her bones. Under a black scarf thrown loosely over her head, her hair was a dirty shade of gray-white, hanging in lank strands around her face. She wore a long, plain black robe with a heavy gray shawl wrapped over it.

"You do not find my appearance pleasing." Lady Augusta sighed. "Neither do I. Nonetheless, it is suitable for what I must show you tonight."

"Is the future so grim?" Carol asked. She thought, but did not say, that Lady Augusta looked ready to attend a funeral.

"You may find it grim," came the sad answer.

"Are we to be observers this time, or will the people we meet be able to see and speak with us?"

"For the few days during which we are there, we will belong to that future time as though we were born into it. Your ability to alter the future exists only in the present, so you will not cause any harm. However, I hope that what you will experience will complete your conversion into a new person."

"I think I have already changed enough for two lifetimes, but if it's your opinion—or the opinion of your superiors—that I need more experience, then let's get this over with." Carol took a deep breath, bracing herself for what was to come. "Take me where you want me to be."

This time Lady Augusta did not embrace Carol, or grasp her hand. She simply rested her pale, bony fingers on Carol's shoulder.

Instantly, the dim light emanating from Lady Augusta faded, and the silent darkness closed in around Carol once more. It was like being smothered in wet black velvet. Carol felt something move. It was not the ground, for that remained steady beneath her feet, but she was aware of a dull, heaving sensation that came from the very bowels of the earth and transferred itself to her body. She suffered a momentary dizziness, and then her head cleared. Lady Augusta removed her hand from Carol's shoulder, leaving her to stand alone.

Sound returned—loud, jarring noises, as if someone were running a rusty piece of machinery, the various parts of which were constantly scraping against each other as the machine worked. Carol put her hands to her ears, but could not shut out the racket.

Slowly the blackness receded until the sky above was a dull gray. Cold rain fell heavily, freezing on the ground.

Carol stared at the machine laboring in the middle of the square. Then she looked at the rest of her surroundings and recoiled in horror.

"Oh, my God." She could say no more. The black-draped figure beside her moved, stretching out an arm.

"Welcome to the twenty-second century," said Lady Augusta. "Welcome to the future."

Part IV.
Christmas
Future.

Lond, 2168.

Chapter Ten

"What is that thing?" The machine in the square looked to Carol like some huge, rusty-red insect. "What is it doing?"

"It is time to erect this year's World Tree," Lady Augusta answered her.

"Is that like a Christmas tree? I don't think it will improve the appearance of the square." Carol fell silent, appalled by what she saw. On all sides once-elegant houses lay in ruins. Only three or four of them looked as if they might still be habitable. Gaps here and there, like open spaces between rotting teeth, marked the spots where individual buildings had been completely demolished. Through one such gap Carol had a clear line of sight straight out to the horizon.

Carol searched for the house that was most familiar to her. When she found it she understood why Lady Augusta had not appeared to her in her room. Her bedchamber was gone and so was Lady Augusta's suite of rooms. What was left of Marlowe House was just one story high. Piles of rubble in front and to either side of the house were apparently the remains of the former upper floors. The front doorway was barred by an assortment of heavy wooden boards reinforced with metal strips.

The square was still an open space, but the grass, the trees and bushes, and the flower beds were all gone, and in their place was a solid gray paving material. In that paved area a few figures wearing heavy layers of dark, tattered clothing were directing the movements of the screeching, unwieldy machine.

Carol shuddered. Everything she could see was a dingy gray or black, broken, ugly, noisy. And cold. Icy rain continued to fall, the drops running off her raincoat in streams. The dampness seeped upward through the thick soles of her sensible walking shoes. Water dripped off her hair and down her neck.

"If this is Christmas in the future," she said, "it certainly does not look like any Christmas I have ever known. And that is no Christmas tree, either."

The object now being lifted into the center of the square by the rusty machinery was not a real tree at all, but a heavy metal excrescence as gray and lusterless as the sky above. Its trunk was at least 20 feet in circumference and three times as tall as the men who were guiding it into place. This bulky trunk had along its length a few crooked projections that might have been intended to represent branches. At its uppermost level the metal monstrosity

214

divided into three sections that spread wide like arms, and each of these arms then separated into five gnarled fingers. The whole thing was wrapped around and around with thick metal cords in grotesque imitation of vines.

"I don't think I have ever seen anything so ugly," Carol said, staring at the 15 upwardly stretched fingers that appeared to be waiting— or perhaps aching—to grasp and hold some huge object.

"Do not let anyone hear you say so," Lady Augusta advised.

"Is this the World Tree you mentioned?" When Lady Augusta nodded, Carol asked, "What is it for?"

"You will need a bit of information if you are not to make dangerous mistakes," Lady Augusta told her. "Here, Christmas is no longer celebrated. A century after your own time it was abandoned, along with all other holidays kept by any faith. The Great Leaders of the People claimed that such celebrations had become too materialistic and commercial, and thus had lost their true meaning. There were also too many holidays, almost two hundred of them in each year. The constant celebrations were cutting into productivity.

"Therefore, when the New Calendar was instituted, all of the old holidays were eliminated in the interest of economic revitalization after a terrible, twenty-year-long depression that brought the world to the brink of chaos."

"What, no Valentine's Day or Halloween to spend money on, either?" Carol's tone was flippant, but after a moment of more serious thought, she added, "I should think abolishing holidays would hinder economic recovery. Eliminating Christmas alone ought to cause a minor recession."

"On the contrary. With no days off and no distractions during the preparations for each holiday, workers have fulfilled the hopes of the Great Leaders by increasing their productivity. The changes have proven to be quite successful."

"But if the workers have no time off at all, that doesn't seem fair," Carol said. "This can't be a very nice world for the ordinary person."

"I am pleased to hear you sounding concerned for ordinary folk. There was a time when you would not have cared. When, in fact, you would have cheered the absence of any holiday, and of Christmas in particular.

"The Great Leaders were not without understanding of the primitive needs of the workers," Lady Augusta continued. "Thus, they designated four major holidays, one at the astronomical beginning of each season of the year. The summer and winter solstices are celebrated, and the spring and autumn equinoxes. Each of these events involves a three-day celebration."

"A long weekend," Carol broke in.

"Precisely, though in the New Calendar there are no weekends. There is simply one day of rest after each ten-day work period, and an extra free day on the first of each new year." Lady Augusta paused to give Carol a chance to absorb all of this information.

"This sounds like a remarkably dreary time," Carol said.

"It may lack charm, but it is a peaceful age," Lady Augusta responded. "After decades of ethnic and religious wars, and of terrorism and economic upheaval, most folk are grateful to be spared further violence, and do not quarrel about repressive laws.

"Most folk," she said again, speaking with a peculiar emphasis. "Not all."

"The economic recovery you mentioned apparently hasn't reached this part of town." Carol glanced from the dilapidated buildings to the rusty machine now pushed to one side, and then on to the ugly sculpture sitting on a low cement base in the exact center of the square. "It's pretty obvious that the Government hasn't cleaned up yet after the last war, or spent money on new machinery, and those workmen certainly don't look prosperous."

"Actually, they are among the more fortunate," said Lady Augusta. When one of the workmen noticed the two women and said something to his fellows, who all stopped talking among themselves to look in their direction, Lady Augusta added, "It would be best if we went indoors at once."

She led Carol through a pile of rubble to the side of Marlowe House, and thence down what remained of the stairs to the recessed area and the servants' entrance. Once there had been a vestibule and a door with four large glass panes set into its upper half. Now the charm of this low entrance was gone. The door had been replaced by a solid wood barricade which blocked the entry to the lower floors of the house. Lady Augusta knocked on the wood. Receiving no response, she banged again, harder this time, and using the same series of knocks.

"Is that a code?" Carol asked.

"It is always best to know who is coming. Where is that man? We could be arrested before he lets us in."

Carol was about to ask why they should be arrested for doing nothing wrong, when the wooden barricade was pushed aside and a middle-aged man with lank, dirty hair peered out at her.

"Let us in, Bas," Lady Augusta commanded. "I have brought a guest to see your master."

"I call no one my master. I am a free man." But Bas moved the barricade a little more, allowing enough room for Lady Augusta and Carol to enter.

In the dark and cluttered room Carol recognized the outlines of the old servants' kitchen. She could see a bed and a chest of drawers in the room beyond, which had once been the servants' dining room and was apparently now Bas's quarters. Bas himself was clothed in layers of dark-colored, worn garments.

"He's in the book room," said Bas, jerking a thumb toward the servants' stairs that led to the upper floor of the house. Without another word he began to pull the wood back across the entrance, blocking it again.

"This way." Lady Augusta started up the steps. Carol followed her.

The one remaining upper floor of the house was reasonably clean, but in need of major repairs. The fine walnut paneling in the hall was badly damaged and the marble floor was cracked in many places. Some of the black and white squares were missing altogether. It seemed there was no electricity, for there were candles or oil lamps set on tables or benches along the hall. The artificial light was necessary because all of the windows were covered with several layers of rough boards, which allowed no daylight to enter.

When she came to the library, Lady Augusta did not pause to knock. With a motion of her hand to indicate that Carol should accompany her, Lady Augusta pushed the door open and went into the room.

Heavy brown curtains pulled across the windows disguised the fact that, like all the other windows and all but one door, these openings to the outside world were covered with boards. Most of the bookshelves were empty. On the desk two candles burned in a chipped pottery holder. The floor was bare of rugs. In spite of the sad changes to its appearance, the room was oddly similar to the library Carol remembered from her years of working at Marlowe House, and from her journey into the distant past. This was the room in which the Earl of Montfort had first kissed her on the night of their betrothal ball.

An unmistakably masculine figure sat at the desk, half turned away from the doorway and with an olive green blanket wrapped around its shoulders against the cold. The man was writing something, but Carol saw his hand go still and his shoulders stiffen as they came into the room.

"Is that you, Aug?" The voice brought Carol to a complete halt.

"It is." Lady Augusta moved forward. "I have

brought a friend with me."

"Your friends are welcome here." The man rose, shrugging off the blanket. He turned, so Carol could see his face and confirm with her eyes what her ears had already told her.

"Nicholas!" she gasped.

"Not quite," the man said. "I am Nik."

"This is the woman I spoke to you about the last time I was here," Lady Augusta said to the man who called himself Nik. "She can be of help to you."

"I will not ask if I can depend on her honesty," Nik responded. "You would not have recruited her if she were untrustworthy."

He put out his right hand and a mesmerized Carol put her own into it, feeling the firm clasp of his long, callused fingers.

"What is your name?" His voice was the same as she remembered, deep and faintly amused. He possessed such masculine power that, between his voice and the touch of his hand, Carol could barely think, and for those first heart-wrenching moments she could not speak one word. Nik put his own interpretation on her hesitancy.

"While you are here, you may use a name other than your own if you wish, but I insist upon knowing how you were originally called," Nik persisted, his fingers tightening around Carol's. "Among my friends, the revelation of a true name is a sign of trust and fellowship."

"I am Carol Simmons." *Call me your love. Tell me you recognize me.*

"You will be Car." He released her hand and Carol felt bereft, lonely, cast adrift in an unfamiliar world. He was *her* Nicholas, and yet

220

he was not. While her heart told her this was the man she loved, she knew in her mind that he was not, could not be, the same person.

Carol took the opportunity to study him as he spoke to Lady Augusta. She could see now the differences between Nicholas, the Earl of Montfort, and Nik, the man of the future. Nik's hair was the same glossy black, but straight instead of curly, and it was fastened into a queue with a cord tied at the nape of his neck. His clothes were worn, dark garments similar to those she had noted on Bas and on the workmen in the square—a heavy black shirt open at the neck, dark gray trousers, a loose gray jacket. There were patches at the elbows and knees, but she could tell the garments were clean.

Nik was taller, leaner, and somehow harder than the man she had loved in the nineteenth century. His cheekbones stood out more boldly. But his wide, curving mouth was the same as she remembered, and his eyes were as sharp and probing as ever, though she missed the sparkle of ready laughter that she was used to seeing. She could understand its absence, though. She did not think there could be much to laugh about in this time and place.

"You will return later for the meeting, then?" Nik said to Lady Augusta. "Take care, Aug. There have been two more arrests since yesterday."

"I will be safe, never fear."

"Are you leaving me?" Carol cried, wondering how she could manage in such a strange place without Lady Augusta to guide her.

"I leave you," said Lady Augusta, "exactly where you ought to be."

"I will see to your safety," Nik told Carol, touching her hand lightly with his fingers. Carol lost herself in his gaze, and when she was able to tear her eyes from his to look around, Lady Augusta was no longer there.

"We should get to work at once," Nik said. "Begin by telling me what your skills are."

"I don't think I have any that would be of use to you. I'm not sure why Lady—why Aug brought me here. What did she say about me?" Carol tried to concentrate. She was sure there was something Lady Augusta intended her to learn here in this future time, and she had to discover what it was.

Unfortunately for Lady Augusta's plans for her, this unexpected meeting with a man so similar to the love she thought was lost to her forever was confusing her. She wanted to fall into Nik's arms, but she knew he would think she was crazy if she did. She kept telling herself that this was not Nicholas, this was a different man, but she could not convince herself. Her every instinct screamed her recognition of him. With Lady Augusta gone, Carol could not ask for confirmation of what she felt. She was on her own in a world which, from what she had seen of it so far, she believed was dangerous.

"Aug told me that you are a remarkable and resourceful woman who would be of great help to me," Nik said. "From her recommendation, I assumed you possessed some specific skill."

"What kind of skill would that be?" She hoped he would give her some information as to what they were supposed to be doing.

What she got was a speculative look that was so familiar it nearly stopped her heart.

"Surely Aug promised you that *you* could trust *me*," he said.

"I need to know more," she hedged.

"So do I." Folding his arms across his chest, he leaned back against the desk. It was all Carol could do to keep from going to him and putting her arms around his neck and kissing him. The need to feel his arms around her was almost overpowering.

"Perhaps you ought to fill me in a bit more thoroughly on just why Aug brought you to me," he said.

"I honestly don't know what Aug's reasons are, or what she thought I could do for you." In the last few seconds Carol had become so certain of her feelings that she said exactly what her heart told her to say. "What I do know is that you and I have met before, in another time and place. I am amazed to discover you here."

He unfolded his arms to grip the edge of the desk in both hands as if he were afraid he would fall to the floor without its support. Or perhaps he feared he would fall through the centuries. He looked at her as if he were recording every bone and blood vessel and nerve of her body, every cell and curving eyelash and strand of light brown hair. For a time he gazed at her lips before he met her eyes and spoke again. Carol had the impression that during those silent moments he had made a long, astonishing journey, and had reached the ending he sought.

"You are from the past," he said, as calmly

and quietly as if he had been speaking of the weather.

"Didn't Aug warn you?" Still his eyes held hers, and it was hard for her to speak sensibly. "Perhaps I shouldn't have said anything." But she knew what she had done was right.

"Aug told me only that I would recognize you."

"Do you?" She awaited his answer, certain in her heart of what it should be, yet scarcely daring to breathe in case she was wrong.

"Oh, yes." His voice was just above a whisper. "I know you well. I have dreamed of you on countless nights. When you came into this room it seemed to me as if you knew me, too."

"I did. Right away. There are a few minor differences, but you are the same man. I'm sure of it now."

"Were we lovers?"

"Only briefly." Carol was surprised to feel herself blushing. "Too briefly."

"Ah." He smiled at her. It was like the sun bursting forth from behind a cloud to put an end to cold and darkness.

"Car," he said, and the short, hard syllable was a warm caress on her ears.

"Hello, Nik." She moved forward until she stood close enough to touch him.

He did not rise from his leaning posture against the desk to embrace her as she expected him to do. He simply lifted one hand and wove it through her hair and pulled her head down to his shoulder. She also raised a hand, to lay it on his chest so she could feel the beating of his heart and know that this was, in truth, her love. They were content to rest so for a long time, until Nik spoke, still without moving.

"Since this is Aug's doing, I will not question your presence any further." His breath was warm on her skin, and she felt the faint scratchiness of his cheek against her forehead. "Aug is a notable witch."

"She is not a witch," Carol murmured into the strong column of his throat. "She's a ghost."

"Do not tell me any more," he responded. "I do not want an explanation of how she brought you here. It is enough for me that the dream of my youth has come true."

"If you have lived before, then perhaps some buried part of your subconscious mind was remembering me and causing your dreams," Carol suggested.

"Hush. I said I do not want an explanation. Reason and common sense have nothing to do with this."

She wished she could obey him, but she could not stop thinking about where she was and what had happened. Nor could she stop wondering what it was that Lady Augusta expected of her in this time.

"Nik." She lifted her head from his shoulder to look directly at him. "What is the danger I sense in this place? Why is everything so grim and gray and bleak?"

"How much did Aug tell you? No, do not misunderstand me," he went on quickly. "I see the change in your expression. This is not evasion on my part. It will be simpler to describe my activities to you if I know what Aug has said."

"She talked about the Great Leaders who apparently restored peace after a violent time. She also mentioned a change in the calendar. According to Aug, most people have cheerfully accepted the wishes of these Great Leaders, whoever they are."

"Wishes?" He gave a short, humorless laugh. "When the Great Leaders speak, it is always laws and demands, and this present Government has been in command for so long that most people do not know what it is to be free."

"Aug did mention that not everyone went along with the Government. Nik, who are the Great Leaders?"

"They are the council of three men who head the Worldwide Government," he said. "When one of them grows old and dies, or is killed by the treachery of the other two, which has happened several times in the last few decades, then a new Leader is appointed by the Government from among their own members. The people have nothing to say in the matter. I, along with some other people, think this system is wrong."

"It's a dictatorship, then," Carol said. "Or more accurately, a *junta*."

"Children are taught only carefully selected portions of history," Nik revealed, "so they grow up not knowing what the world was like before this Government came to power. All but an aged handful of those who can personally recall the earlier time are dead now."

"Aug spoke about violence and wars."

"The last one hundred years before the Leaders took over were a terrible time," Nik acknowledged. "There are some records still in existence, for those who know where to look for them. I have found and read a few of those old accounts. The first group of Leaders did impose peace, that's true, and there were few unwise enough to oppose them because the world was weary of constant bloodshed. We have lived in peace for seventy years, but we paid too great a price for it. There is no freedom now. The Government tells us where we will live and what work we will do, even what clothing we will wear."

Carol spoke up. "There are no more old-fashioned holidays, either, according to Aug. Not since the New Calendar went into effect." She shook her head. "I never thought I would say this, but after watching the disinterested way in which those men in the square outside were raising that ugly metal World Tree, I yearn to see the little *real* tree that used to be there. I miss the Christmas hubbub, and the cheerful spirit that goes with it. So what if the merchants and the media commercialize the holiday? The true spirit of Christmas can't be bought, and anyone with two functioning brain cells knows as much. All the commercial nonsense is just icing on a rich and very solid cake of ancient tradition. A real Christmas involves caring about other people." She fell silent because Nik was watching her with glowing eyes.

"You are just what we need," he said. "What I need."

"We," Carol repeated. "You have mentioned friends. Do they feel as you do about the Government?"

"We are determined to change the way the world is ruled," Nik told her. "We want ordinary people to have something to say about what the laws are and what the punishment for breaking a law should be."

"No one who holds power ever gives up that power voluntarily," Carol warned him. "If you want real change and not just a cosmetic revamping for appearances' sake, then you will have to fight. And you will have to convince more people to join you. This will be too big a job for a small guerrilla group to accomplish."

"We all know it. We are willing to risk our lives in such a cause. Will you join us?"

"I think I already have. But Nik," she cautioned, seeing his expression of joy at her response, "it's only fair to tell you that I don't know how long Lady Augusta will let me stay in this time. She has her own agenda and she doesn't listen to me."

"*Lady Augusta?*" he murmured. "Is that Aug's real name? I have read about noble titles. There are none in this time. All titles and family names were abolished when the Great Leaders took control of the world."

"When I knew you before," she told him, "you were a noble, too. I think you still are."

"You are making a hasty judgment," he said, teasing in a manner that was dear and familiar to her. "You do not know me well yet. I may be a different man now."

"If you were, I wouldn't feel this way about you."

"What way?" His hands were at her waist,

pulling her closer to him where he still balanced against the edge of the desk. "Tell me how you feel about me, Car."

"The point is," she said, trying to resist the strong emotional pull he exerted over her, "Lady Augusta—Aug—may suddenly decide that I have learned whatever lesson she wanted me to understand from my stay with you. If I should disappear without saying good-bye, don't think it was because I wanted to leave you. I may not have anything to say about my departure."

"Perhaps you will not have to go at all."

"Don't fool yourself. I won't be here for very long." It was unbelievably hard to look into his green eyes and say those words without breaking into tears. The knowledge that she would surely lose him a second time was tearing her apart inside.

"In that case, I will see to it that we do not waste a moment." His hands slid downward from her waist along her spine. Cupping her hips, he urged her closer still, until she was positioned between his thighs. Carol put her hands on his shoulders and then around his neck. "Shall I kiss you, Car?"

"I wish you would." She saw his lips curve into an enticing smile. She offered her mouth to him, and he took it, gently at first, tasting her lips as if he were not quite certain he wanted what she could give him.

She understood his lack of sureness. She felt something similar herself. While Nik had dreamed of her, and no doubt wondered if reality could match a matchless fantasy, Carol had actual memories to overcome. She was not foolish enough to think that this was the same physical manifestation of the Nicholas who had once made love to her. She did believe that the soul, or the spirit, of the Nicholas she still loved lived again in the man who was now holding her. While this belief made no logical sense, she knew it was accurate because she did not feel the least twinge of guilt over her rising desire for Nik. If he were not some new materialization of the Nicholas she loved, she would not—could not possibly—want him to make love to her.

He drew back a little, so he could see her better.

"Yes, you are the one," he whispered. "I am certain of it now. I know the sensation of your lips against mine, and I remember the taste of you as if I have actually held you in my arms before today. But you speak the truth when you say you will be taken from me. In every dream I have ever had of you, I have lost you at the end, and I wake up weeping." He let her go. Pushing away from the desk, he walked to the opposite side of the room to stand near the bookshelves with his back to her.

"Tears are not considered a manly thing. However, for this time in which I live, I am not the usual man." He made a gesture toward the few books lined up on the old library shelves. "I read too much and, influenced by what I read, I think dangerous thoughts. I try to calm my impatient heart by listening to antique music. I dream dreams that cannot possibly come true. Yet, one of those dreams is here with me today. If one dream can come true, why not others?

"Your presence gives me new courage, Car."

He turned back to her, his face alight. "If you are here, and we remember what we are meant to be to each other, then perhaps my friends and I can prevail against the tyranny of the Great Leaders and the World Government. Seeing you, I am filled with hope." He broke off, his whole body going tense at the sound of a footstep in the hall.

"It's only us, Nik," a man's voice called out, and Nik relaxed.

"My God, what a way to live," Carol said. "Do you assume every step you hear is that of someone bent on attacking you?"

"Only by exerting great caution have I have survived this long," Nick replied. Raising his voice, he said, "I am here. Come in, Al."

A man bundled in the usual dark and worn garments appeared, followed by a second person. Both were of medium height, and were so well disguised under layers of clothing that at first Carol did not see that this second figure was a woman. Not until she spoke was her gender revealed.

"I told you we would come back safely." The woman swept off a too-large knitted hat to expose tightly braided blond hair. Her blue eyes danced with laughter as she stepped into Nik's arms. "And you were worried."

"I always worry about you." Nik held her so the candlelight fell on her face.

"There is not a scratch on me, or on Al, either." She caught sight of Carol. "Who is this? I have not seen her in Lond before."

"Car is a new recruit. Aug brought her to me this afternoon. Car," Nik said, "this is my older sister, Pen. And her lover, Al."

"Pen?" Carol could tell by the look in Nik's eyes that he had noted her reaction and knew she recognized these people, too. Doubtless, he would ask her about it later. For the moment, he had other concerns.

"Were you seen?" Nik asked Al.

"No. We were careful. However, it might be well for us to show ourselves in public before the sun sets. That way, we won't have to answer questions on our whereabouts yesterday and today. It will be assumed that the ice and rain kept us indoors along with most other people. The weather is clearing now, and the workers have finished with the World Tree, so it will seem natural if we step outside to look at it."

"I'll go with you. You come, too, Car." Nik took her hand. "If we are not seen out of doors with some frequency, the Government imagines we are up to no good and certain unpleasant agents are sent to investigate."

"Are you saying there are Government spies who are continually checking up on you?" Carol asked, horrified by this idea.

"Most of the time, they are scarcely noticeable," Pen told her.

"What a world you have here. It sounds like the old Soviet Union."

"From my reading, I think it is worse," Nik said. "Pen, Al, make your report now, quickly, before we leave the house."

"We met with four other groups," Pen said. "All agreed with your plan. We begin action on the second day after the Winter Solstice celebration."

"I," Al declared, "do not think we ought to

depend upon Ben's group. There are no women in it, and the men are little more than thugs. They may prove to be more trouble than help to us."

"We don't have much choice, not while our numbers are so small. We have to make use of everyone who is willing to work with us." Nik waited until his sister and Al stepped outside the library before speaking again to Carol. "Later, you and I will finish what we have begun here. I do promise you, Car, there will be a later for us."

"Will you tell me then what you and your friends are planning?" she asked. "It sounds to me as if you are organizing some kind of strike against the Government."

"If we are, will you join with us? Aug did say you were sent to help."

"Actually, I was sent to learn, though what the lesson is, I haven't a clue. Yes, Nik." She looked deep into his green eyes, seeing there a warmth to equal the heat racing through her own veins. She thought by his smile that he appreciated the double meaning of her next words. "I will join with you gladly."

Chapter Eleven

The four of them climbed over the rubble surrounding Marlowe House and then walked into the square. The workmen had gone, taking their aged machine with them, but there were a few people standing around looking at the World Tree.

"Does something fit into those fingers?" Carol asked, gazing at the tortured metal branches.

"The Orb." It was Pen who answered her. "At dawn on Winter's First Day, the Orb comes to rest in the branches of the World Tree. It remains there until the Solstice celebrations are over, to let us know a warmer time will return."

"Do not ask more here," Nik cautioned, leaning down to whisper to Carol. "Those hearing you will know you do not belong in Lond."

"Oh, yes, the spies," she whispered back, smiling at him as if they were exchanging romantic words. "I will be careful."

As Al had noted, the weather was in the process of clearing, but the air was rapidly growing colder. A sudden breeze blew a heavy snow squall out of the lingering clouds, dusting the square and World Tree and people with white. Nik looked upward, laughing into the blowing flakes.

"I love the snow," he said to Carol. "For an hour or two it makes everything in this sad world clean and softens the hard edges and the ugliness. When it snows, I could almost believe the world can be made fresh and new again."

"Even that monstrosity in the middle of the square might be a real tree in the dead of winter," Carol agreed, sparing a less hostile glance for the World Tree, where the metal branches now bore a thin coating of white on their upper surfaces. "Look, the sun is shining through the snow."

The air was still full of snowflakes, but the clouds, having dumped most of their burden of moisture, were now too thin to block out the sun. A hazy, diffused yellow glow slowly spread across the sky, while the sun could be seen as if it shone behind a sheer veil. A last burst of snow flurried downward, the flakes glittering in the dim sunlight like particles of solid gold.

"How beautiful," Carol murmured, seeing Nik standing with his face turned up to the shower of snow and the golden light. Snowflakes lay thick upon his black hair. More flakes dusted his forehead and cheeks with bits of gold that melted instantaneously on contact with his body's warmth. She thought she would always remember him like that, standing straight and tall, laughing into the snow, with shimmering drops of golden moisture on his face, his whole form illuminated by haze and sunlight.

His manly strength and beauty, and the love she felt for him, tugged at her heart. She was fully aware that the joy she knew in this precious moment could not last. Soon, inevitably, time and Lady Augusta would separate them. But meanwhile . . . just for now . . .

He looked into her eyes. His smile turned gentle then, and in the green depths of his gaze, for just a moment, she saw Eternity.

"Tell me how the square and the houses appeared in your time," Nik asked later that evening.

The snow showers had stopped with the setting sun, but as the sky cleared the cold arrived in earnest, sending their little group shivering out of the square and into the inadequate warmth of the house. They gathered in the old servants' kitchen, Nik and Carol sitting together on a wooden bench at one end of the room, slightly apart from their companions, where they could speak in relative privacy.

Bas, who seemed to be the twenty-second-century equivalent of butler, cook, and general aide to Nik, was heating up a large pot of stew over an open fire laid where the stove used to be, so the smoke could go up the old chimney. Pen, having refused Carol's offer of help with the remark that it was her turn for kitchen duty, moved from cupboard to table laying out at least a dozen places with cracked dishes and mismatched cutlery, while Al opened a dusty bottle of wine that Bas had just retrieved from the sub-basement. They were talking among themselves, none of them paying any attention to what Nik and Carol were saying to each other.

Quickly, keeping an eye on their companions so she could break off her descriptions of the earlier time if anyone came close enough to hear, Carol described the area around Marlowe House as she knew it.

"Flowers and grass in the summertime." Nik spoke in a pensive voice.

"And colored lights on the tree in the middle of the square at Christmas." Carol went on to describe the decorations and the festive air in London during the holiday season.

"I have never seen a Christmas tree," Nik said.

"If you had asked me a few days ago, I would have told you that I have seen altogether too many of them," Carol responded. "Now, I don't think there can ever be too many Christmas trees. Nik, what would happen if you tried to find and decorate one?"

"No one would know what it was," he said, shaking his head at the idea. "Furthermore, there are no trees in Lond anymore, nor for miles on all sides of the city. Nor, if I could find one, would I be permitted to bring it here. I shall have to be content to see the marvel of a Christmas tree through your eyes, in the same way in which I see the rest of your vanished world."

They could not talk any longer, for more people were arriving. Each newcomer was allowed past the wooden barrier at the entrance only after Bas determined that this was indeed a member of Nik's company. The last to appear was Lady Augusta, who was still wearing her tattered robes, which Carol now understood were chosen to make her blend in with everyone else. However, dreary clothing could not disguise the woman's innate dignity, nor her commanding character. "Aug" was an important part of Nik's little group of rebels.

"She's our resident witch," Pen whispered to Carol. "She comes and goes as she pleases, and no one knows where she is when she is not at Lond. I think she knows a way to make herself invisible. Nik says such spells are impossible. I am not so sure."

There were 14 of them for dinner that night, including Aug and Carol. And they *were* included. No one questioned Nik's decision on the matter of Carol's admission to their group, and everyone spoke openly about their plans in front of her.

"Why have you scheduled your uprising for two days after Winter Solstice?" Carol asked after listening for a while. "Why not on the day itself, when police or other official types will be distracted by the ceremonies?"

"Previous revolts have been attempted during seasonal celebrations, using just that reasoning." The speaker was Jo, a short, red-haired woman whom Carol suspected was fond of

Bas. "As a result of those attempts, the Government now provides extra civil guards for all festivities."

"If we wait until after Solstice, then the Government will have removed its guards and sent some of them away on furlough." That was Luc. Slender, black-haired, with olive skin and dark, languid eyes, he glanced toward Pen, who nodded her agreement with what he was saying. "We have a better chance of succeeding if we strike when the Great Leaders are relaxed and congratulating themselves on another festival peacefully concluded."

Carol was finding the relationships among the conspirators fascinating. She was certain that Luc cared deeply for Pen, yet he was close friends with Al and constantly deferred to the older, tougher man who was openly Pen's lover. All of them ultimately deferred to Nik, and to Aug. But they did listen to the opinions of each member of the group. Thus, Carol felt free to say what she thought.

"What can you hope to accomplish by rising against a worldwide government system when you are so few in number?" she asked. "Even if there are other, similar bands willing to coordinate their activities with yours, there cannot be enough of you to make a real difference. You will be suppressed, and the Government will see to it that no one ever learns what you have done."

"We know the risks and we accept them," Nik said. "We must try. Sooner or later, a rebel group will succeed. Then other groups will arise to join it, and the movement will grow until opposition to the Government is so overwhelming that a change will be made. At last each person will have a voice in the making of laws. We will form a new and better government, one willing to heed the wishes of the governed."

"It won't be as simple as you imagine," Carol cried. "True democracy is a tumultuous thing and you are used to conformity. After listening to your talk for the last couple of hours, it's clear to me that you are in the minority. Under the Great Leaders, most people have stopped thinking for themselves. They are willing to be told what to do. That kind of inertia will be difficult to overcome."

"Still, we must make the effort." Pen's face was alight with the inner vision all of them shared. "We will go forward one step at a time. Our first objective is to bring down the World Government, and we are here to discuss the tactics for our uprising."

"I'm sorry," Carol said. "I didn't mean to throw cold water on your hopes. I just wanted to point out some of the pitfalls ahead."

"We needed to hear your words of caution," Nik responded. "Sometimes, our hopes and dreams for the future carry us forward too quickly."

"I wouldn't want to spoil anyone's dreams," Carol said. "I agree with what you are trying to do. I just don't want to see any of you get hurt."

"There will be sacrifices to be made," Nik said. "Each of us is prepared to give up life itself for our cause. But remember this, Car; when we have won, there will be freedom to celebrate any holiday you want. Then, I promise you, we will raise up a Christmas tree."

"A what?" Pen looked at her brother in bewilderment, but Nik was smiling into Carol's eyes.

She could not avoid smiling back at him. His enthusiasm and hope were inspiring. There was much more Carol could have said on the subject of eliminating repressive governments. There were twentieth-century examples she might have cited, of countries where disparate groups had worked well together until their freedom was achieved, at which point those groups fell to fighting each other with a bloody violence that doomed the weakest and most helpless souls in their societies.

Carol said none of this. Instead, she sat listening during the long evening of discussion, and her heart grew heavier with every word that was spoken. Some, and perhaps all, of those who sat at table with her would die in the struggle to come. Yet they believed the possible cost was worth the gamble, for the prize was political and religious freedom. In spite of her fears for them and her own lingering cynicism, Carol absorbed some of their idealism and their hopes for the future.

Toward the end of the evening, Carol saw Lady Augusta watching her with approval written on her lined face.

"Is this what you wanted me to learn?" Carol asked as the group around the table broke up.

"In part," Lady Augusta said. "There is more to come. The hardest lesson of all will be the last one."

"And what is that?" Carol demanded.

"When the time comes for you to learn it,

you will know what to do."

"Car," Nik interrupted, "Pen and Jo will show you to the women's sleeping quarters."

"But—I thought—" Carol looked at him in confusion. She had imagined they would spend the night together.

"I must leave the house," Nik said. "There are important tasks ahead of me tonight. Do not ask what they are. Go with Pen. She is waiting for you."

"What are you going to do?" Carol cried, seeing Nik, Bas, and Luc pulling on heavy outdoor garments. She immediately envisioned the three rebels attempting to blow up railroad tracks or a power station. Nik seemed to read her mind.

"Nothing violent, I assure you. Among other things, we are going to visit another dissident group, to make some final plans so we won't have to meet during the Solstice, when the civil guards are always especially suspicious." Lightly, he laughed away her concerns. "Aug will be with us, so we shall be safe."

"Can't I go, too?" Carol asked.

"It would be better if you stay here." His hand on her shoulder reassured Carol that he did understand why she was worried. "The three-day holiday begins tomorrow. Then we will all be free for personal pleasures." He waited until Carol bowed her head in assent before he removed his hand.

"Do as he says," Lady Augusta murmured to Carol under her breath.

"Will I still be here tomorrow?" Carol asked her. "Or the next day? I would like to see this famous Solstice celebration."

"We will remain in this time," Lady Augusta replied, "for three, and perhaps for four more days. For as long as is necessary."

"Thank you."

"Spare me your gratitude until you know what the future holds," Lady Augusta snapped with a tinge of her old sharpness in her voice. Gazing at Carol as if she pitied her, Lady Augusta added, "You are as great an optimist as Nik is, and that surprises me. I would not have thought it of you."

The sleeping quarters were underneath the kitchen, in what had once been a storage cellar. The two rooms were clean, but sparsely furnished, and a faint smell of damp earth lingered in the air.

"The women sleep in one room, and the men in the other," Pen explained, showing Carol the way into the women's bedchamber. "Bas closes up the outside door and bars it every night, so we are secure."

"Does everyone sleep in here? I thought Nik said that you and Al—that is, don't you occasionally want privacy?"

"There are rooms upstairs," Pen said. "It is just that we are safer down here."

"This is a terrible way to live."

"I dream of another way," Pen said. "I would like a room with windows I dare to open, to let in a breeze when the weather is hot. Sometimes, I think of bright colors. Once, I saw the wife of one of the Great Leaders when she came to Lond for a visit. She was wearing a long robe the exact color of the sky. How wonderful it must be to dress in colors."

"Why can't you?" Carol asked. "Is it forbidden?"

"No ordinary person could afford dyed fabric," Pen replied wistfully. "If I were to wear such a garment all my friends would wonder where I had obtained it, and what I had done to earn it."

"No wonder you are willing to risk your lives for a better government," Carol muttered. "You people are little more than serfs."

The mattress on her cot was thin, and so was the blanket she was given, but after her conversation with Pen, Carol was not inclined to complain. She found it difficult to relax in her underground surroundings, and the lamp that was left burning at all times kept her awake for hours. In the morning she discovered that Nik and his companions had not yet returned.

"Where were they going?" Carol asked Pen.

"I do not know. Nik takes care not to reveal his activities when he goes out at night." Pen regarded her with a slight smile, then put an arm around Carol's shoulders. And Carol, impelled by an affection born three centuries in the past, returned the embrace. "They will all come back safely, Car. Don't forget, Aug is with them."

"If you want to keep busy," Jo put in, "then come with us to the market. Bas has given me a list of supplies to buy for the Solstice feast."

Curious to discover what this future version of London would be like, Carol agreed, and the three women set out at mid-morning. Because the weather was so bitterly cold, all of them wore extra garments over their usual outdoor gear. Carol was wrapped in an old cloaklike

245

woolen covering worn over her lined raincoat. In addition she had on a knitted hat and thick mittens. She was certain no one seeing her would ever suspect that she did not belong where she was.

They walked. There did not appear to be any public transportation. Carol could not help wondering if this was a deliberate tactic of the Great Leaders, a way of keeping the populace from traveling very far from where they lived, thus preventing people from communicating with each other and perhaps fomenting a rebellion. If such was the intent of the Leaders, they were not particularly successful.

There were great open spaces in the city, but they were not the parks Carol remembered. All traces of trees or grass or public gardens were gone, and large sections of "Lond" lay in rubble. The scenes she saw reminded Carol of photographs taken at the end of World War II. The difference was that the evidence of that earlier war was removed as promptly as possible and new buildings were quickly erected on the bombed-out sites. The damage she saw now was decades old. Pen and Jo told her there were people living in the windowless, half-ruined houses they passed, as Nik and his friends lived in the building they called Mar House.

"At least Buckingham Palace is still standing," Carol murmured, "but it doesn't look to be in very good shape." The wrought-iron fence was gone, half of one wing had been destroyed, and most of the windows were boarded up. A hideous new windowless building rose where once there had been acres of well-kept royal gardens and a lake. This building was the only sign of new construction Carol had seen since arriving in the future. There were still guards at the palace entrances, but instead of the colorful uniforms of Carol's own day, these guards were clad in dark brown overcoats and trousers and they carried wicked-looking weapons and wore metal helmets.

"Those are the Government offices for all of this country," Pen said, hurrying Carol along. "Don't go near those buildings unless you are on official business. I have known people who went in there and never came out again."

The market where they were to shop was set up along the Mall. Here there were crude stalls made out of brick and stone scavenged from ruined buildings. Carol saw a few old doors being used as counters, but most of the foodstuffs lay in baskets on the ground or on top of piles of broken building material. All of the stalls were crowded, for this was the first day of the three-day Solstice celebration and most workers were free to spend their time in preparations for the holiday feast.

"Here, the biggest meal of the year is eaten at the Fall Equinox," Pen said in answer to Carol's questions, "because it occurs in the middle of the harvest season when a lot of extra food is brought into the city. Is it different where you live? Nik didn't mention your home city."

"I think it's best if I don't talk about where I usually live," Carol replied.

"I understand. Discretion is always the safest option." The readiness with which Pen accepted her false response was depressing to Carol. That a young woman whom she knew to be open and

247

sweet-natured should have to resort to such caution—that Pen should have to go about in fear for her life—made clear to Carol why the present Government needed to be replaced with something much better.

"This is the best stall for fresh foods," Jo said, interrupting Carol's unhappy thoughts.

At this winter season the produce displayed was primarily root vegetables. The women bought turnips, beets, and carrots. Pen added a small bunch of greens and some herbs, and then they moved on to the meat and poultry section of the market. Here Jo took charge, saying Bas had told her exactly what to buy.

"Chicken, unless it's too dear," she said, examining the few birds hanging from metal racks. She haggled with the poultry man, ending with the best chicken she could get for the money she had to spend. Carol thought it was a scrawny bird too small to feed all of their group, but she kept quiet, not wanting to embarrass Pen and Jo.

"On to the sweets," said Pen. "They are the best part of the seasonal celebrations."

The provision of sweets was apparently the most profitable business at the holiday, and there were at least a dozen booths selling them. The sweets, formed of hardened, molded sugar, or of a substance that looked remarkably like sugar, were laid out on trays in front of each booth. Carol stared at them.

"Don't they make your mouth water?" Pen asked. "I do so look forward to the sweets. I'd eat them every day if it were allowed. Perhaps it's just as well the Government only lets them be sold four times a year."

"I'm sure the law cuts down on tooth decay," said Carol in a dry tone. She regarded the sweets with a dislike that stemmed from what she had learned about the all-powerful Government. "They are trees. Little sugar trees with an orange-colored sugar ball stuck in the branches. I suppose the ball represents the Orb you were talking about yesterday, Pen."

"We should buy one for each of us," Jo put in. "Nik gave me enough money for fourteen of them."

"When do we eat them?" Carol asked, still viewing the miniature creations with a jaundiced eye.

"Not until Solstice Day," Jo said.

"I'm not sure I can wait," Pen said, laughing. "First the dawn ceremony and then the festival meal. Then, at long last, the sweets." Glancing around to be sure there was no one to hear her next words, she added in a whisper, "After we change the Government, I hope we can still have sweets on holidays."

"If you succeed in changing the Government," Carol told her, "you will be allowed to eat sweets every day of the year. The decision will be yours, along with a lot of other decisions. I hope you have thought about that. Making choices can be exhausting."

"Do be quiet," Jo warned, and Pen smiled and shook her head and did not say anything in reply to Carol's remarks.

Carol found the hours she and the other women spent away from Marlowe House disorienting because of the physical changes that had taken place in the city she knew so well, and saddening because there were so few signs of a cheerful holiday spirit. She missed the sparking white fake snow, the red and green and tinsel decorations, and the brightly colored lights that once had made the shops glow.

She also missed the street lamps, for in this desolate version of London there were none. Pen told her that people were expected to stay home after dark and thus lamps were not needed. In any case, there was no electricity, except in the Government offices and the houses of the most important officials. There were no shops, either, just the booths and, here and there, some goods spread upon the ground without the protection of a booth. It was not long before Carol wished she could hear just one person telling her in a cheerful voice to have a merry Christmas.

Nik, Bas, and Luc returned to Marlowe House in the late afternoon, shortly after Carol and the other women finished unpacking and storing the food they had purchased. The three men sauntered into the kitchen as casually as though their day had been no more adventurous than the women's walk to the market. Aug was not with them, but no one remarked on her absence.

"We will eat the remains of last night's stew this evening," Bas decided, pulling off his outer garments and heading toward the cooking fire, which Jo was presently feeding with bits and pieces of wood. "But tomorrow, we will enjoy a great feast." He launched into a series of questions aimed at Jo, most of them about the food for the following day.

Over the heads of the others now crowding

into the kitchen, Nik's eyes met Carol's. She did not need to touch him or even speak to him to know he had thought about her often during the day. As she had thought of him, for his image had been with her while she gazed at the ruins of a once-great city, and later, as she helped her new friends to carry home the paltry, bruised ingredients for a holiday that meant nothing to her.

The Winter Solstice did matter to the others. Out of a growing fondness for their little company, Carol kept her opinions on the celebration to herself. She sat on a bench beside Nik at the dinner table, increasingly aware of the way his thigh brushed against hers from time to time.

"Our plans are complete," Nik said to all of them. Pushing aside the chipped plate that held the last few scraps of his evening meal, he leaned forward, looking from face to face as he spoke. "There are a dozen other groups like this one, all willing to join with us on the night after the holiday ends. For reasons of security there will be no further contacts among the groups until the uprising begins. So, my friends, enjoy the holiday, but do not drop your guard when you are outside this house, and maintain the usual identification procedures when going in and out of it."

The party broke up at that point. Those assigned to kitchen duty began to wash and put away the dishes. A few members drifted toward the basements, to sleep. Bas and Jo disappeared into his room next to the kitchen, from where Bas could hear anyone attempting to enter the house. Pen and Al headed for the stairs leading to the upper floor. And Nik took Carol's hand, keeping her close to his side as the others dispersed.

Looking up at him, she saw in his eyes the knowledge that lay certain and sure in her own heart. He did not need to ask the question, and she knew she did not need to answer it, but all the same, she did.

"Yes," she said, her voice quiet and calm, and free of all doubts or questions.

Chapter Twelve

"I have a machine that will play recorded music." Nik lit the two candle stubs in the holder on the library desk. "Sometimes when I dream of you, in the dream my favorite song is playing and I hold you in my arms while we move together as though I know the steps to a long-forgotten dance."

"I would like to hear that music."

From a drawer of the desk he removed two disks and a flat black box about the size of his hand.

"This is old equipment," he said. "We found it when we were cleaning out one of the rooms. Luc is clever with machinery; he works with it at the water-cleaning plant, and so he was able to make this player function for me."

Carol expected the sound to be as scratchy as a tune from an antique phonograph record, but obviously Luc had known what he was doing when he repaired the disk player. The music was clear and pure. The strains of an old waltz filled the library like the echoes from a long-ago ball. Carol caught her breath, and her eyes stung with sudden moisture.

"I do not know this dance except in dreams," Nik said, holding out his hands. "Will you teach me?"

She went into his arms, and showed him where to place his hands, and counted out the steps for him. And all the while, her heart was beating to an ancient refrain. The music filled her ears and her mind, drenching her in reawakened happiness.

"It's easy," Nik said after a few minutes. "But then, I have an expert teacher."

It's easy if some part of you already knows the steps, she thought.

When the music stopped he went to the machine and set it to play the same waltz over again.

"Do you always hear the same song in your dreams?" she asked, watching his long fingers moving on the equipment. "Never another song?"

"It is always the same, but I cannot be certain if the music was already in my mind or if I learned it when I was finally able to use the player. The first time I heard the recording, it seemed to me as though the song was familiar."

It was, she thought. *350 years ago, you knew it well.*

The second time they danced, he was much more sure of himself and of the steps for the waltz. He caught Carol in his arms and whirled her around the nearly empty library as if they were on the polished floor of a grand ballroom. Looking into his eyes, seeing his smile, she felt the centuries drop away until once again they were betrothed lovers entranced by newfound desire, caught in hope and in dreams of a bright future together. When the music stopped a second time he stood holding her, looking hard at her, and she knew he had seen the image in her own mind.

"How strange," he murmured, blinking as if to clear his sight. "How wonderful. It was like a waking dream. We were somewhere else, a place beautiful and shining with candlelight."

"I know. I saw it, too." She smiled at him with trembling lips.

"It was not just the music," he went on, "nor the memory of the dreams I've had of you. It was real."

"So is this, the here and now." She could no longer bear the intrusion of the past upon the present. True, he was, in a mysterious way she did not understand, *Nicholas,* but he was also Nik, and the man he was in this future time was a brave and noble person. He, too, was worthy of her love.

She knew they would soon lose each other, but whether he came to her as Nicholas or Nik she would not stop loving him, and the love was what was important. In all the world, in any time, love was all that mattered.

"I have not had a woman for many long months," he told her, his voice low. "Not since well before last Winter Solstice. I have been so consumed with planning, and with making certain all of my friends would be safe, that I have taken no time for myself. For these few remaining days before the uprising begins, will you lie with me, Car? Will you stay with me for the entire night?"

"I have already said yes," she reminded him.

"I thought it best to put it into words so there can be no misunderstanding. You have seen how I live. I own few earthly possessions and my existence is a dangerous one. I can offer you nothing but my heart, and what hope there is for our cause."

"There are no greater gifts than love and hope," she whispered.

He took her face between his hands, smiling when she raised her own hands to hold him in the same way. Slowly, prolonging their anticipation, they drew closer, until at last their mouths met, and held, and melted into one warm and blissful joining of lips and tongues and richly burgeoning desire.

It was a long while until he released her. Leaving her to stand reeling from the effects of his kiss, he took up the pottery candleholder and thrust it into her hands.

"Hold on to this and don't burn yourself," he ordered. Before she could ask him what he intended, he swung her off her feet and into his arms.

"Nik, this is dangerous," she cried, trying to shield the candle flames and hang on to him at the same time.

"It is the least dangerous thing I have ever done," he responded.

He carried her out of the library to a room

that opened off the main hall. He managed it without incinerating either of them, but looking at the flames reflected in his eyes when he put her down on his bed, Carol thought it would not be long before they were both consumed.

With unsteady hands she set the candleholder on the floor beside the bed. Then she looked around. It was a bare little chamber, a space stolen from the back end of the old drawing room. The familiar carved molding along the ceiling stopped abruptly where it met the plain expanse of a more recently constructed wall. There was one long window curtained in olive green blankets. She was sure the opening behind the blankets was covered by boards. There was a small chest of drawers, and a wooden chair with two slats missing from its back. The bed, covered with another olive blanket, was wide but hard and lumpy. That was all—walls, covered window, bed, chest and chair, and two candles. It looked like Paradise to Carol.

Nik sat on the bed beside her. While she was looking at the room he had stripped to the waist. Carol ran her fingers along a wicked-looking raised scar that crossed his chest.

"Where did you get this?"

"It was a gift from one of the civil guards some ten years ago," he said. "I was fortunate. They did not learn my identity, and my friends got me safely away. I have been more careful since."

"You could have been killed!" she cried. "You could still—"

"Not another word," he commanded. "What

happens three days from now is in the future. I will not spoil the intervening days and nights by worrying. Not when I can have you in my arms."

As he spoke he was working at the sash and the buttons of her raincoat. The house was so badly heated that Carol had immediately adopted the habit of her companions, and at all times wore wore as many layers of clothing as possible. She'd added the old cloak Pen had found for her when she went outdoors.

"So many garments," she murmured now, letting him remove the raincoat with its woolen winter lining and then the cardigan sweater. Beneath this she still had on a gray wool turtleneck sweater and matching wool trousers.

"The clothing only makes you appear more provocative," he said. "I have spent many delightful moments wondering what lay beneath it." He paused, looking with some amusement at her plain cotton bra and briefs before removing them, too. Then he waited, giving Carol time to finish undressing him. His eyes glinted with easy male humor when she gulped at the sight of his proud flesh.

Like the rest of the house, his room was cold. Carol began to shiver. With a sound deep in his throat that was part chuckle and part growl of rising passion, he quickly tumbled her under the covers and got in beside her. The thin, patched sheets were cold, the blankets were inadequate. Only Nik was warm. She clung to him as if her life depended on his heat.

"Are you frightened or only freezing?" he teased.

"How could I be afraid of you?" She put her

hands on his chest, running a finger along the ridge of scar tissue. While he nibbled at her earlobe, she sighed with pleasure. "I am cold, but I do believe you will find a way to warm me as quickly as possible."

"I will try." He moved from earlobe to throat to shoulder. He reached her breasts and she arched against him, moaning. Heat filled her and she was vividly aware of his hardness against her thigh. Her need for him was a painful ache. Their teasing banter ended suddenly. Unable to control herself, she grabbed for him.

"Car," he groaned, "I'd be gentle if I could."

"Don't wait." She shifted, giving him ready access to her hot and moist flesh. "You don't have to be gentle, either. I don't feel gentle, myself. I feel greedy. I want—want all of you—Nik!"

She screamed as he filled her, and then she wrapped her arms and legs around him, pulling him closer, ever closer, rising to meet him as he pounded into her in a fury of passion. It was as though he exploded inside her. Carol bit his shoulder, trying with the last fragments of thought available to her to stifle her cries. She was unsuccessful. She gave up the effort to keep some modicum of control over herself because it was too distracting when all she wanted was to follow him into the place where he now was, where blinding, searing passion canceled out all thought of yesterday or tomorrow, where there was no time, but only the present, the moment, and the two of them together, made one in love.

When she recovered enough to think again,

she was still in his arms and he was still part of her. She marveled that she had ever thought his room was cold.

"I'm sorry," he gasped, his rough cheek against hers. "That was too fast. I should have been more careful of you but, Car, I lost my mind. Never—never before—"

"It was just right." She kissed him to stop the unnecessary apology. "Just what I needed. Time enough to be slow later."

"I wish I could be sure we *would* have the time."

"We have tonight." She moved a little, then gasped in shocked surprise. He had not withdrawn from her and he was growing hard again. She closed her eyes, enjoying the sensation.

"It's amazing what a year of abstinence can do," he murmured, and fell to devouring her once more.

Neither of them made any pretensions to innocence. They did not discuss their romantic histories, or talk about the future they knew they could not share. Instead, they devoted the night to enjoying each other, to giving—and taking—as much pleasure as possible in the hours before dawn.

Thus it was that when Bas rapped on Nik's door, to warn him it was time for him to be up and dressing if he intended to be in the square before the Solstice ceremony began, Carol stretched beside her lover, and kissed his cheek and the scar on his chest and then his mouth, and did not feel the least bit injured or insulted when he rolled away from her and got out of bed and began to dress.

She lay watching him in the light of the now-guttering candles, knowing an inner peace and completion she had never experienced before. As during the hours of the night, so now in these few moments before the festival day began, she did not think of any other time or place or person. There was only Nik.

"You'd better hurry," he urged, seeing her with the coarse green blanket pulled up to her chin. "The square becomes crowded and it's often hard to find a place to stand where you can see what is happening."

Breakfast was a simple meal, only a chunk of coarse brown bread left from the previous night and a cup of hot, flavored water that Bas called tea, but that tasted like no tea Carol had ever drunk before. She thought it was a mixture of dried herbs rather than real tea, but without complaint she swallowed it for its warmth and to wash down the dry bread.

With Jo's help Bas was already preparing the feast, and the kitchen was surprisingly warm. Carol noticed that there was an oven built into the chimney, and presumably this oven was being heated in advance. Bas trussed up the chicken the women had purchased the day before and placed it into a roasting pan. With so small a bird there was room left in the pan for plenty of the root vegetables that made up most of the diet at this cold season of the year. Peeled chunks of turnips, parsnips, carrots, and potatoes went in around the chicken. Bas threw some chopped onions on top and Jo sprinkled in a few herbs. Then the lid was secured and the whole thing put into the waiting oven.

"It will cook slowly and be ready to eat by

noontime," Jo said to Carol. "I have made the bread already, and Nik is donating wine from his mysterious cellars down below."

"Then the sweets to finish the meal," Pen added.

"If we took away your sweets, would you celebrate the season as happily?" asked Jo, laughing.

"Probably not," Pen admitted. She sent a wink toward her brother, and winked at Carol, too.

Still laughing, they all left the warmth of the kitchen for the damp chill of the pre-dawn square.

"Is it always so cold in winter?" Carol asked Nik. They were picking their way through the debris that lay around Marlowe House. With the others well ahead of them, Carol did not think anyone would overhear what she said to Nik.

"Sometimes, it's colder," Nik answered. When he spoke, his breath formed a frosty cloud.

"During my time, December is much milder in this city." Carol stopped talking while she negotiated a climb up a mound of broken masonry and a sliding descent along the other side of it. "What kind of bombs were used in the wars? Could the detonations have sent enough dust into the upper atmosphere to cool the climate?"

"I don't know. It may be so." Nik's voice turned bitter. "There is entirely too much we are not told. I hope that particular situation will change soon, so we will have the information we want and need. Car, I must warn you. Be careful what you say while we are outside the house. There will be many civil guards in the square during the celebration. Some of them will not be in uniform."

"I understand. I won't mention forbidden subjects again. May I ask questions about the ceremony?"

"If you phrase them carefully and whisper them to me." They were past the debris and onto the flat, paved expanse of the square. Nik took Carol's arm. "Stay close to me."

There were no artificial lights. Only the faintly brightening sky lit their way as they crossed the square toward the World Tree at its center. A row of civil guards in helmets and brown overcoats kept open a circular area around the Tree, allowing no one to approach the metal artifact. There was no pushing or shoving, and the crowd was for the most part a quiet one. Only the occasional cry of a baby broke through the soft murmur of whispering voices and the shuffling sound made by many pairs of booted feet. The sky grew infinitesimally lighter, and an air of heightened expectation rippled across the crowd.

"Here they come," Pen whispered to Carol. She and Al were standing next to Carol and Nik, but in the semidarkness Carol could not discern the presence of anyone else she knew. Presumably, Bas, Jo, Luc, and the rest of Nik's group had melted into the throng.

At a nod from the officer commanding the civil guards the crowd separated, opening an aisle from one corner of the square to its center. Along this aisle walked a procession of notables. A man in flowing golden robes came first. Beneath his gold headdress his face was solemn as that of any priest, and Carol quickly decided that must be what he was. Behind him walked two women in sky-blue gowns. Since they were not shivering, Carol wondered if they were wearing thermal underwear. Her own hands and feet were fast reaching a state of numbness, and she could not see how anyone could move so lightly while wearing gowns so sheer and loose unless there were an unapparent source of warmth.

"The next person is one of the Leaders." Nik spoke to Carol in a voice just above a whisper. "His name is Fal."

He was a plump, pompous-looking fellow with a slight limp. His tunic, trousers, and boots were all a deep shade of red, and a round medal of some kind hung from a heavy chain to rest on his too-wide chest. He was surrounded by a dozen or so attendants in black and gray. A collection of civil guards in brown and another group of military types in gray uniforms ended the procession.

"The Leader's personal guard," Nik murmured into Carol's ear. "We have only one Leader with us today. The other two are celebrating elsewhere."

The actual ceremony did not take long. This was doubtless because of the astronomical requirements of the Solstice, since sunrise only lasted for a few minutes, but Carol could not help wondering if the biting cold played its part to keep the participants moving through their roles with brisk efficiency. The priest in the gold robes approached the World Tree and began a singsong incantation which, after a few verses, was taken up by the women in blue and then, gradually, by the rest of the people in the square. As if at the command of the man who stood with golden arms outstretched, the sky began to take on a touch of yellowish dawn color. Against this pale shade the fingers of the World Tree arched upward, pleading.

"Our square is used for this ceremony," Nik informed Carol in a low voice, "because, thanks to the destructive wars, from here we have a direct view of the horizon for the midwinter sunrise."

No sooner had he finished speaking than the upper rim of the sun began to rise above the horizon. At the exact moment when the first ray of sunlight shone forth, the Orb appeared.

It came out of nowhere, an enormous golden-orange sphere with a metallic sheen to its surface. Carol heard no sound from it, and while she had admittedly been watching the sunrise and the priest, still she was sure the Orb had not come gradually. It simply materialized in the air above the square as if by magic and hung there, motionless. The people standing beneath the Orb gaped at it, murmuring their wonderment in hushed, reverent voices.

Very clever, Carol thought, appreciating the effect the Orb was having upon the crowd, though she could not participate in the emotions it was evoking in most of the onlookers.

Does it have an engine inside it and perhaps a pilot, or is it moved by remote control, like one of those toy airplanes that people fly in the park on Sundays? Since Carol could discern no break in the smooth surface of the Orb to indicate a door by which a pilot might enter, she decided the object must be moved by remote control. And a very precise control, too, to judge by its subsequent motions.

After a few minutes the hovering Orb began to move. Slowly it descended, sinking toward the square with remarkable timing. Exactly as the disk of the sun stood full upon the southeastern horizon, the Orb settled into the waiting arms of the World Tree. The metal fingers curved around it, holding it securely in place.

A cheer went up from the crowd. Some laughed, others openly wept for joy, still others did both. Carol noted with some cynicism that the Leader and his guards were among the few who stood unmoved by the spectacle.

"And now," intoned the gold-clad priest, speaking above the soft, continuing chanting of the women in blue, "now the Solstice is upon us. Cold winter's end can be foreseen. From this moment onward, the days will grow longer. Now we can be certain that spring will in truth come, and with the returning warmth all life will be renewed." Again he raised his arms toward the Tree.

"Now we see with great thanksgiving the Blessed Orb held within the Sacred Embrace of the World Tree, which will keep it secure for us and not let its warmth and light flee from us."

He went on in this way for some time, but Carol soon grew tired of listening to his repetitious invocations. She tugged at Nik's arm, and when he bent his head to her, she whispered her question in his ear.

"Do people actually believe the sun is held fast like that, in the branches of a tree?"

"I am sure some do believe it," he replied. "It makes a pretty picture. Once in late afternoon I saw the branches of a dead tree against the setting sun, and what I beheld looked much like the Orb resting in the World Tree. Were this ceremony presented to us as a symbol only, I could accept it, for it's true enough that the days will now begin to grow longer. But this worship of Tree and Orb is a state religion and no other beliefs are allowed. Men and women have died for saying it ought to be otherwise."

"So this Government practices religious as well as political oppression."

"Do not say so here," Nik cautioned, and Carol obediently fell silent.

Once the ceremony was over and the officials marched away in another solemn procession, the atmosphere in the square changed. A young man pulled a homemade flute from beneath his jacket and began to play a cheerful tune. Someone else had brought along a small drum, and now began to keep time on it with his hands. A third fellow produced a stringed instrument on which he plucked out a soft harmony to the flutist's song.

A woman began to sing. She was joined by a second and then by a third voice. This was nothing like the formal chanting during the ceremony. This was folk music, cheerful and boisterous, requiring the clapping of many hands. The musicians played louder, providing backup for the song the women were singing.

Then the dancing started. Luc appeared, to

clasp hands with Pen and Carol. Al grabbed Pen's free hand and Nik was on Carol's other side. A woman Carol did not know moved next to Nik, a man joined the woman, and so it went, hands linked into a circle for a community dance. Around and around the square they went, first in a circle and then in a long, spiral line, always with the World Tree and Orb at their center. Knowledge of the exact steps was unimportant. It was only necessary to keep up with the other dancers.

They generated their own heat. A cloud of exhaled breath hung over the square. Above the heads of the dancers the Orb glowed orange-gold where the low rays of the midwinter sun struck it, and seemed to shed both warmth and light on those gathered to celebrate the beginning of its slow return from southern regions.

There followed a period of perhaps an hour when Carol felt at one with the emotions of the people around her who were dancing and singing so joyfully. This future world was so gray and bleak, and so restrictive, that the cold and rain and snow of winter represented a real additional hardship in most lives. The turning of the year brought with it fresh hope. No doubt summer held other miseries—excessive heat, vermin, diseases—but from the depths of winter that other, warmer, season appeared to be one of bright promise, fresh food, and an end to numbing cold and dampness. If they could not drink down the darkness as the ancient Vikings had once tried to do, these people would sing and dance away the year's shortest day and longest night.

Shortly after midday the weather brought an end to outdoor celebrating. For all its golden brightness, the sun was too low in the sky to be able to shed much genuine warmth upon the northern half of the world. After hours in the cold, noses were red and dripping, and lips had become too stiff and blue for more singing. The crowd broke into smaller groups, families or clusters of friends heading homeward for their holiday meal. As if to signal the official end of the morning's celebration, a troop of civil guards marched through the square in tight formation, ignoring the people, staring straight ahead, scattering merrymakers to the left and right.

While adults and teenagers had been dancing, the children too small to join in were left to play at one side of the square under the care of elderly men and women. Now parents hastened to collect their children, and a few of the young ones, seeing mothers and fathers coming toward them, ran to meet their parents.

The civil guards continued their march, knocking down a couple of little boys along the way. A murmur of irritation erupted from the grown-ups. The guards did not stop or change direction, but marched straight on toward the other side of the square. Directly in their path stood a child perhaps three or four years old, so heavily bundled in jackets and sweaters and scarves that it was impossible to tell if it was a boy or a girl. The child appeared to be frozen in place, staring at the oncoming guards out of huge, round eyes.

"No!" Carol saw what was happening and

knew the guards would not stop. They had already knocked down a few children; one more would be nothing to them. They did not care about the civilians in the square. Ordinary folk were unimportant to them. And for some reason—were they too cowed by the guards and thus afraid to react?—Carol knew no one was going to stop the inevitable collision. Nik was talking to someone, his back turned to the scene. Carol could not see anyone else who might help, and time was running out.

She moved forward, running toward the child on cold-numbed feet, pushing aside the few people who stood between her and the innocent who would be knocked to the ground and perhaps trampled.

"Stop, damn you! You bloody lunatic!" She saw the total lack of concern in the eyes of the guards' commander and knew her cry was wasted. The guards would not stop. Throwing out her arms she scooped up the child and kept on running. The guards marched on out of the square.

The whole incident had lasted for only a few moments, and during that time Carol's eyes had connected with those of the guards' commander for but a second, yet she was more chilled by the encounter than she was from hours spent outside in the cold of winter. Something about the commander's indifferent expression and his blank eyes that saw nothing except his path directly across the square tugged at Carol's mind. She did not know the man—had never seen him before—yet in a vague, illogical way she *recognized* him. And feared him as if he had laid a curse on her.

"Car!" Nik was beside her, and with him was the woman who had taken his hand when the dancing started, who seemed to know him.

"Sue!" The woman seized the now-weeping child from Carol's arms. "I didn't see what was happening. I thought she was still with the elders."

"Are you all right?" Nik asked Carol. She nodded, unable to speak for a moment because she was shaking in reaction to what had just happened.

"How can I thank you?" The woman put out a hand to Carol. "Sue is everything to me. She's all I have since my husband died."

Leaving it to Nik to answer the woman, Carol tried to get her emotions back under control. She could not go to pieces here in public.

"I don't think she's hurt." Nik turned his attention from Carol to the child. "She is well padded with clothing and, thanks to Car, the guards didn't touch her. Car, this is Lin, who is—a very good friend."

The emphasis he put on the last phrase of his introduction told Carol that Lin was a member of one of the other dissident groups. Lin would probably be involved in the coming uprising.

"I understand," Carol said, meeting Lin's eyes. "You do not want any harm to come to your child. You want her to be safe, and happy."

Lin nodded, hugging little Sue close to her bosom.

"Take her home and see that she's warm," Nik said. "Do you have a holiday sweet for her?"

"Oh, no." Lin looked a bit embarassed. "I

271

could not afford any sweets. There was barely enough money for food."

"Wait here." Nik sprinted toward Marlowe House, disappearing behind a mound of broken bricks and stone when he ran down the servants' steps. He soon returned, bringing one of the miniature sugar trees from the selection Pen had bought at the market.

"Every child should have a sweet at Solstice," Nik said, giving the sugar tree to Sue. He had taken off his heavy gloves, and now he stroked one finger across the little girl's soft cheek. The gentle tenderness of the action caught at Carol's heart. Sue stuffed the bottom of the tree into her mouth, and Nik chuckled at her obvious pleasure in the taste of it.

"Thank you, Nik," Lin began. He cut off her words.

"Just be certain she's safe," he said, and both women heard the double meaning in his caution. If Lin was going to be a participant in the uprising, her child would have to be placed with people who would be willing to hide her identity in case her mother was killed or captured.

"She goes to a friend tomorrow night," Lin said. Watching her walk away, Nik put an arm around Carol's shoulders.

"Those terrible civil guards," Carol said. "Nik, their commander stared right at me and the look in his eyes terrified me. I could almost hear the wheels turning in his brain. He knew he didn't recognize me and knew I did not belong here. Is there a chance that my presence could cause trouble for you?"

"I don't think it will matter," Nik said.

"People from outside the city come here for the Solstice celebrations. There are always strangers in the square during holidays. One more will make no difference."

"I yelled at him. I cursed him," she persisted. "He will know me if he sees me again." *And I will know him. Why does the thought fill me with dread?*

"There is nothing to worry about. You are cold and tired and upset by seeing a child almost hurt." Nik headed toward Marlowe House, taking Carol along with him, an arm still across her shoulders. "Come inside now. Jo is piling wood on the fire as if we had a room full of logs to spare, instead of just the remains of broken furniture. You will soon be warm, and a glass of wine and a good meal will lift your spirits."

Carol went with him willingly, giving her hearty agreement to the prospect of once more being warm. In the kitchen they discovered the food Bas had put into the oven early in the morning was nearly ready to eat. While the women prepared a salad from the greens Pen had selected on the previous day and Luc and another man set the table, Nik took Carol down to the lower levels of the house.

"There used to be a locked wine cellar down here," Carol told him. "Crampton the butler held the keys to it, and he guarded the wine as if it were gold. I have never been into these rooms before."

"I think they must have been useful as shelters during the wars. The wine is of more recent vintage than your time. Most of it is less than one hundred years old." Nik paused, holding high the oil lamp he had brought with him. Having found the section he wanted, he gave the lamp to Carol while he slid between the dusty racks to retrieve two bottles.

When he came out again he put up his hands, holding a bottle in each. With a wicked laugh and a comical leer he backed Carol against the stone retaining wall that formed the deepest foundation of Marlowe House. There he kissed her.

"You do have a tendency to play with fire," she noted, lifting the oil lamp until its flame was a fraction of an inch away from his chin. "First candles, now this."

"Hold it to one side," he suggested, "and I'll kiss you again more thoroughly."

"If the oil spills, the light will go out and we may be stuck down here for hours."

"Never so long." He was laughing at her. "The others are too hungry to wait for more than a few minutes for the wine to go with their dinner."

"Then we ought to go back upstairs at once."

"Not yet, Car. I have waited all day for this." An instant later his mouth was on hers a second time, and she lost herself in his lips and his tongue and the passionate heat of him. Carol's only regret was that, since he was still holding the wine bottles, he was not free to put his arms around her.

"Nik," said Pen's voice from above. "We are starving. The celebrations aren't over yet but we need our food and some wine if we are to continue." She was interrupted by Jo, who shouted down the stairs over Pen's gentler tones.

"Bas says to tell you he is serving the chicken and if you want any, you are to come at once. Delay and it will all be eaten."

"She's telling the truth," Carol said, laughing now herself. "It is not a very big chicken."

"You are asking me to make the supreme sacrifice," he said, leaning into her, letting her feel his hardness until she moaned softly. "Do not expect me to wait much longer to hold you." He kissed her again quite thoroughly before he released her and motioned for her to light their way out of the cellar and up the stairs.

Chapter Thirteen

Never before had Carol belonged to a group of people who, except for two or three of them, were within a few years of her own age, who joked among themselves and teased each other, and who showed open affection toward one another. The friendly, teasing remarks she and Nik received when they finally reappeared in the kitchen made her blush at first, and then made her happy to be where she was. She entered wholeheartedly into the spirit of the holiday meal.

To her surprise there was enough food. Each of the 12 people at the table received a small piece of chicken, and with the addition of plenty of vegetables and the fresh bread Jo had baked before sunrise, no one went hungry. The wine added to the party atmosphere. No one mentioned what was planned for the day after the holiday. The talk was mostly about social arrangements for the evening.

"There will be more celebrating in the square," Pen told Carol, "and some of us visit friends from house to house. You are welcome to come with us. We won't be home until very late."

"Some of us," said Luc, downing his second glass of wine, "won't return until tomorrow. Some of us have ladies to visit." Two of the other unattached men laughed with him.

"Before you go," said Pen, seemingly unperturbed by this declaration, "we have sweets to finish the meal." She produced a tray on which she had arranged a small forest of the sugar trees, each tree complete with an orange orb entangled in its branches. Pen placed the tray on the table in front of her brother and, with a grand flourish, pulled off the cloth covering it.

"Oh," Pen cried in dismay, "someone has taken a tree. Who would do such a thing?"

"I did," Nik said at once. "Lin had no sweet for Sue. I gave her mine."

"Nik, you would give away your winter coat if someone needed it," Pen declared. "Here, take mine, then. I don't really want it."

"Actually," said Carol, "I don't mean to insult your . . . taste in desserts, Pen, but those candies look absolutely disgusting to me and have since the first moment I saw them at the market. There is no way that I am going to eat one of them. So there will be enough, after all, and you won't have to do without."

"But you are a guest," Pen protested, openly

upset by this idea. "We owe you the best we can give."

"You—all of you—have already given me more than you will ever know," Carol told her. "Don't spoil my holiday now by forcing me to eat something I don't want and expecting me to be polite about it."

"Are you sure?" Pen sounded as if she could not believe this excuse, but she did cast a longing gaze upon the little trees left on the tray.

"Pen," said Nik, repressing a smile, "I have the strangest feeling that Car does not want a sweet."

"Really?"

Carol could almost see Pen's mouth watering. She pushed the tray across the table.

"Eat it," Carol said, "and stop arguing."

Watching Pen nibble at the edges of the sugar tree, tasting it slowly, savoring every bite, Carol was reminded of an earlier version of the young woman. Pen's character was similar to that of Lady Penelope Hyde, and Carol discovered that she felt the same protective affection toward Pen that she had felt for Penelope.

Nik and Carol were given kitchen cleanup duty with Bas that evening, which meant that Jo also remained behind when the others left the house to rejoin the Winter Solstice celebrations. Carol found there was something remarkably pleasant—and oddly romantic— about standing with her hands in a basin of water, washing dishes, and handing them to Nik to rinse in another basin and dry them. Meanwhile, Bas consigned the remains of the chicken to a large pot and began making soup for the next day's meal, and Jo moved about, putting dishes and leftover bread away and sweeping the floor.

"I feel right at home here," Carol said to Nik. "As if I belong. I never did have much of a family, except for a few days once, long ago."

"They like you, too." He accepted the soapy cup she offered, keeping his hand wrapped around hers for a moment more than was necessary. "It would make all of us, and especially me, happy if you were to stay here permanently."

"It won't be allowed." She had not confided to him the actual reason why she was in this future time, saying only that Aug had brought her there and would remove her when Aug decided the time was right. Since Nik was as convinced as every other member of his group that Lady Augusta was a witch with amazing powers, he did not dispute Carol's explanation.

"In that case, we ought to make the most of the time we have." The way he looked at her sent blood into her cheeks and made her knees weak. Her hands went still on the plate she was now washing. Nik's long fingers slid into the basin of warm, soapy water, curling around her wrist and into her palm.

"Nik, stop," she breathed, "or you will have more chipped crockery."

"Do you think it would matter to me?" With laughter crinkling the corners of his green eyes, he began to make little circling motions over her palm and wrist. "Warm and moist and smooth," he whispered, bending a little closer to her.

"Nik!" How could he do this to her, make

her ache for him without bestowing a single kiss on her mouth, without undressing her or touching her body? All of her erotic awareness was concentrated on her left hand and wrist. She thought she was going to faint.

He removed the plate from her unresisting fingers, rinsed and dried it, then turned back to her with an innocent, boyish grin.

"Have you any ideas on how you would like to continue our celebrating?" he asked.

Carol could not answer. She stood with both hands in the basin of cooling water, staring at him until Jo bustled up to them.

"All finished? I'll dump the water, then." Jo picked up the basin and headed for the pantry, where the only functional drain in the kitchen area was located. Because water was available from the taps for only an hour a day on a rotating schedule, the rinse water would not be thrown out. It would be saved in a big old kettle, to be heated and used as dishwashing water after the next meal.

Nik took the dish towel and began to dry Carol's hands. Still she could not speak. She thought he saw the answer to his question in her eyes.

"Well, I don't know about you two," Jo said, bringing back the empty basin, "but I have no intention of going outside into the cold again when I can stay here in the kitchen and be warm."

"I have a surprise for you." When Nik finally took his eyes away from Carol's face to speak to Jo, Carol felt the loss as an emptiness in her chest, as though an important prop had been removed from her. Nik spoke to Jo as if he were completely unaware of the effect he was having on Carol. "The other day I discovered a bottle of ancient brandy down in the cellar. Since this is a special Solstice, I think we ought to open it tonight."

"If you are going into the cellar again," said Jo, "then leave Car here. If she goes with you, we may not see either of you again until morning. If then."

"Shame on you, Jo. You are shocking our guest." Nik disappeared in the direction of the cellar steps.

"Are you shocked?" Jo asked Carol.

"No, just bewildered. I don't understand how he does what he does to me. Sorry," Carol added at once. "That was an awfully personal remark."

"You are not ashamed of what you're doing with him, are you, Car?"

"Not at all," Carol admitted. "In fact, I'm proud of it."

"Then don't apologize for what you feel." After a glance toward the cellar door and another toward Bas, who was tossing leftover vegetables into the soup pot with fine abandon and paying no attention at all to the two women, Jo continued. "I have been with this group for several years, and you are the first woman Nik has taken a romantic interest in. I have always thought his heart was locked away somewhere, hidden behind a barricade more sturdy than the one Bas pulls over the entrance each night. Nik has spent his life working against the Government in quiet, secret ways, and reading and studying old books that might give him clues as to how to invent a better kind of Leadership than the one we presently endure. In these last two days since you have joined us, he is openly happy. We have you to thank for the change.

"We all love him, Car," Jo went on, "but in the same way we love our brothers or our friends, because that has been the only kind of love Nik would allow from us. For his sake, I am glad you are here. Continue to make him happy. Make yourself happy, too, and don't regret what you do together."

"Thank you, Jo." Carol put out her hand to the other woman. Jo took it, squeezed it quickly, and then released her fingers as Nik returned to the kitchen.

"I'll get the glasses," Jo said. "Come on, Bas, you've added every leftover you could find to that soup pot. I thought you were supposed to boil the bones first and put in the vegetables later."

"I am trying something different this time." But Bas did leave his cooking to join the others at the kitchen table. Nik poured out the brandy and Bas sipped judiciously. "Excellent," he approved, nodding.

Carol thought the brandy was much too harsh and strong, and noticed Jo was also only sipping hers, but the men seemed to enjoy it. The tension between herself and Nik remained beneath the surface during half an hour of companionable talk. Nik's hand brushed hers a few times, and his knee pressed against her thigh when he leaned across the table to pour more brandy for Bas and then sat back again. To the casual glance all four of them were relaxed, but Carol could not help wondering if Jo noticed her growing breathlessness or the way she'd ceased to contribute to the conversation. And yet she was oddly content to sit at the table listening to the others and knowing that before much longer she and Nik would be alone together. After a while, as she was certain he would, Nik stood up, drawing Carol with him.

"Take care of the brandy, Bas," he said, indicating the bottle.

"I shall hide it in my room," Bas replied. "Perhaps tomorrow all of us will drink a toast with it to the success of our project."

"Good night." Jo was standing behind Bas with her hand on his shoulder, but her eyes were on Carol and Nik as they left the kitchen.

"This has been the strangest evening," Carol murmured, following Nik up the stairs and coming out at the back of the main hall. She paused, looking around at the cracked black and white marble floor and the old paneling, both lit by the oil lamps kept burning there. "It's as though the dozen or so people who live in this house are family members, as though I have known them for a long time. Bas and Jo are like an older aunt and uncle. And you and I could be—"

"A couple who have lived together for years?" Nik finished for her when she hesitated. "Yes, I felt it, too. To me, the most precious component of your presence here is that it does not seem at all strange." He caressed her cheek with a light, quick gesture.

"What I feel for you, Car, is not just sexual desire, though that particular element can be overpowering at times. But there is something

283

more than desire between us. You are the companion of my heart. If we could live into old age together, even if we should reach a time when we are too feeble for lovemaking, still, just being with you would be joy enough. To see you, to hear your voice and know the touch of your hand on mine, would content me until the end of my life."

He stood back to let her pass into his room ahead of him. Carol stopped just inside the door, thinking that he deserved a better setting than this shabby cubicle of a bedchamber. There was only one thing she could say in response to the passionate declaration he had just made.

"I love you, Nik." It was all she had to give him.

"Then I am blessed," he said. His kiss was light and almost unbearably tender. Carol leaned against him, satisfied for the moment just to have his arms around her. No more was needed. Seldom in her life had anyone spoken to her as Nik spoke. In her past she had heard little praise, so what he said next was precious to her.

"It was a brave thing you did this day, Car. Were it not for you, Sue might have been badly injured by those uncaring brutes of civil guards."

"Anyone who noticed what was about to happen would have done the same," she murmured, her face against his chest. At his mention of the guards she thought again of the cold eyes of their commander. She tried to force the image of the commander's face out of her mind. By thinking only of Nik and what he was saying, she almost succeeded.

"But no one else did take action, Car. Most people are too used to deferring to the guards ever to stand up to them or to protest the way they expect others to get out of their path when they are going somewhere. Only you were courageous enough to defy them." She felt Nik's lips on her hair before he continued. "And then you gave up your sweet so Pen could have one. It was I who should have gone without, since it was my own sweet I gave to Sue."

"I didn't want that sticky thing and you knew it," she said, laughing now. "I am not as unselfish as you seem to think."

"I believe differently." He took her by the shoulders, holding her a little away from him, searching her face for her reaction to his words. "Car, I want a promise from you."

"Anything I can do for you, I will," she said at once.

"Promise me that when you return to your own time, you will do everything you can to keep the spirit of love and friendship and compassion toward others alive, as it is alive in you now. You can change this terrible future into something beautiful, if only you are willing to try."

"You can't really believe I have that much power?" she cried, astonished by what he was saying, and frightened, too, by the responsibility he was laying on her.

"I *know* you have the power," he said. "I believe that is why Aug has brought you to us. She wants you to see what this future world is like, and then she will advise you on how to change it."

285

"Nik—" she began to protest, but he cut her off.

"Why else would Aug bring you to this time?" he asked.

To prove to me what a selfish, self-centered, uncaring creature I had become. To show me how wrong I was, and how little I knew about the important things in life.

"If I could change the future," she said aloud, thinking through the idea as she spoke, "then this time, where you and your sister and friends live right now, would be different—so different that you might not even exist." The realization terrified her.

"I will be here no matter what you do," Nik said. "And we will meet. Perhaps, if you change your time and thus the future, then I will not have to lose you the way I always have in my dreams. The way I will lose you in this life, when the time comes for you to go home." He pulled her closer against him and spoke with a heartfelt intensity that made Carol accept what he was saying.

"Of this I am absolutely certain, Car. Throughout all time, you and I will meet and love again and again. It was meant to be so. And when time is finished and timeless Eternity begins, you and I will be together. Then, our souls will be one, as I believe they were one before ever time began." The hand with which he stroked her hair was infinitely tender.

"I could endure anything," she whispered, "even a separation of centuries, if I thought there was a chance that we could some day be together permanently."

"Believe in that possibility as I do," he said. "And when we are temporarily parted, keep the promise I ask of you."

"I will." She looked into his eyes and smiled through the brimming tears. "Not only because you ask it of me, Nik, but because I have come to understand how intertwined are past, present, and future. And how important every act of kindness is."

"And acts of love," he murmured.

"You are my love. You always have been. You always will be."

"That is exactly what I have been saying."

They undressed each other slowly, oblivious to the frosty temperature of his room. Carol stood trembling on tiptoe to wind her arms around his neck and kiss him. He was a good six inches taller than she and his shoulders were broad and hard with muscle. Overall, he was not bulky despite his strength. He was tough and lean and intensely masculine.

There was no ignoring his masculinity. It pressed hard against her when he drew her upward into his arms. The more thoroughly he kissed her, the harder and hotter it grew, until she felt as if there were a flaming poker jammed between their bodies. She knew how to quench his heat, and knew he would soon take that way.

With his arms still locked around her Nik began a series of dancing steps across the bedroom floor, waltzing Carol backward until her legs touched the side of his bed. When she giggled at the erotic effect of this motion, he kissed her hard and long, drinking in her laughter and replacing it with mounting desire.

Flora Speer

Slowly they sank down together upon the bed. The rough olive blanket scratched Carol's back, but she did not care. Nik's hands were on her, caressing, tormenting, and now she knew what he had been doing all afternoon and evening long. From his delicious, teasing kisses in the wine cellar to the heated looks he sent her way and those secretive touches during dinner, to his playful handling of her while she was washing dishes, and yes, even during the apparently calm conversation over brandy with Bas and Jo—during all of those hours, in the only ways open to him with other people near, he had been wooing her and making her feel safe and secure so that when they reached this moment she would want him as badly as he wanted her. Every cell of her body thrilled to his knowing touch, until she wondered if the brandy she had consumed was flowing through her veins undiluted.

He was on her and in her and she was pulsating to his smallest movement. It was all slow and tender and yet very *determined*. He never stopped moving, but kept stroking firmly in and out of her, and it seemed to her that he could go on forever with the same slow, steady motion. She became aware of the painful way in which her body was beginning to tighten, her muscles automatically growing tense and ready. She smoothed her hands down his spine, arching her back to push herself against him as he came into her once more.

"Closer," she muttered, cupping his buttocks in both hands, pulling him to her. He did as she asked, thrusting deep, then going rigid, poised and waiting.

This time she did not explode. Her climax was more devastating than any mere explosion. She melted. The heat and tenseness that had been congealing so painfully between her thighs in response to Nik's continuing motions flowed out of her and she let it go, a soft moan her only outward indiction of the rhythmic tremors that were shaking her innermost body.

Nik knew at once what was happening. How could he not know when he was buried so deep inside her that he could feel her every quiver? He groaned, calling her name over and over. He thrust hard one more time, and then he lay still above her. They were both trembling, unable to speak. All they could do was touch lips to lips, over and over, drinking from an inexhaustible supply of love and longing, and also tasting in those kisses the certainty of coming separation.

The next day, which was the last of the three-day Winter Solstice celebration, was a quiet one at Marlowe House. Those who had gone out the previous evening slept late. Nor did Nik and Carol rise early, preferring to spend the morning hours in each other's arms in the private world they had created within his room. However, shortly after noon everyone assembled for the main meal of the day. Luc and a couple of his friends were still somewhat bleary-eyed. Pen claimed to be suffering from an upset stomach, which Nik immediately told her was the result of eating too many sweets. Pen recovered quickly when she saw the feast intended for the final meal of the holiday.

Bas first presented a truly remarkable soup. The highly flavored broth contained all the remaining chunks of chicken meat he could pick off the bones, along with a wild assortment of vegetables. The soup alone would have been enough to satisfy Carol's appetite, but there was also a rice pilaf made with spices and herbs and, like the soup, eaten with loaves of Jo's fresh-baked bread. Marveling that Bas and Jo between them could create meal after delicious meal using an inadequate supply of not always fresh food, Carol discovered that she did have room left for the pilaf after her bowl of soup was empty.

The sugar trees having all been eaten on the first day of the holiday, dessert was a baked concoction of apples and raisins, flavored with a bit of the ancient brandy that Nik had left in Bas's care, and topped with cinnamon-spiced crumbs of the previous day's bread.

"There is even some cream to pour over it," Jo said, setting a pitcher down on the table. "But share it, because there isn't any more."

"I have noticed how freely you use spices," Carol said to Bas. "Does the Government by any chance hold the spice monopoly?"

"Who else would hold it?" Bas demanded with cynical humor. "We are encouraged to use all spices freely, but especially cinnamon. The Government must have its profits, though I must say, the spices do improve the flavor of inferior food."

"Just as spices did in the Middle Ages," Carol noted. Bas did not seem to hear her. He went on with his complaints about the available food.

"Last fall we bought a basket of apples and

290

stored them in the cellar, but already they are so bruised and rotting that the only way to use them is to cut them up and cook them in puddings or applesauce. I can remember when good apples would last for most of the winter if they were kept cold."

"Obviously, the Government's food distribution system isn't what it should be. Do you ever get oranges?" Carol thought of all the fresh fruits and vegetables she had seen heaped into the grocers' bins at holiday time in the world into which she had been born. She had always taken such lavish displays for granted. She wondered how Bas would react if she could show him the food halls at Harrods. Bas snorted in disgust at her question.

"If there are any oranges," he said, "the Great Leaders keep them to themselves. I ate an orange once, years ago when I was a boy. I have never forgotten the taste of it."

"There is another reason for wanting to change the present Government," Carol said. "Just think of the dishes you could create if fresh produce were shipped here from other parts of the world in winter. Judging by the meals I have eaten in this kitchen, you have the potential to be a world-class chef, Bas."

"All of which reminds me," Nik said. "I wasn't going to call another meeting before we move tomorrow, but since every one of us is here, perhaps we ought to go through the plan once more, to be sure no one has forgotten his part because of too eager participation in the holiday." He sent a stern look in the direction of Luc and his friends.

"We haven't forgotten," said Luc, "nor did we

talk too much while we were out last night. Our plan is too important for us to chance being caught through carelessness."

"I am relieved to hear you say so." Nik gave Luc a brief smile. "Begin by reciting your part."

Carol listened with growing excitement to what her new friends were saying. Lady Augusta had disappeared shortly after bringing her to this time, but when Carol interrupted the discussion to mention her absence, neither Nik nor the others seemed to think it was odd. Nik pointed out that "Aug" was a witch and thus was free to come and go as she wanted.

Carol had her own explantion for Lady Augusta's absence, though she kept it to herself. There was a lesson Carol was expected to learn in this time, and what that lesson was she would have to figure out for herself, rather than having Lady Augusta direct her. Carol was rapidly coming to the conclusion that the lesson had something to do with Nik's plan. He and his friends were going to attempt on the morrow to begin to fan the underground flames of resentment against a strict and uncaring Government into an open, widespread rebellion, and then into a full-scale revolution they were hoping would produce major changes in the social and political system. Carol believed she was expected to be part of those changes.

When Bas brought the bottle of brandy out of its hiding place in his bedroom and poured a small amount into the cup or glass of each person present, Carol stood with the rest for Nik's toast.

"To the success of our venture." Nik raised his glass.

"We know the cost will be high," Al added, looking from face to face and then putting an arm around Pen. "We believe our goal is worth the risk, and we trust you, Nik."

"Hear, hear," cried Luc.

Upon that signal they all swallowed the fiery stuff. On this evening, in such company, the brandy did not seem to Carol at all harsh or strong. She drained her glass at a gulp, and set it down with a sense of rightness and in complete certainty of belonging.

In late afternoon they all went out to the square again, this time to witness the ceremony as the Orb left the World Tree until the next holiday.

The line of sight was not as clear for sunset as for sunrise, because the remains of several buildings, including Marlowe House, blocked the actual horizon. Still, the same participants marched into the square and took their places as on the previous day. This time the priest was in dark blue robes, and the female chorus of two was gowned in black with silver stars scattered across the fabric. The women glittered with every movement they made. Carol assumed these costumes were meant to represent the night sky that would be visible once the sun had set and the Orb had gone. The obese Leader Fal, who again came with the priest and the women, was wearing for the occasion an outfit in a bright shade of green, which did nothing to compliment his sallow skin.

The priest began to chant, the women joined

him, and just as the sun slipped behind Marlowe House, the branches of the World Tree released their grip on the Orb. Slowly, silently, the Orb rose out of the metal tree and drifted upward into the clear, early evening sky.

Made curious once more by the quiet and effortless motion of the Orb, Carol decided she was going to watch it in order to discover where it went. The priest rattled on, sermonizing about the Orb returning to bless the people at the Spring Equinox celebrations just three months hence. Carol was paying little attention to him or to anyone else. She was keeping her eyes on the rising Orb. The setting sun reflected off its smooth surface, casting a bit of additional light into the square.

Nik gripped Carol's arm so hard that she unwillingly looked away from the Orb to discover what was wrong. Nik's face was set and grim, and he was staring toward the group of officials who were standing around the World Tree. When Carol looked upward again, the Orb was gone.

"Where did it go?" she asked. "It just vanished."

"Never mind the Orb," Nik said. "Don't look toward the Tree, but you are being watched."

"By whom?" Carol froze, not wanting to look anywhere at all until she found out why Nik was so upset that he would hurt her. He was still holding her upper arm in a tight grip.

"The commander of the civil guards," he said, scarcely moving his lips. "The man who was leading the troops who nearly marched over Sue yesterday."

"The man I swore at," Carol added, shivering at the memory.

"The same. He has been staring at you all through the ceremony."

"What shall we do?" Thinking fast, Carol went on. "If I go back to the house with you and he comes after me, you could be in trouble. We cannot jeopardize your plans, Nik."

"I will take you to Lin's house," Nik decided. "She will welcome you and keep you safe. Come with me now."

"No." Carol planted her feet firmly and refused to move. "I am not going anywhere with you, because to do so would show the guards commander that we know each other. At the moment all he knows for certain is that we are standing next to one another, which in this crowd means nothing. If I get into trouble over what I did yesterday and that man thinks there is a connection between us, then you could be blamed, too. You cannot afford to be picked up by the police for questioning, Nik."

"Then I will find someone else to go with you."

"I'm glad you aren't arguing about going with me yourself, but I am leaving this square alone. I won't involve anyone in your group in any trouble I may have with the civil guards," she insisted. "I used to be familiar with London. I'm sure I can still find my way around your Lond. I will go now, before the ceremony ends. That man won't be so likely to come charging after me if he has to make a scene by leaving his official duties to do it. After all, I haven't actually done anything illegal. It's just that he is suspicious of me because I am a stranger. Look the other way, Nik, and I'll slip away now and return to Marlowe House after the ceremony is over and the square is clear."

"Please, Car, be careful." She heard the tension and the fear for her in his voice.

"I'll see you in a little while," she told him, hoping with all her heart that what she said was true.

Chapter Fourteen

Carol stepped behind Nik's taller, heavily clothed bulk. He moved to stand squarely in front of her, so his body would block her from the sight of anyone standing near the World Tree. With Nik shielding her, it was easy enough for her to work her way backward among people who were all focused on the ceremony. No one gave her more than a glance and she kept her face down, hoping thus to make identification more difficult. If it came to that; if the guards commander demanded to know who she was. At the thought of confronting the man dread blossomed anew within her, along with a premonition of coming horror. There was no time to dwell on such thoughts. Her immediate aim was to get out of the square.

She reached the corner of the square. Marlowe House lay half a block away on her left. In Carol's imagination the house beckoned to her, promising a safety she was not willing to seek. If she were being watched, the last thing she wanted to do was draw attention to the house where Nik and his friends lived. A street opened before her, leading away from the square. It headed westward and Carol took it. The crowd thinned out as she put more distance between herself, the World Tree, and the ceremony taking place at the foot of the Tree.

By now she was fairly sure the guards commander would not know where she had gone, but she wanted to stay well away from Marlowe House for a while. And, she reminded herself, she would have to be extremely careful not to be seen by the commander a third time. There was something about the way he looked at her with his cold, almost mechanical gaze that sent chills along her spine. Her every instinct told her the commander was a man who would listen to no excuses and who would show no mercy.

It was growing darker by the minute. The ceremony must be completed by now. This supposition on Carol's part was confirmed by the number of people who began to hurry past her. They all wore a deflated, post-holiday air about them that was much like the after-Christmas letdown she had noticed on the faces of people in her own time.

Carol had always felt superior to those sad souls. Since she did not believe in celebrating Christmas and expected nothing from the day, she was never disappointed by a lack of holiday cheer in her own life, and thus the days immediately following the end of the festive season were the same to her as any other day of a monotonous year.

Now she was sorry for the poorly dressed, shivering folk who were wending their way homeward through the steadily increasing cold. Furthermore, she was aware of a sense of kinship with them. She was as haphazardly attired as any of the people around her, and she was shivering, too.

She picked up her pace, wanting to lose herself in the anonymity of the growing throng pouring out of the square. Since the official celebrants and the civil guards apparently used only one route for their processions to and from the World Tree, Carol did not think she would be followed along this other street, but it seemed a good idea to try to make herself appear to be just as dejected as everyone else at the end of the holiday. Not having any real destination in mind, she continued on toward the west.

After a while she noticed that the press of people around her was thinning out as men and women turned off the main road and into smaller streets and alleys.

"Better get out of the way," cautioned a man who brushed by her with a child in his arms. "Here come the guards. You don't want to be caught blocking their path."

"Thanks. I wasn't paying attention." Quickly Carol followed the man into a dark side street.

"You lost?" the man asked, not pausing in his rapid stride when he glanced at her through the shadows.

"I took the wrong street out of the square,"

Carol said. "After the guards go by I'll head back again. I'm sure I can find my way home."

"Just be careful of the guards, and get indoors as soon as you can. You know how tough they can be on stragglers after a holiday ends."

"Right. Thanks again." Carol watched the man and his child fade into the darkness and disappear. Wanting no meeting with the civil guards, she took his warning to heart and waited, pressed tight against the side of a building, until the sound of tramping, booted feet passed away into the darkness. On returning to the wider street she saw how few people remained on it. Making a hasty decision she hurried across this street.

Reasoning that if she periodically located the broad street she knew it would keep her on course even in the bewildering darkness, she began to work her way back toward Marlowe House along narrower, secondary streets which would offer better shelter than the main road to anyone who wanted to stay out of sight.

She had reckoned without the winding alleys and the dead-end mews. Certain sections of London had undergone great changes in 175 years. The main thoroughfares might be the same, but the side streets once so familiar to her had been bombed out and rebuilt several times before the last bout of general destruction. Ruined buildings and the inevitable heaps of broken stone and brick impeded her progress. The twists and turnings she was forced to take around these obstacles were confusing her sense of direction. She was sure several hours must have elapsed since she had left Nik, and she knew he would be worrying about her.

At last admitting she was lost, Carol decided her best option was to continue in what she by now could only hope was the right direction and pray that she would soon come upon a familiar landmark. In the meantime, though being careful would slow her down, she would have to try to keep out of sight. In one way, it would be easy enough to do. There was almost no one abroad to notice her. On the other hand, if any of the civil guards came along they would see her at once and she would be arrested.

"I hate this," she muttered under her breath. "I used to walk all over this part of London without worrying about meeting policemen. Then, I thought of the police as friends and protectors of honest citizens. What a disgusting world this has become. And if I don't get back to Marlowe House soon, Nik will be so upset. My absence might even cause him to delay the beginning of his plan. Where in this messed-up city *is* Marlowe House? Oh, at last!"

This exclamation burst from her as she walked into an open square. Almost immediately she saw it was not the square she sought. Here, the houses were not damaged. There were no piles of rubble for her to pick her way around, but instead a smoothly paved street. The square itself contained no World Tree. What Carol saw was a collection of large vehicles parked in neat rows filling up most of the open space. Each of these machines looked as if it could transport six or eight people comfortably.

"Limousines," Carol said, peering through a windshield to look inside one of them. "Not exactly like the twentieth-century version, but so luxurious they couldn't be anything else."

It did not take much guesswork to discover the reason why so many limousines were parked in one place. In one of the fine houses fronting the square there was a party in progress.

After ducking behind a car so she would not be seen, Carol made a quick survey of the area. There was a bonfire at the side of the square most distant from her, and around the blaze a group of men stood or sat. From their neat outfits in various dark colors, very different from ordinary clothing, these men appeared to be the chauffeurs of the parked limousines, awaiting the call to drive their employers home at the end of the evening. They had a good supply of food and drink available, and were talking and singing rather loudly. A half-dozen men in the brown uniform of the civil guards kept a casual watch on them.

Unlike the neighborhood around Marlowe House, here there was electricity. The square was well lit by ornate street lamps and every house blazed with light. Directly in front of Carol was the mansion in which the party was being held. Through the wide front windows she could see people moving about inside. Curiosity making her bolder, she lifted her head to look over the top of the car.

That the rooms inside the house were warm was obvious from the clothing worn by the women present. Sheer, gauzy gowns revealed arms and throats and, in several cases, great expanses of snowy bosoms. All the women flaunted glittering earrings, necklaces, bracelets, rings, and tiaras. The men were adorned with heavy, jeweled gold or silver chains over their costumes of tunics and tight trousers, and their hands were beringed with more colorful gems. After days of seeing only dark and tattered garments on everyone she met, Carol's eyes were briefly dazzled by the many bright colors confined within the silk-covered, gilt-trimmed walls of that room.

There were still people arriving. The front door of the mansion was wide open to admit the guests, though a pair of uniformed guards stood on the step, keeping a sharp watch on all who entered. Trying to see better, Carol changed her position, creeping along the side of one of the parked cars, keeping her head low when a new set of headlights swung into the square.

The occupant of this newly arrived limousine was the Leader, Fal, who had been at the Solstice ceremonies. Fal climbed out of the car somewhat awkwardly. He was still wearing the unbecoming bright green tunic and trousers in which he had attended the late afternoon ceremony, but in the interval since then he had added several heavy gold chains around his neck, each chain bearing a jeweled medallion. At the Leader's appearance, the civil guards at the entrance all snapped to attention—and jumped again when the second person in the car alighted. This man was plainly dressed in a brown uniform and no extra adornments. Recognizing the commander of the civil guards, the very man she least wanted to meet, Carol quickly lowered her head. Almost immediately, compelled by a terrible fascination, she once again peered over the hood of the car behind which she was hiding.

In contrast to Leader Fal's short roundness, the commander was tall and slim. His uniform, combined with his pale face and starkly slicked-back brown hair, made him look to Carol's eyes like a dangerous thug. It horrified her that out of all the streets in ruined Lond, she should have fled away from him to the one place where he would be. There seemed to her to be some unearthly design in this near meeting. Nor was her apprehension eased by the conversation she now overheard.

"Come on, Drum," she heard Leader Fal say to the commander in a querulous voice. "I have repeatedly told you, there is nothing to be concerned about. It is just a rumor, and we have heard many rumors of possible trouble before this. None of them have meant anything. Neither does this rumor. Put extra guards on the streets and then forget it."

"I know every person in that area by sight," the man called Drum responded. "Yet twice I have spotted a stranger there. What does it mean?"

"It probably means," said Leader Fal, "that someone invited a country cousin to the city for the holiday. I will wager every chain I am wearing that you never see your mysterious stranger again."

"I have learned to trust my instincts," Commander Drum insisted. "First a persistent rumor, and then someone out of place, someone who evokes a most violent reaction in my heart."

"I didn't know you had a heart." Leader Fal

304

laughed in an insinuating way. "Tell me, was this stranger a man or a woman?"

"What difference does that make?" Commander Drum snarled, displaying a remarkable lack of respect for his Leader. "I recognize trouble when I encounter it and I tell you, I have twice in two days smelled trouble in that square."

"And I tell you, we can easily handle any problem that may arise. Now, will you kindly allow me to attend the party being given in my honor? Really, Drum, you are worse than those womanish priests. The people are well subdued and will remain where they belong—at the bottom of our social ladder. They have their little entertainments and I have done my part on their behalf on this day. Now I want to relax."

"If you are wise," said Commander Drum, "you will never relax your vigilance."

"No, no, Drum," Fal corrected him. "Vigilance is your task. Mine is to lead."

Still grumbling at each other, the two men climbed the steps, where the guards stood at stiff attention until they entered the house. They left Carol desperate with fear, for she had finally recognized Commander Drum. It was little wonder she had not done so before. His face was greatly changed from that of the man she had once known and, in her youthful innocence, believed she loved. But in his cold and disrespectful attitude toward Leader Fal and in the flat blankness of his eyes, Carol had just seen the spirit of the man she had hoped never to meet again.

Robert Drummond. She did not think he had seen her just now, but all the same, Carol began to tremble as if the man were deliberately pursuing her across the centuries.

She now had serious cause to fear for Nik and for her friends at Marlowe House. She was not surprised to hear from his own lips confirmation that she had been noticed by Commander Drum, but she was deeply disturbed to learn that there were rumors circulating about trouble in the immediate future. She did not think anyone in Nik's group would betray him by accident or by deliberate plan, but she did not know the people in the other groups who were to join Nik and his friends. It was possible that someone, having taken too much strong drink during the Solstice celebrations, had let slip a word too much about the scheduled uprising.

Carol knew she ought to leave the square at once and try to locate Marlowe House as quickly as possible so she could warn Nik. But first she wanted to see if she might learn anything more. Carefully she worked her way forward until she crouched behind the car nearest to the windows of the mansion. Another pair of late arrivals was at the door, diverting the attention of the guards, and the men at the far side of the square were paying no heed at all to the partygoers. Carol stood up and craned her neck to see inside the house.

In the warm, gilt-decorated room a band of musicians was playing a tune she could not hear. There were flowers everywhere, huge vases of them set on the floor and towering six feet high and other, smaller vases placed on tables or on chests. In one corner of the room potted palms and miniature trees were arranged around a splashing fountain of white marble. Within this artificial bower a few guests strolled, talking and laughing and, occasionally, pausing to exchange lengthy kisses and the sort of caresses that are usually reserved for more private places.

"And Marlowe House gets one hour per day of running water," Carol growled angrily, glaring at the fountain.

Elsewhere in the large room guests were helping themselves from a long buffet table set against one wall. It was this table that next caught and held Carol's attention. Staring at it, she swore under her breath at what she beheld.

The cloth was made from some glittering, gold-colored fabric and most of the dishes were gold or silver. There was a giant haunch of roasted meat, which a servant was carving. There were baskets of fine white bread, and bowls of salads and vegetables, and platters of various meats already sliced for the taking. Entire poached fishes lay on nests of shredded green leaves. The centerpiece of this display of culinary splendor was a huge golden compote piled high with oranges, grapes, pomegranates, and peaches, the whole extravagant design stuck through at intervals with long branches of fresh purple orchids and topped with the largest pineapple Carol had ever seen.

It was the fruit that did it, that made her so angry she wanted to throw a rock through the window. The unfairness of the scene before her struck Carol like a blow to the stomach. While Jo was forced to bargain for a bony chicken that was meant to feed no more than two or three people at most but that had to be stretched to fill a dozen hungry stomachs for a Solstice feast, while Bas made soup out of the leftovers and spoke of having eaten only one orange in his life, in a world in which Lin could not afford to buy even a single holiday treat for her child, these people, the so-called Leaders, were living in decadent luxury. And denying it to others. Refusing to share what they had. They even rationed the water supply to ordinary folk.

No wonder they needed squads of civil guards to keep the peace. No wonder Nik and others of like mind were planning to revolt.

"I will do everything I can to help them," Carol vowed.

"Hey, you! What are you doing there?" One of the guards at the far side of the square had seen her. His voice rang out with absolute assurance that he would be obeyed. "Come over here at once."

For the space of a heartbeat Carol did not move. She stood frozen where she was, not looking toward the guard who'd ordered her to present herself to him, but still with her gaze fixed on the scene inside the mansion.

"I said, come here!" The guard raised his voice a notch. The two guards standing at the mansion entrance turned their attention toward the rows of parked limousines, searching for a view of the miscreant who did not jump in instant response to an order from one of their comrades.

Inside the brightly lit house Commander Drum paused on his way to the buffet table, turned, and headed for the wide front window as if a sound from outside had penetrated the luxurious warmth of the party. He stopped by the window to peer out into the square.

Carol thought he saw her. She was still standing upright with one hand resting on the hood of the limousine behind which she had been sheltering. Across the darkness she looked right into Drum's eyes. Cold possessed her, a chill more bitter and heart-numbing even than Lady Augusta's embrace. In that moment Carol knew how a trapped rabbit felt, paralyzed, terrified, unable to do anything but wait for the hunter to pounce.

And then a noisy group of revelers surged into the square, half a dozen of them, laughing and singing. Some carried wine bottles. All were well dressed. They headed for the mansion where the party was being held and demanded entrance of the guards at the door.

With the arrival of these newcomers the terrifying spell holding Carol in her place was broken. She could move again, and she did so. Down behind the cars she went and, keeping her head low, ran out of the square by the way she had come into it.

Once in the narrower side streets, she no longer worried about discovery or about which direction she took. Pursued by the sound of booted feet, she simply fled as fast as she could, turning corners so she would be out of sight, squeezing herself into tiny spaces between buildings, slipping into dark alleys. When she suddenly found herself at the brink of a narrow canal, she jumped over it without a thought and kept running. Once she disturbed a little knot of people in ragged clothes who huddled in a lightless arcade.

"Help me," she gasped, risking her life on the chance that they were no more fond of her pursuers than she was. "The civil guards are after me."

"Hah! Them. Come this way." Without questioning her they handed her along from person to person in the dark, finally pushing her through a gate into an alley at the rear of the arcade. The gate closed behind her and she was alone again.

Here all was silence and, freed of the requirements of haste, caution returned. Her way was darker now, and from what Carol could distinguish of it, the area where she found herself was in a sorry state. There were no electric street lamps burning, nor well-kept houses. In a black quietness disturbed only by the scurrying of the occasional rat or the snarls of a pair of fighting cats, she crept along, not knowing where she was, but too frightened to stop lest she be discovered and taken by the civil guards.

She would never be able to explain by what route she arrived—perhaps there was some supernatural hand in it—but suddenly she walked into an open space and saw before her the World Tree with its empty, grasping fingers and, directly across the way, Marlowe House.

Carol came to an abrupt halt. Commander Drum had spoken to Leader Fal about having seen her here, so it was possible that he had sent some of his guards to watch for her. But she had to get home—for Marlowe House *was* home and it represented all that existed of security and warmth in this hideous future world.

And Nik was there, in Marlowe House. She

could not lead Drum's men to him, but she had to get to Nik, to warn him. At this point she scarcely knew anymore what it was she wanted to warn him about, but the need to feel his arms around her was a burning ache in both her mind and her heart. Perhaps, if she went very carefully, and if she were lucky, she could reach the house without being seen.

She slipped into the deeper shadows of a broken stone wall, all that remained of an elegant old building. Slowly she began to edge her way around the square toward Marlowe House. She was half frozen from the cold, worn out after a night without sleep, and so frightened that her wits were as numb as her hands and feet. Which was why she did nothing when she first heard the soft step behind her.

It was the lightest, faintest crunch of a foot upon broken stonework and mortar ground into dust. Then silence. Nothing. Not even a breath came out of the darkness. All the same, Carol was certain that someone was standing directly behind her. She could not turn around. She could not move at all—or breathe—and her heart had stopped beating.

A wool-covered hand clamped down over her mouth, stiffling the scream she was unable, from sheer terror, to utter. An arm wrapped around her chest, pinning her hands at her sides before she could raise them to fight off her attacker.

Carol felt her knees begin to buckle. Her stomach lurched. She knew she was going to faint. Blackness swirled around her as she crumpled against the person who was holding her.

Chapter Fifteen

"Where in the name of all the worlds have you been?" demanded a low, harsh voice in her ear. Made frantic by fear, Carol gasped, struggling against restraining arms, trying to get her feet down on the ground so she would have more leverage to push away from the man who held her. Blind terror gripped her. Though she could not see him, she was certain he was a member of the civil guards, sent by Commander Drum to lie in wait for her.

"Stop fighting and answer me, damn it. We've all been sick with worry looking for you. Where were you?"

"*Nik.*" Recognizing him at last, she went weak and limp with relief. But only for a moment. There was no time to indulge herself in weeping or hysterics. There was too much that she ought to tell Nik at once, lest he inadvertently betray his friends and his cause by carrying her directly home.

"The guards commander—Commander Drum—Nik, he saw me again and he recognized me. His men chased me. I tried to lose them, but I'm not sure I did. He talked about having seen me here, in this square, during the ceremonies. He may have sent guards to look for me in case I return, and if they find us together you will be in trouble, too."

"All the more reason to get you safe inside." Nik did not seem to be the least bit disturbed by Carol's information.

"Didn't you hear me?" she cried. When she tried to wriggle out of his arms so she could stand up and confront him, he only held her more tightly. "Nik, you could be in serious danger."

"I don't think so. Car, surely you know that we have our own watchmen, and our own system of monitoring the movements of the civil guards. There is no one in this square who should not be here."

"Oh." Of course he would have sent out his own people to stand watch. Nik was not a careless planner and he held many lives in his hands. She felt foolish for her nearly hysterical warning. "I was so frightened," she whispered, her face pressed hard against the coarse cloth of his outdoor coat.

"You are safe now." He carried her across the square to the broken steps at the side of Marlowe House, then past the barricade that Bas moved aside at his call, and on into the servants' kitchen. There he set her down in one of the chairs at the table.

"She's over-chilled," Nik said to Jo. To Bas he added, "Call the others back. They'll be glad of a hot drink and their beds."

"You have all been out looking for me, when you should have been safe here, planning for tomorrow. I am so sorry for the trouble I've caused you." Carol felt like crying. Now that she had reached her destination, she was weak and trembling all over again, and her hands and feet began to ache as they warmed from a state of near frostbite.

"Drink this and stop apologizing." Jo thrust a cup into her hands. Carol tasted brandy mixed with hot water and herbs. "We'd have done the same for any other member of our group. You were trying to divert the guards' attention away from our headquarters, and we appreciate the risk you were running for our sakes."

"I learned something that may be of use to you," Carol said, her eyes on Nik. Quickly she recounted the conversation she had overheard between Commander Drum and Leader Fal. She did not, however, mention what she believed about Commander Drum's real identity. That particular piece of information was important only to her and, possibly, to Nik and Lady Augusta. To her other friends, the most important news of the evening was what she had learned that might affect their plans for the following day.

"I don't think Leader Fal is particularly bright," Carol said, finishing her report on her activities since leaving the square that afternoon, "but Drum is sharp as the proverbial tack, and I do not imagine for a minute that he is the kind of man to take chances when it comes to security. And he did see me outside that house where the party was being held. I'm sure of it, Nik. Drum will probably send extra guards to this area just in case I show up here once more."

"It won't matter," Nik told her, "because we will all stay indoors until it is time for the uprising to begin."

"They could make a house-to-house search," Carol insisted, recalling the history of her own century with frightening accuracy. "They could arrest everyone they find in any house on this square and hold all of us for days—or for years. From what I've seen of this time, the authorities don't worry too much about civil liberties for ordinary people."

"We will be safe until tomorrow," Nik repeated.

"How can you be so certain?" Carol cried.

"Because Aug has returned with news of the other groups she has contacted. And when Aug is here, she protects us."

"Where is she?" Carol wasn't sure she wanted to see Lady Augusta again. Not yet. She was afraid of what the ghost's presence would mean to her. She wasn't ready to return to her own time, not even to escape Commander Drum. And the prospect of being forced to leave Nik was unbearable.

"Aug is with Al and Pen and the others, searching for you." Jo refilled Carol's cup with more brandy and hot water. "She will return soon. Meanwhile, you ought to get out of those clothes and into something like a blanket or a robe that has been warmed by the fire. And from the look of you, a few hours of sleep would be in order, too."

"How can I sleep, knowing my presence here may put all of you in danger?" Carol demanded. "Or knowing what we are going to begin in just a few hours?"

"Jo is right, Car." Nik lifted her out of the chair where she still sat. "You need to rest and so do I. I will take care of her, Jo. When the others return, tell them to go to bed, and you go, too. There is no need for any of us to rise until mid-morning. We are less likely to become nervous and get into trouble if we are all asleep. Of course, some of us manage to get into a fair amount of trouble while in bed." With a chuckle worthy of a man who had no more on his mind than a few free hours ahead of him to spend as he pleased, Nik carried Carol up the steps and along the hall to his own room.

"I don't think you understand what is going on here," Carol warned. "You are in danger because of me."

"No," he corrected her. "I am in danger because of what I and my friends plan for later today, but we planned the revolt, and its timing, long before you came to me. What you have done, Car, is make these last few days both beautiful and precious. I will never forget them. Or you." He set her down on her feet and stood holding her with his hands at her waist. Carol leaned against him, loving him, wanting his touch.

"Take off these cold clothes," he whispered, working at the buttons on her raincoat. "I have a robe you can use until you are warm again— until I remove that garment, too."

He had to take off her shoes for her. Carol's fingers were still too numb to untie the laces for herself. She sat on the edge of his mattress, wrapped in the scratchy woolen robe he'd found for her to wear, and let him chafe heat and feeling back into her feet. And her ankles. And her calves and knees and thighs.

"I want something of you," he murmured, his mouth against her right knee.

"Anything." She was ready to sink down on his bed and let him take her there and then, in any manner he chose, so long as he stayed with her. She was afraid to let him out of her sight.

"Dance with me." Amazingly, when he lifted his head to see her reaction there was mischief in his eyes.

"Dance," she repeated blankly. Then, understanding. "As in waltz?"

"Wait here." He was gone only a moment, just long enough to give her reason to begin to panic for fear he would not return. She told herself her nerves were playing tricks on her. Here with Nik she was safe. Commander Drum would not find her. Lady Augusta was still away from the house. All the same, she sighed with relief when Nik reappeared, his eyes on the portable disk player, his fingers working the controls. He set it for the tune he wanted. When the music started he held out his hand to her. Carol rose from his bed.

In her bare feet, in a bathrobe fashioned from one of the common olive-green woolen blankets that were used whenever a warm, sturdy fabric was required, she went into his arms and once more they danced as if they

317

were in a ballroom, wearing formal evening dress, with a full orchestra playing.

"Never forget me," she pleaded. "Nik, I don't know why I am so frightened. If something happens to either of us in the uprising tomorrow, know that I love you."

"Hush." His lips caressed her forehead and her eyelids. With a soft laugh he attempted to tease her out of her gloomy mood. "I do not want to think about *that* uprising, only about the one I am personally experiencing at this moment."

"It's not even tomorrow," she corrected herself, so obsessed by the deadly fear chilling her veins and her heart and brain that she scarcely heard him. "It's today. Just a few hours from now."

"Woman, will you be silent? Or must I compel you? I do not want to worry about what may, or may not, happen later today. For the next few hours, I want to hold you in my arms and dance with you one last time before we move on to a grander place. When next we dance together, Car, it will be in the Leaders' palace, and we will be free, all of us. But I want this waltz to stay in my memory, so I never forget what it is like to live here, in this house, with you."

His voice dropped to a lower, more thrilling note, capturing all of Carol's attention. He had the power to make her forget her serious concerns about the future. Nik could make her think only about the present moment.

"When this waltz is over," he said, "I want to lie down on my bed beside you, and put my hands on you, and kiss your lovely breasts and your soft belly and then your beautiful, rosy entrance, where you always welcome me so deliciously. I want to push myself into you slowly and hear your sigh of pleasure when I fill you. There is no other sensation on earth so marvelous as the one you produce when you tighten and convulse around me while I am deep inside you, when you give yourself to me completely while I am still hard and barely able to control my own reaction to your approaching release. The way your face softens and glows with an inner light, the way your breath catches, the taste of your lips and then your mouth when I put my tongue in you. Do you know how eagerly I wait to hear you moan at that last moment when I can restrain myself no longer and I dissolve into your sweetness?"

"Nik. My dear love." They were no longer standing as a couple dancing the waltz should stand, a little apart from each other so they had space to move for the dance steps. Instead, Nik pulled her close until they were touching body to body. He was clad only in shirt and trousers, having removed his outer garments when Carol took off her clothing. The front of the robe she wore slipped open, so a narrow strip of her quivering flesh was pressed against him. She could feel his hot hardness against her abdomen. She moved restlessly, wanting him closer still.

Every word he spoke raised her temperature, and he talked on in that hypnotic voice, describing everything he was going to do to her, and each wild, hot thing he wanted her to do to him in return, until Carol's legs would no longer hold her upright. She hung in his arms, which were all that supported her, and listened to him, and trembled uncontrollably, and went slowly mad with the ache of wanting him inside her. But all he did was speak softly, just above a whisper, and kiss her face and her ears and throat. And all the while, the strains of the antique waltz swirled around them.

"Please," she whispered. "Nik, please."

"Ahhh." His lips brushed across hers once more. She wanted him to take her mouth with roughness and thrust his tongue into her as he had promised he would. "I knew you would respond to music and to words and kisses. Are you warmer now?"

"For heaven's sake," she gasped.

"Ah, no," he murmured into her ear. "For your sake. For mine."

He pushed her down onto the bed, the edges of her robe falling apart to reveal her entire body from throat to ankle. There on his bed she writhed in helpless desire, her eyes on his hands. For he was slowly—oh, much too slowly!—opening his trousers to free the huge mound of swollen manhood that strained against the dark fabric. Then his rigid masculinity sprang boldly forth and Carol moaned at the sight of it.

He did not undress. There was not time. Carol opened her legs and lifted her arms, inviting him, and he fell onto her, into her, and she clutched at him, pulling him deeper, ever deeper. Rough cloth scraped across her sensitive skin. She did not notice. All she knew was the heat where their bodies joined, the driving movement, the tight friction, and at the last, the soaring, blinding delight.

* * *

Not until much later did she undress him completely, before the two of them climbed beneath the bedcovers, pulling them high to keep warm.

"You devil," she murmured, snuggling against him. "You did it all with words."

"Not, precisely, *all*," he responded with a decidedly lewd chuckle. "Though I will admit, I took unfair advantage of you by translating your passionate fear into desire. I think you are no longer so frightened as you were a while ago."

"Nor so cold, either." She teased him with one hand and kissed his muscular chest and let him gather her close with softly intimate laughter. Her fear was not entirely banished, but it was manageable now, lying deep within her so she could pretend it was gone. "Tell me, sir, what were all those fascinatingly lurid promises you made a little while ago? I should like to see them fulfilled."

"So you shall, one by one, though your fulfillment leaves me a broken and drained man. Where shall I begin?"

"Wherever you like. Just don't stop."

He knew no inhibitions. With hands and lips and tongue he made love to every part of her body. And he did it repeatedly.

"But, Nik," she protested hours later, "you don't always—you haven't—I mean, you let me, but you—" He interrupted her with a kiss.

"Half my pleasure lies in watching you," he said. "I have been enjoying all the passion a mere man can handle in a few short hours."

"But I want—"

"I know," he murmured. "One last time before we must leave this room, this palace of love we have created."

"Show me again how best to pleasure you," she begged. "This last time should be just for you."

"Together, or not at all." He took her hand and put it in a place where she had not thought to touch him before that moment. Groaning and sighing in delight he whispered, "This will be for both of us, Car. Together."

And they were. Staring into his eyes at her last instant of sanity, she could almost believe they would always be one in this way, with their bodies completed by each other and their hearts and minds and souls blended into one glorious acceptance of a happiness that knew no limits of time or space. Then Nik moved in her and Carol could think no more.

"I want to be a real part of the uprising." Seeing Nik with his sharp profile outlined by the light from the little oil lamp as he bent over to fasten his boots, Carol knew that no matter what might happen on this fateful day, she would always remember him like this. The dark colors of his shirt and trousers, the contrast of focused lamplight and deep shadows burned themselves into her brain, imposing this more mundane image next to the sublime sight of Nik's features softened by the transports of passion.

It was amazing that while she desired him with a violent need that did not cease when each episode of lovemaking was finished, she also treasured this aspect of their time together, the talking and planning. She liked being with him when his friends were present, too. She loved their times alone and in private, but those hours were only a part of her attachment to this man. There was a balance to their relationship, a completeness in all areas of her present existence, that made their private moments even more precious. Carol was determined not to be parted from him on such an important day, unless it was because she was actively helping him.

"If Pen and Jo can go with you, then so can I," she told him.

"Pen and Jo have personal reasons for what they are doing." Nik stood, buckling his belt around his slim waist. "Pen in particular. She has a sister to avenge."

"Sister?" Carol repeated. "I didn't know. What happened?"

"She died of pneumonia in a year when fuel rationing was unusually strict. Many of the very young and the very old died of cold and hunger during that bitter winter." His voice was cool and unemotional, but Carol was not fooled by his indifferent pose. There was a sadness in him when he spoke of that loss. "She was two years old. I am not certain how much Pen actually remembers about El, but I'm sure she must feel the absence, since they were twins."

"Her name was El?" When he nodded without answering, being busy taking several pieces of equipment out of the chest of drawers, Carol went on. "She was your sister, too, and you are five or six years older than Pen. You must remember her."

"Where Pen is long and lean with a character

323

that is a bit sharp at times," he said, pausing in his preparations with a weapon in one hand, "El was round and plump and laughed a lot. She was a cuddly child. They weren't identical twins, you see."

"El's death must have hurt you, too."

His eyes met hers, and in their sudden blaze of green fire Carol saw all the reasons why he would lead that day's revolt. It had really begun with the death of his sister, when he could not have been much more than seven or eight years old. She knew the pain of that childhood loss must have gone deep because, although he had told her much about his life in the interludes between their lovemaking on several nights, he had never mentioned El until now. But he wanted her to know El's name, and to understand the most intimate, most secret, of his reasons for what he was doing.

She could not think of anything to say. She could only go to him, to put her arms around his waist and her head on his shoulder, to hold him thus for a while, until his arms came around her, too, and they stood bound together by the knowledge of loss, and by love.

And then it was time for them to go down to the kitchen and join the others, to make their last preparations for the battles that lay ahead.

"I don't care what you say, Nik, I do not want to be protected. I am going to have some part in this," Carol told him. "After what I have seen and heard in the last three days, and especially after what I witnessed last night at that digustingly luxurious party for Leader Fal,

324

I *must* be involved in the uprising."

"If you go out," Nik responded, "if Commander Drum sees and recognizes you, he will order you imprisoned—or worse."

They were all in the kitchen, sitting around the table over the remains of a late morning meal, their last before they went forth to do battle with the Government. Even Lady Augusta was there, returned from her mysterious absence. In her tattered gray and black robes she truly looked like the witch Nik and the others believed her to be. Carol turned to her, hoping to draw Lady Augusta into the argument on her own side.

"You said once that your mission was to teach me to care about others and to want to help people," Carol said. "Well, now I do care. Can't you convince Nik to change his mind? I'm sure he will listen to you." She broke off because Lady Augusta was looking at her with a particularly penetrating gaze.

"It is true you have changed in deep and positive ways," said Lady Augusta. "But are you prepared to accept the final transformation required of you?"

"I can't answer your question until I know what the final change is going to be," Carol said. "What I do know is that I am a part of these people—of all of them, even those like Lin and Sue who are not immediate members of this one group. We are *family*. I can't explain my feelings about this. It just *is*. We are all part of a whole."

"Just so." Lady Augusta nodded her approval of the sentiment Carol was expressing.

"Which is why I cannot stay here, safe and

warm, with food at hand," Carol declared, "while my friends go out into the cold to do battle for reasons that are so right and clear, not knowing if they will live to return home. It would break my heart if I could not go with them. I feel that I am *meant* to be with them today."

During this impassioned speech Lady Augusta never took her eyes off Carol, and it seemed to Carol that her glance was warmer than it had ever been. When Carol fell silent, Lady Augusta turned the same warm look on Nik.

"I do not think you can prevent her," Lady Augusta said to Nik, "unless you intend to practice physical restraint on her."

"Tying her up probably wouldn't work," Pen said, cutting into the dispute. "Car is a resourceful person. She will find a way to do what she wants to do."

"I say, let her go with us," said Jo. The others around the table added their agreement, outvoting Nik. Still, he was their leader, and Carol knew if he flatly refused to let her join them, they would accept his decision, however grudgingly.

"Aug." Nik turned to Lady Augusta. "Can you promise me that Car will be safe throughout the fight that's sure to happen today?"

"Why should I be safe if no one else is?" Carol cried. "Give me something constructive to do and I will take my chances with the rest of you."

"You could always come with me," Luc suggested. "Do you know anything about pyrotechnics? Or demolition work?"

"I can learn." Carol's response was immediate.

"No." Nik's reaction was just as quick. "She cannot go with you, Luc."

"I don't intend to blow myself up, you know," Luc said to him. "Or anyone else, either. An opening salvo is all I plan. Just a bit of distraction for those uncivil civil guards."

"Anything we do today carries some danger with it," Jo remarked. "Let Car go with Pen and me."

"What will you be doing?" Carol asked her.

"Directing innocent people out of the line of fire," Jo said calmly. "We will be using weapons to protect them if it becomes necessary."

"Aug." Nik looked at Lady Augusta again. "Tell us what you foresee."

"I cannot reveal the end of this day's events," Lady Augusta answered. "I can tell you that Car's future will be exactly what it has always been meant to be. So will yours, Nik—and the futures of all the others who sit at this table."

Nik stared at her as if he could decipher her cryptic response by sight alone.

"It doesn't matter what you say, Nik, or what Aug has to say, either," Carol told him. "I *am* going to be in the square with you." She did not add that Lady Augusta's answer to Nik had left her shivering with a new and undefined fear. She wasn't only afraid for herself. She was terrified for all of them, for she had learned in just a few short days to love each person in that room.

The vacuous face of Leader Fal in his tight green outfit and the cold, determined countenance of Commander Drum rose into her

Flora Speer

consciousness, the two faces of an uncaring Government that must be overthrown if there was to be any hope of a better future for her friends.

"Yes," Carol said again, "I don't care how dangerous it is, I am going to be where I am supposed to be."

Chapter Sixteen

They filtered out of the house into the square singly or in pairs. At Nik's insistence, Carol went with Lady Augusta. They were to meet Pen and Jo a short time later.

"Then I will leave you," Lady Augusta said to Carol in a low voice so no one else would hear her.

"You won't be there?" Carol asked, surprised. "Has Nik given you some secret, magical assignment to carry out? You have all of them convinced that you are a witch, you know. I might believe it myself if I didn't already know you are a ghost," she added under her breath.

"I will do what is necessary," was Lady Augusta's only response.

"Riddles again," Carol muttered. "I never know where you are going to appear next, or what you plan to do to me. I warn you, do not

329

try to interfere with my activities today, or I will see to it that your attempt to change my character fails miserably, and then where will you be for all eternity?" Lady Augusta did not seem to be upset by this threat. She only gave Carol a strange little smile and turned away.

Carol pulled a knitted mask over her face. Nik had insisted that she wear it, and Luc, who had been out on a mysterious mission long before dawn and who had only returned in time to eat with his friends, had agreed the weather was so bitter that many people would be similarly attired. Carol's disguise would help her to blend right in with the rest of the populace. She did not think the mask would keep her identity hidden for long from the searching eyes of Commander Drum, but she was not going to mention her doubts to Nik. She did not want him to change his mind about letting her join Pen and Jo.

"Car." Nik's hand was on her shoulder. "Take care."

"I will. You, too." She was no longer afraid. All of her fear had vanished in the same moment when Nik agreed to allow her to take part in the day's events. What Carol felt now was excitement mixed with anticipation. Yet at the same time she was oddly calm, as Pen and Jo were calm when they bid Bas good-bye and walked out of the house. Like her friends, Carol would do what was required of her and pray that all of them would meet again in victory. Al and most of the other men were already out there in the square, moving into position and waiting for the signal to begin. Carol was eager to join them.

"Go now, Luc," said Nik.

"I will see you again in an hour," Luc replied, grinning at Carol. "I hope you will enjoy the fireworks I have designed." With a cheery salute to Nik and a quick handshake for Bas, Luc slipped out of sight around the partially opened barricade.

"We're next," Bas said to Nik a few minutes later. "Aug and Car are to go out last. Aug, be sure you close the barricade. You know how. We don't want any desperate civil guards hiding themselves in here and ambushing us when we return."

"Good luck," Carol said to them. "We'll meet again soon."

"Yes," said Bas, smiling at her. "We will."

Nik's hand tightened on Carol's shoulder. She knew he would not kiss her, but the glance they exchanged was worth a dozen kisses. For a moment she covered his hand with her own. Then Nik was gone, following Bas past the barricade, and Carol was alone in the kitchen with Lady Augusta. Carol was tempted to ask again if Nik and his friends would come safely through the next few hours, but she did not think Lady Augusta would give her a straight answer.

"It is time to go," said Lady Augusta. She motioned to Carol to leave the house first.

Carol heard the barricade slide shut behind her. Quickly she went up the steps and climbed across the first mound of broken materials before she turned around to reach down a hand to help Lady Augusta up beside her.

Lady Augusta was not there.

"Is this a good sign, or not?" Carol wondered. She paused, looking around in case Lady Augusta had somehow gotten past her, but if she had, Carol could not discover her whereabouts.

There was an inch of fresh snow on the ground, and it was quickly being churned into gray slush by the two dozen or so civil guards who were pacing about the square with a false air of casualness that could not have fooled anyone. They were not deployed in a group but were moving individually, and they appeared to be greatly interested in the activity at the center of the square, as if that were the reason for their presence.

The noisy old machine was back and with it, the same bunch of workmen whom Carol had encountered on her first day in this future city of Lond. Beneath dismal gray skies, in bone-chilling cold, the men were in the process of removing the World Tree.

"I guess it's like an artificial Christmas tree," Carol said to herself. "They put it up at the beginning of the season, and then dismantle it when the holiday is over. I wonder if the branches unscrew from the trunk. Or if they have an attic to store it in."

She did not watch the workmen for long. They did not seem to be working very hard or accomplishing much for their half-hearted efforts, and Carol had her own duties to think about. She was supposed to join Pen and Jo, and to operate under Jo's direction. She could see her friends just a few yards away, talking to Lin. After a last glance at the World Tree and the workmen Carol strolled over to the other women, trying to appear natural.

"Where is Sue?" she asked Lin, mindful of the civil guard who stood near.

"Gone to stay with my sister for a few days." Lin responded with a wink the guard could not see, to let Carol know she understood the need to make their conversation sound ordinary, and that she also understood Carol's concern for the little girl's safety. "It's a good thing, too. I have fallen behind in my work over the holiday."

"You'll be back in the rhythm of it in another day or two," said Jo with just the right touch of indifference toward boring work. "Oh, look, the tree is about to come down."

The men operating the machine were maneuvering it so that its long, rusty arm reached toward the trunk of the World Tree. The jaws at the end of the arm opened and then began to clamp themselves around the trunk, preparing to lift the metal tree off its base. Everyone in the square stopped to watch, including the guard who was standing near Carol and her three friends. This was the moment they had been waiting for, when the attention of the guards was distracted by a routine and unremarkable event. All around the square other rebels were silently poised for action, though they, too, appeared to be watching the removal of the tree.

Jo made a quick gesture with one hand and at her signal Pen moved toward the nearest guard. Carol could see that Pen was holding a stunner weapon in the hand that rested beneath the folds of her heavy coat as if she were seeking warmth. The charge generated by the stunner would not hurt the guard, it would simply make him unconscious for several hours. By the time he awoke the action should be over, and he would be given the opportunity to join the rebels. Nik had told Carol that many of the guards were as opposed to the present Government as anyone else, but were kept in line by threat of harm to their families if they did not follow orders. Nik believed these disaffected guards would go over to the rebel side as soon as it became clear that the Government was going to fall.

"Luc's surprise is overdue," Jo murmured, displaying the first sign of nervousness Carol had seen in her.

"Give him a moment or two more. Luc is dependable." Lin's voice was as low as Jo's, but Pen must have heard her, for she glanced backward and wiggled her eyebrows at Carol. Carol grinned and held her breath, grateful for Pen's tension-breaking sense of humor.

When the rumbling started, Carol thought at first that the noise was coming from the machine standing next to the World Tree and that something was wrong with the machine. She realized her mistake when smoke began to pour from the end of every branch of the tree. Flashes of red and blue light followed the appearance of the smoke. From where Carol stood it looked as if the metal fingertips of the tree were hurling out miniature bolts of lightning. The noise was certainly loud enough by now to be mistaken for thunder.

Carol did not know precisely how Luc had created this show of light and sound, but it produced exactly the effect Luc and Nik had intended. The men who were working on removal of the World Tree began to back away from it, talking anxiously among themselves and looking frightened. Then the rusty machine waiting to lift the tree began to belch and shake, and the workmen moved more quickly, putting distance between themselves and the machine.

With the eyes of most people in the square directed toward the machine and the World Tree, the moment for action was at hand. Pen released the safety catch on her weapon, aimed it at the guard in front of her, and leveled him with a single burst. The buzzing noise the stunner made reverberated unpleasantly in Carol's ears for several seconds after Pen was finished. The guard lay unmoving. Jo reached down and removed his weapon, taking it for herself. They left him where he fell, comatose but unharmed. All across the square similar incidents were taking place and, for a moment or two, no one appeared to notice what was happening. Carol saw Nik not far away, leaning over to take the weapon from the guard he had personally sent into involuntary sleep.

"Start moving the bystanders out of the square now," Jo ordered. "Anyone who isn't going to fight along with us will have to leave or risk being hurt."

"Look!" Lin pointed, laughing. Fiery golden pinwheels were shooting out of the World Tree from all angles.

"When Luc said fireworks, he meant it," Carol remarked. "What a brilliant idea to distract the guards."

"Not for long," Pen noted. "And don't let Luc's

contribution distract *us* from our work. I see a couple of elderly women over there who ought to be sent home where they will be safe. We only have stunners, but the guards have killing weapons and they won't hesitate to use them on anyone who gets in their way." Pen started forward and Carol went with her.

Out of the corner of her eye Carol saw one of the civil guards who was standing near the World Tree pull out his weapon and adjust the setting. Taking aim, he fired at one of the twirling pinwheels. A flash of electric blue light enveloped the World Tree.

Carol had not gone two steps more before a violent explosion roared through the square. She was so stunned by it that she could not move, could not have saved herself if it were necessary. She saw the machine beside the World Tree disintegrate into a thousand pieces of jagged metal that rained down on the square, carrying with them injury and, in some cases, death. And then, with a second roar that shook the ground, the World Tree itself exploded.

"Come on!" Pen yelled, pulling at Carol's arm. "Let's get those old women, and the children, out of here."

"Lin?" Carol shouted. She looked around, expecting to find Lin right next to her. But Lin was lying facedown over the stairs leading to a ruined house. A long shred of twisted metal protruded from her back. Jo bent over her, then lifted her head, weeping.

"There is nothing we can do for her," Jo said, not bothering to hide her grief. Bravely she tried to pull herself together. "We knew there would be losses. Let's keep them to a minimum by getting those innocents away so we can come back and join the fighting with clear consciences."

They tried, pushing terrified, crying old people and mothers with young children toward the avenues that led to safety. It was not an easy task. There were a lot more people running into the square than attempting to leave it and it was difficult to open a path, but eventually everyone who was not to be directly involved in the revolt had been convinced to go home. Then Carol, Pen, and Jo hurried back to the square, where the civil guards were doing their best to restore order. They were not succeeding. In fact, the guards were quickly losing control of the situation. One by one they went down, felled by the stunner weapons in the hands of Nik's friends.

Carol did not know when the serious weapons fire began, but all at once the air was full of the buzz and crackle of killing sidearms and around her in every direction people were screaming.

"Get down!" Jo pushed Carol hard and she hit the pavement. A split second later a large, solid building stone directly behind her burst into tiny fragments.

"What happened to the World Tree?" Carol cried. "Why did the machine blow up?"

"That stupid guard who shot at the tree ignited all of Luc's fireworks at once," Jo answered. "Luc was there, near the tree, firing the fuses. I don't know how he could have survived those explosions."

"Oh, God, not Luc, too," Carol whispered.

Then: "Where is Pen? She was here with us a moment ago."

Carol looked around. She could see Nik crouching behind some stones with Bas beside him, so she knew they were still all right. She did not recognize anyone else, but perhaps the other rebels were as well concealed as Nik.

"Car, I think Pen is hurt," Jo said. "Let's try to reach her."

Crouching down they ran to where Pen sat on the ground. White-faced, looking as if she was going to be sick, Pen clutched at her left shoulder.

"This wasn't done by a stunner," Pen said through gritted teeth. "One of those cursed guards got me with a killing weapon. I'm just lucky he wasn't a very good shot."

"Can you walk?" Jo asked her. "Car and I will get you back to the house. You will have to take care of yourself after that, because we are needed here."

"I can manage," Pen grated, wincing when she tried to move her left arm. "I know where the medical supplies are stored and I know how to use them."

"Let's go, then. Car, you help her up and I'll provide protection. I'm sure to be better with a stunner than you are."

Carol wrapped an arm around Pen's waist, steadying her. Pen groaned once, but stiffled any other sound of pain. Together the three of them stumbled toward Marlowe House. Meanwhile, Carol could hear weapons firing in the far distance outside the square, a sure sign that the revolt had spread to other areas of the city.

"Do you hear it?" she said to Pen. "We aren't alone. The other dissident groups have joined us, just as they promised they would."

"We need their help," Pen gasped. She stopped dead, forcing Carol to stop, too. The two of them stared in disbelief as four armored vehicles as big as twentieth-century tanks rumbled into the square. They bore the Government's markings. Formidable-looking guns bristled from every side of the vehicles.

"Oh, no," Pen cried. "What has happened to the demolition teams? They were supposed to eliminate the Government's heavy arms."

"Obviously, something went wrong." Carol tried to pull Pen toward the house and safety.

"Al was with one of those teams," Pen said in a desolate voice.

"Perhaps they were only delayed for a while," Carol suggested, trying to offer hope. She was aware of how badly Pen was sagging against her, and she began to worry that Pen's shoulder wound was more serious than they had previously realized.

"Come on, hurry," Jo urged. "There is a major battle shaping up and I want you inside, Pen, before it starts."

Out of the armored vehicles leapt dozens of men, reinforcements for the few civil guards who were still standing. The new arrivals fanned out across the square, shooting as they went. Amid the confusion, the smoke, the cries of the wounded and the shouted orders, an all-too-familiar figure in a plain brown uniform stepped down from the lead vehicle as coolly as if he were once again leaving a limousine to attend a fashionable party.

"Commander Drum." Carol felt a cold hand tighten around her heart. "Pen, come *on*. Move it, will you?"

"I can't. My legs—too weak." Pen fell to her knees. "Leave me. Take shelter, Car. You, too, Jo."

"Are you crazy?" Carol screamed at her. "We aren't going anywhere without you." She cast one more quick look in the direction of Commander Drum, and then she tried to hoist Pen to her feet.

"I can't." Pen's voice was growing fainter. "My entire left side is numb."

"Al warned us the guards are using a new kind of bullet in their sidearms," said Jo, talking fast. "According to him, it inflicts paralysis as well as a wound. Pen, we will have to carry you."

"No! Leave me, please, Jo. I can't help the revolt, but you and Car can."

"Shut up, Pen. We aren't going to leave you." Carol still had her arm around Pen and now Jo supported Pen's other side.

"We'll never get her down those steps to the house," Jo panted as they dragged Pen along. "But Nik and Bas have taken shelter, so let's join them."

The men were hunkered down behind a pile of large stone blocks. As Carol and Jo dragged Pen toward them, Carol saw Al race across the square, dodging the guards' fire all the way. He leapt over the stones to join Nik and Bas. Just as he took cover, two of the armored vehicles exploded into pieces.

"Did you see that?" Carol yelled into Pen's

ear. "Al is all right. You'll be with him in just a minute."

Pen did not answer. She was by now nearly a dead weight, unable to help herself, but Nik had seen the women. At once he left the safety of the stones to run toward them.

"One of those new paralyzing bullets got her," Jo explained. "I don't know if she'll recover or not."

"You two get behind the stones," Nik ordered, taking his sister into his arms.

Staying as close to the ground as they could, they all ran for the cover of the stones. Pen cried out when Nik laid her down, then was still. Now it was Al's turn to hold her. He knelt, rocking her, whispering what comforting words he could.

"We can't stay here," Nik said. "Al, what about those other two vehicles?"

"They should blow at any minute," Al said. "When they do, I'll take advantage of the confusion to carry Pen into the house. Sorry for the delay on the vehicles, but I'm not as clever at demolition work as Luc was."

"He's dead," Jo said. It wasn't a question, just a bleak statement of fact.

Al nodded. "When the tree went up, Luc went, too. He couldn't get away in time." Even as Al spoke, two loud explosions rent the air.

"That will be the other two vehicles," Al said to Nik. He picked up Pen, holding her close. "Cover me till I get her inside," he said, and started for the steps leading down to the servants' entrance and the familiar kitchen.

Al had not gone three steps before a loud buzzing noise sounded. With a cry of pain, Al stopped abruptly, dropping Pen. Al fell next to her, and they lay there like two inert bundles of rags.

"Pen! No!" Heedless of the danger to his own life, Nik was out of the shelter of the stones, kneeling next to his sister.

To Carol's eyes, what happened next happened in terrifying slow motion. She went to Nik, to crouch beside him and try to help him drag his sister to the steps that led to safety within Marlowe House. Jo and Bas stood with their backs to Nik, Carol, and Pen, firing away at the guards who were trying to kill all five of them.

Al was dead; Carol could tell that much without touching him. But she did not have time, even in slow motion, to think about Al's fate. They had to get Pen away to safety, for she could not help herself.

Nik was pulling Pen into his arms, lifting her, preparing to make a dash for the steps, when Carol heard Jo scream. Turning, she saw Jo go down on one knee and then onto her face, while Bas fired at the man who had shot his love. Then Bas was lying across Jo's body, his leg so badly wounded that Carol wondered if he would ever walk again. Carol looked up from Bas and Jo to meet the eyes of their opponent . . . and the hair at the back of her neck rose in terror.

Commander Drum's cold, impersonal glance skimmed past Carol, not recognizing her because of the knitted mask she still wore, disregarding her in favor of Nik and the burden he held. Nik could not defend himself, not with Pen lying helpless in his arms. Carol saw the flash of deadly amusement in Drum's dark, shadowed eyes, and knew he was going to kill both Nik and Pen with one blast from the long, gray metal weapon he held so carelessly in his right hand.

Never had Carol imagined that anyone could enjoy the act of killing but, watching Commander Drum, she could not deny he was relishing the thought of what he was about to do. Still in slow motion, the dreadful scene unfolded before Carol with terrible deliberation.

Apparently understanding that there was no time in which to escape, Nik did the only thing he could. He turned away from Commander Drum. As he turned, he bent over to shield Pen's body with his own and thus take the full force of the blast himself. Commander Drum lifted his weapon, taking slow, careful aim.

Nik. He was going to kill Nik. Her love. Her only love. And Pen, her sister and friend. Carol did not have to think about what she was going to do next. A deadly joy blossomed in her heart. What she did, she did gladly, willingly, out of a pure and compelling love and a belief that Nik and Pen deserved to live.

"Stop!" Carol leapt forward, placing herself squarely between Nik and Commander Drum. She spread her arms wide in a protective gesture. If he wanted to kill Nik and Pen, Drum was going to have to go through her body first. "I won't let you do this! You must stop!"

Commander Drum's eyebrows went up, but at first he showed no other sign of surprise at her action. Then he looked right into Carol's eyes and she watched the slow light of recognition dawn in him. Carol understood at last why the two of them had been fated to meet in this particular time . . . and knew that Commander Drum understood it, too.

"So," Drum said softly, almost tenderly. "My nemesis. I know you of old. But you will not haunt me any longer."

"Car!"

Carol heard Nik's desperate warning shout. She saw the long, slow flame erupt from Commander Drum's weapon and make its leisurely way toward her. And in Drum's cold eyes she saw her own death, watching her.

From behind Commander Drum, Bas struggled to a half-sitting position and fired his stunner. Drum went down, sinking to the pavement in a peculiarly graceful paralysis. Bas collapsed again, his eyes on Carol.

There was a hot, grinding pain in Carol's chest. She could not breathe, and the ground came up to meet her with such a jolting shock it tore a cry of anguish from her lips.

With the sound of her own scream, the slow motion stopped. Normal speed resumed, and suddenly everything was happening much too fast. Nik turned her over, holding her. When Carol's head fell back across his arm, she saw the still-paralyzed Pen weeping silent tears . . . and a circle of poorly clad people—Nik's friends joined with allies from other rebel groups—all standing shoulder to shoulder facing outward toward the civil guards, defending this little space where she lay in Nik's arms . . . . She could hear shouts and screams in the background, and the continuing sound of weapons fire.

"Car." Nik's face was wet, though it was

not raining. "Car, why did you do it? I'd far rather it were me. How can I live without you?"

Still she could not get her breath, and the pain in her chest would not go away. There was a hot, sticky fluid pouring down her left side, but she was unable to stretch out her hand to reach beneath her raincoat to discover what it was.

"Nik." It was so difficult to speak. Nik's face was growing blurry, in a way she had seen once before . . . long ago.

"Car—Car, my love." Nik's voice sounded so broken and desperate that she wanted to put her arms around him and tell him everything was going to be all right. But she could not move. "Car, don't leave me!"

"I love you." She wasn't sure he heard her. There was a roaring noise that blotted out mere voices, and there was a sickening darkness enveloping her.

Carol felt as though she were being dragged away to another place, but she had not heard Nik shout an order for her to be moved. And the pain . . . never had she experienced such fiery, lancing pain.

She could bear the pain. It would not last for long, and Nik and Pen were still alive. That was what really mattered, not her own temporary discomfort. Her lungs ached for the air she could no longer draw into them. Carol struggled to breathe and found she still could not.

The encroaching blackness grew closer and heavier, pressing down on her, driving the life out of her pain-wracked body. The last thing she heard was Nik's howl of agonized loss as his dream of love with Carol turned into a reality more devastating than any nightmare could ever be.

"Car! Noooo!"

Part V.
Noel.

London, 1993.

Chapter Seventeen

"Be careful," warned Lady Augusta, "or you will trip and fall."

"Where? . . . what?" Carol stared into thick fog. There were pale halos around the street lamps, and the lights on the Christmas tree sent forth a ghostly, multicolored glow. "I'm still in the square. But it's so quiet. What has happened to the weapons fire? And where are the others?"

"Your former companions remain in their own time." The words came out of the darkness. Carol could just barely see Lady Augusta as a slightly more distinct shape than the formless, shifting fog.

"Nik," Carol cried. "Pen. The others. What happened to them?" She was beginning to understand that she was not dead, though she had willingly given up her life. Instead, she had been returned to the world in which she belonged. The change had been so abrupt that now she could not stop thinking about those whom she had left behind. Or was it left ahead? She was too confused to reason through the answer to that question, and Lady Augusta's response only added to Carol's distress.

"Do you mean, what *will* happen to them?" asked Lady Augusta. "Are you certain you want to know?"

"Of course I want to know! I love them! Stop playing tricks on me and tell me the truth for once."

"If you wish, I will let you see for yourself what their future will be."

"Yes. Show me." Carol placed a hand on her chest where the fatal wound had been. There was no wound now, and no flow of blood. Her raincoat was intact. Yet beneath her hand her heart beat at an alarming rate, and a terrible pain still lingered in the form of a rending sensation of loss.

"Since you desire it so passionately," said Lady Augusta, "I will vouchsafe one last vision to you. Prepare yourself, Carol."

There was a movement in the fog, and once more Carol was plunged into a dizzying, empty blackness. She was not completely alone. She sensed the presence of Lady Augusta, though she could not see her ghostly guide.

"Where am I?" Carol asked.

"Watch." Lady Augusta's disembodied voice came out of the void surrounding Carol. "Watch, and learn the final lesson."

In the darkness there slowly developed a circle of light. Carol could see into it as though she were looking through the wrong end of a telescope. While everything she saw appeared to be far away, she was able to make out a gray stone wall, three wooden poles in front of the wall, and a few men in brown civil guards uniforms. Commander Drum stood at their head, waiting in a gray and cold dawn.

As Carol watched, more guards appeared, supporting three bundles of rags. The bundles moved in short, jerking steps, and Carol realized that the three objects were human beings—or what was left of humans after unspeakable tortures. She understood now the purpose of the three poles. The pitiable creatures being dragged forward were unable to stand alone and were going to be tied to those stakes.

"Why are you showing me this?" Carol demanded of Lady Augusta.

"You insisted upon seeing it. This is the final act, the last scene for you to observe," came the doleful answer.

With a rising sense of horror Carol comprehended the significance of the series of rusty-brown stains on the wall behind the stakes. When the prisoners were secured to the stakes, Commander Drum stepped toward them, cloth in hand.

"No blindfold," rasped the person tied to the center stake.

"Nik!" Carol screamed. "No, this can't be happening."

"No." The figure at Nik's left side also shook its head, like her brother refusing Commander Drum's offer of a cloth to cover her eyes.

"Pen! Lady Augusta, stop this! Make Drum stop."

"I cannot change it," said Lady Augusta. "So long as the present and the future remain unaltered, this will be their fate. Only you can make the difference, Carol."

"I suppose you intend to be as foolishly brave as your companions and also stare death in the face?" said Commander Drum to the remains of a person on Nik's right. This distorted shape could barely gasp out a single word.

"N-n-no c-cloth." So tortured was the sound that Carol was convinced his larynx had been broken. But like his friends, he struggled to stand as upright as he possibly could, given his terrible injuries.

"Bas!" Carol cried, weeping for pity. Bas had tried to save her when Drum was determined to kill her, and she was sure Commander Drum had seen to it that Bas suffered accordingly for daring to shoot his stunner at the leader of the civil guards.

"There is no need for last words," snapped Commander Drum, moving away from the prisoners to stand with the other guards. "No one will hear what you say except me and my men, and we won't care."

Nik pulled himself a little straighter, fighting against the ropes that held him and lifting his head to glare proudly at his executioners. Despite Commander Drum's cold-blooded declaration, Nik spoke with as much defiance as any man could be expected to muster under such dreadful circumstances.

"We do not die," Nik declared between labored breaths. "We love—we hope—we still dream—of a better world. We will live on."

"A charming theory," sneered Commander Drum, "but faulty logic, I fear. When we kill you, that will be the end of you."

"No," Nik choked. "Not—not the end."

"Oh, God!" Carol screamed. "Help them! Someone, help them!"

"Guards, raise your weapons," Commander Drum ordered with a bored calmness of manner that was utterly appalling to Carol. "Aim. Fire."

"No! Stop!" Carol's desperate pleas had no effect on the scene before her. The grating buzz of the guards' hand weapons filled her ears. The figures lashed to the poles each jerked once and then went perfectly still.

"You have seen what you wanted to see." Lady Augusta's voice was a solemn whisper of sound in the deadly quiet following the executions. "Remember it well, Carol."

The circle of light in front of Carol's eyes grew smaller and smaller until it vanished and all was blackness once more. . . .

And in Carol's bosom, beneath the hand she still held over the spot where once a selflessly accepted wound had bled, her heart quietly shattered into an infinite number of tiny, excruciatingly sharp and painful splinters. . . .

Chapter Eighteen

Carol was alone. Lady Augusta had vanished, leaving her in the middle of the square. At first all was silence. Then, slowly, sound returned. The first noise Carol heard was a car horn, followed by the cries of a small child having a tantrum and the cajoling voice of the child's mother.

Bewildered, Carol stared at her surroundings. The fog was lifting and the street lamps were lit. The small bulbs on the Christmas tree shone with multicolored holiday brightness. On all sides of the square the old houses rose, whole and well cared for. Wreaths graced many of their doors and lights glowed in the windows. Directly ahead of her stood Marlowe House. All four stories of it and the roof were solid, complete, undamaged by warfare or time.

354

Reaching out, Carol touched the Christmas tree, feeling with a new delight its prickly needles and the heat of an electric bulb.

"You're real," she said to the tree, "not metal, and not something thought up by an uncaring Government. You *mean* something. Thank God for Christmas!"

She did not enter Marlowe House by the servants' entrance. She knew Nell would probably be in the kitchen with Mrs. Marks and Hettie, and she did not want to talk to anyone for a while. There would be time enough for conversation later, after she'd had a chance to assimilate everything that had happened to her.

She found her house key in the purse that was still slung over her shoulder and, mounting the front steps, went in by the main door. She paused for a moment in the hall, looking at the clean black and white marble floor and the paneling that Nell did her best to keep well polished. There was no one in the hall. Crampton was probably in the kitchen with the women. Carol crossed to the drawing room entrance and opened one of the double doors.

The room was unchanged and unused since Lady Augusta's funeral. The walls were still pale yellow silk, the carved paneling accented with white and gilt paint.

Her sense of time having been distorted by supernatural events, Carol was forced to count the days on her fingers in order to determine exactly how long it had been since she had stood in this same place during the reception after the funeral and rudely refused to make a donation to St. Fiacre's Bountiful Board. It was three days ago. And only last night—no, 175 years in the future—she and Nik had danced in the small, partitioned section at the far end of this room before falling upon his bed to make intense, passionate love. And in the morning they had left his room and gone out to fight and die.

Carol walked across Aubusson carpets, past gilded Regency chairs and tables, to the rear of the long, narrow drawing room. There she stopped, noting that the window which would one day be the single window of Nik's small bedroom was not covered with layers of wood for security reasons, but instead was draped in heavy yellow silk and gold fringe.

"Oh, Nik," she whispered, her voice breaking. Gently she touched the windowsill, and then the wall where the head of his bed would one day be. "No. I can't let it happen. The future has to be different. I will do anything I can to save him from that terrible end. And Pen and Bas, too. All of them."

"Good evening, Miss Simmons." Crampton stood in the drawing room doorway. "I thought I heard you come in."

Carol did not respond. The lump in her throat prevented her from speaking.

"Will you be wanting a late supper, miss?" asked Crampton.

"Late?" Carol repeated. "What time is it?" *An interesting question,* she thought, *and in a metaphysical sense, an unanswerable one.*

"It is just past nine o'clock, miss."

"Oh. I see. Well, I did eat a rather substantial tea at a late hour, so I think I will skip another meal tonight. I am going to bed now, so you may as well lock up the house."

"Yes, miss." Crampton showed no sign of surprise at her claim to have eaten elsewhere when she took almost all of her meals in her own room, but then Crampton rarely showed any emotion at all.

For the first time in her almost six years at Marlowe House, Carol wondered what the butler really thought: about his late employer, about Marlowe House itself, and about the end of his career, for it seemed certain that he and Mrs. Marks would retire when the house was closed after Lady Augusta's estate was settled. On her way out of the room she went past him with a curious look, but Crampton, who was pulling the double doors shut behind her, did not appear to notice her interest.

On the upper floors of the house the corridors were lit only by single bulbs in wall sconces. The emptiness and the deep shadows did not bother Carol. After her recent experiences she was beyond fearing anything. Even death could not frighten her now. Opening the door of her own room, she reached out and pushed the light switch. Lamps sprang to life beside her bed and next to the wing chair by the fireplace, illuminating the familiar room that at the moment appeared entirely strange to her.

A guest awaited her. Across the hearth from the wing chair Lady Augusta sat upon her invisible sofa.

"Shut the door and take off your coat, Carol. We have much to discuss."

"I wondered when you would show up again." Carol took her time undoing the buttons and the sash of her raincoat and hanging the coat in the closet. She needed those few minutes to collect her thoughts. She was not as calm or as unaffected by recent events as she pretended to be. She was very much afraid that Lady Augusta knew this and would take advantage of her weakness.

"Do sit down, Carol. You are wasting time."

"I thought you had all eternity."

"Certainly not. I explained to you on my first visit that I have been given only until Twelfth Night to convince you to change your ways. I said, sit down!"

Carol was planning to remain on her feet, but Lady Augusta gave her no choice. She felt herself being moved to the wing chair, felt her body bending and an invisible force pressing her downward until she sat as she was bidden. Once she was seated the force released her.

"Very clever," said Carol, glaring at her visitor. Then, intrigued, she looked more closely at the ghost. Lady Augusta's gray hair was no longer hanging around her face in lank strands. Instead, it was piled into her usual neat chignon. She was still robed in the same gray and black she had been wearing during all her time in the future with Carol, but the robes had undergone a subtle transformation. They were not so heavy as they once were, and the long streamers of dark fabric no longer looked so much like tattered rags, but now assumed a more elegant, drifting appearance, like chiffon dyed to the color of dark smoke or of thick, swirling fog. These garments were never still. The skirt and the long, loose sleeves and the newly sheer cloak around her shoulders all lifted and blew gently in a nonexistent breeze, and then settled back around Lady Augusta's figure, only to rise again a moment later. The effect was both ghostly and disorienting. Carol suspected Lady Augusta of wanting it that way.

"How are you, Carol?"

"How do you expect me to be? I'm not sure whether I'm dead or alive." Lady Augusta did not respond to this deliberately provocative statement, but only sat watching her, and after a minute or two Carol added, "I want you to tell me what I can do to prevent the tragedy I just witnessed."

"As I recall it, you were a willing participant in those tragic events. You were willing to give your life to save those whom you loved."

"*Love*," Carol corrected. "I love them still and will until I . . . but I've already done that, haven't I? I have already died. Much good my sacrifice did them. You saw their final fate. That's what I want to change, and you have to tell me how."

"You have learned the lessons I intended you to learn." Lady Augusta moved, sending a flurry of sheer black and gray fabric into the air. To Carol's eyes, the colors seemed to be fading into lighter shades even as she regarded her visitor with growing frustration. Nor did Lady Augusta's next words shed more light on any possibility of changing the future. "The rest is up to you, Carol. You have only to look into your own heart. There you will discover all you need to know."

"I want Nik to live," Carol cried. "And Pen—and Bas and Jo and Al and Lin. Luc, too. All of them, all of my friends in that time."

"Then you must take immediate action, for if you do not change the present, when time moves on to Nik's day, he and all his friends will die in that failed uprising or will be executed after it is put down. Only you can change the future you saw this evening. If you wish it to be so, Nik and his friends will live under a democratic, representative government. No uprising will be necessary because there will be no repression. Nor will the cities of the world be in ruins or the weather patterns changed by the weapons used in terrible wars. And Christmas—along with all other holidays—will still be celebrated. The future depends upon you, Carol."

"You are being unfair," Carol said, feeling more frustrated than ever. "One person alone cannot solve all of the world's problems."

"You are not expected to do so. What you *are* expected to do is care about those whom you know you could help. Begin with those around you and go on from there, always doing the best you can. The slightest change can make a bigger difference than you realize."

"My best," Carol repeated thoughtfully. "I haven't always done my best in the past, have I?"

"Do it now. It is never too late to begin." Lady Augusta rose, her garments floating around her. "Sleep now, Carol. The pain of this second parting from your love will ease, especially since you know that you have the means within yourself to save him a second time. And to save the life of Car."

"Are you telling me that there will be a Car?"

Carol stared at her. "A *real* Car?"

"I thought you were the real Car." Head tilted to one side, Lady Augusta regarded her with a piercing look. "Didn't Nik explain all of this to you when you first arrived in that future time? Surely he mentioned the dreams he had, foretelling your meeting?"

"Yes, he did." Carol sighed, remembering. "I listened to his beautiful words, but I didn't really understand them until this minute. Is it true, then? Nik and I will meet again in the future, and we might both live beyond those days when I was there? And Pen and the others, too?"

"Whether possibility becomes reality is up to you, Carol." Lady Augusta raised one hand and Carol began to grow sleepy. It was all she could do to keep her eyes open. She yawned, too weary to lift her own hand to cover her mouth.

"Sleep will mend your present grief," Lady Augusta said.

"Don't go. Will I see you again? Didn't you say . . . ?" Carol was so sleepy that she could no longer remember what Lady Augusta had said.

"I am heartened to learn that you now desire my company where once you despised it." There was amusement in Lady Augusta's fading voice, and a kindness and warmth Carol had not heard from her before. "I will return once more. For the moment, my presence is required elsewhere. You have until Twelfth Night, Carol. Do your very best, child. Remember, I am depending upon you."

The voice grew fainter and fainter, until Carol

could just barely hear the last words. She sighed and turned over, snuggling down beneath the bedcovers. Questions floated through her mind, but she was too tired to ask them just yet. Tomorrow would be soon enough. For the moment, her pillow was soft and the bed and her flannel nightgown were warm.

Pillow? Nightgown? Hadn't she been sitting by the fire?

Chapter Nineteen

Christmas Eve Day was Carol's 27th birthday. She gave the fact only the briefest thought as she rose from her bed at an early hour. When she finished washing her face in the bathroom down the hall, she stared at herself in the mirror over the sink, expecting to see in her visage the marks of the great changes that had taken place in her. However, except for the faint hint of a smile lingering about her usually downturned lips, her face looked the same as it always did.

"After what I've just been through," Carol said softly to herself, "I ought to be red-eyed from crying all night. But I slept better than I have for years, and I can't see any outward signs of severe emotional conflict. Why not?"

It did not take much thought before she knew the answer to her question. Though they were real enough to her, the horrors of the future had not yet actually occurred, so they could not mark her. Nik was not yet born; thus, he had not died by order of Commander Drum. Nik, his sister, and his friends might never have to face the terrible deaths Carol had witnessed. She could make the difference for them.

"And I will," Carol told her damp reflection. "I have the power to change the future. Lady Augusta said so, and I believe her. The only question is, exactly where to start."

By the time she had applied her makeup and dressed, her plan of action was formulated. It was still early. Nell brought her breakfast on a tray every morning at 7:30, but today Carol did not wait to be served. She hastened below to the kitchen.

"Oh, miss," cried Nell, catching sight of her, "I was just fixing your tray."

"There is no need for you to climb all those stairs," Carol told her. "I will eat right here, at the kitchen table. Unless I'll be in your way, Mrs. Marks? You look very busy."

"Eat where you like," said Mrs. Marks, somewhat ungraciously.

"Thank you, I will. I would like to talk to you, Mrs. Marks. And to you, too, Nell."

"What about?" asked Mrs. Marks, slamming two pans of freshly baked bread down on the table.

"First," said Carol, "if the invitation is still open, I would be very happy to join all of you for Christmas dinner tomorrow night."

"I thought you had other plans." Mrs. Marks was turning the hot loaves out of the baking pans onto racks to cool, but she paused to send a sharp glance in Carol's direction.

"Well, my original plans have—er—they've fallen through," Carol said. "Besides, it might be nice if the entire staff ate a meal together on what will almost certainly be our last Christmas at Marlowe House."

"Oh, yes," said Nell. "Oh, that would be lovely, wouldn't it, Mrs. Marks?"

"If you want to eat with us," Mrs. Marks said to Carol, "then you are welcome. It is Christmas, after all. But I still don't understand why you want to."

"She just told you why," Nell cried.

"No, she didn't." Mrs. Marks frowned at Carol, who suddenly grinned at her. Mrs. Marks stared, too taken aback to say another word.

Carol had just recalled an old adage. *If you want someone to be your friend, don't do a favor for him. Instead, let him do a favor for you.*

"Mrs. Marks, I have a great favor to ask of you," Carol announced.

"Now we come to it," said Mrs. Marks with another of her hard looks.

"Yes, indeed." Carol was still smiling. "Do you know St. Fiacre's Bountiful Board?"

"Everyone in this part of London knows about St. Fiacre's," said Mrs. Marks. "The Reverend Mr. Kincaid and his wife do a lot of good there."

"I agree." Carol extended her smile to include not only Mrs. Marks and Nell, but also Crampton and Hettie, who had come into the kitchen while she spoke and who both looked very surprised to see her sitting there at the table. "I think we should help Lucius Kincaid and his wife in their efforts to feed the poor. I am sure they could use more food, and extra hands to help serve this evening's meal would also be welcome."

"Help them?" Mrs. Marks looked doubtful. "Well, I don't know. I have so much work to do in preparation for our own Christmas dinner tomorrow."

"Don't be silly," said Nell. "Only half an hour ago, you were bragging to me how you had preparations so well in hand that there would be nothing left for you to do from breakfast time today until late tomorrow morning. And just think of all the cookies you've been baking for days. Who you intended them for I'll never know. The five of us can't eat all of them before they go stale. We might as well donate them to St. Fiacre's, where they'll be appreciated." When Nell paused for breath, Crampton cleared his throat.

"If I may make an additional suggestion," said Crampton, "I believe canned goods are always acceptable at such establishments. If they are not used for tonight's meal, they can be easily saved to be served at some future time. Hunger is not confined to the holiday season, and St. Fiacre's Bountiful Board serves meals all the year round. Now, the cellars below this kitchen are filled with food that will be useless if Marlowe House is soon to be closed. The executors of Lady Augusta's estate will be forced to find a means of disposing of all of those cans. We could carry some of them to St. Fiacre's today."

"I don't think Lady Augusta would approve of your idea, Crampton," said Mrs. Marks in a stern tone of voice.

"Believe me," Carol told her, "the Lady Augusta I know would wholeheartedly endorse Crampton's wonderful idea."

"Do you really think so?" Mrs. Marks appeared to be puzzled by Carol's assured tone, but after a moment she nodded, accepting the notion that Lady Augusta might have been more generous than her cook had ever realized. "Well, in that case, seeing that this is the holiday season, I could make another batch of bread and send it to the church."

"Thank you." Carol paused, then asked, "If I buy a turkey to contribute to the cause, could you have it cooked in time to take it to the church hall late this afternoon? I'm not certain what time the dinner is to be served. And, I confess, I wouldn't know how to roast a bird on my own."

"Here now, I'm not sure about all of this," Mrs. Marks began, puzzled again and a bit upset by so many unexpected suggestions.

"The doors of the Bountiful Board open at five o'clock this afternoon," Hettie stated. "Oh, Mrs. Marks, let's do it. I know Lady Augusta was never one for charity work, but Mr. Kincaid has always been nice to me. I go to St. Fiacre's every Sunday," she confided to Carol.

"I suppose we could do our bit to help out, just this once, since it is Christmas Eve." Mrs. Marks looked at the small, plain roll on Carol's plate and at the cup of tea Nell was pouring for her. "That's not much of a breakfast. I could cook an egg or two for you, if you'd like."

"I would love it." Carol sat back in her chair, well satisfied with the response of Lady

Augusta's staff to the first part of her plan to change the future. "Two eggs, scrambled, if you please. And thank you very much, Mrs. Marks."

Carol spent the morning in a burst of last-minute Christmas shopping. The first order of business was the turkey. She bought the biggest, plumpest bird she could find and carried it back to Marlowe House herself.

"I wanted to be sure you would have enough time to cook it," she said to Mrs. Marks, "so I didn't wait for the delivery service."

"Hah. At least you know how to shop for a crowd." Mrs. Marks regarded the turkey with satisfaction. "That ought to feed a fair number of people. I'll fire up the big oven, the one we used to use for great roasts in the days when Lady Augusta's father was alive and still entertaining. Now, where are you going? I thought you were going to help us." This last exclamation was addressed to Carol's back.

"I never learned to cook," said Carol, one hand on the door knob. "I leave that to experts like you, Mrs. Marks. I have more shopping to do. I will be back in time to assist in carrying everything to the church." She did not add that she was feeling increasingly nervous about this charitable project of hers, or that she was comforted to know the servants would be with her so she would not have to meet the Kincaids on her own.

"While you are gone," Crampton put in before Carol could leave the kitchen, "I shall call the Reverend Mr. Kincaid and inform him of our intentions. He should know of them in advance, for it may be that with our additions to his menu, he will be able to invite more hungry folk than he originally planned to feed."

"That's a good idea, Crampton. I'm glad you thought of it." She was more relieved by his suggestion than Crampton could possibly guess. It was cowardly of her to let him smooth the way for her with the Kincaids, but Carol was afraid the rector and his wife might not be glad to see her after her rudeness to them on Monday afternoon. The episode after Lady Augusta's funeral seemed years ago to Carol, but to the Kincaids it was only a few days in the past. They could not have forgotten it. With a silent prayer that she would be forgiven her earlier sharp words and permitted to do what she could to help the good people of St. Fiacre's, Carol let herself out the door before Mrs. Marks could think of any reason why she ought to stay and help with the cooking. Now, with the turkey in the cook's capable hands, Carol could begin the rest of her errands. She headed toward Bond Street first and then to Regents' Street.

Within a very short time she bought a bottle of toilet water and a jar of hand cream in the same scent for Nell, whose hands were often red and rough from housework and who Carol suspected often longed for feminine pleasures she could not afford. For Crampton, Carol purchased a book about the historic houses of England. Next she selected a pretty blouse for Mrs. Marks. Finding a gift for Hettie was a bit of a problem, since the scullery maid did not seem to have any interests beyond her work at Marlowe House and Carol knew from the vision of the servants' holiday dinner shown to her by Lady Augusta that Hettie could not read very well. A book would not suit but, recalling Hettie's remark that she went to St. Fiacre's every Sunday, Carol at last settled on a felt hat decorated with a sprightly red feather.

It had been years since she had bought a gift for anyone, and in those earlier, youthful days Christmas shopping had always seemed like an unpleasant chore. It was not so today. Every present she bought represented in some way a gift of love, and the cheerful "Merry Christmas" that she regularly heard during those hours was music to her newly blossoming spirit, a sound almost as joyous as the Christmas carols being played in the stores she visited.

"This is fun," Carol said to herself with a sense of wonder. "I never guessed that shopping for presents to give to someone else could make me feel so wonderfully happy." She knew it would be even more fun if the man she loved could be with her, but she refused to think about her own longings. She was engaged in a project to ensure that same man a long and happy life. Knowing that she was succeeding would be enough for her.

Her arms filled with packages, she paused outside a confectioner's shop. She thought Lady Penelope Hyde would have appreciated the gaily decorated and cleverly arranged boxes of chocolates and other sweets in the window. The Pen who lived in the far future loved sweets. Taking a chance that Abigail Penelope Kincaid also had a sweet tooth, Carol went into the store and selected a large box of assorted candies.

"A merry Christmas to you," the shopkeeper called after her as she left.

"Merry Christmas," Carol replied, giving him a bright and totally sincere smile.

She stood outside the shop for a moment, trying to balance all her parcels and realizing that she could not possibly carry anything more. Hailing a taxi, she returned to Marlowe House a second time, to sneak in by the front door and carry everything up to her bedroom, there to hide the packages in her closet in case Nell should come into the room for some reason. Having deposited the gifts on the closet floor, she straightened to look at her wardrobe. It was not large, and all of her clothes were in shades of brown, black, or gray.

"Not very cheerful," Carol noted. "I will have to do something about that. And I still need decorations for St. Fiacre's hall and for the church. Do I have enough money left?"

After scraping together every pound note and coin she could find, she went out again. This time she bought a packet of pretty but inexpensive wrapping paper and some ribbon, then purchased a green silk scarf and a bright lipstick for herself, before ending her Christmas shopping at the florist's shop where she had purchased roses and narcissus just a few days previously. There she selected an assortment of red and white flowers and holiday greenery for the altar at St. Fiacre's Church, a table arrangement for the buffet, and three wreaths with red bows on them.

"We can deliver these," said the shopkeeper

when Carol explained why she wanted so many decorations. "I am closing the shop in half an hour, and I will be happy to take everything to St. Fiacre's myself. In fact, I'm helping to serve the dinner tonight."

"Then I'll see you there," Carol said.

"If you are working with Mrs. Kincaid, you certainly will." The young woman smiled at her. "Merry Christmas."

"Oh, merry Christmas!" Carol cried. "Until later, then."

Back at Marlowe House, the kitchen was filled with the good smell of roasting turkey and sage and thyme. Hettie was packing cookies into large tins for transportation to St. Fiacre's, Nell was wrapping loaves of still-warm bread, Crampton was sharpening a carving knife, and a slightly frazzled-looking Mrs. Marks was bustling about giving orders to everyone.

"I don't know how we will get that turkey to the hall," Mrs. Marks fussed.

"I shall carry it," Crampton told her, "and I shall carve it, too. You have done a lovely job on it, Mrs. Marks. The bird will provide the perfect centerpiece to the main course."

"They already have two turkeys, you know," said Hettie, closing the last tin of cookies. "There are people in the kitchen over at St. Fiacre's carvin' them right now."

"Nonetheless, *I* shall carve this one where everyone can see it," Crampton responded. "The sight of an entire bird beautifully roasted to a perfect shade of brown will add to the festive air of the meal."

"Exactly right, Crampton," said Mrs. Marks. "I suggest that you ladies retire for twenty minutes or so, in order to prepare yourselves, and then we will leave," Crampton said.

Smiling to herself at the way in which the formerly standoffish servants were warming to the plans she had instigated, Carol hurried to her room to hide the last batch of parcels in her closet. She pulled out a simple gray wool dress and changed into it, wrapping the new green scarf around her throat and fastening it with a gold pin in the shape of a leaf. It had once belonged to her grandmother and for sentimental reasons, Carol had refused to part with it when she gave up all other traces of past luxury.

The group from Marlowe House made a merry parade through the streets to St. Fiacre's Bountiful Board, where the rector greeted them at the door. Carol quickly discovered that she need not have worried over the way she would be received. Lucius Kincaid gave her the same friendly smile he bestowed on the others with her. Carol also found that his almost Victorian manner of speech no longer irritated her. Rather, knowing now the kind of person he really was, she thought his speech was charming.

"Good heavens," Lucius Kincaid said, surveying the food they carried. "I knew you were coming to help us, but I never expected all of this. My friends, you have made Christmas immeasurably happier for many souls tonight.

"And please do notice," he added, waving an arm to indicate the decorated front door and the interior of the hall, "that an anonymous donor has sent us wreaths and flowers. It's quite remarkable, really, to find someone so sensitive and so generous. Few people remember that even those who live in the direst poverty can appreciate beauty when it is shown to them. Of course, we need food to nourish their bodies, but we ought not to forget to feed their spirits as well."

"Amen to that." The florist with whom Carol had dealt earlier in the day had spoken from behind Lucius Kincaid's back, and she winked at Carol.

When the Reverend Mr. Kincaid moved away to show Crampton where to put down the turkey, Carol stepped closer to the florist.

"Thank you for your discretion on the subject of the decorations," Carol murmured. Looking around, she added, "But I never ordered this many flowers. There is a bouquet on every table, and there are wreaths on all the walls and even on the door into the kitchen."

"Isn't it amazing how much pleasure can be derived from giving a gift to someone who has no idea who sent it?" said the florist, laughing. "I wish I had discovered that simple fact of life before today."

"Are you saying that you donated the extra bouquets?" Carol asked, wondering how she was going to pay for this largesse if the additional flowers were not a donation.

"You inspired me," the florist answered. "My shop will be closed for the next two days. Anything left there this afternoon will surely be dead by Monday morning, so I thought, why not bring all the flowers here, for these people to enjoy? They are just leftovers, you know, but Lucius Kincaid was so happy to have them that I felt guilty for not doing this long ago. I think from now on I will send all of my unsold flowers here to St Fiacre's. I'm sure Mr. Kincaid will know who would appreciate them. Perhaps I could donate bouquets for the altar each Sunday, too, if it's agreeable to him."

"I'm sure it will be. That's very kind of you."

"The idea was yours, Miss Simmons, and it was a good one. Will you excuse me? I am supposed to be helping in the kitchen."

With moist eyes Carol looked after the young woman, astonished to discover how quickly her own modest gesture had affected someone else's behavior. Surely, this was what Lady Augusta meant when she said that the smallest change in the present could make a major difference in the future. True, it was only a few flowers, yet the gesture might lighten someone's heart enough to produce a correspondingly kind chain reaction in a more important area.

Then Carol spied Abigail Penelope Kincaid, in bright red skirt and green turtleneck sweater, just as she had been dressed in Carol's vision of this night. Clutching the box of candy she had brought along, Carol hurried forward to intercept the rector's wife.

"Merry Christmas," Carol said. Not knowing exactly what to say next, and still more than a bit embarrassed over her unkindness at their last meeting, she thrust the decorated box into Mrs. Kincaid's hands. "This is for you. Please be just a little selfish and keep it for yourself. I want you to have it."

"You and the others from Marlowe House have already been so generous," Mrs. Kincaid said. "Lucius and I were quite surprised. Oh, dear, I shouldn't have said that. It's just that when we met the other day, you weren't at all interested in what we are trying to do here."

"I wasn't myself the other day," Carol said. "Not my true self, the self I am supposed to be. I'm not making much sense, am I?" She ended on a nervous little laugh.

"Perhaps more sense than you think." Abigail Penelope Kincaid gave her a shrewd look. "You are different now. If you were to ask my opinion, I would say that you have had a revelation of some kind."

"You would be very close to the mark," Carol told her. "Perhaps one day, when we know each other better, I can tell you exactly what has happened to me since Monday and Lady Augusta's funeral. You and your husband are among the few people who might believe me."

"Of course we will believe you. And I have a feeling that we are going to become very good friends." Abigail Kincaid linked her arm through Carol's. "Now, come and help us serve this wonderful dinner that you and so many other generous people have helped to provide."

Carol went with the rector's wife and did her best to be useful. After serving up vegetables at the buffet table, she helped to clear off the empty dishes and then set out the donated pies, cakes, and cookies. Meanwhile, Mrs. Marks's cooking skills and Crampton's carving ability were much admired. Mrs. Marks's cookies in particular were widely praised, and every last one of them was eaten, a fact which pleased the cook enormously.

Someone from Marlowe House—Carol never

discovered who it was, but she suspected Nell—had whispered the secret of her birthday to Lucius Kincaid. At the end of the main course, and just before dessert was served, the Reverend Mr. Kincaid rapped a spoon against a glass and called for attention.

"We all know that this is a blessed night, the holiest night of all the year," he said. "For one of our contributors here with us at this feast, December twenty-fourth also has a personal significance. It is her birthday. To the well-named Miss Carol Noelle Simmons, we wish the happiest of birthdays, and a joyous year ahead."

The company did not sing "Happy Birthday." Instead, they offered three cheers to her. As "Hip, hip, hurrah!" rang through the hall, Carol stood between Lucius and Abigail Kincaid and tried her best not to cry.

"Speech, speech," called a voice from the crowd.

"They will expect you to say something," Abigail Kincaid whispered to Carol.

"Thank you, and a merry Christmas to every one of you," Carol responded to her audience. "This is easily the best birthday I have ever had. But there is a far more important Person whose birthday we will celebrate in just a few hours. I hope to see all of you in church."

"I second that particular sentiment," declared Lucius Kincaid, to general laughter. "Miss Simmons, why don't you cut the largest cake? Symbolically, of course, since it is not, strictly speaking, a birthday cake."

"It is the very best kind of cake," Carol told him, "because it was made and carried here in a spirit of love and generosity."

Following the serving of desserts, Carol, Mrs. Marks, the florist, and Abigail Kincaid took charge of pouring coffee or tea for the grownups and milk for the youngsters. Later, when the meal was over and most of the guests had left, there were dishes to wash and put away, while Hettie and Nell helped to sweep the floor and a few male volunteers folded up and stored the chairs and tables. Everyone worked with a cheerful will, but all the same, they just barely got to the church in time.

Carol had been standing for hours, and her feet were aching, she was tired—and she had rarely in her life been so contented or felt so completely possessed by the Christmas spirit. Nor was she alone in being affected by the evening and by the welcome they had received at St. Fiacre's.

"Hettie isn't the only one who comes here," Mrs. Marks confided to Carol in a remarkably friendly way. "I try to sneak out for early service each Sunday."

"It's a lovely old church," Carol whispered back, "but it needs a lot of work."

"There's little money in this parish," said Mrs. Marks. "And what there is goes to meals like the one you saw tonight. At one time I hoped that Lady Augusta would leave something to St. Fiacre's in her will, but I should have known better."

"Perhaps it's not too late," Carol murmured. She watched Abigail Kincaid and her three little children arrive and take their seats, a signal that the service was about to begin.

In the church Carol could see evidence of

her own good intentions, for the flowers and greens she had ordered for the altar now filled the lovely old vases—and there were extra vases of white chrysanthemums, which she had not ordered, sitting on either side of the pulpit. She glanced toward the florist, now standing with a young man who had joined her during the course of the evening. The florist looked at Carol and smiled, letting Carol know that the white flowers were her contribution.

"There is hope," Carol said aloud.

"Perhaps there is," answered Mrs. Marks. "Every Christmas I believe that anew."

Then they stopped talking because the choir began to march in and the strains of "Oh, Come All Ye Faithful" filled the old church.

It was nearly one o'clock in the morning before the contingent from Marlowe House returned home.

"A most rewarding evening," remarked Crampton, setting down the turkey platter and the carving set. "I am glad we participated."

"So am I," said Mrs. Marks. "Thank you for suggesting it, Miss Simmons."

"Yes," said Nell. "And the church service was beautiful, too."

Hettie's only comment was a long, noisy yawn.

Wishing each other some rather sleepy variations of "Merry Christmas," they separated then, but Carol stayed up until well after two o'clock, wrapping the Christmas presents she had bought earlier in the day.

She slept long and well that night, entertaining no ghostly visitors and not plagued by visions of Christmases in the past, present, or future. When she wakened at mid-morning it was to the sweet scent of paperwhite narcissus. The red bowl of bulbs she had purchased three days earlier and set on the table beside her bed now presented flowers in full bloom, and the fragance filled her chamber.

"No matter where I may be during the rest of my life," Carol said, touching a petal with one gentle finger, "the smell of narcissus will always remind me of this incredible Christmas. Fresh, pure flowers blooming in the dead of winter to symbolize a new beginning. In fact, a whole new life."

She swung her feet out of bed and hastened to dress, eager to meet whatever possibilities this special day might bring to her. She pulled on a beige skirt and matching sweater and slid her feet into low-heeled beige pumps. For a bit of cheerful color she added the green silk scarf, once again fastening it at her throat with her grandmother's pin.

"We all got up so late," Nell whispered to Carol when she finally reached the kitchen, "that Mrs. Marks has decided to serve the Christmas feast in early afternoon, so she can skip making lunch. She says we can be satisfied with just tea later, instead of a regular dinner."

"From what I have seen of her preparations for today's big meal, a cup of tea will probably be all any of us will be able to swallow by nightfall," Carol responded. Raising her voice, she added, "Mrs. Marks, can I help you in some way?"

"You can set the table," came the prompt

answer. "Crampton will show you where everything is. Make certain you do it right." Hearing this admonition, Carol and Nell grinned at each other, smothering laughter.

Except for the addition of a small Christmas tree decorating the sideboard—a joint contribution from Nell and Hettie—the holiday meal that followed shortly after noontime *appeared* to be just as Carol had seen it when Lady Augusta showed it to her in the second of her remarkable nights with that ghostly apparition. However, there was a definite change in the spirits of those who gathered in the servants' dining room.

"After last night I do feel much more in the spirit of the holiday," Mrs. Marks declared. "This meal reminds me of the Christmas dinners my dear mother used to make when I was a child."

"Indeed," said Crampton. "This has been a most memorable Christmas. I no longer feel quite so useless as I once did when contemplating the retirement soon to be forced upon me. I had begun to believe that I would be put out to pasture, so to speak. I thought there was no place for a man of my years in today's busy world. But last night the Reverend Mr. Kincaid asked if I would be interested in overseeing the production of meals at St. Fiacre's Bountiful Board. He says the meals have become so popular that he and his wife no longer have time to do the work involved and still keep up with parish affairs and their many other duties."

"Crampton," exclaimed Carol, "your experience as a butler should make you ideally suited to that job."

"I told Mr. Kincaid I would seriously consider his offer," Crampton responded. "However, since for lack of funds it must be a volunteer position rather than a paid one, I fear I cannot afford to accept it. My pension is too small to allow me to continue to live in London. It is a pity, for I would like to be of some use to my fellow man." He ended on a sigh.

"Perhaps something can be done to enable you to take the job," Carol murmured.

"I do not think so. But it is enormously cheering to discover that my services could still be of use despite my advancing age. Now, let us not dwell upon the uncertain future," Crampton urged. "Let us instead enjoy this Christmas to the fullest. Allow me to propose a toast to the five of us who, most unexpectedly during the last few days, have, I believe, become friends."

Crampton poured out the brandy—Lady Augusta's finest stock, just as in Carol's vision of this scene—and they drank the toast to themselves.

"And to Lady Augusta," said Nell, lifting her glass a second time. When Mrs. Marks snorted her disapproval of the suggestion, exactly as Carol expected her to do, it was Carol who interceded.

"I have only recently begun to appreciate what a fascinating woman Lady Augusta was," Carol said. "I never troubled myself to learn about her early personal life or to discover why she was so difficult and so miserly. I think now that she had a wounded heart and hid her pain beneath a shell of nastiness. Perhaps she wished for someone who would love her in spite of the unpleasant front she presented."

"If anyone had tried," Mrs. Marks stated bluntly, "Lady Augusta would have pushed that person away."

"Perhaps you are right," Carol said. "But we aren't here to analyze her. Let us just drink to Lady Augusta's memory and wish her spirit well, wherever she may be tonight."

"Certainly," said Crampton, refilling glasses all around. "In the spirit of Christmas, let us drink to Lady Augusta."

With my very best brandy.

Carol could have sworn she heard the echo of a ghostly voice that no one else in the servants' dining room discerned.

With the brandy glasses still half full and a fresh pot of tea steeping, Carol brought out the presents she had purchased the day before and gave them to her new friends.

"I never thought," exclaimed Mrs. Marks, "I mean to say, we have never exchanged gifts before and I did not expect—Miss Simmons, I have nothing to give you in return, and I'm sure Nell and Hettie haven't, either."

"I don't want anything in return," Carol said. "I enjoyed chosing each gift. And the friendship you have given me is worth more than anything that comes in a package."

"Oh, my." Mrs. Marks tried to wipe her eyes without anyone noticing. "What a Christmas this has been. *What a Christmas!*"

"It ain't over yet," noted Hettie, who, upon opening the box from Carol, had immediately donned her smart new hat with the scarlet feather on it. "Mr. Kincaid says Christmas lasts till Twelfth Night."

"He's right about that," Carol told her, thinking of Lady Augusta's claim that she had been given until Twelfth Night to change Carol's character.

"We shall make the most of the joyous season," declared Crampton. "More brandy, anyone?"

"I do believe just a small drop more would be in order," murmured Mrs. Marks.

"Who could we toast next?" asked Nell, holding out her glass to Crampton.

"Who needs a toast?" Hettie giggled. "Drink up. Drink up."

"Now, now," cautioned Crampton. "Moderation at all times, if you please."

With amusement and genuine fondness Carol watched these new friends of hers. She still sorely missed both Nicholas and Nik, and she knew she always would. But she was not sorry she loved them, and she found that her emotional anguish had diminished somewhat as she tried to make the holiday a happy one for others. It scarcely mattered to her now what her own personal future might bring. She would continue to do the work she had set for herself and pray that in doing it she would improve the future for those she loved. Perhaps, some day, Lady Augusta would find a way to let her know if she was succeeding.

To Carol's surprise, the dignified Crampton now produced a supply of Christmas crackers, those paper-wrapped party favors so beloved of the English for their holiday celebrations. The cardboard tubes were covered with red and green tissue paper and decorated with gilt. When a long strip of paper at one ruffled end was pulled, a loud *pop* could be heard, after which it was possible to extract tiny treasures from within—and a funny paper hat.

"We must all put them on," declared Hettie, who, after imbibing a bit too readily during the toasts, could not seem to stop giggling. "Oh, Mrs. Marks, yours is a crown."

"How very appropriate," said Nell, upon which the two younger women fell into fits of laughter. Unabashed, Mrs. Marks did place her crown upon her gray hair.

"I note that I am a dunce," said Carol, unfurling a bright blue tissue-paper cap with a long point that stood straight up when she donned it. "Open yours, Crampton, and let us see what you are to be."

"Did you hear something?" asked Crampton, holding up one hand. "Hush, please, and let me listen. I thought I heard someone at the front door."

Into their startled silence fell the loud noise of the seldom-used door knocker.

"Who could that be so late on Christmas Day?" asked Mrs. Marks.

"There is only one way to find out." Straightening his jacket and smoothing his hair as he went, Crampton left the servants' dining room and headed for the steps to the upper level of the house.

"Well, I'm sure I wasn't expecting guests," said Mrs. Marks. "Were you expecting anyone, Miss Simmons?"

Carol did not answer, but only shook her head because she was listening intently. She could hear voices from the entrance hall above. Crampton and another person were talking together. The second voice sounded oddly familiar, though muffled as it was by the intervening walls, she could not place it exactly. Automatically, without thinking about what she was doing, Carol put up her hand and removed the blue paper dunce's cap. Then, intrigued by the continuing sound of male voices, she left the servants' dining room and went into the kitchen, intending to go up to the front hall to discover who was there. Just as she put a foot on the bottom step Crampton came through the door at the top. Behind him loomed a taller figure.

"Crampton?" said Carol. "Is anything wrong? Who is that with you?"

"There is nothing wrong," Crampton informed her. "It is only that Mr. Nicholas Montfort has arrived somewhat earlier than expected." Crampton moved down a step, making room for the person behind him, who advanced to the upper landing, where Carol could see him more clearly.

He was tall and rather slender, although she could not doubt that beneath his well-cut suit there were hard muscles. His hair was black and straight and his eyes were green. That strong, thrusting jaw, that long slash of nose—it was, and yet it was not. . . . Carol grabbed for the banister, praying she would not faint.

"Good evening," said Nicholas Montfort, looking straight at her with no sign of recognition. But then, why should he recognize her? He had never seen her before in his life.

"Oh, my God," Carol gasped. "Lady Augusta, why didn't you warn me about this?"

Chapter Twenty

"Yes, thank you," Nicholas Montfort replied to Mrs. Marks's question. "I would appreciate some dinner. Airline food is not especially satisfying."

"As I have explained to you, Mr. Montfort," Crampton said, "we were told that you would not arrive until Tuesday at the earliest. Marlowe House is, however, prepared in expectation of your coming."

"I cleaned and aired Lady Augusta's rooms myself," Nell said, contributing her part to Crampton's assurances. "There's even clean towels in the bathroom."

"Thank you," Nicholas Montfort said again. From his position on the topmost step he gazed upon the little group below him, his eyes gleaming with amusement when they lit on Hettie with her brandy glass still in hand, on Nell's flushed, eager face, and on Mrs. Marks, who in her excitement had forgotten to remove her gold paper crown. Only Crampton really looked like a proper servant, and even his cheeks were a bit more pink than usual, thanks to several glasses of good brandy.

"I am afraid I have interrupted your holiday celebrations," Nicholas Montfort said.

"Not at all," Crampton responded. "We have finished with our dinner. Mrs. Marks will be delighted to prepare a meal for you."

"Hmm." Nicholas Montfort's eyes were once again fixed on the glass in Hettie's hand. Carol half expected him to demand to know exactly whose brandy the girl was drinking. Then he turned his attention to Carol. "I assume you are my late aunt's former companion. Miss Simmons, isn't it?"

"That's right." Carol was amazed to discover she could still speak, for she remained in a state of shock at the sudden appearance of the man whom she had loved in both the past and the future but had never expected to encounter in the present. Lady Augusta had not bothered to warn her of this unexpected development.

"Perhaps you will join me in the dining room while I eat, Miss Simmons," Nicholas Montfort continued. "Before I speak with the solicitors there are a few questions I would like to have answered about my aunt's last weeks."

"Of course." Carol met the green eyes directly. Deep inside her a glorious excitement was building, a sense of unlimited possibilities. This man's presence at Marlowe House was Lady Augusta's doing. Carol was certain of it. Therefore, his arrival must be connected in some way to the changes she was expected to make in both the present and the future.

"Did you take dictation for my aunt?" The question was a little abrupt, but Carol was not offended.

"Occasionally," she said, adding, "I am probably not as proficient at shorthand as you might want."

"I will only require you to take a few notes," he said, his eyes still on hers. "Find your notepad and some pencils and meet me in the dining room in thirty minutes. Now, Crampton, if you will see to my baggage, I would like a bath before I eat. Mrs. Marks, I will expect my dinner in one hour."

He was gone, Crampton following him. Mrs. Marks moved toward the stove, muttering to herself about possible menus using the leftover roast turkey.

"Who made him king of the hill?" asked Hettie, still gaping at the door through which Nicholas Montfort had left the kitchen.

"You put down that brandy glass, girl, and come and help me," Mrs. Marks ordered. "He may not have a title before his name, but I know a nobleman when I see one. Mr. Montfort will expect the very best service and the best food I can prepare."

"First," said Nicholas Montfort, watching Carol scribble hasty notes on her pad, "there will be two more guests arriving late on Monday afternoon. Have the servants prepare rooms for them."

"Right." Carol put down her pencil to take a sip of tea while her companion applied himself to a plate heaped high with creatively transformed, reheated roast turkey and vegetables. "Will one of the guests be Mrs. Montfort, and if so, shall I tell Nell to make up the room next to Lady Augusta's bedchamber? I believe it is in suitable condition. Nell takes very good care of all the rooms."

"There is no Mrs. Montfort. I am divorced."

"I'm sorry to hear that." She was not sorry at all. She feared her heart would have broken if he had said he was married.

"Don't be. I'm not," he responded to her politely insincere remark. "It was best for both of us. We never matched well together. Something was always—always *disjointed* between us." He stopped, fixing her with an inscrutable look. "Now, why the devil should I feel compelled to tell you such a thing, when I never discuss personal matters with my employees?"

"I am not exactly your employee," Carol said. "I worked for your aunt."

"May I assume that you know Aunt Augusta's solicitors?" he asked, turning his attention to a list in his own handwriting which he had put next to his plate for easy reference.

"Yes. She used to send me to their offices carrying sealed messages she did not want to discuss over the telephone."

"That sounds like Aunt Augusta. She never trusted anyone that I knew of. Do you think she trusted you?"

"Not at first," Carol said. "But recently, yes, she put great faith in me. I hope I never disappoint her."

"Why do you say that? Did she leave some particular instructions with you?" His glance was sharp. "It is my understanding that she left little or nothing to the people who worked for her."

"Not in her will, no." Carol took a deep breath, preparing to state facts that were not true in any legal sense, but which she knew to be Lady Augusta's deepest desires. "Mr. Montfort, I do think she meant to do much more for her servants. She did understand how difficult their lives would be if they were turned out of their positions. Crampton and Mrs. Marks are too old to find new employment, and Nell and Hettie are not especially well educated. Hettie, in particular, can barely read. They are not likely to find good jobs elsewhere. Then there is St. Fiacre's—"

"Are you telling me that my aunt was fond of these people?" he said, interrupting. "I find such a claim difficult to believe."

"How well did you know your aunt, Mr. Montfort?" Carol demanded. "I have worked for her for nearly six years. During that time, I do not recall any contact between you."

"Because there was none. Her estate was left to me only because I am her sole remaining relative. Now let me ask *you*, Miss Simmons—how well did you know my aunt?" When Carol, trying to decide how much she should tell him, did not respond at once, he went on. "You did not know her at all. Oh, you may have seen her every day for six years. You may have done her bidding, perhaps even to her satisfaction, though I doubt if she would have told you so if you had. Lady Augusta Marlowe did not make friends of her employees, nor was she ever generous to them. Do not attempt to convince me that her character was otherwise, or I shall begin to suspect you of some unscrupulous intentions in spite of your security clearance. She did have a security check done on you, did she not? I would expect it of her."

"Yes, she did, but she wasn't as suspicious as you think. At least, not—not—"

"Not at the end, when her mind was failing?" he suggested, frowning at her.

"How dare you imply that I tried to influence a senile old woman? That is what you are saying, isn't it?" Carol felt like crying. How could this man look so much like the Nicholas and the Nik she knew and loved, and yet be as cold and suspicious as Lady Augusta at her worst? "Your aunt and I understood each other. As for you, I think you don't care about anything but her estate. If you cared about her, you would have made an effort to see her once in a while."

"She would not have allowed me to enter the house. Did she never tell you the scandalous tale of her quarrel with my mother?"

"Perhaps you ought to explain that business to me." Carol was rapidly growing annoyed with him. "All I know about the great Marlowe family feud is that Lady Augusta and her sister once got into a major fight and stopped speaking to each other. Then your mother married and went off to Hong Kong, and the two sisters never made up their quarrel and never saw each other again."

"Those are the basic facts," Nicholas Montfort agreed.

"Why did they fight?" Carol asked, speaking more softly now in hope of coaxing him to tell her all about it. "I don't know why I feel the way

I do about this, but it seems to me to be vitally important that I should know what caused the quarrel between your mother and your aunt. Perhaps then I could better understand what motivated Lady Augusta."

"I remember her, you know." Nicholas Montfort's face softened with a smile. "We all lived in this house when I was a little boy. In those days, my grandfather was still alive. When my father died, Grandfather insisted my mother should return home, to stay with him and Aunt Augusta. She was older than my mother. I was missing my father and she was remarkably patient with me."

"I know Lady Augusta never married," Carol prompted gently.

"She had a beau. That's what she called him. He had been a dashing pilot in the Royal Air Force during the war. Afterward, he went into his family's business. He came here to lunch one day, shortly after we arrived. He took one look at my mother and promptly forgot all about Aunt Augusta. There was a bit of a dustup about it," Nicholas added dryly, "and a battle royal when my mother decided to follow him to Hong Kong and marry him there."

"I can imagine." Carol let out a long breath. "So that's why the two sisters never spoke again. If Lady Augusta's heart was broken by her own sister's actions, it would explain why she became such a crusty, suspicious old spinster. I can't blame your mother, though, not if she loved your stepfather."

"She did. And he loved her. I have seldom seen two people so happy together. He died a week after she did, and I truly believe his death was caused by a broken heart. He just did not want to go on without her."

"Did you go to Hong Kong with your mother?" Carol asked, to change the fascinating subject a little without entirely leaving it.

"Not immediately," he said. "I went to school here in England. Afterward, I started in the London office of my stepfather's business. Later, I went out east to work directly with him, as his partner. I took full control of the company on his death. Now, with Hong Kong scheduled to be returned to the Chinese in just a few years, I have been considering moving our headquarters back to England."

"You could live in the old family homestead."

The suggestion elicited an amused chuckle from him. "You have a peculiar effect on me, Miss Simmons. I seldom talk so much. Or perhaps it is the result of returning to this house and finding myself quartered in rooms that were my grandfather's when I was last here. On the other hand, it could be no more than jet lag that is making me so talkative."

"You haven't said anything very shocking, and I won't repeat a word of it," Carol murmured. She was acutely conscious of the warm, quiet room with its candlelight and gleaming silver and crystal. Nicholas was seated at the head of the long, mahogany table, and she was at his right with the silver tea service in front of her.

"Is that a decanter of port I see on the sideboard?" he asked. "Would you care for a glass, Miss Simmons?"

"Thank you." Carol did not usually drink

port, but she would seize any excuse to remain with him like this for a little longer. She noted with pleasure the easy grace with which he rose to lift the decanter of wine off the sideboard. The way he moved had not changed from either the past or the future.

Nor was there any change in her heart in regard to him, whether he called himself Nicholas Marlowe the Earl of Montfort, or Nik the leader of a band of rebels, or plain Mr. Nicholas Montfort. She had been steadily falling deeper and deeper in love with the same man under wildly different circumstances. Now here he was, in her own time, and her love for him meant nothing at all, because he did not know her. Carol considered her extraordinary situation for only a moment before she became aware of a slight nudging sensation within her mind.

No, Lady Augusta, she thought in response to the sensation, *I won't forget what I have to do.*

"This is the third time you've done that." Nicholas set a stemmed crystal glass of port down in front of her. "First you look desperately sad, as if your heart were broken, then you smile as if you have just remembered a wonderful secret."

"Perhaps I have, and perhaps I ought to reveal at least part of it to you," she murmured. Raising her eyes to his she said in a crisper voice, "You won't be able to do any business tomorrow because it is Sunday—or on Monday, either, because Boxing Day has been postponed until then. You can't meet with Lady Augusta's solicitors or make any official decisions about her estate until Tuesday at the earliest. In the meantime, I would like to show you a few things. Call them my secrets if you like. Will you go to church with me tomorrow?"

"Church?" He laughed. "I haven't been to church for years, but yes, if you like, I will go with you. It is the season for churchgoing, after all."

She told him the time of the service and then she rose, using the late hour and his long journey as an excuse to end the evening. The nudging in her mind was growing stronger, urging her to leave the dining room before she was actually ready to do so. As a result of this peculiar sensation she hoped—indeed, she prayed—that Lady Augusta would be waiting for her in her bedroom when she got there, because she wanted an explanation for the events of the last few hours.

Her room was empty. Only the scent of paperwhite narcissus greeted her. Carol looked around, unable to believe she was alone. Surely Lady Augusta was present, even if Carol could not see her.

"Am I right, then?" Carol asked the air. "Have you sent Nicholas Montfort to Marlowe House at this exact time because you want him to help me change the future?" Having received no response to these questions, Carol nonetheless continued speaking aloud to an empty room.

"Lady Augusta, are you going to provide some help, or do you expect me just to fumble around until I figure things out on my own? Come to think of it, that is what you let me do in the other times, isn't it? You took me to the past and the future and gave me a few pointers for getting along in each, and then you disappeared and let me learn my lessons for myself. And in both of those times you did nothing to stop me from falling in love. Can it be that loving Nicholas and Nik was part of your overall design for me?

"In case you don't know it yet, Lady Augusta," Carol went on, "just in case you can't read my mind, I ought to tell you that tomorrow I am going to introduce Nicholas Montfort to the people at St. Fiacre's Bountiful Board, and I am going to try to convince him to make a large donation out of your estate."

There was no need for an introduction. Nicholas already knew Lucius Kincaid.

"We went to school together," Nicholas said to Carol as soon as he saw the rector march in behind the choir and take his place at the altar. "What is he doing in a place like this?"

"I plan to show you what he's doing, right after the service," Carol whispered in reply. A short time later she noted with great interest the startled look on Lucius Kincaid's face when he saw Nicholas kneeling beside her at the altar rail, and then the happy grin he tried to keep under control as he went about his priestly duties. Even more interesting was the way in which the two men greeted each other after the service was over. Laughing, pounding each other on the back, they utterly destroyed all of Carol's preconceptions about Englishmen being reserved.

"I never thought to see you here," Lucius Kincaid cried. "Has the Far East lost its glamor? Are you home to stay?"

"I am considering taking up permanent residence in London," Nicholas responded in a mock serious tone totally unlike his usual voice. "Yes. Harrumph. The matter requires serious, not to say, lengthy, thought."

"I had forgotten how well you do that. You have just heard a perfect imitation of Old Foggy, our tutor at Oxford," Lucius Kincaid informed his wife and Carol, who were both watching this display of schoolboy comradeship in stunned disbelief.

"Lucius, my dear," said Mrs. Kincaid, "we ought to be in the hall at this very minute. People are waiting for us."

"Come with us, Nicholas." The Reverend Mr. Kincaid gave his old friend a hearty shove on one shoulder to direct him into the churchyard and thence to the back entrance of the parish hall. Carol and the rector's wife followed them. Inside the hall the Sunday morning edition of St. Fiacre's Bountiful Board was in full swing, with volunteers serving a breakfast of coffee, tea, or juice with sweet rolls.

"I wish it could be eggs and kippers and the occasional platter of bacon," said the rector. "Unfortunately, this is the best we can afford, and I must say, we hear few complaints."

"What, exactly, is this program?" Nicholas asked. The two men moved off, Lucius Kincaid talking rapidly as he explained the purpose of the Bountiful Board.

"Mr. Montfort seems to be a nice man," Abigail Kincaid commented, watching carefully to see Carol's reaction to her words.

398

"If he is your husband's friend, then he must be a decent fellow," Carol said as casually as she could manage. She was longing to tell Mrs. Kincaid all about her history with Nicholas Montfort, but she sensed that it was not yet the proper time to do so.

"Like Lucius, Mr. Montfort is apparently not without a sense of mischief." Abigail Kincaid's blue eyes were laughing. "By the way, Lucius has eaten at least half of that box of candy you gave me. He says he prefers the nuts and the tough, chewy ones."

"Of course he does. I would expect nothing less." Their eyes met. Suddenly, with an instinctive yet unspoken understanding of the mysterious connection between them, both women burst into laughter.

"Luc," said Nicholas a short time later, "you cannot possibly continue this work on your own. You must agree to let me help." Pulling out a checkbook, he began to write.

"My dear fellow, I did not bring you to this hall to solicit money from you," cried Lucius Kincaid.

"No, you did not," said Nicholas, smiling a little. "It was Miss Simmons who brought me to St. Fiacre's, and I am grateful to her. Here you are. I believe I can also promise continuing support in the future." He handed the check to his friend.

"Oh, I say!" Lucius Kincaid stared at the paper in his hand. "Nicholas, this is quite magnificent. Almost unbelievable, in fact."

"Nonsense." Nicholas's hand rested on his friend's shoulder for an instant. "You did me a good turn once. It is only fair for me to return the favor, and with interest, since it was so many years ago.

"Luc saved my life," Nicholas told Mrs. Kincaid and Carol. "While we were at Oxford, he pulled me out of the river after a boating accident. Now, Luc, I do want something from you in return for this check. I would like you and Mrs. Kincaid to come to Marlowe House for dinner on Tuesday night. My assistant and his wife will be there, too. You do remember William Bascome?"

"Will? I wondered where he had gotten to. So, he has been working for you." Lucius Kincaid grinned. "It will be a reunion of old school chums who have not seen each other for far too long."

Later, walking back to Marlowe House from St. Fiacre's, Carol filled Nicholas in on the Christmas Eve dinner at which she and the servants had assisted the Kincaids.

"Those good people are struggling to keep the Bountiful Board going," she said. "I hope you can continue to help them." When he did not answer, she was silent for a while before adding, "The church could use some restoration work, too."

"A *lot* of restoration. I am capable of noticing such things on my own, Miss Simmons." He spoke in a severe tone, but his eyes were dancing with green fire when he stopped to catch her shoulders and turn her around to face him directly. "I suppose you want me to restore Marlowe House to its former glory, too?" he teased.

"It would be lovely if you could. Such a

beautiful old house should not be allowed to fall into ruin."

"I have always been fond of the place. Perhaps I will keep it instead of selling it as I first planned to do."

"I know Lady Augusta would be pleased to hear you say that."

"Once again you pretend to know her thoughts and her wishes." He looked distinctly skeptical.

"It is not pretense. I am telling you what I *know* about her."

"Really?" From his amused expression Carol could not tell what he thought of her claims.

"Believe me or not, as you please," she said. "It really doesn't matter so long as you help Lucius Kincaid and also do something for the staff at Marlowe House."

"Why, Miss Simmons?" he demanded. "Why is this so important to you? Is it because of something my aunt said or did? I am fairly good at reading character, and I think you are hiding something from me."

He was still holding her by the shoulders and looking deep into her eyes. Carol gazed back at him, wishing she dared to move a step or two closer to him and lay her head upon his chest. The desire to feel his arms around her tore at her heart. But he was awaiting her response and she gave him the only one she could.

"I can't get into this at the moment," she said. "I don't want you to imagine that I have lost my mind, which is what I am afraid will happen if I say too much before you know me well enough to believe my story. I promise, I will tell you when the time is right."

"I thought at first that you might be a con artist, someone who was trying to get money for herself from my aunt's estate, after having failed to convince her to write you into her will." He continued to look at Carol as if he could read her very soul and he spoke as if he were talking to himself.

"I can't blame you for thinking along those lines," Carol said. "After all, you don't know me. But Mr. Montfort, I assure you, I would not know how to begin to be dishonest."

"You haven't asked for anything for yourself," he said. "It is all for other people. What is this mystery, then? What motivates you?" Still he did not remove his eyes from hers. Carol was only dimly aware of cars moving along the street and of people waking past them and glancing curiously at the couple who were gazing into each other's eyes so intently.

Nicholas, her heart sang. *Nik, Nicholas, Nik. My Love.*

"Miss Simmons?" he prompted.

"Call it a spiritual renaissance," she whispered.

"Yours, or my aunt's?" he asked.

"Both," she breathed. "Both of us have changed beyond recognition, beyond returning to what we once were."

"You are real," he said, his hands tightening and then loosening on her shoulders as if he wanted to reassure himself that his assessment of her was correct. "You are not a ghost, and something tells me that you are not an angel, either."

"I am alive," she responded. "As I have never been alive before."

"You make it sound like a miracle."

"It is," she said. "Dear Mr. Montfort, it *is* a miracle. Now all I have to do is convince you of it."

"Crampton said you wanted to see me." Carol paused in the library doorway, looking around at the shelves crammed full of books, at the oriental rug on the floor and the polished desk.

Nicholas raised his head from the papers he was working on. A pair of narrow reading glasses was perched on the end of his nose and his face was serious.

"Come in. I have a few more questions for you." He waved a hand, indicating the chair placed directly across the desk from where he sat. "Tell me, Miss Simmons, what are your plans, now that your employer has died?"

"I don't know," Carol said. "I have been wondering what to do, but I haven't decided yet."

"You appear to be well acquainted with my aunt's affairs. Would you consider staying on to assist me here at Marlowe House?"

I would stay anywhere, do anything, to be with you. Acknowledging to herself her fear that he might not find her work acceptable, Carol was completely honest when she answered him aloud.

"I did act as Lady Augusta's secretary when she needed one, but I must warn you, Mr. Montfort, I do not have much in the way of office skills. I can barely type, and if you were to show me a computer, I would probably run away from it."

"You won't need to type, or to file. That is not the kind of job I meant. Perhaps Joanna

Bascome can teach you to use a computer, but it won't be absolutely essential." He leaned back in his chair, watching her every reaction to his next words. "Miss Simmons, I detect in you a remarkable sensitivity to the needs of others. Having made a large fortune, I now feel duty-bound to distribute at least part of it in ways designed to do the most good for people who could use some help in getting their lives onto the right path. Would you be interested in acting as my assistant?"

"Oh, yes. It's exactly what I want to do. To make people happier, to improve their futures and thus, perhaps, to change the future world for everyone who comes after us—I can't think of anything more wonderful. But Mr. Montfort, how can you make such a hasty decision? You don't know anything about me. I might be an embezzeler who will steal your entire fortune." Carol stopped when Nicholas began to laugh. The carefree sound made her heart leap with pleasure.

"Miss Simmons, if Aunt Augusta hired you to work for her, I am certain she ordered a complete security check done on you. The results are probably in her solicitors' office. Of course, I will have you checked out again, just for my own records, but for work of this kind I do prefer to trust my own judgment— and my judgment tells me that you are exactly the person I need.

"Now," he went on, apparently assuming that she was already hired, "tell me what you know about Aunt Augusta's servants."

Quickly, Carol sketched the situation for him, pointing out Hettie's illiteracy and the desperate need of both Hettie and Nell to find new jobs when their present ones were terminated.

"I don't think either girl has much chance of getting a well-paying job," she said, repeating essentially what Lady Augusta had revealed to her during their invisible excursion into the servants' quarters. "Crampton and Mrs. Marks are slightly better off because they do have small pensions, but I don't think they will be able to live very well after they retire." She went on to tell of the offer Lucius Kincaid had made to Crampton, and Crampton's sorrowful comment that he would have to refuse it. As she spoke, an idea took shape.

"Mr. Montfort, this morning you told Lucius Kincaid that you wanted to continue to help his efforts at St. Fiacre's. The poor man is much too busy. Could you set up a fund to pay a supervisor for the Bountiful Board? Then Crampton would be able to take the position, possibly with Mrs. Marks as his assistant. If they were in charge of the soup kitchen, Mr. Kincaid would be free to concentrate on his pastoral duties. All three of them would be relieved of a great deal of stress, and thus they would all be much happier people.

"As an added benefit, Abigail Kincaid wouldn't have to work so hard, either. At the moment, she is the one who does most of the planning for those meals. And, if you fund the Bountiful Board, perhaps the Kincaids wouldn't feel obligated to put so much of their own money into feeding the poor and Abigail could occasionally buy something brand-new for herself or her children to wear." Carol finished in a rush of excitement.

"This is exactly the kind of creative thinking I want to hear from you." Nicholas sounded enthusiastic. "Miss Simmons, I do believe that you and I are going to make a very good team."

Later, Carol, Nicholas, and Crampton inspected Marlowe House from its attic to the sub-basement. Crampton pointed out repair work that needed to be done, and Carol made notes.

"It's such a shame the original house was divided into two," Carol said. "The old Marlowe House was so lovely and spacious."

"So it must have been." Nicholas was looking at her as if he was wondering how she could possibly know what kind of house it originally was.

"I have heard rumors," said Crampton, "that the lease on the house next door, which once was part of Marlowe House, will soon become available. The information might be pertinent to your future plans, Mr. Montfort."

"Thank you, Crampton." Nicholas looked thoughtful.

That Sunday afternoon and again on Monday morning, Carol put her limited typing skills to the test. Under Nicholas's direction she made up a list of necessary repairs for the house, and then typed a proposal for a fund to aid St. Fiacre's Bountiful Board.

"I believe Lady Augusta would want a portion of her estate to go into the fund," Carol said to Nicholas.

"It will take quite a while to settle her estate,"

Nicholas replied. "Therefore, we will begin with my money."

"Could you set up the fund in her memory, then?" Carol asked.

"What a persistent woman you are, and how certain of what my aunt would have wanted. Very well, we shall call it the Lady Augusta Marlowe Memorial Trust Fund. Is that grand enough for you?"

"It sounds perfect. I know she will be pleased."

"Wherever she may be," Nicholas added in the dry tone she was coming to know well.

When Carol was finally freed of office duties she hurried down to the kitchen. She was afraid that Mrs. Marks, who could be temperamental, might be upset by the additional work involved in having three extra people living in the house after Nicholas's associates arrived on Monday evening, and further annoyed by the festive meal for six that was scheduled for the following night. To Carol's surprise, Mrs. Marks appeared to be energized by these challenges. In fact, she was in her glory, ordering Hettie around the kitchen until the poor girl was thoroughly confused, and driving Nell half mad by insisting that only the best china, silver, and crystal should be used but that every piece must be washed and polished first.

"I can see you have everything under control," Carol said to the cook.

"It's time this old house came to life again, if only for a little while," Mrs. Marks responded. "I'll show Mr. Montford some fireworks—culinary fireworks! I'm not ready for retirement just yet. Oh, we will have a grand feast tomorrow night. Hettie, where is that copper pan I wanted?"

William and Joanna Bascome were, as Carol expected, twentieth-century versions of the Bas and Jo whom she had known in the future. She recognized them at once, although like Nicholas, they did not know her. In Will Bascome, Carol also saw a resemblance to the Earl of Montfort's butler who had unwillingly let her into the earl's house on a December afternoon in the distant past.

I must remember to ask Lady Augusta about this, Carol thought. *Does it always happen this way, with the same people coming together again and again over the centuries? If so, why was Penelope Hyde in love with Alwyn Simmons in the past and Pen with Al in the future, yet in this time, she is married to Lucius, who will one day be Luc? It's very confusing.*

To Carol's delight, Will and Joanna Bascome were soon chatting with her as if they were all old friends. They enjoyed an early dinner and then the new arrivals retired, blaming the inevitable jet lag after their long trip from Hong Kong.

"By way of Majorca," Joanna said. "We stopped to visit my parents, who are retired there, which is why we did not arrive with Nicholas."

Some time later Carol mounted the steps from the kitchen, where she had been conferring with the servants on the schedule for the next day. Still smiling at Mrs. Marks's bustling rejuvenation, she stepped into the main hall, then paused, listening. From the library at the back of the house came the strains of a well-remembered waltz. Carol hurried toward the sound.

Nicholas was sitting behind the desk, reading some papers. He had put on Lady Augusta's stereo and was playing one of her old records. He glanced up as Carol came through the door.

"Is there a problem?" he asked, peering at her over the rims of his reading glasses.

Carol found his quizzical expression endearing. If only she dared to go to him, to put her arms around his shoulders, perhaps to sit on his lap and rest her head upon his broad chest. How wonderful it would be if he would hold her in the tender embrace for which she longed. Telling herself not to forget that so far as Nicholas Montfort was concerned they were still strangers, she responded to his question as coolly as she could with a hauntingly familiar tune filling her ears.

"No problem at all," she said. "I heard the music and I couldn't resist coming in here so I could hear it better. I love that waltz."

"So do I. It is odd, because I usually prefer something more modern, but that old song has always had the power to move me. I don't know why." Tossing down the papers he had been reading, he rose and came around the desk to her. "Since you like it, too, would you care to dance to it, Miss Simmons?"

Carol could not protest that a library was a peculiar place in which to dance, for she knew better. When Nicholas Montfort held out his arms, she went into them like a weary traveler who has finally returned home. His strength, his graceful movements, the sparkle in his green eyes, the touch of his left hand clasping hers, the way his right hand on her waist guided her easily around the room, all raised images in her mind of past and future moments with him that blended together into a few exquisite minutes in the present. It seemed to Carol as if the very walls of the library held music and tender memories.

Carol was not sure whether Nicholas Montfort felt the same breathtaking pleasure in the dance that she did. They moved perfectly together, as she had known they would, but when the music stopped, Nicholas dropped his arms at once and stepped away from her.

"You must excuse me now," he said. "I have several hours of work still to do. Thank you for a charming diversion at the end of a busy day and evening." He kissed her hand lightly before he went to the door, to hold it open for her. There could be no question that Carol was being dismissed—politely and kindly, but dismissed all the same.

"Good night, Mr. Montfort." Hiding her hurt and disappointment, Carol left the library and made her way upstairs to her own room, there to contemplate a dismaying question.

What would she do if, in this lifetime, Nicholas Montfort was not for her? If Penelope-Abigail-Pen was not with the same man in every period in which she lived, could the same fate befall Carol?

Carol knew the answers to those questions as if they were engraved upon her heart. She would always love Nicholas, but if he could not love her, then she would work with him for as long as he allowed her to and she would see to it that they helped as many people as possible. And she would always try to remember that in a future world—a *different* future world from the one she had known—she and the man she loved *would* be together. If in this lifetime she was not fated to know Nicholas's passionate love, then she would earn his respect.

Nor would she be alone. She would have friends, the Kincaids, Nell and Hettie, Mrs. Marks and Crampton, the Bascomes if she were lucky—and perhaps even Nicholas's friendship, too. It was not all she wanted, but it might have to be enough. Knowing there was more to come in another lifetime, she would learn to be content.

"This is the gift that Lady Augusta has given me," Carol whispered, "and for it I shall be forever grateful. *Forever*. Thanks to her, I know that this life is not the end."

Chapter Twenty-One

Nicholas's dinner party for the Kincaids and the Bascomes was a great success, the three men enjoying themselves with tales of their school years which Carol suspected were highly embroidered. While the men talked the women got acquainted, and by evening's end Carol was sure they were going to be friends. Which, from her point of view, was exactly as it should be.

In fact, the evening was similar in spirit to the ones Carol had enjoyed in the Lond of the future, in the kitchen of a ruined version of Marlowe House. This time, the conversation was a good deal more cheerful.

"I have begun inquiries as you wanted," Will Bascome said to Nicholas. "I believe it will be possible for us to acquire the lease on the house next door."

"Are you planning to rejoin the two halves

of Marlowe House once again?" Carol asked Nicholas.

"It would create too big a house to be practical, and who knows what the needs of the future will be?" he answered. "We might want two separate houses. I did think, Will, that you and Joanna might like to design your own flat on the top two floors of the building next door, and we could use the lower levels as offices for the Montfort-Marlowe Charitable Trust. Perhaps Lucius will have some people among his flock whom we could hire to do the work. Talk to him, Will, he knows them all and knows who needs a job." This last was said with a mischievous grin in Lucius Kincaid's direction.

The week following the arrival of Nicholas Montfort in London was a busier one than Carol had experienced for some time. She had never realized how much work was involved in spending large amounts of money. In company with Nicholas she visited Lady Augusta's solicitors, where she did not hesitate to voice her opinions as to what her late employer would have wanted done with the money she had left behind. It quickly became clear to her that Nicholas was right when he told her it would take time before Lady Augusta's estate could be settled and all the taxes on it paid.

Thanks to Nicholas's quick action in regard to his own fortune, which was entirely within his control, by the end of the week arrangements were well in hand for continuous funding of St. Fiacre's Bountiful Board. When Nicholas approached Crampton and Mrs. Marks about taking positions at St. Fiacre's, their responses were immediate and positive.

"I do not doubt that you would prefer a more youthful butler and cook if you intend to remain in London," Crampton said to Nicholas, "and while Mrs. Marks would never admit to such a thing, I believe she has found the last few days rather tiring."

"Indeed not," that worthy lady protested. "I could continue as I am doing for years to come, but I do feel I could be of more use at St. Fiacre's. However, neither I nor Crampton will leave Marlowe House until a new cook and butler have been installed."

"Thank you, Mrs. Marks." Nicholas's response to this speech was as serious as the cook could have wished. "I am grateful to you for your consideration. If either of you should happen to learn of anyone qualified to join my staff, please let me, or Miss Simmons, know of it."

Nell and Hettie were to be kept on at Marlowe House at increased wages, and Hettie had been signed up for a course in remedial reading at Nicholas's expense.

"You are being very generous," Carol told him.

"I will be paid back in loyalty and better service," he responded. "If those two young women are as intelligent as you think they are, they won't remain lower-echelon servants for long. I take great pleasure in promoting deserving employees."

Repairs to Marlowe House were to begin shortly after the new year, and Nicholas was discussing with Lucius Kincaid and Will Bascome just what ought to be done to restore

St. Fiacre's Church to good condition. A donation would soon be made to cover most of the
restoration bills.

Carol was pleased with all of these changes,
which she believed would have a positive
impact on the future. It was the present
that disturbed her, for Nicholas continued
to preserve his cool, professional demeanor
with her. Nor had he played that haunting
waltz a second time on Lady Augusta's old
stereo. It was almost as though he felt no
personal connection to Carol at all. She began
to wonder if she would, as she feared, have
to resign herself to being only his business
associate in this present lifetime.

At mid-week a strange little incident occurred
that left Carol perplexed and eager to question
Lady Augusta at their next meeting. Will
Bascome announced that he had obtained
four tickets to a popular play for the following
night, which was Thursday. He invited Nicholas
and Carol to join himself and Joanna.

"It's a wonderful idea, Will. We could all use
a break. We will go on to dinner afterward,"
Nicholas decided. "Miss Simmons, would you
mind informing Crampton and Mrs. Marks of
our change in plans? Perhaps the servants
would like a night off, too."

"Certainly, Mr. Montfort." Silently cursing
his formality and her own, Carol hastened to
the kitchen. There she discovered Mrs. Marks
with a large knife in hand, attacking a boiled
lobster as if it were a personal enemy. Without
comment Carol delivered her message. She
knew Mrs. Marks well enough by now to be
aware that she would not have to wait long

before she was told exactly what was troubling the cook.

"I'm sure I could use an evening to myself," said Mrs. Marks, taking a vicious whack at the lobster. "There's others what would also enjoy an extra night out on the town. Nell has started seeing that young man she met at St. Fiacre's on Christmas Eve. Mrs. Kincaid says he's a decent enough fellow, but he hasn't got a job. Nell pays for the cinema and for their tea afterward, too. In my day, a respectable man would never let a lady pay his way. Mrs. Kincaid says times have changed, but I say, not for the better."

"What young man?" Carol asked, disregarding Mrs. Marks's other complaints. "I didn't know Nell was dating anyone."

"She wasn't, till this week. Here they come now," Mrs. Marks hissed in a stage whisper.

Out of the servants' dining room issued Nell, her blond curls dancing and her plump cheeks pink with an emotion Carol could not immediately define. A tall, fair-haired young man was right behind her. Crampton followed the couple into the kitchen. He was finishing what sounded to Carol like a serious lecture.

"I will expect you to have Nell home by eleven o'clock at the latest," Crampton warned the young man. "I stand in the place of her late parents and I feel responsible for her, so I will hold you to this time-honored household rule."

"Sure, Mr. Crampton. I'll see she's back in time," said the young man in an offhanded way.

"Oh, Miss Simmons," said Nell, catching

sight of her, "this is Allen Symms. Al, this is the lady I told you about."

"*Al?*" When the young man stuck out his hand, Carol took it, but she could think of nothing else to say to him. He did not appear to notice her tongue-tied condition, nor did Nell.

"We're off to see that new movie," Nell told Carol, adding in a low voice, "You'd think Crampton and Mrs. Marks were my grandparents, they're so fussy about where I go and what time I come back."

"They care about you," Carol said. "Have a good time." As the young couple went through the servants' entrance and up the outside steps, Carol stared after them.

"Nell and Al together?" she murmured to herself. "There is no way in heaven or earth that I will ever understand this development. I wonder what Lady Augusta would say?"

"An interesting question, Miss Simmons, and one with which I quite agree." Crampton was standing closer to her than Mrs. Marks and he had overheard her remark, but he could not possibly have known why Carol found the pairing so incomprehensible.

"There's no accounting for young people's activities these days," Mrs. Marks put in. "If you ask me, that boy is just not right for Nell."

Carol was left with a sense of bewilderment. She was unable to understand why two couples—the Kincaids and Nell with her new friend—were so mixed up when they ought to be paired off differently. And yet Lucius Kincaid and his wife seemed to be perfectly happy in their marriage. Perhaps couples did not always find each other in every lifetime. It was a depressing idea.

Whatever her concerns about her friends, Carol soon put such thoughts aside in order to concentrate on her own relationship with Nicholas Montfort—or rather, her lack of a relationship with him. Throughout their evening with the Bascomes, at the theater and the dinner afterward, Nicholas behaved toward her with the same air of polite but detached formality that permeated all their activities together. Carol was beginning to believe he felt nothing at all for her.

After a nightcap in the library on their return to Marlowe House, the Bascomes decided to retire. Nicholas and Carol followed them up the stairs, and they all said their good nights in the upper hall. Their bedroom door closed behind Will and Joanna, leaving Carol and Nicholas alone.

"Good night, Mr. Montfort." Carol started up the second flight of stairs toward her own room.

She never knew what made her suddenly look over the railing toward Nicholas in the hall below. Perhaps it was the sudden faint whiff of lavender in the air, or possibly it was the fact that Nicholas did not respond to her words.

He was standing by the door into Lady Augusta's old suite, with one hand on the polished brass lever. She caught him by surprise, with all of his polite, professional barriers down. He was gazing up at her with such an expression of stark longing on his face that Carol stopped dead, gazing back at him.

"Nicholas?" For the first time she used his given name.

"Carol." His voice was a whisper, but still she heard him. With his eyes locked on hers he drew nearer to the staircase where she remained standing, unable to move. Reaching up, he placed one hand over hers on the banister as if to keep her where she was. He spoke again in the same harsh whisper. "Who are you?"

"I am Carol Noelle Simmons."

"That is not what I meant and you know it." His voice was rough, as if he were fighting against an emotion he did not want to acknowledge. "*Who* are you? *What* are you, that you can have this effect on me?"

She did not answer in words. Instead, she bent forward to caress his face with her free hand. Nicholas caught his breath—and caught her hand, holding it tightly so she could not pull away from him.

"We have met somewhere before," he said. "That must be it. I can't think of another explanation for what has happened to me in the last few days."

"And what is that, Nicholas?" Carol moved down one step and then another, slowly returning to the hall where he stood. She paused on the second step. "Tell me what you feel."

"You are—*significant* to me." Then, as if he could maintain his rigid self-control no longer, he burst out in a low, ragged voice, "My God, how do you expect me to feel? Since the first moment I saw you, all I can think about is taking you in my arms, taking you to my bed. On Christmas night I did not know you, I had never seen you before that I could remember, but I could not get you out of my mind. I don't think I have slept an hour since I reached London. And every day, seeing you, working with you, having to hide what I'm feeling—"

"No one would ever suspect." Carol was amazed to discover that she could keep her voice so level when Nicholas was losing control. She held on to his hands and looked straight into his eyes. "I didn't guess. I thought you were indifferent to me. I could only hope that one day you might regard me as a friend."

"Friend?" he choked. "Far more than that. This isn't supposed to happen! I am a sensible, practical businessman. What I am feeling belongs to fairy tales and medieval legends. Intelligent men do not fall madly in love at first sight or imagine that they have known someone else since the beginning of time. I think I must be going mad," he concluded.

"Could you entertain the possibility that we might be meant to be together?" she asked.

"Do you mean fate? I have known people in the Orient who believed in such things." He looked even harder at her. "Is that what you believe? Do you feel the same way that I do?"

"Since the moment when I looked up and saw you standing at the top of the servants' steps," she said, "I have known there was a deep connection between us. I was only afraid that you would never know it—at least, not in this time."

"Carol." He did not remark on her last words. Perhaps at a later time he would ask her about them. If he did, she would answer him honestly, for she could never lie to him.

She watched him move to the bottom of the staircase, still holding her hands in his over the railing, until he faced her directly, from two steps below her.

He lifted her hands to his lips. It required only a little tug on Carol's part to make him release her hands so she could put them around his neck and entwine her fingers in his thick, dark hair. She leaned downward, balancing herself against his shoulders. His arms went around her, holding her above him for a long moment while he gazed at her as if to assure himself that this was what she wanted, too.

"Nicholas," she whispered in response to his silent question, "hold me. Don't ever let me go again."

Slowly, deliberately, he let her body slide along his until they were face-to-face. Another long moment passed as they looked into each other's eyes, learning eternal truths that would for the present remain unspoken. And then their mouths met in a bruising kiss that released all the pent-up passion each was feeling. When it was over they were breathless.

Carol threw back her head, moaning her pleasure as Nicholas's mouth skimmed along her throat. Eagerly she clutched at his shoulders, and cried out a second time when she felt the touch of his tongue on the sensitive skin just beneath the slashed neckline of her dress.

"Hush," he cautioned, "or we'll waken Joanna and Will. I don't want company just now, do you?"

Carol could not answer. She only nestled her face into his shoulder and let him touch her where he would. It was a relief when he picked her up and started for his bedroom. She did not think she could have stood on her own feet for much longer. Her knees were decidedly weak.

He shut the door with his shoulder and carried her across the room to the huge old bed. There he laid her down and bent over her to unfasten the buttons at the front of her dress. His mouth followed his fingers all the way down to her waist. Carol stretched luxuriously, kicking off her shoes.

"This room," she murmured, "is where Lady Augusta used to sleep."

"It is the bedchamber of the master of Marlowe House," he corrected her. "When I was a boy, this suite was my grandfather's. It is mine now."

"I don't know about your grandfather," she said softly, pulling his head downward as she spoke so she could kiss him again, "but somehow, I don't think Lady Augusta would mind in the least if she could know we are here together."

There followed a long pause while Nicholas indulged himself in the taste of her lips and her inner mouth, and Carol responded eagerly to what he was doing. His hands were working at the front of her dress, unbuckling her belt, unfastening the last few buttons, pushing fabric aside. Carol scarcely noticed what he did. She had spent the last five days and nights in an agony of longing for this man, and now she was reveling in the wonder of his lips on hers. She whimpered at the loss when he removed his mouth from hers to raise his head and gaze down at her.

"Carol, my sweet, how beautiful you are." She

was surprised to note that he had removed her clothing down to her plain white slip and her bra. In a reflexive act she crossed her hands over her bosom.

"I wish," she whispered, "that I were wearing something glamorous made of silk and trimmed in yards of lace."

"The wrappings don't matter." With a slow, sensuous motion he laced his fingers into hers and gently tugged her hands away from their protective position, spreading her arms wide upon the bed. In the same deliberate manner he pulled the straps of her slip downward and unfastened her bra to reveal her breasts. "It is the package inside that counts and you, my dear, are a rare gift. Never before have I met a woman as generous and tenderhearted as you are. Will you be generous with me tonight?"

"Tonight and always," she murmured. So sure was she of him that she felt no need to be cautious in words or deeds. "I have waited for you all of my life. And on Christmas night there you were, looking at me from the top of the stairs, the most wonderful Christmas gift I have ever received."

"And here I thought you were my Christmas present," he responded with a chuckle. "Carol . . ." His lips brushed hers again, their breaths mingling in a sigh of recognition and joy.

All of their movements were slow, as if they had all the time in eternity. Carol unbuttoned his shirt and slid it off along his arms, her every motion as she removed it speaking of tenderness and desire. Slowly she caressed Nicholas's shoulders and his chest. He lay quietly, allowing her to do whatever she wanted to him.

"You have no scars," she murmured, touching a place where once a ridge of reddish tissue had snaked its way across his torso—*would snake in the future—might not scar him at all if she did her work well in this lifetime*. Her fingertips traced smooth skin over hard muscles, and she rejoiced in the sound of his groan of mounting desire. "I have dreamed of touching you like this."

"Touch me here." He took her hand and put it on himself, letting Carol feel his strength and his throbbing, eager heat. In return he touched her, and kissed her until she was trembling and tossing her head upon the pillow and begging him to take her.

He was all the men she had loved—the men she loved still—in past, present, and future. He was the *same* man, for though his body might change slightly, his spirit and his courage were unalterable by time or changing circumstances. Her own spirit always recognized him. He was her only love and he would be through all eternity. And she was his. In this present time they would not be parted. She knew it with absolute certainty.

She looked into his eyes as he moved into her with a sure, bold stroke. She returned his passion with her own, freely giving to him everything he needed, everything he wanted of her. He gave to her in equal measure, holding back nothing, taking her with him as his passion soared until at the end they cried out the triumph of their everlasting love with one voice and one heart.

Chapter Twenty-Two

It was the night between the fifth and the sixth of January, the time which is called Twelfth Night and which is generally acknowledged by traditionally minded folk to be the end of the Christmas season. It was also the night on which Lady Augusta had promised to make her last visit to Carol.

Nicholas did not stir when Carol slipped out of bed shortly before midnight. Nor did he move when she caught up her robe and slippers in one hand and let herself out of his bedroom. She paused to scuff her feet into the slippers. It was chilly in the hall. Carol shivered a little as she pulled on the robe and fastened the sash at her waist.

She did not expect to meet anyone else wandering about Marlowe House so late at night. The servants were all asleep in their own quarters, and Will and Joanna Bascome were away from London on a week's visit to Will's family, who lived in Cornwall. As for Nicholas, Carol could only hope he would not sense her absence from his side and begin a search for her.

The upper floor of Marlowe House seemed even colder than usual to her, but that might well have been because she had just left Nicholas's warm embrace. Carol's old room was positively frigid. It was also empty. No ghostly apparition awaited her. The paperwhite narcissus were dead and gone, although a trace of their fragrance lingered on the still air.

"I guess Lady Augusta is going to be late." Carol pulled a blanket off the bed. Wrapping it around her shoulders, she sat down in the wing chair. Minutes passed. Nothing happened. Carol shivered, looked about the room, stared into the empty fireplace. No one joined her. Her feet were freezing. She pulled them up beneath her, tucked a corner of the blanket around them, and continued to wait. After a while her eyelids began to droop.

The light appeared suddenly, flooding the room with brightness. Carol's head snapped up, her eyes opened wide again, and all her senses came alert. She blinked at the brilliant yet soft pulsations now surrounding her.

"Good evening, Carol." When Lady Augusta stepped from the light to stand before her, Carol rose to her feet. There was no way that she could *not* stand upon encountering such a resplendent creature.

Gone were the gray and black tatters of Lady Augusta's most recent materialization.

Gone, too, the lavender chiffon of her first appearance and the rich red velvet of her second. This time, Lady Augusta was garbed in a gleaming, iridescent robe that contained within itself all the colors of the rainbow along with every conceivable shade of each of those colors. And yet, the overall effect of that multiplicity of colors was to create a soft, pearl-like white. The sleeves of the robe were long and loose, and the ever-drifting folds of the skirt fell to Lady Augusta's feet. A cord of mixed gold and silver bound her waist.

This version of Lady Augusta was tall and slim and youthful-looking, her face unlined and shining with an unearthly joy. Her long, loose hair was pure white, and a wreath of white roses sat upon her brow. The scent of roses surrounded her.

"Is that really you?" Carol whispered, awestruck.

"Amazing, isn't it?" Lady Augusta's voice was different, too, having acquired the rich tones of a finely cast bell. The sound, though quiet, reverberated in Carol's mind.

"Well," Carol said, making one last attempt to retrieve her former assertive and falsely casual attitude when dealing with this ghost, "it looks to me as if you have finally achieved your proper place with my help, just as you wanted. I guess we can both relax now."

"Not at all." Lady Augusta shook her lovely, shining head and the light in the room pulsated and shimmered in response to the motion. "There can be no laziness for me in that place where joyful work in service to others is the most sincere form of worship. Nor can you ever revert to your former indifference to other people.

"You have done well thus far, Carol," Lady Augusta went on. "You have transformed yourself and you have begun to change the world around you. You must continue with this work, for with it you are also changing the future into what you hope it will become."

The unexpected compliment destroyed the final remnants of the cleverness and the too-smart attitude to which Carol had been clinging. In her heart she knew she did not need tough defenses when dealing with Lady Augusta. What she needed was unflinching honesty.

"If my character has improved recently, it is largely your doing, and I know it." Carol spoke with more humility than she had ever felt before. "Left to myself I would have stayed exactly as I was, a miserable human being. But the awful truth is that I am still a selfish person. For example, I know that leaving here to take your proper place is what you want and what we have both been working for, but I wish you did not have to go. I will miss you terribly and I would keep you with me if I could. You never thought you'd hear me say that, did you?" She ended with a short, broken laugh that came close to degenerating into a sob.

Lady Augusta nodded in regal acknowledgment of the tribute paid to her. "I, too, have been altered by our time together, Carol. As you have learned from me, I have been learning from you. Each of my visits to you has taught me a little more about the true qualities of love between men and women. I have also learned how valuable friendship can be. I do have a few lingering regrets about the lack of both emotions during my own most recent time on earth, but I believe those particular problems will be resolved at a future date."

"I am glad our association hasn't been entirely one-sided," Carol said. "It is a great relief to me to know that you finally have the place you wanted so badly." She would have said more, but was stopped by the wry chuckle that accompanied Lady Augusta's next words.

"The proper place which I so eagerly sought upon first reaching the hereafter is not at all what I expected it to be. In fact, the full revelation of my exact place came as a startling, though not altogether a displeasing, surprise to me." Lady Augusta appeared to hesitate, considering, before she spoke again. "Which is why I have a final request to make of you, Carol."

"Of course. Anything I can do. Just name it."

"Ah, child, you make me ashamed that I did not value you at your true worth when I was alive."

"I wasn't worth much then. I was a different person. I still have relapses, as you may have noticed a few minutes ago."

"The seeds of goodness were within you, though they were buried deep and required nourishing. Continue to nourish them, my dear. You now have friends to help you when you fear you will falter.

"Very well, then," Lady Augusta went on. "This is my request. That you name your first daughter Augusta. Raise her with love, teach her to have a generous heart, and when she is grown you will discover in her a friend as constant and loving as I ought to have been to you when I was most recently alive."

"Are you saying what I think you're saying?" Carol exclaimed.

"There are some things," responded Lady Augusta, "which I am forbidden to explain. All the same, I believe you do understand what I cannot speak. You always have understood me in the past—and in the future."

"I wish I could touch you," Carol whispered. She stretched out her hand, but her fingers encountered only a cool, transparent light.

"You will touch me again, in time. In good time," Lady Augusta said. Her figure was beginning to fade, as was the glorious light surrounding her. "Good-bye for now, Carol . . ."

"Don't go. Please, stay with me for just a while longer. There is so much I need to ask you." Tears were pouring down Carol's cheeks. "Please . . . stay. . . ."

"Later, Carol. . . ."

"Carol, love, for heaven's sake, wake up!"

"What—where—?" Forcing her eyes to open, Carol looked around. She was curled up in the wing chair with the blanket tucked around her feet, and Nicholas was kneeling before her, talking to her and attempting to wipe the flowing tears off her face.

"Where is she?" Carol demanded.

"Where is who? Carol, your hands are cold as ice. What have you been doing alone in this unheated room?"

"I am not alone. Nicholas, didn't you see—?"

She grabbed at his upper arms, holding on to him until the world around her settled down and stopped spinning. "I must have been dreaming."

"It sounded like a nightmare, from the way you were screaming. I heard you all the way down in my room. Are you sure you're all right?" He pulled her to her feet and held her close as if to warm her with his own body heat.

"Yes, I'm fine. I came up here to think, and fell asleep and had a bad dream, that's all." It was not all, and Carol knew it. She was beginning to understand so many wonderful things. She smiled at Nicholas, her love.

"Let's go back to my room, where it's warm." His arm around her shoulders urged her toward the door. "I want to make love to you again."

"I would like that very much." She would decide later exactly when and how much to tell him about her adventures with Lady Augusta's ghost. He might not believe her until he knew her as completely as she knew him—and after all, a wife was not required to reveal everything about her past life to her husband.

Nicholas would be her husband, when the time was right for them to marry. She was absolutely certain of it. This man had been her love in the past and would be her husband again in the distant future.

Carol knew beyond any doubting that her life had been on the wrong track when Lady Augusta's ghost first appeared to her. Cold and distrustful as she had then been, she had almost destroyed her own future along with the future prospects of everyone for whom she now cared.

Lady Augusta had saved her. At the image of that once-cantankerous lady and the amazing possibilities she had suggested, Carol could not help smiling.

"What are you thinking about?" Nicholas paused in the doorway of Carol's old room to kiss her. With one gentle finger he traced the new upward curve of her lips.

"I was thinking about Lady Augusta," she said, casting a last glance backward into the room as Nicholas shut the door on it. "She is the one who brought me to Marlowe House, and who then brought you here, to me. All of it was meant to be, exactly as it happened."

"I will always be grateful that you were here to meet me," he whispered as they went down the stairs to his bedchamber.

"So will I." Carol sighed, sinking into his arms so that he was obliged to pick her up and carry her the rest of the way to his bed. "Always and forever, Nicholas. *Forever*. Merry Christmas and many Happy New Years to come, my love."

Part VI.
Merry
Christmas.

Lond, A.D. 2168.

Chapter Twenty-Three

It was snowing again, though not enough flakes floated downward to cause difficulties for travelers. On this Christmas Eve there was just enough snow to lightly frost the evergreen in the center of the square and make it look like the tree in a classical Christmas picture. It was an enormous tree, so tall that during the summer months birds nested in its uppermost branches in complete safety far above the vigorous city life that went on in the square even in the hottest of weather. On those hot, sunny days, children played in the shade beneath the tree or climbed along its trunk as high as their parents or their nurses would allow them to go.

Every Christmas the tree was decorated with lights. It had grown so tall that placing all the colored bulbs had become a long and tedious project, particularly when the weather turned blustery. In a recent year, the Government had suggested that the tree be cut down and a smaller one planted in its place. This, the Government claimed, would make holiday decorating easier and more efficient. The outcry of those who lived in or near the square had been so immediate and so loud with outrage that the Government at once withdrew the suggestion, bowing as usual to the will of the people and leaving the beautiful old symbol of a cherished holiday untouched for all to enjoy.

Car turned from the front window and contemplation of the decorated tree outside to give her full attention to the gathering in the drawing room of Mar House. Everyone she loved would be there. Dear friends Bas and Jo and their children sat beside the Christmas tree that almost touched the drawing room ceiling. Lin and Sue and Lin's husband, Tom, were helping them to sort through a box of antique Christmas ornaments in preparation for the decorating party that was about to begin.

Out in the hall the most recent arrivals, Nik's twin sisters, were pulling off their winter coats in eager expectation of joining the fun. Through the wide doorway Car could see the very pregnant Pen leaning against her beloved Al while the two of them listened to El's new husband, the ever-smiling Luc, tell a slightly naughty joke.

"They don't look like twins, do they?" Nik said, sliding an arm around Car's waist. "I sometimes think the midwives mixed them up with someone else's babies at birth."

"I don't," Car responded. "Their characters

are remarkably similar. Outer appearances can be deceiving."

Pen was tall and slender save for the bulge of the child she carried within her. Her hair was pale blond and her eyes were blue. El was shorter and plump, with darker, curly blond hair and gray eyes. While they might not look like identical twins, they did look like sisters and their tastes were so similar that, to the utter despair of their brother and the frustration of their would-be lovers, they had traded Al and Luc back and forth between them for several years before finally deciding which sister would marry whom.

"Here is Aunt Aug." Nik hurried forward to assist the elderly lady who had just appeared in the doorway to remove the old-fashioned cloak she insisted on wearing. Beneath the cloak Aug had on a bright red velvet dress trimmed with small bunches of artificial holly and mistletoe. Her thick white hair was pinned into a neat knot at the back of her head, with a small piece of mistletoe tucked into it.

"You look wonderful," Car said, answering Aug's usual question before she could ask it. After hugging her aunt and kissing her cheek with great fondness, Car inquired, "How did your meeting with the Prime Minister go?"

"Rather well," Aug responded. "I do believe that Drum has seen the error of his recent autocratic ways and will in future pay much more attention to what the citizens of this country want him to do—and not just at election time, either."

Flora Speer

"He's a hard man, our Prime Minister," Car agreed, "but he is a fair man, too, and he wants to do what's best."

"He doesn't have much choice, with you two females harrying him at regular intervals," Nik teased.

"This time, it was Aunt Aug, not me, who convinced him to change his policy," Car said. To the older woman she added, "You are a wonder."

"Yes." Aug gave her a knowing grin. "I certainly am. Now, tell me, my girl, when do you intend to give me a great niece to carry on my name? I am not going to continue in this present life for much longer and I would like to be sure my successor is on the way before I leave you."

"If we must remain childless to keep you with us," said Nik, "then I shall send Car to the attic to sleep and make my own bed in the sub-basement."

"Now, there is an arrangment that could not last for more than two hours at the most." Pen had joined them in time to hear Nik's joking words. "Aug, I beg you, stay with us. We need you. I cannot think how any of us would manage without you."

"Especially Prime Minster Drum," Car added, laughing, though the eyes with which she regarded Aug were shadowed by the certain knowledge that, at one hundred years of age, Aug could not live much longer.

"But my dear," Aug said, patting Car's arm, "I will always be with you. You couldn't get rid of me if you tried. I thought you knew that by now.

438

"Enough of serious talk," Aug went on, raising her voice to speak to all of the guests. "It is time for laughter and feasting and goodwill to everyone. It is time to celebrate Christmas. You young people, start singing. I expect to hear a few good old-fashioned Christmas carols from you. I, of course, intend to be the one to place the star on top of the Christmas tree. Someone bring a ladder."

About the Author

Flora Speer is the author of six historical romances, three futuristic romances, and four time-travel romances.

Born in southern New Jersey, she now lives in Connecticut. Her favorite activities include doing the research for her books, gardening (especially flowers and herbs used in medieval gardens), needlepoint, amateur astronomy, and following the U.S. Space Program. She also loves cats, long walks, and the pleasures of good conversation with dear friends.

She enjoys receiving letters from readers, and faithfully promises to answer each one. Readers may write to:

Flora Speer
P.O. Box 270347
West Hartford, CT
06127-0347

Please include a stamped, self-addressed envelope.

TIMESWEPT ROMANCE
A TIME-TRAVEL CHRISTMAS
By Megan Daniel, Vivian Knight-Jenkins, Eugenia Riley, and Flora Speer

In these four passionate time-travel historical romance stories, modern-day heroines journey everywhere from Dickens's London to a medieval castle as they fulfill their deepest desires on Christmases past.

_51912-7 $4.99 US/$5.99 CAN

A FUTURISTIC ROMANCE
MOON OF DESIRE
By Pam Rock

Future leader of his order, Logan has vanquished enemies, so he expects no trouble when a sinister plot brings a mere woman to him. But as the three moons of the planet Thurlow move into alignment, Logan and Calla head for a collision of heavenly bodies that will bring them ecstasy—or utter devastation.

_51913-5 $4.99 US/$5.99 CAN

Three captivating stories of love in another time, another place.

MADELINE BAKER
"Heart of the Hunter"

A Lakota warrior must defy the boundaries of life itself to claim the spirited beauty he has sought through time.

ANNE AVERY
"Dream Seeker"

On faraway planets, a pilot and a dreamer learn that passion can bridge the heavens, no matter how vast the distance from one heart to another.

KATHLEEN MORGAN
"The Last Gatekeeper"

To save her world, a dazzling temptress must use her powers of enchantment to open a stellar portal—and the heart of a virile but reluctant warrior.

Timeswept passion...timeless love

A LOVE BEYOND TIME

FLORA SPEER

When he is accidentally thrust back to the eighth century by a computer genius's time-travel program, Mike Bailey falls from the sky and lands near Charlemagne's camp. Knocked senseless by the crash, he can't remember his name, address, or occupation, but no shock can make his body forget how to respond when he awakens to the sight of an enchanting angel on earth.

Headstrong and innocent, Danise is already eighteen and almost considered an old maid by the Frankish nobles who court her. Yet the stubborn beauty would prefer to spend the rest of her life cloistered in a nunnery rather than marry for any reason besides love. Unexpectedly mesmerized by the stranger she discovers unconscious in the forest, Danise is quickly arroused by an all-consuming passion—and a desire that will conquer time itself.

_51948-8 $4.99 US/$5.99 CAN